The Seed Collectors

Scarlett Thomas

CANONGATE
Edinburgh · London

Published in Great Britain in 2015 by Canongate Books Ltd,
14 High Street, Edinburgh EH1 1TE

www.canongate.tv

1

British Library Cataloguing-in-Publication Data
A catalogue record for this book is available on
request from the British Library

ISBN 978 1 84767 920 8
Export ISBN 978 1 84767 921 5

Typeset in Perpetua by Palimpsest Book Production Ltd, Falkirk, Stirlingshire

Printed and bound in Great Britain by Clays Ltd, St Ives plc.

The SEED COLLECTORS

Also by Scarlett Thomas

Fiction

Our Tragic Universe
The End of Mr Y
PopCo
Going Out
Bright Young Things

Non-Fiction

Monkeys With Typewriters

For Sam and Hari

'Crown yourselves with ivy, grasp the thyrsus and do not be amazed if tigers and panthers lie down fawning at your feet. Now dare to be tragic, for you will be redeemed.'

Friedrich Nietzsche

Ah! sunflower, weary of time,
Who countest the steps of the sun,
Seeking after that sweet golden clime
Where the traveller's journey is done;

Where the youth pined away with desire,
And the pale virgin shrouded in snow,
Arise from their graves and aspire;
Where my sunflower wishes to go.

William Blake

Family Tree

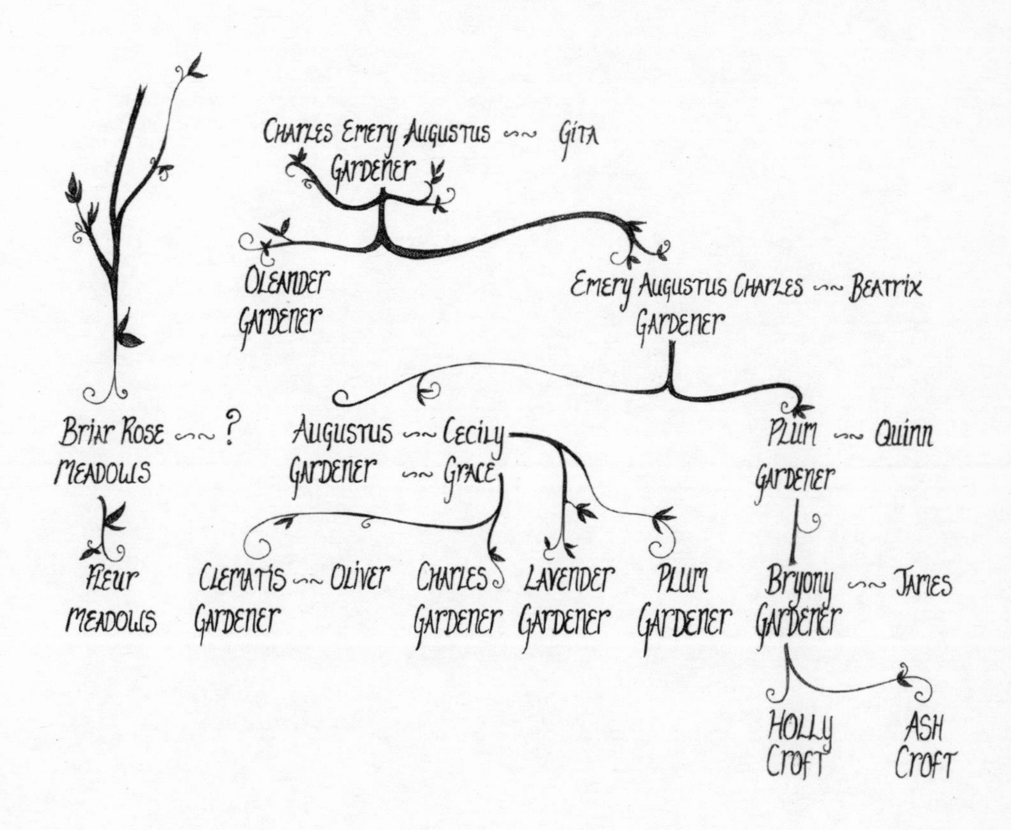
Charles Emery Augustus ~ Gita
Gardener
Oleander
Gardener
Emery Augustus Charles ~ Beatrix
Gardener
Briar Rose ~ ?
Meadows
Augustus ~ Cecily
Gardener ~ Grace
Plum ~ Quinn
Gardener
Fleur
Meadows
Clematis ~ Oliver
Gardener
Charles
Gardener
Lavender
Gardener
Plum
Gardener
Bryony ~ James
Gardener
Holly
Croft
Ash
Croft

Funeral

Imagine a tree that can walk. Yes, actually walk. Think it's impossible? You're wrong. It's called the walking palm. Its thick dreadlocky roots rest on the ground rather than inside it, and when it has had enough of being where it is, it quietly uproots itself, like a long-wronged wife, and walks away, at a speed of just over one metre per year. In the time it takes the walking palm to flounce out, nations will fall, people will die of old age, ancient secrets will be told, and new-born babies will grow into actual people who . . .

Bryony and the children have gone, and Fleur is now listening to her friend Clem Gardener on the radio talking about the walking palm, *Socratea exorrhiza*, and the challenges of filming its journey. It took over ten years to film it walking just fifteen metres, out of the shadow of a recently erected logging station. On the time-lapse film it staggered along desperately like something that had just been born or was just about to die. But the walking palm certainly knows how to travel. It does not need tickets, or require transfers, or have to fill in visa forms. It does not put so much hand luggage in the overhead compartment that it falls on people. It just goes. Most species in Clem's Academy Award-nominated documentary *Palm* find some way of travelling, of course. If they can't move themselves around, then they produce seeds and get birds to move them, or animals, or us. And some plants have amazing ways of producing seed. The talipot palm, *Corypha umbraculifera*, which can live to over 100 years old and only flowers once in its life, produces the biggest inflorescence in the world, made of millions of flowers. Now there's a real commitment to the next generation. Some of the 2,400 species of palms around the world are known to actually flower themselves to death. It's called hapaxanthy . . .

'You mean they *commit suicide* by flowering too much?' says the presenter.

'It's quite common,' says Clem, in her low, underwatery voice. 'They put all their energy into flowering – or, in other words, attempting to reproduce – and there's nothing left for anything else. Their roots wither and die.'

'So it's not just because it's beautiful?'

'Nothing in nature is "because it's beautiful", not really,' says Clem.

Fleur is finishing her tea. It's a homemade blend of dried pink rosebuds, passion flower, cinnamon and honey. It's very soothing. Since Bryony and the children have gone, she has also added some of the opium she grows in the garden. She looks out of the window of the old dowager's cottage that Oleander gave her on her twenty-first birthday and raises the antique teacup to the robin she has kept alive for the last seven winters. He cocks his head. Fleur is still in the cottage. If she goes out to do some gardening, there might be live worms, or the slugs that she sometimes puts in a saucer for him. But Fleur won't garden today. He'll have to make do with the dried fruit she put on his table yesterday.

'Oleander is dead,' she tells him through the window. 'Long live Oleander.'

She drinks deeply from the cup.

The robin understands, and begins to sing his oldest and most sorrowful song.

'Mummy?'

Bryony barely hears the word any more.

'Mummy?'

'Hang on, Holl.'

'OK. But, Mummy, just quickly?'

'I'm trying to listen to Clem, Holly. You should listen too. She's your godmother.'

'Yeah, I know, and she's also like my millionth cousin, a thousand times removed.'

'She's your second cousin, once removed. My cousin.'

'We could have stayed at Fleur's to hear her.'

'Yes, but I think Fleur wanted to be on her own for a bit. And anyway, we've got to get home. Daddy'll be making dinner. And you've got homework to do.'

Bryony turns up the car radio, but Clem has stopped talking. Now there's a guy who had to be rescued from somewhere, possibly Antarctic Chile, although Holly was *Mummy*ing over that bit. The format of this programme is supposed to be a group discussion, but Bryony knows that Clem probably won't speak again. At school she had a habit of saying one clever thing in every class, and then drifting off to God knows where while Bryony highlighted all her notes in one of three fluorescent colours and Fleur learned mindfulness by stabbing herself with a protractor. Every so often the biology teacher said something about how sad it was that these three weren't at all like their mothers. In fact, at fourteen, their mothers – frail, beautiful Grace, bold Plum and the legendary Briar Rose – had also been terrible students, interested only in the Rolling Stones, but no one remembers that, because it doesn't fit the story of how they become famous botanists. Or famous-ish. Or famous-ish mainly for disappearing while on the trail of a miracle plant that probably never existed, or possibly killed them all.

'Mummy? Am I a tree? She said that people aren't like trees, but I am, in a way, aren't I?'

'Yes, Ash. You are, in a way.'

'More than I'm a *village* anyway.'

Having a son called Ash, while living in a village called Ash, hadn't seemed anything worse than a bit cute when they named him. There aren't that many botanical names for boys, after all, and at least Ash could be short for Ashley if he ever wanted to get away from the plant thing. Bryony's husband James was very keen on the old Gardener family tradition, though, and in the end it came to a toss-up between Ash and Rowan. Ash himself has since pointed out that they could have chosen Alexander, William or Jack (in-the-hedge). On that occasion – Ash's eighth birthday, or perhaps it was his seventh – James told Ash he was lucky not to be called Hairy Staggerbush, Fried Egg Tree, Thickhead or Erect Lobster Claw, all of which are apparently real plants.

Bryony and James have no idea of the stupid conversations Ash has pretty much every day at school when someone asks him, yet again, why he's called Ash when he lives in Ash, as if he named himself. Being named after a grandfather or a footballer or a TV character is fine. But a whole village? All kids know that no one should be named after the place they live, unless they are Saint Augustine or something, or Saint Stephen or Saint George – but in those cases you become famous first and *then* someone names a place after you. On his own, Ash likes being named after a tree that has magical powers. But he's hardly ever on his own. He is dreading going to secondary school in Sandwich or Canterbury, where people will ask his name and where he comes from and both answers will be the same, which will make him sound retarded. He is already practising shrugging and saying 'Oh, just some boring village', but it's not that convincing. Maybe the house will burn down, on some lucky day when there are no people or cats inside it (which is virtually impossible: there's always life in Ash's house), and they'll have to move.

'Clem doesn't make cakes like Fleur,' says Holly. 'And she wears really weird clothes. But then I suppose that's because she makes documentaries, and . . .'

'Don't you think Fleur wears weird clothes?'

'No. Fleur's pretty. She wears dresses. And *interesting* combinations of things.'

Bryony sighs. 'Well, yes, I suppose everyone knows that dresses make you pretty.'

'What does that mean, when you say it like that?'

'Like what?'

'Is it irony?'

'How do you know about irony?'

'Er, *school*? Anyway, Mummy, you wear dresses.'

It's true. But while Fleur wears things you'd see in the thicker magazines, or on the size-zero celebrities she works for, Bryony usually wears a version of the clothes Holly wears but better cut and in darker colours: jersey dresses or big jumpers over leggings, all made by Backstage, Masai or Oska. What Bryony used to think of as fat people's clothes. Yes, yes, of course all the styles come in S and even XS, but it remains unclear why thin people would need clothes with elasticated waists and asymmetric folds around the middle. Almost everything Bryony now wears goes in the washing machine at forty degrees and doesn't need ironing. Bryony loves fashion, but it doesn't love her. She'd like to be a Jane Austen heroine – or actually even one of the heroine's shallow friends who only cares about fashion and won't go out in the rain – but she's way too fat for that. This season it's all about clashing florals and colour blocking. You can clash florals if you're a thin seventeen-year-old. If you do it at Bryony's age you look as if you don't own a mirror. If you colour block at Bryony's size you look like a publicly commissioned artwork.

'Mummy?'

'I'm still trying to listen to this.'

'Can't you go on *Listen Again* later when you're filling in your food diary?' says Holly. 'Anyway, Mummy?'

'Hang on.'

'Mummy? How many calories are there in a cake?'

'What kind of cake?'

'Like the cakes Fleur made.'

'Did she make them? I thought she bought them. Or didn't she say that Skye Turner sent them?'

'No, Mummy, she said Skye Turner sent her cakes *once*. But they were like weird low-carb brownies or whatever. She made these ones. They were spicy and everything – not like stuff you can buy. Anyway, how many calories do they have?'

'You shouldn't be worrying about calories.'

'I'm not worrying. I'm just interested.'

'About two hundred, I think. They were quite small.'

'So in a day, you could eat, like . . .'

In the rear-view mirror, Bryony can see Ash screw up his eyes like a little potato.

'Don't say "like", Ash. Say "around" or "roughly" or something.'

'Like, seven and a half cakes,' says Ash. 'Wow.'

'Yeah, but only if you eat basically nothing else,' says Bryony.

'Awesome,' says Ash, in something like a loud whisper.

'Cake is for babies,' says Holly. At the party all the girls made sugar sandwiches with white bread and huge slabs of butter and honey to help the sugar stick and the grown-ups didn't even stop them. The grown-ups were too busy smoking at the bottom of the garden and talking about whether they would rather fuck a fireman or an anaesthetist and looking at pictures of holidays on someone's phone. Holly's insides now feel a bit gluey. And the thought of the butter she ate – yellow shiny poo – makes her want to vomit.

'How many cakes does Fleur eat, Mummy, do you think, in a typical day? Or a typical week. Would you guess at closer to ten, fifty or a hundred? Mummy?'

'As if anyone would eat a hundred cakes a day, you total spaz,' says Ash.

'Mummy?'

'What? Oh, who knows? I think she makes a lot more than she eats. I think she likes the way they look more than the way they taste.'

'Mummy?' says Holly. 'Is that why Fleur's so thin in that case, if she only looks at cakes but doesn't eat them?'

'Who knows? Maybe she's just got lucky genes. She's always been thin.'

Lucky genes. Is that what it comes down to? Or maybe Fleur doesn't eat family packs of Kettle Chips when no one is watching. Maybe she doesn't add half a bottle of olive oil to a pot of 'healthy' vegetable soup like James and Bryony do, or use three tins of coconut milk (600 calories per can) in a family curry as James does. Maybe she's still on the Hay diet, like Bryony's grandmother Beatrix, who always talks of 'taking' food, never 'eating' it, and has given Bryony some kind of food-combining cookbook for the last three Christmases. Food combining means not eating protein and carbohydrates together. That would mean no Brie with crusty bread, no poached egg and smoked salmon on toast, no roast chicken and potatoes. Bryony feels hungry just thinking about it.

'Mummy? Have I got lucky genes?'

'Depends what you think is lucky.'

They have left Deal and are driving on the main road back towards Sandwich. It's a warm day, and very bright. Spring is certainly coming. On the right, somewhere beyond the flat fields and the country park built on the old colliery slagheap, is the English Channel, with its wind turbines and ferries and migrating birds. On the left, more fields, full of scarecrows. In the distance Bryony sees the reassuring old Richborough Power Station cooling towers huddled together like three fat women on an eternal tea break. Then, in one of the fields on the left, she suddenly sees something hovering, perfectly balanced above the scarecrows.

'Mummy, why are we stopping? Arrrgh . . .'

'Oh. My. God. Mummy, you are even worse than Daddy.'

Both children wave their arms and legs about, pretending they are having a car crash, as Bryony pulls into a farm's small driveway.

'Look at that,' she says softly.

'At what exactly, Mummy?'

A huge bird of prey. Swooping. It's beautiful, and it's just . . . there. Bryony struggles to remember the names of local raptors that James has told her. Could it be a hen harrier? A marsh something-or-other? A kestrel? Or do you only see kestrels in Scotland? It doesn't matter; she can look it up in the bird book when she gets home. Maybe they can all look together.

'Oh, I must tell Daddy . . .'

She begins noting its features. And then she sees the wire holding it up.

'What are we supposed to be looking at?'

'Nothing.' Bryony restarts the engine. How stupid. How could she not have seen the wire from the road? The raptor is a fake, like the scarecrows. Even the starlings aren't fooled; hundreds of them are flying around everywhere.

'Mummy, did you think that was a real bird?'

Ash and Holly start to giggle.

'Mummy, you're a right wally.'

Which is exactly what James will say.

'So how was your swim today?'

'Fucking awful.'

Clem is rooting around in the drawer for something. They have finished listening to the repeat of her radio programme and the kitchen is suddenly very quiet. Ollie is not going to try asking about Oleander again. Or if he does he will make sure he does not mention the inheritance, which made him sound like a total cunt before.

'What have you lost?'

'My vegetable peeler.'

Despite being married, they have separate vegetable peelers, just as they have separate gym memberships at separate gyms with different swimming pools.

Ollie shrugs. 'I haven't had it.'

Clem sighs. 'What went wrong at the swimming pool this time?'

'This time.'

'What?'

'Well, you say it as if I'm some kind of twat who can't even go to the swimming pool without some major drama, and . . . *What*?'

'Nothing.' She has now found her vegetable peeler, that minimalist piece of stainless steel that looks as if it would slash your wrists in an instant. Ollie's peeler has a sensible rubber grip. With Clem's you can peel every which way, as if you were fencing, or literally doing battle with your vegetable, really fucking killing it. Ollie's just peels sensibly. Clem starts killing something. It's a butternut squash.

'Anyway . . . ?'

'Well, OK, so basically I'd just finished in the gym when the bus turned up. And – don't look at me like that – I know this is going to sound cruel but I totally wasn't in the mood for twenty – yes, *twenty* – and no, I'm not going to say the word "spaz", or "flid", OK? – people with "learning difficulties". Obviously I'm sure they are all lovely and wonderful and I'd fucking hate their lives but they don't have enough helpers. And they don't wash them before they put them in the swimming pool. And that pool is disgusting enough to begin with, as you know. Like, for example, the clump of hair is still there. After a YEAR. Stop looking at me like that. And try not to slash your wrists with that thing. You think I'm exaggerating? OK. Right. One of them was literally a woman with a hunchback – WHICH I AM NOT JUDGING, OK – but she was also covered in hair. I mean she looked like a *yeti*. A hunchback woman *yeti* in my swimming pool. The guys are also all perfectly lovely, I'm sure, although my personal preference would be to have them wash before getting into a pool with me, but one of them not only does not wash, he wears these huge corduroy shorts that probably still have things – like used tissues, if he actually used tissues – in the pockets, and he goes to the deep end and just bobs up and down picking his nose while I'm trying to swim. And then there's this other one who is huge and black – YES, I KNOW IT DOESN'T MATTER BUT I AM TRYING TO PAINT A PICTURE FOR YOU – who does this superfast front crawl which is quite impressive really, but he keeps his eyes shut and his head entirely underwater so he spends his whole time mowing down babies and the elderly while the yeti shakes with fear and sort of moos in the shallow end. I mean, can't they just shave her?'

'Can you pass me the Le Creuset roasting tin?'

Ollie goes to the wrong cupboard and gets the wrong tin.

'I mean, is it unethical to shave a yeti-woman if you have one in your care?'

'I am not responding to this.' Does she almost smile then? Maybe not. 'I mean, you don't shave before you get in the pool.'

'Ha! You *have* responded. The woman hath . . .'

'You've got a hairy back. That's the wrong tin.'

'My back isn't that hairy. And I'm a man. Which one do you want?'

'The Le Creuset one.'

'I don't know what that means.'

'Yes, you do.'

'No. Unlike you I don't carry an inventory of our bourgeois cooking equipment around with me in my head at all times. What does Le Creuset even mean?'

'Don't be a dick. It's the one with the handles.'

'If you mean the third-degree-burn pan, why don't you say so?'

Clem sighs. Ollie gets the right roasting tin. And a beer.

'They could wax her. How traumatic would that be? She could go to Femme Naturelle.' Femme Naturelle is the beauty parlour that has just opened up around the corner from their house in Canterbury. If she's in a good mood Clem sometimes jokes about going there for a Brazilian, or even a Hollywood. Her pubes are perfect as they are, of course: a little black triangle of something like AstroTurf or . . . The image is going wrong so Ollie abandons it. '*Yeti Naturelle*.'

'That was almost funny before you spoiled it.'

When they get in, Ash snuggles up in the conservatory with his nature book. Holly gets the spare laptop and loads a DVD onto it: something with a 15 certificate about bitchy schoolgirls that her uncle Charlie got her last Christmas. Bryony suggested this on the way home, mainly as a way to stop Holly pointing out every other fake bird that they drove past. The house smells of baking bread, as usual, and also chocolate. James must have made a cake too. So much cake in one day.

'Why is she doing that?' asks James, when he comes in from the garden.

'Mummy,' wails Holly from the conservatory. 'Tell him you said I could.'

'I said she could.' Bryony kisses him. 'How are you?'

'I'm fine,' says James. 'Been baking.'

'I can smell. Something lovely that I shouldn't eat.'

'Chocolate and beetroot brownies. Beetroot from the garden!'

Bryony doesn't ask if it's for a newspaper assignment. James bakes all the time: bread every day and cakes twice a week. Once James baked 'the most calorific cake in Britain' from a recipe in one of the tabloids so he could construct a witty piece about how he didn't think his organic eco-kids would eat it, but of course they did. Holly was actually sick: brown and pink vomit all over her bedroom. Bryony can't remember what caused the pink that time. Can't have been beetroot. Must have been jam. And why has James used fresh early-season beetroot in brownies? Couldn't he just have roasted it? Everyone loves roasted beetroot, and it roasts so quickly when it's so fresh. He could also have put it in a salad.

'Good to get more veg in the kids,' Bryony says.

'That's what I thought. And you can have one, can't you?'

She opens the fridge and gets out the Villa Maria Sauvignon Blanc she started last night. There's only about a third of the bottle left, so she finds another white and puts it in the freezer just in case. She walks across the room and selects an unchipped Dartington Crystal glass from the dresser. It's three minutes past six. The clocks went forward this morning, so in some way it's really only three minutes past five.

'Do you want one?' she asks James.

'No thanks.' He looks at his watch. 'How was your afternoon?'

'All right. Ash still won't go near the deep end when the wave machine's on, after whatever it was that happened last week. The party was pretty boring. Poor Fleur's in a state but not talking about it. Oh, and after we left Fleur's Holly remembered she'd left her blue scarf behind so we had to go all the way back to Deal. A lot of toing and froing, and she's basically had way too much sugar. Cake at the party of course, and some disgusting-looking sweet sandwiches, cake at Fleur's . . . But I guess at least she's eaten something. She's pretty scratchy now, though.'

'How is watching an unsuitable DVD going to help?'

How is giving her even more cake going to help? But Bryony doesn't say this.

'At least she's quiet.'

Bryony pours the wine. What is it about the first sip of a crisp Sauvignon Blanc on a mild early spring day? It's like drinking a field full of cold, slightly shivery flowers.

'And you say Fleur isn't good?'

'Well, as usual she didn't say anything at all about how she was feeling. I wish she wasn't all alone in that huge cottage. It must be so stressful having to suddenly take all responsibility for Namaste House and all the therapy and yoga and everything. And all the famous people who are always hanging around there . . . Although I suppose whoever inherits the place will probably sell up quite quickly, but then what will she do? It's all she's ever known. Of course she owns her cottage, but presumably whoever inherits the house will do some kind of deal with her so that the estate can be sold whole . . .'

'When's the funeral going to be?'

'A week on Thursday. They need time to get in touch with everyone. Potentially people could be coming from India, Pakistan, America . . .'

Bryony goes to the rack to find a bottle of red to open for dinner. Should she open two? No, one will be fine. But why not make it the 15.5% Tempranillo in that case? Get a bit of spice and warmth in her before the week ahead. She starts looking for the corkscrew, which is never where it last was. One of the things Bryony's father taught her was that you should always open a bottle of red wine an hour before you want to drink it, or longer if it's more than five years old. Bryony vaguely remembers the evenings when he used to open two bottles at once, and her mother would drink one of them by herself, before dinner, looking vampiric and oddly expectant. After dinner her father smoked hash and her mother drank the second bottle of wine and they talked about going back to the Pacific to continue their study of the Lost People while Bryony read Jane Austen and wished for the phone to ring.

'Do you want to come and see something?' James says.

'What is it?'

'Come and see.'

She sighs. 'Hang on. I want to get this open. And I'll have to change my shoes.'

Bryony uncorks the wine, takes off her boots and puts on a pair of dirty blue Converse trainers that she has set aside for gardening; not that she ever has time for gardening at the moment.

'Holly? Ash?' calls James. 'Do you want to see what Daddy's made?'

'They're all settled down,' says Bryony.

'Do we have to?' calls Holly.

James sighs. 'No, but you'll miss something exciting.'

The kids put on their shoes and everyone walks to the bottom of the garden to admire the bird table that James has put together this afternoon, presumably between digging up beetroot and baking. Bryony doesn't ask why he hasn't been writing, and doesn't say anything about the cats. She'll have to get them bells. Then again, birds come to the garden anyway, and the cats kill them anyway, and she's never actually bothered to get them bells before. Then there's bird flu, although no one's said anything about bird flu for ages. Why can't she just like it? It does look nice where James has put it.

'That's lovely,' Bryony says, kissing James again. 'We can watch the birds from the kitchen. But you didn't do it all today, as well as making brownies and digging up beetroot?'

'You are so unbelievably gross,' says Holly. 'When will you be too old for kissing?'

'Never,' says Bryony. 'We'll still be kissing when we're a hundred.'

'It could be a lot worse,' says James, raising an eyebrow at Bryony. 'Eh, Beetle?'

'Yuck! That's even more gross. I know what you're thinking, and I know what it means when you make your eyebrows do that. And when you call Mummy "Beetle".'

The kids slink back off to the conservatory.

'Remember the goldfinches?' says James.

'Oh God, yes. Of course. How could I forget something like that?'

How indeed? Although when you are working full-time and studying part-time it's easy to forget things. But of course the goldfinches were amazing. One day last autumn – it must have been just before Halloween – ten of them turned up in the back garden. Given that there had never been any goldfinches in the garden this seemed to be something of a miracle. And they were so impressive with their bright red heads and wing flashes of pure gold, like peculiar little superheroes, all masked and caped. James declared them his favourite bird, and Holly said she thought they were too 'bling' but nevertheless ended up spending hours watching them through the binoculars that Uncle Charlie bought for her. The lunchtime after they arrived Bryony got chatting to the woman from Maxted's who recommended sunflower hearts and niger seed, and a proper feeder for the niger seed, and a little hanging basket for the sunflower hearts, all of which Bryony bought. How unlike Mummy it was to come home with something that was not clothes, shoes, chocolate or wine! Anyway, these offerings also went down well with the goldfinches, and Bryony, James and the kids spent the next day trying without success to take just one good photograph, but the little buggers would not keep still, and . . .

Such strange, slow little birds, gathering their gold capes around them, pulling their red masks down over their eyes and settling down on the niger seed feeder for what seemed like hours, as if it was some kind of opium den. And the next day another ten showed up. And the same again for the next three days until there must have been fifty goldfinches regularly visiting their garden. They would all eat slowly and seriously for quite a long time, sometimes getting a bit flappy and knocking each other off the feeders but mainly just chomp-chomp-chomping like superhero-puppets controlled by very stoned puppeteers. Then they would all take off and fly bobbing and tweeting around the village sounding like the ribbon on an old cassette tape being rewound. This went on for about a week, and then they were gone. Bobbing and tweeting their way across the Channel to Europe in a group of over 350, according to the Sandwich Bird Observatory.

'I want to be ready for them this year, if they come back.'

'They were so beautiful.'

'Like you.' James strokes Bryony's face. 'It's still light,' he says, 'and warmish. You could put on a cardigan and bring your wine out here. I'll get one of the deckchairs out for you.'

James is always trying to get Bryony outside in the fresh air. Perhaps more fresh air will help her become more like ethereal, perfect Fleur, who has been known even to sleep outside when the moon is full. Although he has never said this, of course. He says Bryony is beautiful. He says Bryony is beautiful and then Bryony begins to think poisonous things like this. Anyway, James will bring one deckchair out and Bryony will sit in it alone, while James cooks dinner. That's the offer. Is it a good offer or a bad offer? Would it be better if she decided that she wanted to come and sit outside and got the deckchair herself? Once James told her she made too much of things, adding meaning that was never there. Bryony laughed and reminded him that being an estate agent meant having to do that all the time and that she couldn't help it if it was now in her nature to make cupboards sound like spare bedrooms. Although of course what he was objecting to was her tendency to make spare bedrooms sound like cupboards.

'This isn't for your column, is it?' asks Bryony.

'What?'

'I don't know. Making a bird table. I mean, the goldfinches won't come back until October or November. If they come back at all. In the meantime are you going to write about how hilarious it is when one of the cats brings in a bird? How Daddy has to deal with it because Mummy's too grumpy, or too squeamish, or late for a viewing, or at a seminar . . .' Or hungover, but that sort of goes without saying these days.

James's column is on page four of the glossy magazine of the biggest selling liberal weekend newspaper. It's called 'Natural Dad'. On the facing page there's a column called 'City Mum'. The idea is that James, once a well-known nature writer but now better known for his column, writes about living in the countryside with his two down-to-earth children and his increasingly bad-tempered wife. City Mum writes about her children's friends' ten-grand birthday parties in Hampstead, and wonders whether to buy her offspring shoes from Clarks like her parents did, or Prada, like her richest friends do.

'Hey, chill, Beetle. What's the matter?'

'Nothing. Sorry, I . . .'

'It's not as if you *have* ever cleared up after the cats in your life.'

'I do when you're away. It's horrible.' She sighs. 'Anyway, look, I don't want to start anything. I'm sorry. I'm knackered, and upset about Oleander, and I've still got to do all my reading for Thursday.' As well as being a partner in the estate agency, Bryony is doing a part-time MA in Eighteenth Century Studies. 'I just worry that you spend too much time on that column. I want you to be able to do your serious work, that's all.'

'I know you do.' James touches her arm lightly. 'But work doesn't always have to be serious. Come on, I'll get you a deckchair. I'm making a Thai green chicken curry for dinner. And then of course there's brownies. I'll do the washing up and you can get on with your reading.'

'Well, that's enough of my boring life. How about you?'

Charlie frowns. 'Well,' he says, 'where to start?'

Who goes on a blind date on a Sunday night? Even Soho has a kind of Sunday feeling, as if it has stayed in its pyjamas all day and just can't be arsed with all this. Charlie looks at Nicola, sitting across from him in the too-trendy, contemporary Asian restaurant she probably booked online. The music's too loud. She's wearing a silky dress in a kind of wine colour that makes her look faintly leprous. She's a mathematician doing a postdoc at King's. At home Charlie has a new orchid book that came just before he left (no, there isn't post on a Sunday: it was delivered to Mr Q. Johnson next door by mistake two days ago). He wishes he were at home reading it, with an espresso from his beautiful Fracino machine. He almost says something about the orchid book. He almost says that the thing about him, the main thing, really, although definitely not the thing you'd notice first, especially not if you happened to be blindfolded while he was fucking you, is that he loves seeing orchids in the wild in Britain. Apart from the bit about the blindfold, that would be a great line for a first date. Or maybe it all sounds a bit off-putting? The blindfold would be silk, and from Liberty, and – of course – handwashed between uses. He says nothing. He actually just wants to get this over with.

'I'll nip to the loo while you think about it,' says Nicola.

She slips on a tiny cardigan that stops under her arms. She's wearing very high heels. Every woman in here is wearing very high heels. She's probably been here before, perhaps with an ex, or with students from her undergraduate days. Charlie sighs. He can't be bothered with all this tonight. He sees a footballer he recognises walk in and joke with the doorman, who slaps him on the back. He picks up his phone and finds a text from his father telling him that his great-aunt Oleander is dead. Well, that's . . . Gosh, poor Fleur. Charlie texts her. Then he texts his cousin Bryony to ask how she and the family are. Then he begins composing a text to his sister Clem that combines sadness about Oleander with congratulations on her radio thing. But it's too hard, so he temporarily abandons it and flicks quickly to MyFitnessPal to add the carbohydrate grams he just accidentally had in his starter. Checks his hair in the reverse camera, not that he cares what Nicola thinks about his hair. Charlie often checks his hair when he is alone. It's quite nice hair. He likes it. Especially this latest haircut, which . . .

Nicola's back. Through the uncertain fabric of her dress he can see her knickers digging into the flesh of her otherwise OK bottom. Charlie likes a biggish bottom, but ideally on a much skinnier girl. How can she bear to be out in public like that? A thong would not solve the problem. He hates thongs. But there are lots of seamless knickers nowadays and . . .

'So,' she says.

Charlie puts his phone away. The main courses arrive. He has ordered halibut with Malaysian chilli sauce, which is probably full of sugar that will give him a headache and rancid vegetable oil that will give him cancer. She is having monkfish with Chinese leaf cabbage and jasmine rice. Charlie does not eat rice.

'Well, obviously you know I work at Kew.'

'That must be amazing. Do you get to go and hang out in the glasshouses whenever you want?'

'In theory. But no one really does.' And no one uses the libraries either, in case they bump into eager ethnobotany students who want to talk about different kinds of latex, which is the white gunge that comes out of some plants when you cut them, or be reminded whether it's paripinnate or imparipinnate leaves that have a lone terminal leaflet. Charlie always buys his plant books from Summerfield, Amazon or Abe, and then no one else can touch them or make them dirty or try to talk to him about them. He often feels like a lone terminal leaflet himself. Quite an elegant one, naturally, and on a very rare plant.

'So what do you do exactly? What's your job title?'

'I'm a family type specialist.'

'What does that mean?' She smiles. 'I know nothing about plants.

except sometimes from Izzy's drunken ramblings. She's always going on about mint and herbs and stuff.'

Izzy, aka Dr Isobel Stone, is the mutual friend who has set them up. She's a world authority on Lamiales, the order of angiosperms that contains mint and herbs and stuff. Charlie first got talking to her in the tea room about a year ago after an incident involving a member of the public and a rather mangled herbarium specimen that turned out simply to be *Lavandula augustifolia*, one of the most common plants in the UK, if not the entire universe. The member of the public wrote around seventeen letters about his 'mystery plant', each one more offensive than the last, eventually accusing everyone at Kew of being 'blind, intellectually stunted bastards'. Since then Charlie and Izzy have often had morning coffee and/or afternoon tea together, and Izzy has become the colleague that Charlie would never really fuck, but about whom he will masturbate if his fantasy happens to take place in a work setting. On Thursday Izzy gave him the address of this restaurant and a phone number and raised an eyebrow, and Charlie wondered if he *could* in fact fuck someone from work until Izzy said that her friend Nicola was expecting to meet him there at 8 p.m. on Sunday. It was all a bit awkward because Charlie had said he was available before he knew who he was meeting. And then Izzy told Charlie that Nicola had not stopped going on about him and his 'great body and beautiful eyes' since seeing him in a picture Izzy put on Facebook. Of course, desperate, fawning women of this type will often do *anything*. Which in one way makes the whole thing less . . . but in another way it becomes so . . .

'Um,' says Charlie, 'well, say you've gone to the rainforest and collected a plant but you don't know what it is and you send it to Kew for identification, I'm the person – or one of the people – who decides what family it's in, and therefore which department it should go to for further identification. Like if its leaves are a bit furry and it smells of mint I send it to Izzy. Or one of her team.'

'So you get mystery plants?'

'Yeah, all the time. But mostly we solve the mystery quite quickly.'

'That's so cool.' She pours more wine. 'So what's a botanical family again? I last did biology at GCSE. Plants are too real for me.'

'It's a taxonomic category. One up from genus. From the top it's kingdom, phylum, class, order, family, genus, species. Well, that's the basic structure anyway. The rice you're eating now has the Latin name *Oryza sativa*, which is its genus and species. Its family is Poaceae. Or, basically, grass.'

'Rice is a type of grass?'

'Yep.'

She sips her wine. 'What's a human a type of?'

'Monkey. Well, great ape. Hominidae.'

'Oh yes. Of course. I knew that. Everyone knows that. What about this cabbage stuff then?' She holds up a forkful of wilted greens.

Charlie frowns. 'You're not going to make me identify the whole meal, are you?'

'No. Sorry. I'm being silly.' She smiles weakly. 'Forget it.'

'It's probably *Brassica rapa*. Chinese cabbage. In the family Brassicaceae. The mustard family.'

She puts some in her mouth and chews. 'Cabbage is a type of mustard?'

'Yeah, kind of. The mustard family is sometimes known as the cabbage family.'

'So cabbage is a kind of cabbage.' She laughs. 'Wow. Excellent. OK, next question. Where are you from?'

'Originally? Bath.'

'Oh, I love Bath. Gosh, all that lovely yellow stone – what's it called, again? – and those romantic mists. Do you have any brothers or sisters?'

Charlie doesn't tell her that Bath stone is called Bath stone. 'I've got a sister. And a cousin I'm very close to. And, I guess, two half-sisters I hardly ever see, because . . .' He doesn't really know how to end this sentence, so he doesn't bother. Instead, he looks at Nicola's wrists. He tries imagining them bound with rope. Cheap, itchy rope. He imagines them bleeding. Just a little. Perhaps just a tiny blue bruise instead. One on each wrist from being held down and fucked. Face-fucked? No, just fucked. Obviously she'd have consented to all this, but it's amazing how many women do. In fact, a lot of women have only slept with Charlie because he's offered to tie them up. You know, as one of those jokes that aren't really jokes. But he doesn't really fancy Nicola, with or without rope etc.

There's quite a long pause.

'God, you're hard work, aren't you?' She grins. 'Don't look so serious. I'm teasing. What are their names?'

'Clematis. That's my sister. We call her Clem. Bryony's my cousin. My half-sisters are Plum and Lavender, but they're just kids still. My father remarried after my mother went missing on an expedition . . .' Nicola doesn't respond to the missing mother thing, which is odd, so Charlie explains about the family tradition of giving a botanical first name to anyone not certain to keep the famous Gardener surname, although of course Clem kept the Gardener name anyway when she married Ollie. Then he explains about his great-great-grandfather, Augustus Emery Charles Gardener, who was a famous horticulturist, and his great-grandfather, Charles Emery Augustus Gardener, who was supposed to be overseeing a tea plantation in India but ended up falling in love with a Hindu woman and founding an Ayurvedic clinic and yoga centre in Sandwich, of all places. And then his grandfather, Augustus Emery Charles Gardener, who . . .

'Can I tell you about the desserts?'

Nicola immediately looks up at the waiter, and Charlie realises he has been boring her. Good. Maybe she'll leave and this will be over. He has had enough to eat, and definitely enough carbs, but agrees, after some pressure, to share an exotic fruit platter. He'll have a bit of kiwi or something. But he insists on ordering a glass of dessert wine for her. He likes watching girls drinking dessert wine for reasons that would probably be disturbing if he ever thought about them. He has a double espresso, which won't be as nice as the one he could have at home.

'So why are you on a blind date?' Nicola asks him.

Charlie shrugs. Right, well, if she doesn't want to know any more about his family, she won't hear about his great-aunt Oleander, who just died, and who used to be a famous guru who even met the Beatles. She also won't hear about his mother, who is not just missing but presumed dead, along with both Bryony's parents and Fleur's terrible mother. And the deadly seed pods they went to find in a place called – really – the Lost Island, far away in the Pacific. And that's Nicola's loss, because it's really a very exciting story, with loads of botany in it and everything. But then all girls like Nicola want to talk about is how many people you've slept with and what your favourite band is and how many children you want.

'I don't know,' he says. 'How about you?'

'Izzy sort of took pity on me because I got dumped.'

'Sorry to hear that.'

'What's your history . . . ? I mean, when did you . . . ?'

'I got divorced about ten years ago.'

'Mine was last month.'

'Was it bad?'

She shrugs. 'We'd only been together for three years.'

'Yeah, but I mean, did you, were you . . . ?'

'What, in love? Yes. Well, I was. How about you?'

'I suppose I was. Yes. Just not with my wife.'

Nicola pauses. Sips her wine. Puts her finger in her mouth, and then in the bowl of salt on the table, and then back in her mouth again. Why on earth is she . . .

'So who did you fuck instead?'

Charlie's cock stirs ever so slightly at the sound of the word 'fuck' coming out of her full, quite posh, red-lipsticked mouth. She reapplied her lipstick when she went to the loo. He likes it when girls bother to do that.

'It's complicated.'

She sighs. 'Right.'

'How about you?'

'What, did I fuck anyone else?'

Again, a very slight emphasis on the word 'fuck'. The consonance of it. Another small stir.

'Yes.'

She smiles. 'I can't tell you that. I hardly know you.'

Eyebrows. Smile. 'We could change that.'

'Really? How?'

'Go out to the fire escape and take off your knickers.'

She pauses, looks shocked, but probably isn't. Laughs. 'What?'

'You think I'm joking?'

'I'm not sure. Er, most men wouldn't quite . . .'

'But what if I'm not?'

'Surely we could find somewhere more comfortable to . . .'

'But the excitement is all in the discomfort.'

'Well . . .'

He looks at the door. His watch. 'I mean, if you have other plans . . .'

'Take off my knickers.' She acts like this is a joke, could still just about be only a joke. 'Right. OK. So I'm standing on the fire escape in the freezing cold with no knickers on. And then what?'

'You put them in your mouth.'

'I'm not doing that.'

'Why not?'

'Well, why should I?'

‘So that people are not disturbed by your moans of pleasure. Or pain.’

‘I’m going to feel really stupid anyway. I can’t . . .’

‘Well, just take them off then. I’ll pay and then come and join you in a second.’

‘And you won’t be long?’

‘No.’

She flushes a little and gets up. ‘OK. Don’t be long. I can’t believe . . .’

Is it always this easy? Yes, when you actually don’t care.

Afterwards, Charlie drives his green MG back to Hackney. The house is just off Mare Street on a long road of huge Victorian houses in various states of renovation. Charlie and his ex-wife Charlotte (how much fun that was when they met: ‘I’m Charlie,’ ‘Hey, so am I!’, although it became complicated later on when they started opening each other’s letters by accident and one of them was That Letter from Bryony) split the proceeds on their flat in Highgate in a way that only their lawyers understood, and he ended up with just enough for the deposit on the Hackney place. He worked out that unless he asked his father for money, he could just about afford to continue living in London only if he bought a tired old student let, did it up a bit, and advertised for some housemates. He took two weeks’ holiday and painted all eight rooms, including the ceilings, while a friend of a friend with a sander did the floors for a hundred quid. So now here he is, living with two art students, a fashion blogger and a jazz musician. The main problem with the place is that the previous owner, Mr Q. Johnson, who now lives next door, insists on Charlie still keeping garlic on all the windowsills to keep bad spirits out of the house, and drops in every few days to check that he does. He has also not changed his address with the Labour Party, *Disability*, *Spin*, Saga and various other companies, so most of the post that comes to Charlie’s house is for him. It seems particularly unfair that Charlie’s post often goes to Mr Q. Johnson for no reason at all, especially when it is clearly marked number fifty-six.

When Charlie gets in, the band is practising in the basement. He watches a bit of *La Dolce Vita* on BBC2, then makes a cup of fresh mint tea and takes it to bed. He should have left Nicola on the balcony without her knickers. It would have been a hilarious thing to tell Bryony next weekend. But, mainly out of politeness to Izzy, he gallantly went outside, stuffed Nicola's knickers in her mouth and fucked her. She was quite pissed by then, so he managed to get his dick halfway up her arse before she realised what he was doing. But, again because of Izzy, he was super-polite and took it out like a nice, well-mannered boy and reinserted it in her vagina. Which is why he doesn't understand the text message he now has from Izzy: *How could you???* He texts back, *Be more specific?*, but does not get a reply.

It's very complicated, trying to organise a wake. Fleur has no idea who is even coming to the funeral. But afterwards, everybody should be invited to Namaste House for food. Of course they should. But there could be ten people or a hundred. How is Fleur supposed to know who will come? If even Augustus and Beatrix are going to come then anything could happen. Oleander changed a lot of people's lives over the years. But many of them must be dead now: dead, reincarnated and living completely new lives. Could you contact someone who . . . ? Fleur shakes her head. How stupid. Because it's so complicated organising a wake she is watering all the plants in Namaste House for the second time today. This is something Oleander and Fleur used to do together each evening. Doing this makes Fleur feel almost as if she *is* Oleander, and of course you don't have to miss someone if you are them, and . . .

The orangery is attached to the west wing. At this time of day it is filled with the soft colours of sunset with only a whisper of moonlight. Fleur has looked after the orchids in here since she was a teenager. Some of the ones she propagated are getting on for twenty years old, but there are others that are much older. Their roots reach out like the thin arms of the starving and desperate, although it's all a big act because they know that Fleur knows exactly how they like to be misted, and when. Fleur waters the frankincense tree in the centre of the room, touches its bark, as she always does, her hand coming away smelling of the heat and damp of faraway places. The orangery is where the celebrities come to relax by day, to breathe air produced by rare plants and to look out at the orchard with its wise, old trees. The orangery is vast, but the celebrities won't share it. If one celebrity finds another one already here then she, or more probably he – for some reason the residential ones are usually male – will instead go all the way to the east wing where they can choose the cool Yin room with the peppermint water fountain, the small, hot Yang room or the Dosha Den, full of black velvet cushions stuffed with down and dried roses.

Sometimes one of the newer celebrities will make an observation about the lack of a coherent spirituality in the house. The massages are Ayurvedic, because Ketki does them. Ish, Ketki's husband, does both Ayurvedic and macrobiotic consultations, and is also a trained acupuncturist and cranial osteopath. The food is mostly Indian, sometimes Ayurvedic, and made by Ketki's ancient aunt Bluebell. She specialises in kulfis – Indian ice creams made with condensed milk, cardamom pods and saffron – but which she often makes into the shape of Daleks. Everything else is a jumble of Buddhism, Taoism, Christianity, Hinduism, Wicca and who knows what else. Oleander famously believed in 'everything'. There's a tapestry halfway up the west-wing staircase with a profound religious significance that no one can quite pin down, not even the Prophet, who has an eye for such things.

After checking the first floor again, Fleur goes down the east-wing staircase – avoiding not just the tapestry but also the White Lady, who often comes out on a Sunday, or after someone has 'moved on' – and through the library with its huge peace lilies and rubber plants and that tarry, tobaccoey smell of old leather bindings, and she wonders where on earth Ketki could be. She checks the orangery again, and the kitchens, with their unmistakeable smell of fenugreek, coriander and, of course, the curry plants, which Fleur now waters for the third time today. All around are big Kilner jars of yellow split peas, red, brown and green lentils, four different types of rice, whole oats, sultanas and desiccated coconut. Silicone Dalek moulds, but no Bluebell. A half-drunk mug of Earl Grey tea, but no Ketki.

This is infuriating. There is, after all, so much planning to do. Ketki has said she'll make curries for the wake if Fleur will help. She has also suggested that her two daughters might come up from their professional lives in London and do some cooking. Unlikely, frankly. And Fleur herself is actually going to be quite busy on the day of the funeral and . . . Fleur sighs. Goes up to the second floor, with its long corridor of guest suites with the original servant bells that she had mended years ago, and then to the third floor, to the original servants' corridor where the 'servants' still live and in which the bells sometimes still tinkle, late at night, if one of the celebrities has overdosed, become enlightened or wants a cup of hot chocolate. Now, of course, it's just Ketki, Ish and Bluebell up there, but years ago Fleur and her mother had their cramped little rooms at the north end of the servants' corridor. And, after her parents' disappearance, Bryony stayed in one of the old servants' rooms for almost a year until James's parents took her in. Ketki's daughters – dramatically rescued from somewhere in the Punjab region, by Oleander, who saved them from almost certain abduction, rape and forced marriage – to Muslims, *imagine* – grew up in the house. They were joined at the south end of the servants' corridor by their cousin

Pi, who was himself rescued, but from something else entirely, quite a lot later.

Of course no one has suggested that Pi, who moved out of his tiny room years ago and is now a famous author in London, should come and make curries. No one has suggested that *his* eldest daughter should take time off from *Vogue* photo shoots to come and make curries. His wife never comes to Namaste House so at least that isn't an issue. But anyway, why not get Clem, Charlie and Bryony – Oleander's actual relations, who are presumably about to inherit everything – to come and make the curries? The Prophet has, to Fleur's knowledge, never even been in the kitchen, but that doesn't mean he couldn't help in an emergency. But some things never change; however much time you spend with supposedly enlightened people, in a house so brimming and glowing with enlightenment it's sometimes like being in one of those fish tanks that . . . *Shut up, for God's sake*. Fleur closes her eyes. Enlightenment is so difficult and tiresome, and Fleur isn't sure she's going to get there in this lifetime, but she could really do with a stiller mind. As usual, when she tries to stop her thoughts, her ego goes into a sulk for about one second and there's peace. Then the whole thing starts up again.

She eventually finds Ketki folding towels in Treatment Room 3. It's almost as if the old woman has been avoiding her.

'There's still time to get it catered,' Fleur says. 'We've got the money.'

Indeed. Those packages that the Prophet still sends off. And Fleur's big ideas, like those huge clouds floating above everyone until suddenly, splat, you are covered in rain. There's absolutely no shortage of money. Even after the Inland Revenue came round a couple of years ago. Especially when one of them went away with his own mantra, a yin/yang necklace, a shaved head and a fondness for chickpeas.

'I want to do this for Oleander,' says Ketki. 'She would have liked . . .'

'She would have liked you to be able to relax and grieve for her in peace. We've got no idea who's going to turn up for this. There'll be the press as well. I mean, not in the house, obviously, but causing trouble around the place. You know what they're like. I mean, let's face it, *Paul McCartney* might come. He probably won't, but . . .'

'Paul McCartney.' Ketki bobbles her head and almost smiles. She and her family arrived at Namaste House not long after George Harrison had been there, at least according to the tabloids, for a two-week meditation and yoga retreat with Oleander and some notorious wise-woman Fleur barely remembers but who used to live in the rooms looking down on the orangery that the Prophet now has. Fleur has a dim memory of patchouli oil, guitars and smoke, although most of her childhood was like that, especially before her mother disappeared. But by then there were mixing desks and DJs as well. The wise-woman grew the rare, impossible frankincense tree from seed, Fleur remembers. She put a spell on it, or said she did. If someone sold this place then what would happen to the frankincense tree? No one else would know how to look after it. Perhaps a botanical garden would take it, although moving it would probably kill it. Fleur will have to ask Charlie.

'Well . . .' says Ketki.

'And I'll have some people back to the cottage afterwards.'

'What people?'

'You know, Clem, Bryony, Charlie, if he comes. Pi. I guess just anyone who's around and wants to stay up late chatting. I'll do a small supper. That way we won't disturb you, Bluebell and Ish.'

Ketki knows that 'chatting' means drinking too much, and 'staying up late' means having sex and taking drugs. She's read her nephew's novels. She knows what Fleur does in that cottage. She turns back to the towels.

The room smells of the oils Ketki uses in her massages. For a long time she made her own essential oils from flowers in the garden and grew marigolds to use in her aromatic face packs. In fact, once upon a time Fleur was her assistant, and learned how to make all the classic

Ayurvedic plant remedies, massage oils and balms. Together they used to grind sandalwood and cinnamon sticks, and make their own besan flour from chickpeas, although Bluebell often insisted they use her flour, which was a bit more lumpy. They grew and harvested hibiscus flowers, marshmallow roots and chamomile. They even grew their own turmeric in one of the greenhouses. Now Fleur runs the whole show and insists that most of the oils and dried plants come by mail order, although she does still let Ketki help collect the rosebuds, lavender and rosemary. The only thing Fleur harvests is the opium which, yes, Ketki also knows about.

'I suppose there's James,' Fleur says. 'He'd probably help. He's a good cook.'

'Who is James?'

'You know. James Croft. Bryony's husband.'

James is just one of several people Ketki believes Fleur to be involved with, secretly.

'Help with what?'

'Make curries for the wake, if that's what you really want to do.'

'I just think that we should.'

Oleander always said that the word 'should' should always be ignored. Then she laughed until whoever she was talking to noticed the paradox.

'OK,' says Fleur. 'I'll do a big soup, then, as well.'

'Lentil soup I think,' says Ketki. 'And several carrot cakes.' She bobbles her head again, which means it's all settled.

When Fleur leaves the room she thinks of going to see Oleander, and then remembers that Oleander isn't there any more. She sighs. Ketki's husband Ish is in the meditation area, reading the *Observer*. Fleur half tries to catch his eye, but he doesn't look up. Ish doesn't hear very well now, and it's possible that he just has not sensed her in the room. Then he does look up.

'Go easy on her,' he says. 'She has lost her oldest friend.'

'I know,' says Fleur. She does not add that she has now lost almost everyone, and is probably about to lose almost everything.

Here's what Fleur's ego says, stirred by these thoughts. It says, What about *me*? What about what *I've* lost? It also says, Lentil soup and *carrot* cake? But that's what they make for the retreats. That's what they make for the spa weekends. That's what they *always* make, even though basically everyone who comes to Namaste House now requests a low-carb diet, and absolutely no one eats pulses of their own accord any more apart from Madonna and Gwyneth Paltrow. And anyway, Oleander is dead. She is *dead*. Can they not, *just this once*, do something different? Can they not have . . . (even the ego sometimes needs to pause and think, although this is often just for effect) cocktails and canapés? No. Of course not. Well, *Fleur* will have cocktails and canapés over at the cottage. She'll cook aubergine and homemade paneer wrapped in poppy leaves and intricately flavoured with her homemade black spice blend, and then a fragrant pistachio korma with soft white rice, and little mousses made from bitter chocolate and quail's eggs. In the cottage they will see off Oleander in style, whatever Ketki wants to do in the house. Fleur tells her ego to shut up. Of course she does. But she has to acknowledge that it has come up with a lovely menu. And it would be good to make the thing in the cottage different from the thing in the house. And have something for all the gluten-free, low-carb people like Skye Turner – if she comes – and Charlie – if he comes. She will hand-make some chocolates too. Rose creams, and hibiscus truffles.

Back in the cottage, she starts making a list, remembering what Oleander has been saying so much recently: on the level of form, nothing matters. In this world, you can do what you like. *Doing* is not what makes you enlightened. This is good, after all the things Fleur has done. She may have put off enlightenment for now, but she hasn't put it off forever.

On Monday morning there's a knock at Clem's door. It's Zoe.

'Hey,' she says. 'You busy?'

'I wish the university server would explode again,' says Clem. 'Or whatever it did last time it lost all my emails. Come in.'

Zoe comes in but doesn't sit down. She is very tall and always has her blonde hair tied up in a ponytail that would make anyone else look eight, or a bit backward. Today she is wearing ripped jeans, cheap pink flip flops (even though it is only thirteen degrees outside) and a faded yellow Sonic Youth T-shirt. She has a ring through one nostril and never wears make-up unless there's something official going on, like her job interview, for which she wore black eyeliner only on her top lids, sheer red lipstick and an oddly intoxicating perfume that smelled like a bag of sweets left in a men's locker room for too long. She teaches screenwriting.

'I'm just on my way to staff development,' Zoe says. 'Do you want me to steal you some Jammie Dodgers?'

'What is it this time?'

'Dignity in the workplace.'

'How can anyone be dignified in any workplace?'

'Yeah. I'll definitely make that point.'

'God.' Clem stretches languidly and slowly spins her chair away from her computer. 'I'm being smothered in family.'

'In what way?'

'Oh, sorry, don't worry.' She smiles, and shakes her head as if she had water in her ears. 'Thinking out loud.'

'No, go on. Your family is always interesting.'

'Oh, OK, well, my great-aunt just died – no, don't worry, it's all right, I barely knew her. She's the one who took in my cousin and my best friend when our mothers went missing – you know about that, right? And she used to hang out with the Beatles and everything . . . ? Anyway, my grandmother Beatrix, who's about a hundred and fifty and should not know how to use email, is basically driving us all mad making arrangements for her and my father to come to the funeral, even though they totally hated her. They thought, or think, that Oleander – that's my great-aunt – was responsible for the deaths of my mother, my aunt, my uncle and my best friend's mother.'

'Why? What did she do to them?'

'No one knows. Back in the late eighties they went off to find a miracle plant and never came back. We think the plant has this seed pod that looks like vanilla and has supposedly magical or mystical properties – only no one knows how to get the good effects without dropping dead. Oleander wasn't even there.'

'Wow. Now there's a screenplay.'

'Or a nature documentary.'

Clem's office smells lovely, but in a way that Zoe can't quite fathom. It's not any particular one of the lavender candles, or the large succulent plants, or even all of them together, although they probably contribute to it. Today there's also a scuffed cardboard box containing small plants with white flowers, but they are new and the smell is always there. What is it? It could be Clem herself, perhaps. It's damp forests, but in a good way. Perhaps a touch of the tropics. Clem is the only person in the department to have bare floorboards in her office instead of the institutional carpet. She has also had all the fluorescent lights removed from the office. Yes, *removed*, which is about a thousand times more weird and interesting than just deciding not to turn them on, which is what a normal person would do. Instead of the lights she has various old Anglepoise floor lamps that she says she found in a forgotten cupboard somewhere in the basement. And instead of having an institutional computer whirring away all day, she has a silent, beautiful, tiny laptop that she brings from home in a thin canvas bag. Sometimes she even puts it away in a drawer and works in sketchbooks instead. Zoe only started working at the university in September, and so far her office contains not much apart from the desk, chair and beige computer the department gave her. She has a bright orange carpet that, apparently, her predecessor actually *chose*. She aspires to something like Clem's office, but with an iMac and a bit less sadness.

'This place would be improved if there were fewer emails in general – like a ban on any emails from family, friends and partners, for a start. And, of course, students.'

'Don't let them hear you say that,' Zoe says. 'They love you.'

It's true. The students do love Clem. They love the fact that she directs real documentaries, and therefore can tell them how to do it. Clem also replies to their emails, even if she often takes a couple of days – OK, sometimes a week – to get around to it. But some lecturers never reply to emails at all, which is pretty shit when you're paying over three grand a year to do a course. Clem never tells anyone off for anything. She makes low-key jokes. She doesn't patronise them. When she hears them talking about sex instead of lighting ('Oh. My. God. You actually slept with her and no one told me? I don't care. I'm SO happy for you') she simply raises an eyebrow and watches them all explode into giggles. She has never been late for a class, and always gives them fun things to do, like those spoof nature documentaries where they get to do the worst possible voiceover to go with their footage of rabbits or blackbirds on campus ('*The blackbird is now surely thinking, Why is that Emo tosser pointing a camera at me?*'). She's old enough for them not to be aroused by her. She certainly doesn't freak them out as much as Zoe, who is much closer to them in age and appearance and has worked on things they actually watch. Most of the students know that Clem was nominated for an Oscar, but they haven't seen any of her documentaries, not even *Palm*. But several of the boys in the class have wanked themselves silly to things Zoe has written, especially that teen lesbian drama set in Wandsworth. It's pretty crazy, being taught by someone whose words have made you, well, do *that*.

'How have you even got time for staff development?' Clem asks

Zoe. 'I mean, I hope you're not being too stretched. I don't remember this coming up in your probation plan.'

Zoe shrugs. 'It's new. Different. Defamiliarising, probably. I might get something to put in a screenplay. Also, of course, I'm working towards my Very Important Equal Opportunities Certificate.'

'We should probably add that to your next probation report. It'll look good.'

'Yeah. Anyway, I just wanted to see if you're maybe around for coffee later.'

'What time does it finish?'

'Four thirty, I think.'

'A whole day?'

'I believe there are case studies. And role play.'

'OK, well, knock on my door when you get back. I'm sure I'll still be here. At this moment I feel like I'll be here forever.'

'Cool. By the way, what's in the box?' Zoe asks.

'Chilli plants. Do you want one?'

Zoe shrugs. 'Sure. Well, I mean, are they hard? I so do not have green fingers.'

'They're easy. They're just annuals, as well, so . . .'

'What's an annual?'

'They just have one growing season and then they die. One of my PhD students needed them for his film so I brought some in. Now they're looking for homes. They grow really nice chillies. Quite hot.'

'I do love chillies.'

'Yeah, I'm kind of addicted too. I'll bring you one later.'

Cocks.

Hundreds and hundreds of cocks. Perhaps three of them are in fact birds with feathers and beaks and so on, looking rather ridiculous in this context. But the rest . . . Some of them are in men's mouths. Some of them are in women's mouths. Some of them are in teenagers' mouths. Some of them are in men's anuses. Some of them are in women's anuses, hands, or stuffed between their breasts. Most of them are in women's vaginas. Some women have one cock in their vagina and another in their mouth. Some have yet another cock in their anus. The images are accompanied by captions, for example, 'Young teen gags on hot cock' or 'MILF takes it both ways'. Beatrix meant to type 'clocks' into Google Images, but here she is, looking at cocks. To be properly accurate, it was last month that Beatrix meant to type 'clocks' but actually typed 'cocks', at which point she was prompted about what level of safety mode she wanted. Since Beatrix has never much cared for being protected from things, she switched safety mode, whatever that even was, off. And. Well. *That* was a strange afternoon.

Today she meant to type 'cocks' (although if she was discovered, then, of course, 'clocks' was what she really meant . . . *Very* shocked indeed . . . Can't imagine what sort of perverts would actually choose . . . Unmitigated filth . . . etc. etc.). In fact, for the last month she has been doing this almost every morning after early trading is over. It's not ideal, though, now that she's used to the images. She wants something more, but she doesn't know what. There are too many black cocks on Google Images. Beatrix liked them at first, but now they seem vulgar, and she has realised that at least some of them must be fakes. Some of them are as long as an arm. Beatrix has discovered that she likes medium-sized white cocks: the kind of cock she imagines her husband would have had. She never saw it erect in all the years they were married. She felt it enter her and withdraw from her but she knew she shouldn't touch it or acknowledge it in any other way. He did the minimal amount of touching needed to get it into her. She tried to manually stimulate him once, but he moved her hand away and she had the impression for some weeks afterwards that he thought she was some sort of . . . Well, some sort of whore.

Black whore. Asian Whore. Teenage whore. Whores gagging for it.

Cartoon whore.

Now *they* are strange.

Beatrix's orgasm flutters through her like a tired goldcrest. Afterwards, she gets up and makes herself a pre-lunch gin and tonic. In the kitchen, the laptop showing one of her ADVFN stock-market monitors flickers blue, red and green. Mostly blue today, which is good, although that often means red tomorrow. Once the blood goes back to wherever it came from, Beatrix finds she can't quite believe that she just looked at all those pictures of miserable looking people being, frankly, violated (she has to be honest with herself and admit that 'in the moment' she likes the miserable ones best, but anyway). Beatrix feels very flat at this time of day, around about the time she used to take Archie for his walk. She could still go on her own of course, but she doesn't. At first she enjoyed seeing other people out with their dogs, but now she doesn't. She used to feel like a dog-owner who had lost her dog (in relation to Archie she can't say the word *died*, and even the word *death*, used so frequently about friends, relatives and even a husband, a word that she previously felt was clean, to-the-point and brave, is so wrong in this situation; just as it was about her beautiful daughter Plum) in some sort of temporary way, but now she doesn't; now she's just an old woman doddering about on her own, and it's as if she never had a dog. It was two years ago when he . . . Well, anyway, it was not long after that when she began scrapbooking her investments (a strategy taught by that incredibly tall man at that strange seminar she went to in London), which was why she was looking for pictures of clocks, sort of, but never mind that. Beatrix can't possibly hold the thought of what she just did at the same time as thinking, however fleetingly, about Archie. She sips from her drink and gets one of the scrapbooks down from the shelf. The tall man (what was his name?) had suggested scrapbooks based on sectors: travel and leisure, perhaps, or food and drug retailers. But grandchildren works for Beatrix. Not precisely as they are in real life, but . . .

This is her favourite one, really. In Clem's scrapbook she is not married to ghastly Ollie. Clem is married to Bill Gates, who is not just rich and powerful but surprisingly easy to cut out. This gives Clem a potential budget of billions. What would she do with all that money? Quite clearly, she'd change her life completely. Of course she wouldn't want simply to be Bill Gates's trophy wife. In the scrapbook, Clem has decided to leave her lecturing job in London, get a PhD in Botany and set up her own botanical garden somewhere in the West Country. Her father Augustus, alone again after the sudden death of his young second wife Cecily – from something viral, Beatrix imagines, something old-fashioned and messy like Spanish flu – will pick up his gardening gloves again and become Chief Botanist. Yes, it's based on the Eden Project, and that's what Beatrix has used for her scrapbook, but in her mind it is much more beautiful, and is closed to the public on one day a week when Clem gives tea parties and talks about science and the latest plant research projects. Instead of going off to silly places in JEANS to film palm trees wandering about (which Beatrix doesn't really believe in) Clem spends her days floating around orchid houses in perfect white dresses. She never has periods. Occasionally she gives press conferences in lemon Capri pants. The Capri pants are from Dior, of course. And from about 1982. But that doesn't really matter. Sometimes Beatrix puts things in her scrapbooks simply because she likes them.

Beatrix has a copy of this month's *Vogue* and a pair of scissors and is planning Clem's outfit for the funeral on Thursday. There's a Reiss dress worn by Kate Middleton that would work, although is it too cheap for someone married to Bill Gates? Then again, if it is too cheap for a billionaire, then maybe it's within the range of a relatively well-off grandmother taking her granddaughters to London for shopping and lunch (Saturday) and art galleries (Sunday). Last time they went to an art gallery Clem made her look at a skull covered with diamonds and a sun made of dead flies. This time Beatrix will choose. Perhaps those botanical illustrations at the V&A. They won't be able to get an outfit in time for the funeral, of course, but that's fine; since Beatrix's scrapbooks exist outside normal conceptualisations of time and space, the outfit can be added much later. And the scrapbooks are to help visualise investments anyway. Not that Reiss is listed on the Stock Exchange, but still. Maybe one day it will be. Beatrix wonders where a busy young woman like Clem – either the imagined version or the real one – might buy a funeral outfit in a hurry. Then she buys some shares in ASOS.

After she has checked her email – nothing from Clem, Augustus or Charlie – and moved on to Bryony's scrapbook – now there's a problem – the Schubert begins again. It's not that Beatrix does not like Schubert. She does like Schubert very much. Sometimes when she's searching for c(l)ocks on the internet she does it with Schubert's String Quintet in C Major playing on the stereo system that Augustus bought her for her ninetieth birthday. Schubert's String Quintet in C Major is, to use a word that Beatrix has learned from the internet, 'dirty'. It is also quite 'rough', the last movement in particular. But she likes to choose when she hears it. Not that the person upstairs ever plays the String Quintet in C. It's always the piano sonatas. Because of the c(l)ocks, Beatrix has missed *You & Yours* on the radio, which is just a lot of old people moaning, really, but can be helpful when she is in the mood for shorting. But she has no intention of also missing *The Archers*. Would the kind of person who thinks it appropriate to listen to Schubert at full-blast at midday also be the kind of person who would remember to switch it off in time for *The Archers*? Perhaps not. Beatrix goes back to her study and Googles 'spying on neighbours'. Around a million hits come up, but most of them are just more pornography.

'Right, so here's the dilemma. A colleague has made it clear that he has feelings for you, and you have made it clear that you don't have feelings back. Then he gives you a gift. Is that harassment?'

'What's the gift?'

'That's what I said! They were all like, *Yeah, this is total harassment*, without even knowing what the gift *was*.'

'I mean, if it's the *Kama Sutra*, then yeah, I guess that's probably harassment.'

'But it could be like a Polo or something.'

'Do people still eat Polos?'

'Who knows? Also, what's the *context* of the gift? Has he given lots of people gifts? I mean, you could just imagine some twat going to Human Resources to complain that this guy's given her, I don't know, a copy of his new film or something, even though he's given it to everyone else in the department and put it on YouTube.'

'Or it could be Christmas,' Clem says.

'What a long day.' Zoe sips her soya latte. 'My God.'

'But you've got your certificate now?'

'Yeah. But guess what? It needs updating every five years. I'm going to have to go through all this again before I'm thirty.' She groans. 'Obviously I'll have to make it in Hollywood by then.'

'Is that what you want to do?'

'No. Well, sort of. I don't know.'

The staff common room is almost empty. It has a strange old municipal feel to it despite the posh vending machines and bright red sofas. Zoe has taken her hair down and put on some sheer lipstick, because, well, it is conceivable that she might be meeting people afterwards. Between Clem and Zoe on the table is a chilli plant in a rolled-down Waitrose carrier bag.

'So anyway, what do I do with this?' Zoe asks Clem, touching the bag, but not the plant.

'Put it on a sunny windowsill. Give it a lot of water – like twice a day. It'll prefer being in the garden if you've got one, but aren't you in a flat? Anyway, the only semi-complicated thing you'll need to do if you keep it inside is hand-pollinate it. Don't make a face. It's easy. I'll show you. You take your little finger like this and rub it in the flower gently and look, it's covered with pollen. Then you rub the same finger – gently again – into another flower and that's it pollinated. Now you want to go back to the first flower with pollen from the second. Then to a third flower. See? Keep doing it whenever you see flowers. It can be a bit random. Just pretend your finger is a bee.'

'Don't bees know what they're doing, though?'

'No. It's completely accidental. They go to the flowers for nectar and accidentally pollinate the plants. A little finger is as good as a bee.'

'And this pollen stuff? It's not like poisonous, is it?'

Clem laughs. 'It's the plant's version of sperm.'

'Yuck,' says Zoe, but she starts gently rubbing her finger in one of the flowers and smiles when it comes away covered in yellow dust. She gently pushes her finger into one of the other flowers. 'Have I basically just enabled this plant to have sex?'

'Yep. Exactly,' says Clem.

Zoe pulls the plant towards her. 'I'll look after you,' she says to it. 'You'll get to fuck all the time.'

'Oh, guess what I heard today?' Clem says.

'What?'

'They're going to do the UK premiere of *Palm* at Edinburgh in June. And it's up for their big documentary award. They sent me an email last week which I totally would've missed if I hadn't had a good blitz today. Honestly, someone emailed earlier asking if he could come and do a PhD at our "illustrious universe". And I've had another three from my grandmother since I saw you this morning. Apparently someone won't stop playing Schubert in the flat upstairs from hers, and this is why she's coming to the funeral in the end. It's like . . .' Clem sighs.

'I know. Fucking family, right? But that's amazing news, though.' Zoe strokes a leaf on the chilli plant. 'I mean about the award.'

'Yeah. Thanks. And I'm going to be on the judging panel for the nature documentary prize while I'm there. Should be really interesting. Feel a bit like I've fallen behind with what people are doing at the moment. The last nature documentary I even watched was Heidi Cohen's *Snow*. My god. That was actually last year. Shit. What happens to time?'

'You go to the Oscars. You sit on planes next to plants.'

'How do you know about that?'

'You told me. It stuck in my head. What was it?'

'An Echinacea. I'd completely forgotten. God, that guy who put his whole family in Economy and then sat in Business with his Echinacea plant on the seat next to him.'

'Anyway, it's all in the screenplay I'm writing about your life.'

'Be serious.'

'I am. I'll ask for your permission when it's done, obviously. And check all the plant names or whatever.'

'God.' Clem groans, but does not look displeased.

'Anyway, all great for the REF. Esteem indicator thingies, or whatever. I mean award nominations and panels and stuff.'

The Research Excellence Framework is basically what the World Cup would become if academics organised it. It comes around every six or seven years in some form or other but it's always changing its name and its rules. But essentially whoever publishes the most and best books and does the most glamorous things with the biggest audiences wins. What do they win? Government funding for their department. This has been so vastly reduced in recent years that even the maximum amount is not even worth getting any more, at least not if you're in the arts or humanities. But the more funding the department gets, the better everyone thinks it is. The winners will always be Oxford and Cambridge so the pressure is on to get that third place, which last time went to the London School of Economics. Being on TV, as Zoe's work has, is particularly good. But she'll need to get at least one more film out before 2014. Clem has *Palm*, which is better than anything anyone else in Film has. Of course, she still needs to finalise her whole entry. She'll put in *Palm* and that new documentary she's working on, *Life*. And then she'll probably have to write a couple of journal articles to make up her four outputs. Zoe can get away with two – maybe even one – because she is so new.

'So are you going to celebrate with Ollie?'

'What?'

'The documentary award nomination.'

'I don't know. I've got my great-aunt's funeral to go to next Thursday and by the time I've recovered from having all my family in one room at once it'll probably be too late. Anyway, we celebrated the Academy Awards thing, and everything else. I've done too much celebrating this year.' She downs the last of her double espresso. 'Sorry, that makes me sound like an idiot.'

'Invite me next time. I'll help you celebrate properly.'

'Yeah, I will. Thanks. But you know, at the moment it would just be great to have some peace and quiet. I mean, it's been an amazing year with the film doing so well, but I just want to switch it off now. You must understand. You must have had that with *Wet*, for example?'

'I didn't almost win an Oscar for it.'

'No, but still.'

'You are happy, though, surely?'

Clem smiles at Zoe. 'No, not really.'

Fleur is sitting on a huge sofa in the drawing room of the Soho Hotel doing an echo breath, which is where you breathe out, hold, and then breathe out some more. It's supposed to help undo the ego. It hasn't undone Fleur's ego but at least it's got rid of some of the stale crap from her lungs: a few atoms from Marilyn Monroe's last breath, perhaps, which apparently we all have in our lungs at any given time. Fleur has just had what was supposed to be an hour with Skye Turner, but somehow turned into an hour and a half. Skye's assistant had originally booked yoga and meditation, but in fact Skye just wanted to vent about her manager and so it became a kind of therapy session. Of course, that's fine – listening to people vent is also what Fleur does – but she does get frustrated when people don't follow her advice. It's worst when she says something amazing that Oleander has said in the past to her – like 'What does your heart say?' or 'What would Love do?' – and it has no effect, or the other person just says, 'I don't know'.

People always know what their hearts say and what Love would do, even if they don't want to admit it. Your heart might say 'I want to fuck my neighbour', or 'I want to leave my job', and you might not like it but it's always a good idea to get it out, put it on the table and have a proper look at it. Your heart, not your mind, is what connects you to the universe. And maybe you *should* fuck your neighbour. After all, what you do on the level of form does not matter one little bit. Fleur said something like this to Skye Turner before and Skye suddenly stopped talking and her eyes went clear just for a moment and she *got it*. She was connected, just for a second. Then, *poof*. Skye Turner does sort of want to fuck her neighbour, as it happens, or at least her parents' neighbour; but as her parents' neighbour is on prime-time TV every Saturday night, Fleur is not sure it counts as a heart-universe situation, even though everything is supposed to be equal. Or maybe it was the neighbour's son? She sighs.

Oleander was never impatient with people. Oleander realised that her clients might get stuck with the same problems for months or years or even lifetimes and she gently told them things that she accepted might not actually register for a very long time. Fleur is not a very good therapist really, and certainly isn't a qualified one. She isn't a qualified yoga teacher either, although she's better at that, having taught classes at Namaste House since she was sixteen. Celebrities pay for her advice because she supposedly knows everything Oleander knows. She doesn't know a tenth of what Oleander knew. Well, OK, she knows a lot about making tea. And Patanjali's Eight Limbs of Yoga. But that's it.

The man she is waiting for walks in, wearing faded boot-cut jeans, a pink shirt and an old black wax jacket. He looks both younger and older than his age: sixty-eight. He's always been too thin and he has always walked too fast. He will have parked his silver Mercedes 300SL on Soho Square. He drives everywhere – also too fast – and always finds a parking space, despite all the terrible karma he believes he has.

'Augustus. How are you?' Fleur stands up and kisses him on both cheeks.

'Fleur.' He kisses her back. 'You look very, well . . . very *bright*, to be honest, darling. You'd certainly stand out in a crowd.'

Fleur is wearing a dress that someone's stylist gave her last week as a thank-you present. The top part is a block of cerise and the bottom part is a block of orange.

This, already. 'You think we'll be seen,' she says to Augustus.

'It would be very awkward if we were. Cecily's not fantastic at the moment.'

She follows his eyes as he looks around the large room. A female journalist with a Mulberry Bayswater and old-fashioned Dictaphone is interviewing a young woman at one of the tables, but there's no one else here. The doorway is on the far side of the room, and beyond that is the hotel lobby and the bar. People don't come in here; although on the other hand, of course, they do. Last time Fleur was here there was a celebrity sitting on the opposite sofa playing Top Trumps with a boy of about ten. Fleur thought this boy was his son, and the large dark woman his wife, until it became clear that the woman was from a charity and the boy was terminally ill. The celebrity pledged £10,000 and rewrote a speech the woman had written all while Fleur was sitting there working out a daily yoga routine for the ex-wife of a rapper called The Zone. But celebrities don't give a shit about other people; so, really . . .

'I don't think my dress is going to make any difference. We can go somewhere else if you're not comfortable here. Not Blacks though because of Clem, so I don't really know where else there is. Or maybe this is just a bad idea altogether . . .' Fleur gets up. She didn't used to be like this with Augustus but she is now. She feels as if she's been stuck at the end of the cul-de-sac that is their relationship for a million years.

'Don't be silly. Sorry, darling, you know I get over-anxious. It's on your behalf as well. And Cecily, like I said, isn't . . . Anyway, sit down. Let's have tea.'

Fleur sighs, sits down and breathes out some more. She looks at the menu. It's beautiful. Everything in here is beautiful, which is why she comes. If she was on her own she would probably order a whole afternoon tea with savouries and scones and clotted cream. But Augustus wouldn't understand her ordering all that and then taking three quarters of it home for the birds, so Fleur simply orders a plate of fruit and thé pétales. Oh, and some macarons, at least two of which she will sneak away for the robin, who is quite partial to them. Augustus orders a slice of fruit cake, an English Breakfast tea and a large glass of Bordeaux. He frowns when Fleur gets out her mini jar of pink Himalayan salt and her special herbs that she adds to everything.

'Well,' he says. 'How are you?'

'Sad. Very sad. Not surprised, of course. She's been so ill. I'm still working but everything seems so different. How are you?'

'The same.'

Augustus is always 'the same', whatever that even means. Fleur waits for him to say something about Oleander, but he doesn't. He won't. Fleur doesn't even know why he and Beatrix are planning to come to the funeral, as they haven't spoken to Oleander since 1989. Does he hope to inherit Namaste House? But that wouldn't make sense, because . . . She closes her eyes and opens them again. Sees the frankincense tree first, and then for some reason all the cushion covers she and Ketki sewed.

Augustus frowns again. Rubs his eyes.

'What's wrong?' Fleur asks.

'Oh.' He pauses. He smiles weakly. 'Everything. The usual.'

How many years does it take to stop missing your first wife, your sister and your two closest friends who have gone missing in India – or possibly the Pacific – while you stayed at home with a bout of malaria? More than he's had, that's for sure.

'Well . . . I'm sorry.'

'Don't worry, darling. How's the garden?'

He really isn't going to say anything else about Oleander.

'Good. A bit bare in places. The poppies are coming up. And I actually remembered your seeds this time.' Fleur pulls a small brown envelope out of her bag. 'These are from the best one. Really deep purple. I can't believe I actually let it seed. But then again . . .'

'Thank you, darling. I'll put yours in the post. We keep forgetting.'

'We do.'

'I expect we're very busy.'

Fleur smiles. 'I expect we are.'

The afternoon tea arrives. When Augustus picks up his fork Fleur notices that his hands are shaking. He started growing opium to give to Cecily after her breakdown, but now he takes much more than she ever did. Much more than Fleur does. He says it helps his malaria, but who takes opium for malaria? The last time anyone seriously took opium for malaria in this country was in the sixteenth century. But at least it's something they have in common. Some reason for choosing nice cards to send each other. Although Fleur isn't allowed to sign hers with her own name.

'So is this the fashion?' he asks her, still looking at the dress. 'I'll have to tell Cecily.'

Fleur thinks about the story of the two celibate monks who come to a flooded piece of road. There is a beautiful woman there, and so one of the monks lifts her and carries her past the flood. The other one can't believe he has done this, and sulks for miles. Eventually, he confronts his friend and asks him why he did it. His friend simply replies, 'I put her down several miles ago but you, my brother, seem still to be carrying her.'

'It'll be over by the summer,' says Fleur. 'I wouldn't bother.'

Actually, it won't quite be over by the summer. According to Skye Turner's stylist, colour is going to go on into Autumn/Winter and possibly even beyond into S/S12, although there's also a sixties vibe in the air that she thinks may come to something. Maybe a pencil skirt thing. Fleur learned this earlier on when she was waiting for Skye to emerge from the larger of the two bathrooms in her hotel suite. There were handbags everywhere, about £30,000 worth, that Skye had been sent for free just that morning. She didn't want any of them because one of them was named after a celebrity more famous than her. The stylist was going to take the lime green one for herself, but offered Fleur the yellow one. Fleur didn't want it. Being surrounded by Hindus all the time makes leather kind of awkward. 'Are you mad?' the stylist said. 'Take it and put it on eBay.' But Fleur couldn't be bothered. She probably should have got it for Bryony, though. Now she wants to stop this awkward conversation Augustus is planning to have before it even starts. Cecily, presumably, has her own ideas about clothes. Fleur sees her gardening painfully in white nightdresses at midnight, or visiting the doctor in linen trousers that sag around the arse, or grey asymmetrical dresses that make her look about twenty years older than she is. Fleur hears bits and pieces about her from Clem, who doesn't really feel comfortable having a step-mother only five years older than she is, especially one who can barely walk and so must be pitied a little.

'Really, fashion isn't worth trying to keep up with.'

'Well, you certainly seem to keep up with it.'

'I don't. I just wear what random stylists give me, or what gets left behind at the house. Honestly, being around celebrities all the time would turn anyone off fashion.'

'How is the business?' asks Augustus.

'Good. Great, really. Although who knows what's going to happen now that . . .'

'But the place is making enough money?'

'Yes, of course. For now. With Oleander gone I'm having to do a lot more of the one-to-one stuff, you know, like the therapy and the yoga and . . .'

And helping the Prophet make his parcels now that his one arm isn't so good.

A bit of watering sometimes in the room above the orangery where no one goes.

Because if the universe didn't want her to do this, then the universe would not have set it all up like this, and her mother would not have gone on that trip to meet the Lost People and would presumably not have become such a Lost Person herself. Although in some way she was always lost, which was what started it all. Fleur doesn't know where the Prophet's packages go; he has spared her that. But she's been happy to bank the proceeds. But will they be enough? Because if Namaste House is sold then . . .

'Don't they say people aren't spending money any more? I mean luxury spas and designer gurus are a bit, well . . . With the credit crunch and everything, surely people are cutting back?'

'Celebrities will always spend money on feeling better about being sent thirty grand's worth of handbags that are named after another celebrity.'

Augustus snorts. He's not poor himself – far from it – but he looks down on people who make money from singing about having sex on the floor, or on the beach, even though he has had sex on lots of floors and also on the beach. In fact, sex on the beach was almost certainly what got him into this situation with Fleur in the first place.

'No, I'm serious. It's really hard to cope with a life that's so absurd,' Fleur says. 'Imagine this. You've grown up on an estate in Folkestone, dirt-poor but beautiful. You've never had any money. You've been on one holiday with your mates to Ibiza that cost under a hundred quid and it was the best time you've had in your life. Your friends become hairdressers and waitresses. You get some work doing backing singing and save up to buy yourself one of those' – Fleur points at the journalist's Mulberry – 'which costs eight hundred quid but then you realise that more famous models and actresses and pop stars are being given these things for free, because the companies want their stuff pictured with celebrities. Anyway, to cut a long story short, you make it. You become famous. You release an acclaimed album and you're savvy enough to pick up a stylist as soon as possible and before you know it you're walking for Dior even though you're not a model. You do a duet with the most famous indie singer in the country. *Now* you get sent bags. You get flown first class. You stay in five-star suites. It's great, but you realise you can never go back to Ibiza with your mates again. You can never get excited about earning enough money for a handbag again. The more money you earn, the less things you actually pay for. Everything becomes worthless. Meaningless. But you have to stay famous because the only thing worse than your current life would be to go back: back to poverty and having to take buses and buy frozen food and make your own doctor's appointments. But nobody stays famous. Some people are famous for three years, but that's about it unless you're actually Tom Cruise.'

Augustus puts three, no, *four*, lumps of sugar in his tea. Fleur continues.

'So one day your assistant books you an economy plane ticket by mistake and they won't let you in the executive lounge. You protest and are removed. You try to upgrade but there are no available seats left on that flight. You don't even know how to buy a plane ticket any more. You actually use the dreaded words that you used to joke about with your mother: "Do you know who I am?" They don't. Well, they do, but they're not going to upgrade you now your mascara is running. And there was that thing in *Grazia* last week, and you've put on a couple of stone since you stopped touring. You want to kill your assistant, really kill her, but instead you fire her by text message. You sit in the economy cabin sobbing because for the next three hours you are going to be normal. You may as well be dead. Your lowest point is when you go to use the business-class toilet – because that's the one you've always used before– and the cabin crew politely but firmly steer you back to economy.' Fleur pauses. 'That's where you find spirituality. Right in that moment. That's when you are most ready to be filled with light.'

'You are so like her.' Augustus shakes his head. 'It's uncanny. But be careful, though, darling. Make sure you're prepared for all the stories to surface again now that she's dead.'

Fleur almost says, 'Yes, Daddy.' But she's never called him that.

'Anyway, how's everything in Bath? How's the malaria?'

Augustus frowns. 'Painful. Unpredictable. The same. My mother sent me to an acupuncturist last week. It didn't help. It just hurt.'

'I don't think it's supposed to hurt. Did you say something?'

'No. That kind of thing never works on me anyway. There's no point.'

'So why did you go?'

'You know my mother . . .' Actually, Fleur did not. But she knew all about her.

'How's Cecily? And the girls?'

'Cecily's the same. On a new medication, but can't get up before midday and still won't speak to my mother. Beatrix has made quite an effort lately, but it hasn't made any difference. And the girls, well, Plum's delightful. Reminds me a lot of Clem when she was that age. Lavender's dreadful. I don't know what to do any more. She wants things all the time and sulks if she doesn't get them. Sometimes I wish we'd stopped with Plum. I mean, in terms of Cecily's health, we *should* have stopped at Plum, or even before.'

'It must be a phase,' Fleur says. 'I'm sure Holly went through something similar. Didn't Plum? I mean, marketing to children is such a huge industry now.'

'It's the way Lavender asks for things, though. That's what gets me. She sits on my lap and looks into my eyes like some sort of prostitute – I'm sorry, but that's exactly what it reminds me of. "Darling daddy, *please*," she says, all fluttering eyelashes as if she was Marilyn Monroe or something. Where on earth did she learn to do that? It's just embarrassing.'

Maybe it's the effect of the atoms. Or maybe she was Marilyn in a previous life.

'Does she have friends?'

'Yes, of course.'

'Do they have sleepovers?'

'Sometimes. I think they're too young, but Cecily says it's normal.'

'So she saw another girl do it to her father. Or she saw it on Nickelodeon or a Hollywood film. She's probably trying to impress you. Show you how grown up she is. Show you how much she knows about the world.'

'Yes, but then there's this awful wailing when I say no.'

Fleur shrugs. 'I guess that's just what it's like having kids.'

'You were no bother,' Augustus says.

No. No, Fleur wasn't any bother to Augustus. He quietly paid her school fees and kept his distance and may never even have admitted he was her father if he hadn't thought she was about to have sex with Charlie – her actual brother. He never changed her nappies, and he never bought her a birthday present and she never sat on his lap. Not once.

The third-floor seminar room is windowless and hot. If there were windows you would definitely be able to see Canterbury Cathedral from up here. Seeing the cathedral is one of the top three reasons people come to this university, but once here students usually find themselves in these poky windowless rooms looking not at the cathedral and the pretty town around it but instead at the incomprehensible notes that the seminar leader before theirs has left on the whiteboard. The large dining room downstairs has a perfect view of the cathedral but this view is usually screened off. There doesn't seem to be any reason to screen it off, except perhaps because students sitting there eating their £3.40 meals are deemed unworthy of something so aesthetically pleasing and must have it removed in case it ruins them in some way. Or before they ruin it. Before class Bryony went there for a snack, and she walked around the screens and sat there looking at the cathedral and waited for someone to come and stop her. They did not.

The group is arguing about a piece of dialogue from *Northanger Abbey*. Ollie lets them go on for far too long, as usual, and is not even definitely listening. At this moment the group isn't even supposed to be discussing this passage, but should be finding instances of metafiction in the text. Helen, dreadlocked, dungareed, bisexual, argumentative, thinks it's *highly* insulting that Henry Tilney tells Catherine Morland what flowers she should like, and finds him, and in fact the whole novel, *highly* condescending. Grant, the big-chested American scholarship student, says that in his opinion Henry is trying to liberate Catherine, and other women, by getting them to see beyond the simply domestic. Helen thinks women don't need liberating by annoying toffs, thank you very much. And so on.

Bryony doesn't join in. She simply reads the lines again. 'But now you love a hyacinth. So much the better. You have gained a new source of enjoyment, and it is well to have as many holds upon happiness as possible. Besides, a taste for flowers is always desirable in your sex, as a means of getting you out of doors, and tempting you to more frequent exercise than you would otherwise take. And though the love of a hyacinth may be rather domestic, who can tell, the sentiment once raised, but you may in time come to love a rose?' Bryony sighs. Who wouldn't fall in love with a man who teased you as gently and sweetly as that? Who wouldn't fall in love with a man who could see such different things in a hyacinth and a rose? Henry Tilney knows that loving a hyacinth and loving a rose are two entirely different things. He's really talking about two different seasons, not just the indoors and the outdoors. He's really talking about darkness and light and . . .

But Bryony would rather die than join in one of these discussions. Sometimes she imagines herself saying something, and it's like when you give yourself vertigo by imagining falling off something very high. Everything fizzes up – her heart, her legs and, for some reason, embarrassingly, even her sexual organs – and in a way it's almost enjoyable because she knows that this is a private fantasy, like throwing herself off a cliff, or sleeping with Ollie, and she would never do anything about it. Bryony tells herself that she doesn't really want to sleep with Ollie. It's just because he's her seminar leader. She always wants to sleep with anyone in authority; it's fine. She never does it.

Although of course they did sleep together once, a long time ago, when she and James had a bad patch and before Ollie and Clem were together. Long before the children, or anything that really mattered. But no one knows about that, and it could never happen again. She's too fat, for one thing. And he's married to Clem.

And of course there's still James. James knows the difference between a hyacinth and a rose. James would understand this passage. For a moment, Bryony aches for him, his too-sweet curries and the way he stirs his penis into her as if she were just another concoction bubbling in one of his cast-iron pans – not that he puts his penis in the pans of course – and how that is also too-sweet, as if he'd once read that this is the way women really like it and does it to please her. Bryony can't bear to tell him that she hates it, that she wishes he would just pin her down on the bed and fuck her like a real man. Would Ollie fuck her like a real man? Unlikely. He'd probably do that stirring thing now too. Clem probably likes it. Does Henry Tilney fuck Catherine Morland like a real man? Now there's a seminar discussion. Bryony thinks that he would. He wouldn't be too dominant though; he would simply be assertive, although possibly a little brisk. And as for Darcy . . . To be properly fucked by a real man you'd need Darcy who, to be honest, would probably go down on you as well. First, of course. In his damp shirt. Oh . . .

Bryony stays behind after everyone else has gone. She stays behind most weeks to ask Ollie something or other, even if it's just how Clem is. She hasn't seen Clem much lately and is worried about her. Is she working too hard? But Ollie never says much. Ollie doesn't even acknowledge her until all the other students have left the room. Even then, it can take a few seconds to get his attention. He is often busy rolling a cigarette, or checking his email – or whatever it is he does – on his phone. And then he's always in such a hurry to get away.

'Of course, next week I won't be here, so . . .' she begins.

Ollie puts his iPhone into the inside pocket of his soft brown leather briefcase. The screen of the phone is cracked, and has been since the beginning of term. Sometimes when Ollie gives them some activity to do he sits there looking at things on it with no expression on his face at all. Bryony has wondered why he doesn't get his screen repaired. Surely he'd have had it insured? Or maybe he likes it like that.

'Do the reading anyway, if you can,' he says. 'I think you'll enjoy it.'

How can Ollie have any idea of what she enjoys or doesn't enjoy now? She never says anything in class, and hasn't taken up her supposedly compulsory tutorial. She and James haven't socialised – well, not properly – with Clem and Ollie for quite a long time. Everyone's just so busy. Bryony enjoys – just about – standing in a classroom like this with Ollie, with nothing between her and the door, knowing she can leave at any time. The idea of sitting in a room with him for fifteen minutes? No. What if she blushed? What if she broke his chair? What if she suddenly said something like 'Can I see your penis?' instead of what she actually meant to say? Not that she wants to see his penis (again); it is smallish, mushroom-coloured and rather crooked, but . . .

'Will the class still be going ahead?'

'What, without you and your insightful contributions?'

Bryony blushes. 'No, of course I didn't mean . . .'

'Well, I'm not going to the funeral, so . . .'

'Oh. OK. Well . . .'

He sighs and looks up from his briefcase. 'I did offer. But Clem doesn't *need* me to come. Turns out I'm good for buying flowers for Grandmother Beatrix's Grand Arrival, but not required at the funeral itself.' He smiles wanly. 'I never said that, of course. I realise – as I've been reminded – that if I had normal reading weeks like everyone else this wouldn't have been a problem. But then again, reading weeks are supposed to be for reading, not going to funerals.' At the University of Canterbury, where Ollie works, and the University of Central London, where Clem works, it is usual to have reading weeks in the middle and at the end of the autumn and spring terms. But this term Ollie decided to cancel the one in Week 24 so that his students could discuss eighteenth-century philosophy in the light of Derrida. Bryony isn't that sorry to be missing it. She has tried to read Derrida before. It's very interesting, of course, and who doesn't love Derrida? But it takes her around an hour to read a paragraph and by the time she gets to the end of it she's forgotten what was at the beginning and sort of wants to go to bed. When Jane Austen says something clever, everyone – or almost everyone – can understand it, even after a few glasses of wine. Why can't Derrida be more like Jane Austen?

More pertinently: why is Ollie confiding in Bryony? It frightens her. *He* frightens her, with his slightly cold eyes and the new flashes of silver electrifying his hair and his stubble. He and Clem are both greying stylishly of course. Despite now living in Canterbury, they both still go to their old hairdresser in Shoreditch who gives them jagged, asymmetrical cuts that somehow emphasise their wisdom, rather than their age. Bryony is sure that Clem still books all Ollie's hair appointments. She probably pays for them too.

'I'd better go,' she says, looking at her watch.

'I'm off to the bar. Fancy a drink?'

'I can't. I mean, I'd love to, obviously. But, you know, the kids.'

'Let James put them to bed for a change.'

Bryony frowns. In reality, James will already have put the kids to bed. In fact, he puts the kids to bed almost every night because of Bryony doing her reading, or her valuation reports, or having drunk a bit too much.

'He wouldn't know how,' she says.

'No?' Ollie shrugs. 'OK, well, I'm going to go and have a drink anyway.'

'Where do you even get a drink on campus at this time of night?'

The bar is dark, uncomfortable and almost empty. All the furniture is cheap, sticky and has sharp, thin edges that would kill a toddler in less than five minutes. There's football: Germany are playing Australia on a screen that covers most of one wall. Germany are winning, of course, but Bryony can't see that from where she's standing. Bryony wouldn't be able to spot the German football team if they walked into this bar. She watched all England's matches in the World Cup last year – yes, including the one against Germany where the ball went over the line but wasn't a goal – and she even pretended to like it, and actually did understand the offside rule when Holly explained it to her, although she's forgotten it now; but, really, *football*? Sometimes she has said to James that her love of fashion is like his love of football, and she has to admit that there is something gendered and therefore unfathomable about it all. Both football and fashion have beautiful patterns that you seem to need the right kind of chromosomes to see, although as James has repeatedly pointed out, fashion requires a lot of time and money and football just requires a subscription to Sky Sports or a nice local pub.

Ollie hands Bryony her large white wine without looking at her and picks up his pint of IPA without looking at it. He looks, with the same expressionless expression he uses when looking at his phone, at the big screen. As Bryony follows him to a table, she can just about see that one of the teams has scored one goal, and the other has not scored any goals.

'Nice to see Australia losing something,' says Ollie.

Bryony mumbles something indistinct that could be 'That's good', but might equally be 'That's interesting', or even, if you analysed the tone closely enough, 'I really couldn't give a shit.'

'Shame the Germans don't play cricket,' Ollie says.

'But then wouldn't they beat England at that too?' says Bryony.

'Do you like sport?'

Bryony can't work out whether the emphasis in that sentence has fallen on the word 'you', the word 'like' or the word 'sport'.

'Not really. I quite like tennis, I suppose, but that's only because of Holly.'

She sips her wine. It's too sweet and too warm. At home she has most of a bottle of 2001 Chablis in the fridge. It cost around thirty pounds, but that's worth it, right, for a bottle of wine to drink at home, when you'd pay that for a bottle of really crap wine in a restaurant? Anyway, the Chablis is cool and crisp, of course, but with just a hint of hay bales in the early morning – don't laugh – and, to be honest, well, just a touch of horse manure. Bryony loves wine that tastes of barnyards or stables. She's been looking forward to that Chablis all day. Now she has 250mls of this crap, Pinot Grigio or something, to get through, and she feels slightly dizzy from not eating since half past five. Why the fuck did she order a large glass of white wine in the first place when all it's going to do is get warmer and warmer? And she has to drive home. And not say anything stupid.

'So I guess you're not my teacher any more,' she says to Ollie.

'Yeah,' he says. 'Now we can fuck.'

What? OK. Bryony has gone bright red. She must have done. Ollie is still looking at the football. She looks at what he is looking at. Someone in a white shirt kicks the ball to the goalkeeper. It's all a bit blurry. He's not trying very hard to . . . Oh, of course. It's the goalkeeper on his own team. Bryony does not understand why people kick the ball to their own goalkeeper when surely they should be trying to get it to the other goal. But . . . Now someone's blowing a whistle. Everyone stops running. It's half time.

Ollie looks at her. 'Er, *joke*. Sorry.'

'No, it's OK. It's . . .'

'Anyway, what about the PhD? I'll be supervising that, surely? You can't fuck your supervisor. You've applied, right?'

'What?'

'*Joke*.'

'I know.'

'So?'

'Yeah. I applied online at the weekend.'

'And for funding?'

Bryony frowns. 'Yeah.'

Ollie sips his IPA.

'OK. Look, don't take this the wrong way, but do you actually need funding?'

'What?'

'I mean, do you actually need funding more than, say, Grant, whose father lost his foot in an accident in a factory that won't pay him any compensation? Or Helen, who grew up on a council estate in Herne Bay and whose head-teacher once had to buy her a coat because her parents spent all their dole money on smack? I mean, I don't want to put you off or anything, but . . .' He laughs. 'Well, to be honest I do kind of want to put you off. I mean you guys are pretty minted, right, you and James?'

Ollie says all of this as if it's another joke. He even adds some ironic gravity to what he says about Grant and Helen so that Bryony knows that he knows that their narratives are just that, *narratives*, and that reality is so much more complex and dignified than tired old sob stories. The only thing is, it's also obvious that he's totally serious, so . . .

'Well, actually . . .'

'And of course – and I don't mean to be harsh, but it's happening, right, so we might as well admit it – there's Great-Aunt Oleander's estate to be divided up. What's that house worth? A million or two? Plus the business.'

'She's probably left it all to Augustus,' Bryony says. She has already had this conversation with James. What is it about men? Can people not just be sad for a few days before starting to talk about who gets what? But the fact is that, to be blunt, Bryony has spent most of what she inherited from her parents on clothes, wine, shoes and stuff for the kids, and she and James don't have that much money any more. Well, they have some money. But not so much that Bryony can blow £950 in ten minutes in Fenwick on eye-shadow and moisturiser as she did on that hot, peculiar day last summer. They don't have enough money to live like Augustus and Cecily, or Beatrix, of course, with all their property and bonds and God knows what. Bryony and James have enough money to go to the Maldives at Christmas, which is what Bryony wants to do, but not enough money to buy a forest just outside Littlebourne, which is what James wants to do. If Bryony does inherit part of Oleander's estate, she has promised to buy James the forest on the basis that, yes, of everything a person could choose to do in the entire fucking world, she really wants to spend every summer in a dark, damp forest, picking poisonous toadstools and getting wet all the time and DYING. Even if she doesn't die, her thighs will chafe, which people think is funny but is not funny. But maybe James will get a book out of it. And Bryony will be thin by the time they have to actually go to the forest, which means that everything will be different. She'll be like a woodland nymph, dressed only in pure white cobwebs, and . . .

'What are you and Clem going to do with your share? I mean, if there is a share, which I still think there probably won't be.'

'Probably a teaching buyout for me, so I can finish my book.' Ollie finishes his IPA. 'It's just so fucking busy here all the time. Clem wants a pond in the garden. Wants to make a film about it.' He looks at Bryony's wine. 'You want another one? I'm going to get another one.'

Bryony shakes her head. He goes to the bar. Bryony wants to pee, but she can't leave while Ollie is at the bar. Perhaps he'd think that she'd walked out on him because of what he said about fucking, or about the scholarship. Perhaps then he'd leave too. Would that be such a terrible thing? Then Bryony could go home and start again on her evening, and drink the Chablis instead of this Pinot Grigio and love James like a real wife would. There are 165 calories in this glass of wine, but Bryony won't log it in her food diary later because it isn't very nice and she didn't really mean to have it. When she gets home she'll have 250mls of Chablis and she'll log that instead. She also won't log the sausage roll and chips she had in the dining hall before this evening's class, because, after all, she wouldn't normally have something like that, and now that term is more or less over she is confident that she will never even go to the dining hall any more, and after all where else would you find sausage rolls and chips? Fuck it. She just won't fill in her food diary at all today. She'll start afresh tomorrow. That means she can drink all the Chablis when she gets home. And she could have a packet of crisps now. Could she eat a packet of crisps in front of Ollie? No. Well, maybe. Actually, what Bryony really wants is a cigarette, but that would just be nuts. She gave up for the last time over three years ago. No calories in fags, of course. But James hates her smoking, and so do the kids. Last time Bryony smoked, Holly cried all night and threatened to kill herself.

Ollie comes back with a pint of IPA and a medium glass of white wine.

'Here,' he says. 'Sorry I'm being a bit of a cunt. It's been a long day.'

175 ml. Another 130 calories. And it will be warm by the time she gets to it. Warmer. What she should do, what she should really do, is wait for Ollie to go outside for a cigarette and then tip the rest of the large glass away somewhere and start again on the slightly cooler and smaller new glass. OK, how would she actually do that? She could just take it back to the bar. She could take it back to the bar and explain that she really shouldn't drink this because she's driving and could they just get rid of it for her, please, but in such a way that the man she's with doesn't see? Or she could just return it because it's shit. She could go up to the bar and say, 'Your wine is too shit even for students,' or something cleverer that she would think of. But then they'd just give her more of something else. It's so hard

to lose weight when all the time people are giving you things full of calories. Ollie starts rolling a cigarette.

'Actually,' she says, 'can you do me one of those as well?'

The football is back on. Improbably, Australia scores a goal.

'Fuck me,' he says. 'Game on. You coming?'

They smoke by the university duck pond. Bryony wants to vomit, but she has to admit that once she is over the initial nausea, the cigarette tastes amazing. She feels mellow, all of a sudden, almost the way she felt that time she made tea from the wrong caddy at Fleur's cottage. She'd forgotten it was like this. She was thinner when she smoked as well. How could she have ever stopped doing it? Smoking was like having a best friend who always listens and never judges you.

'It would be nice to have a garden pond,' she says. 'I guess now the kids are a bit older, but they're so expensive and . . .'

'If you get a scholarship you could afford a pond.'

'That's not what I mean.' She sighs. 'Anyway, yes, all right, fine. I'll pull out. I don't need the scholarship as much as Grant and Helen need it. Point taken. But the main thing is that they're better students than me, so why would I waste my time going up against them?' She sighs again. And draws deeply on the cigarette.

Ollie screws up his face. 'Why do you think they're better students than you?'

'They say more.'

'You got the top mark for your essay.'

'Did I?'

'Yeah. So you'd probably get the scholarship. But they need it more. And they won't come without it, so you'd basically be doing them out of their doctorates. You'll come anyway, of course.'

'I guess so. Well, no pond then.' And no forest. 'Never mind. Hope you get yours.'

'No kids to drown in ours,' Ollie says. 'Never will be.' He throws his cigarette end in the duck pond. 'And because of that, my wife has started hating me. But you'll know all about that.'

Bryony does not have any idea what he's talking about.

'I don't have any idea what . . .'

'Look, ignore me. I'm being a total cunt. Sorry. Fuck it. Let's go back.'

Inside, Australia have scored another goal. A penalty. It's 2–1.

'Well,' Ollie says. 'Miracles do happen.' He goes to buy another drink.

Bryony should have left by now. She hasn't even texted James to tell him she'll be late. Why has she not even done that? She could have done that while Ollie was at the bar, or while he was outside smoking, if she hadn't been outside smoking with him. She should do it now. When she gets in she'll have to clean her teeth before saying hello to anyone. That might sort of fool the kids, but it won't fool James. Whatever she does now, he'll know she's been drinking, and smoking. At this rate she won't even be able to finish the lovely Chablis because James will probably be in bed reading, and what kind of wife sits up drinking while her husband lies in bed reading?

She quickly texts him now: *End of term drinks. No reception until now, sorry. Home soon as I can get away. Love you.* Somebody, probably Fleur, was telling Bryony recently about an app people get that writes their text messages for them. In order to do this, it has a database of the things people always say in text messages. *Sorry. See you soon. Leaving now. I love you.* It must have been Fleur. Yes, it was over tea on Sunday while they were not talking about Oleander's death and how Fleur felt about it. One of the celebrities had told Fleur about this app, expecting her to disapprove. But for Fleur there was no difference, not really, between an app supplying the words 'I love you' and one's fingers typing what are essentially just words anyway. Bryony surprised herself by saying something back about Derrida, and arguing that it's not that words are meaningless: quite the opposite. Words separate things. They create meaning. Without words we wouldn't know the difference between a table and a planet. Without words, would anything exist at all? Then Fleur, being Fleur, said there's no difference between a table and a planet anyway because the whole universe is just an illusion. Then Holly rolled her eyes and said, 'OK, you are both officially mad.'

'Clem doesn't hate you,' she says to Ollie when he comes back. 'How could she? I mean, you're very attractive – I'm saying that objectively, of course – and your book is going to be amazing, and . . .' Bryony touches Ollie's arm in a way that is supposed to be reassuring. Bryony doesn't touch many men's arms, at least not any more. She is surprised to find how firm this one is. Ollie's biceps are incredible: rocks the size of tennis balls. Bryony's intellectual mind retreats into what could be an endless ellipsis while her vaginal walls immediately start producing fluid. Biology is such an easy lay.

'Maybe she thinks she doesn't,' he says. 'But underneath, she does.'

'No. That's not right. She's lucky to have you.'

He sighs. 'I don't know.'

He's probably right. Bryony was the lucky one, getting James. He has already texted her back: *No hurry. Hope you have fun. Kids in bed. Drive safely. Love you forever.*

When Ollie gets in, Clem is asleep. Or pretending to be asleep to make him feel bad about staying out. Or perhaps some mixture of the two. He shits in the spare toilet before joining her. Here's the game: he is being REALLY, REALLY quiet so as not to disturb her because she is so clearly REALLY, REALLY asleep. She cracks first.

'Hello.'

And he does love her. That's the thing. He adores her.

'Hello.'

'Are you having an affair? Do I need to start shaving my legs more or something?' She yawns. 'Please tell me it's not a student.'

'No, no. You're quite safe. I was out romancing Frying Pan.'

This is what he calls Bryony. How do these nicknames start? Well, Bry rhymes with Fry, obviously. Bryony and frying pan have the same number of syllables. They are both dactylic, which means that the stress falls on the first syllable of the three. The nickname is also metonymic, because Bryony is fat, and frying pans represent, or in some way stand for, fat. But you can analyse these things too much. Clem knows who he means, and while she never joins in his nicknaming, she doesn't stop him doing it either. It's basically because she must still believe that he is taking the piss out of himself when he does it, and not the other person. And his nicknames aren't that good, to be honest. If Clem comes up with something it's brilliant. If Ollie does it's usually just a bit weird. Like all his book proposals.

'God, I must give Bryony a ring about next Thursday.' Clem rolls onto her back. 'How was your class?'

'Fucking awful.'

Ollie can see Clem's Forever Fish swimming bag neatly packed for the morning on the yellow wooden chair on her side of the room. The neatness is partly to spite him, just as the neatness all around the house is partly to spite him. The yellow wooden chair on his side of the room is empty. It is empty because their cleaner, Alison, insists on putting everything away. Anything that is left out is dumped, hidden or imprisoned in whatever cupboard or on whatever shelf happens to be nearest. Ollie looks and finds yesterday's gym shorts hanging up in the wardrobe. This is stupid because, first, who hangs shorts in a wardrobe? Second, they stink. Ollie would report this to Clem, but she would just lazily say something about how he isn't a child and can he put his shorts in the washing basket if he wants them washed rather than put away. Under the reign of Alison, these are the only two things that can happen to objects in this house: they are either washed, or they are put away. Clem has no qualms about telling Ollie off, but will never mention how she really feels to Alison. But of course, if Clem feels really strongly about something she never actually says it to anyone. This is why Ollie reads her journal. And because she knows he reads her journal, she never writes what she really feels in it (and sometimes goes so far as to actually lie, for example all that stuff about how she REALLY, REALLY loves him).

But anyway, even if half her journal is bullshit, he knows how she feels. He knows that she genuinely wants him to be a success – not as much of a success as her, of course – but enough of a success that he is no longer embarrassing. Can't produce a book, can't produce the right sort of sperm . . . Ollie imagines Clem in the swimming pool, in her red swimming cap with her turquoise goggles. That swimming cap . . . He imagines making love to her while she is wearing her swimming cap, and her sensible turquoise-and-white Speedo swimsuit. He'd pull the swimsuit to one side, as if they were both teenagers, perhaps leaning up against a tree . . . He'd get her to give him a blow job with her swimming cap on, and then he'd come on her head. Ollie's erection subsides as he pisses for the last time before bed. Can he not even get a sexual fantasy right? He imagines telling her about it, and then Clem laughing, just once, and asking why she'd be leaning against a tree in her swimsuit and explaining where the whole fantasy had gone wrong. *That bit about the swimming cap . . .* But it's rubber, isn't it? Of course men are going to feel that way about rubber. *But coming on my head? That's a bit, well, a bit odd, wouldn't you say? Especially as you're infertile. I mean, who wants a load of dead spunk on their head?*

Clem yawns, and starfishes her legs under the covers.

'So why did you go for a drink with Bryony?'

'I totally persuaded her not to go for the scholarship. It was so easy, and . . .'

'Isn't that a bit immoral?'

'Not if I get two PhD students for the price of one. Or three, if

I can get Grant and Helen to split the scholarship between them. They can't not promote me if I have three PhD students and loads more time to . . .'

'How can they split a scholarship?'

'The eighteenth-century one is like twenty-five grand a year. For that you could easily get two sets of tuition fees and two lots of rent with some left over for a Pot Noodle every so often, or some lime and soda down the pub. They'll do some teaching. They won't starve. I mean it's not as if these . . .'

'But isn't the point of that scholarship to give a student a really good PhD experience because that's what Esther would have wanted. I mean, didn't her husband say . . .'

Ollie rolls his eyes. 'It's great being dead, isn't it? I mean, dictating what everyone . . .'

Clem twists her hair around a finger. 'Don't be a fucking idiot.'

Again, the way she says it. With a little lazy smile so he can't get pissed off. Like when a beautiful cat scratches you and you can't really be cross. Although Clem is not cat-like. She's a mermaid. A smiling, singing, beautiful and deadly thing from the sea, twisting her hair around her finger like . . . Like, who *does* that during what could become a really exciting argument, with crying and everything?

'Don't call me a fucking idiot.' And because of her, he can't even say this the way he wants to say it and has to make it sound like something from a meditation tape. Ollie takes off his shoes, which should have been taken off downstairs. He drops his socks on the wooden floor, and his boxers on the yellow chair. He sucks in his stomach as he unbuttons the yellow shirt that Clem bought him. This goes in the washing basket, although the wrong one (there is one washing basket for delicates, to be washed only by Clem, which this shirt, costing £189.99, definitely is; and another washing basket for things which are not delicate and can therefore be washed by Alison, who puts everything on the Easycare cycle regardless of what any of the labels say). Ollie folds his jeans over the back of the chair, but they look wrong there, so he hangs them up. Then he puts his socks and boxers in the non-delicate washing basket and moves his yellow shirt to the right basket. Why is life so fucking complicated?

'Anyway, didn't her husband say that the bequest was to make sure a student could do a PhD without having to work as a waitress on roller skates, or whatever bizarre thing Esther had to do?'

'Topless on wheels, selling her body for . . .'

'Oh, come on.' She sighs. 'Don't be such a dick.'

'Well, she . . .'

'She's been dead for less than a year. She was our friend. Why does everything have to end up being about . . .'

'Oh, right. And now you're going to pretend you were really close to Oleander too.'

'Ollie . . .'

'What?'

'Why are you being such a dick today?'

Of course she calls him a dick, rather than a cunt, because her cunt works and his dick does not work. At least, his dick works, on the rare occasions when it is given the chance, but his balls are a tangled mess and because of that . . .

'Why is it always me?'

'I don't know why it's always you.'

'Oh, so you won't even admit . . .'

'I think I'm going back to sleep now.'

'I see, so you won't even . . .'

'Goodnight.'

And how does she do that? She just rolls over and goes to sleep. Just like that. Like a seal or something, rolling over in the water, or into the water from a grassy bank or wherever seals go when they're not in the water. She doesn't even moan about having to get up so early in the morning because she WORKS IN LONDON when they

LIVE IN CANTERBURY. And it is quite late, after all. It's 23.15 and she likes to be asleep by half past ten. Can you lose an argument on the basis of simply not scoring enough points? Or is going to sleep in the middle of it basically a KO against the person who is still awake?

Somewhere in the grounds of Namaste House, a pop star is loose. Not Paul McCartney, who evidently couldn't make it. It's only Skye Turner, nowhere near as famous as Paul McCartney of course but currently a respectable number 7 on the Top 40 compiled from iTunes and Spotify figures (but not YouTube, where she has yet to make her mark). She is not just loose but lost and alone in the white garden, which is not yet white. She has been to the house thousands of times but has never made it beyond the orangery and into the grounds. And now Oleander is gone. About half an hour ago Skye Turner saw a copper sculpture of a horse that she would like to buy. It was standing in the middle of something called the 'wildflower meadow', although there are no wildflowers yet. Would such a thing be for sale? You don't know unless you ask. But now she can't find it again. At first the sculpture horrified her: it was half horse, half skeleton. But now she would like to buy it. She would like to buy it, but she can't find it. And now Oleander is gone.

Who was Skye Turner crying for, at the funeral this morning? Was she crying for Oleander, who was old and had not been in much pain and in any case not only believed in reincarnation but did not want to be reincarnated, which is a win-win, really? Or was she crying for herself, for what she had lost? There's Fleur, of course, Fleur remains, but . . . Skye Turner sighs. Oleander was a mystical recording studio, and all the tapes that Skye Turner made there are now lost. Burned. Erased.

She walks through an old wooden door and finds herself in a small walled garden. In the centre of the garden is a stone plinth with another copper sculpture on it: a toad. Facing the sculpture is a moss-covered bench with a robin on it. The robin stops digging around in the moss and starts watching her. The dried remains of last year's poppies – even Skye Turner can recognise a poppy – are scattered around like faded decorations from a long-ago party. And there are green shoots everywhere. Things are growing, despite the cold. There is a faint smell of chamomile. She turns again and is no longer lost: there is Fleur's cottage, looking like something from a book, with its big, sleepy-eye windows and huge, sad door. Ivy beards it all over like a green man's face. And there's Charlie Gardener, the great-nephew, hovering. He is thin, angular, slightly wizard-like. A young, dark magician who might see her and chase her through the tangled forest where she would fall and . . . Skye Turner moves away, back towards the white garden, followed by the robin, who is singing something that sounds like, but can't be . . .

How exactly does a pop star come to be in the garden of a house on the very edge of England, in a slow, small medieval town that, long ago, was a busy port before the sea curled up like an old woman with no lover and became a tiny, shallow river with little boats and moorhens and samphire growing on its banks? You can take a helicopter, which is what the Beatles did all those years ago. You can land at the small airport a couple of miles away. But the more normal route is two trains and a taxi. It takes forever. On a map Sandwich looks close to London. It is in Kent, for goodness sake, a county that bleeds into London, is right next to it. But it takes Skye almost as long to get here as it takes to get to her parents' place in Devon, which is almost five counties from London, the way the train goes. From here to her parents' place in Devon it's roughly seven hours. And then there's Greg somewhere in the middle.

And now Oleander is gone.

Skye Turner walks on, through the small forest and around to a larger path lined with trees. From here she can see Namaste House: big, red, old; perhaps slightly wiser than the sad cottage next door? The large white door with the crescent-moon steps leading up to it. The orangery to the right. All the flowerbeds and kitchen gardens and greenhouses and the old brass sundial. There are flowers everywhere in this part of the garden. Skye Turner can't name most of them, but in the summer they are delicate purple things and fragile red things and trembling blue things and things that climb up without checking what the way down might be. Clinging to the side of the house is a plant that could be clematis, with large buds. And inside, she knows, through the white door, there will be the faint smell of chlorine from the indoor pool and the hum of the generator – or whatever the hell it is – that runs the sauna and steam rooms. The pale ceramic jugs of lemon water everywhere: alkaline, purifying. Curries for lunch. Wholemeal cakes. And then through the library and up some stairs and there she always was. Oleander, wearing something ridiculous – a robe covered with stars and planets once and a silver shell suit another time – with a sweet, deep warmth that was like something you'd drink if you were really ill, and of course Skye Turner was really ill when she first came here and . . .

And now Oleander is gone.

The doorway to Fleur's cottage smells of lapsang souchong, black cardamom and roses, which is a bit how Fleur herself smells, although with Fleur there are layers and layers of scents, each one more rare and strange than the last. Her perfume, since they discontinued Givenchy III because of something to do with the oak moss in it, is Chanel's 31 Rue Cambon. She is peppery, woody . . . She is the essence of chypre. She is deep, green, magical: something you'd find naked by a remote lake. Something that would let you, no, encourage you, to do whatever you . . . Beyond the doorway, where there are pre-dinner smells of chocolate, fruit and fresh spices, Charlie can hear someone crying, probably Bryony. His sister Clem never cries. And then Fleur's voice.

'I had to let you know as soon as possible, basically.'

'It's just, I mean, I'm thrilled for you. But why?'

'I think . . . I mean, I do feel a bit awkward.'

'But let's face it, though, our husbands *would* want to sell it.'

'James wants a bloody forest.'

'Ollie doesn't know what he wants, really. Or what I want. But he definitely wants money.'

'I do think that's probably why.'

So *Fleur* has inherited Namaste House. Well. Oleander must have known, then. She must have known that Fleur is Augustus's daughter. But why not give a share to anyone else? Charlie can see Fleur biting her lip in that way she does, trying to explain, trying to find a way of telling her oldest friends that she is unbelievably rich and they are not, when it was supposed to be the other way around. But they must appreciate that she has worked there for free for almost fifteen years, using her strange, quiet instinct for business to take the place out of danger of bankruptcy. And . . . well, actually, for God's sake, why has no one ever seen it? The family resemblance is so striking it is almost embarrassing. Or it would be if anyone bothered to look. She and Charlie resemble twins found huddled together approximately twenty years after being abandoned in a remote jungle. Or maybe Harrods. In any case, if you left twins together for that long, alone, perhaps it's inevitable that they would . . . But anyway, they are hardly together any more, and everyone else is so wrapped up in themselves that it's likely that no one will ever notice, and no one will ever know. Which hurts Charlie in a way he can't quite . . .

'What, because Ollie's such an idiot?'

'No! Of course not! But yeah, I guess I will keep the whole thing going and look after Ketki and Ish, and Bluebell, and the Prophet, for the rest of their lives. Oleander knew I'd do that. I've been trained to do that for, like, forever. I'm not going to sell up because running Namaste House is literally the only thing I know how to do.'

'But she gave you no idea she was planning . . .'

'No. Well, not exactly. You know what she was like. But then she didn't tell me that she was going to give all of us a seed pod each either. Or that Quinn left a journal. And then of course there's that amazing hunting lodge on Jura. I didn't even know we – she – even owned that. You and Charlie will have to work out what you're all going to do with it. I mean it's got to be worth loads as well, right? It looked way bigger than Namaste House. It must be so exciting! So we've all done OK really, not that we should see it in that way, because of course we'd all rather have Oleander back and everything. It's just so strange the way that . . .'

It is strange, Charlie thinks. But Oleander must definitely have known. She knew all about Augustus and Briar Rose and their secret daughter. No one thought it was odd when Oleander let Fleur stay on in the house after her mother disappeared. Fleur had grown up in that place after all. Where else was she supposed to go? And where was Oleander going to get another yoga teacher that she wouldn't have to pay? But now all the extra responsibility she gave Fleur makes sense. And of course the huge gift of the cottage. She must always have known Fleur was one of the family; that Fleur had Gardener blood in her. But leaving Namaste House – the whole operation – to her? What the fuck is that about? Charlie is pleased for Fleur, of course he is, but what are Beatrix and Augustus going to say? And what in God's name are they all – the younger generation, the ones left behind – supposed to do with a seed pod each? What was Oleander trying to say there? Go kill yourselves? Will there be something in Quinn's journal that explains further? But if

Oleander had things and knew things that were important then why hide them for the last twenty-odd years? Clem has already asked to read the journal, and Bryony has shrugged and said yeah, for sure, but she just wants to read it first, as Quinn was her father after all. Which basically means no. And as for this hunting lodge on Jura, which he, Clem and Bryony now own, and which Fleur is still trying to make sound exciting and even better than Namaste House, no one knows how that came to be in the family at all. They'll go and visit it in July, they have decided. It's two plane rides away in the depths, if such a thing exists, of the Inner Hebrides, off the west coast of Scotland. And then to make things even more confusing there is this woman lurking about called Ina who turned up at the funeral from the Outer Hebrides . . . She was saying something about the frankincense tree before and . . .

Fleur's voice has long since trailed off. There's a long pause followed by the sound of a teaspoon hitting bone china just slightly too hard.

'Will you have to get some kind of qualification now? I mean, if you're going to take over running all the therapy and yoga and everything?'

'Bryony!'

'Well, she's talked about it often enough. And I've really enjoyed going back to uni. I just thought . . .'

Charlie pushes the open door and calls 'Hello?' to let them know he's coming, and to give the impression that he's only just arrived and hasn't been listening to their conversation for the last ten minutes. His Vans don't make any sound on the black-and-white Victorian tiles in Fleur's entrance hall. He wore a suit for the funeral itself but has since been back to Bryony's and changed into his favourite Acne faded corduroy trousers and a white T-shirt with a yellow Alexander McQueen cardigan over the top. 'You look like an old person,' is what Holly said when she saw him. So he tried the Acne blazer that was his second choice but a bit matchy-matchy with the trousers. 'You look like you've been to Debenhams,' she said. 'You are basically an old person who goes to Debenhams, and even has lunch there, with slimy peas and gravy.' She sort of had a point; he could see that. But maybe you have to be over eleven to understand that fashion is not only – or even – about looking good. At eleven it is impossible to understand why grown-ups wouldn't want to be happy all the time and go around in ball gowns drinking fruit juice and eating chocolates and spending their wages on puppies, kittens, board games, picnics, trips to the cinema and visits to the donkey sanctuary. Charlie supposes that if Holly were ever in charge of a budget there'd have to be a tennis court too. And cut flowers. He suddenly sees her holding vast bunches of pale pink peonies, weighing more than she does, probably, with early-summer sunlight glinting off her almost-black hair.

The women are in the drawing room on the right. Charlie breathes deeply, as he always does when he enters this room, as if to actually take it into his body: the polished oak floorboards; the Sanderson Grandiflora wallpaper in eggshell and bronze; the antique sofas that Fleur reupholstered herself using various old Liberty fabrics, all with botanical, slightly otherworldly prints. The large vase of pussy willow on the apothecary-style coffee table. Fleur herself is sitting in the rocking chair, which has a print of dark pink and purple organisms that are almost, but not quite, recognisable flowers. Clem and Bryony are sitting together on the pinker of the two George Walton sofas. In front of them Charlie is pleased to see the Wedgwood Golden Bird tea set he bought Fleur for her thirtieth birthday. He, of course, is still wearing the labradorite pendant she made for him all those years ago. They've hardly spoken for months after that argument about Pi last July, although of course they saw each other earlier at the funeral, but from opposite ends of a row. Now here he is.

'Hello,' says Fleur. 'I'd offer you a cup of tea but actually we're due to have cocktails in half an hour when the others arrive so unless you're desperate . . .'

The smell of Fleur's lapsang souchong blend. But . . .

'I'm fine. Can I help with anything?'

'Yes, actually,' says Fleur. 'Come and help me pick some mint.'

There is a frost on the morning after Oleander's funeral. When the robin wakes up, his wings are glary and frozen, and he has to shake himself for several seconds to free them before he can even think about flying. When he gets to the large stone birdbath he finds that there is no water, just a large slab of ice that he can't drink or bathe in. But there is something on his table, at least: not dried mealworms; not slugs. The robin likes spelt pastry but does not like smoked salmon because it tastes of fire and danger. Norman Jay does not like smoked salmon either, and the no-name woodpecker doesn't even come to the bird table. The bad-luck magpie will have to eat it when he comes later in the morning, or else the bigfat pigeon will have it, or his mate will.

After he has eaten several poppy seeds and the remainder of his pink macaron, the robin flies to the other birdbath on the steps leading up the side of the cottage, where it is warmer. He drinks slowly, and then washes, his lacklustre wingflap signifying that he does not want what is coming soon: finding a mate, nesting, providing. He is tired: it is his eighth spring. Through the bedroom window he can see that Fleur is nesting. Fleur often nests. But she never lays any eggs. That man in her nest has made it yblent. Did he make Fleur put out the firedangerfish? Did he eat the other macarons? Did he make her cry out in the night, as she so often does now? The robin heard nothing, so perhaps this is the one who makes her silent. The one with feathers like a blackbird, although he has not been in Fleur's nest for years. The robin suddenly wants to be alone, so he flies to the top of the holly tree, puffs out his chest and sings his most violent song. The song, roughly translated, tells of hard beaking, in both a sexual and non-sexual way. It has woodness, but also intense fertee.

Fleur is not asleep. Fleur is not really awake either. She is wondering about the Scottish woman, and all those things she said. And how she wants to give her something in the morning, which is more or less now. She said she had something else from Oleander, that Oleander couldn't give Fleur while she was still alive. Fleur can hear the robin singing something deep and far away. The woman – Ina, her name obviously the end of something else, hopefully not Nina, for obvious reasons – had travelled from her croft on the Isle of Lewis, in the Outer Hebrides. Oleander used to go on mysterious 'Scottish trips', setting off on a sleeper train roughly twice a year. But she never talked about who she saw or what she did. Fleur had imagined her in Edinburgh, Miss-Jean-Brodieing around castles and tweedy shops before meeting sad, wildered celebrities in hotel suites or mansions overlooking the Firth of Forth. She was wrong.

At the funeral Ina talked about the first time she'd met Oleander, at a festival in 1968 at which Oleander gave a spontaneous workshop involving a projection of a Super 8 film of the inside of a tree stump. Everyone – bearded guys on acid, their children, their wives who, when not attending festivals with them still cooked them their 'tea' and whom they called 'love' – gathered around to watch the jerky footage of small rodents inside the tree stump fighting over scraps of cheese, fruit or whatever people put there for them. Oleander stood there, mice and voles and the occasional stoat fighting grainily over everything behind her, all inside this tree stump, and she apparently said, 'That's you,' to everyone watching. She said, 'That's you when the girl you love sleeps with yet another man. That's you when your mother tells you to get a job, yet again. That's you when that man on the tube tells you to get your hair cut. That's you when your best friend buys the dress you wanted. That's you when you run out of fifty pences for the meter. That is the violence you feel inside. That is the violence of your mind, as it separates you from your brother or your sister and condemns them. You may not ever resort to actual violence. Indeed, most of us probably never will be violent in the world of form. But your mind is violent, and your thoughts are violent and with your thinking you murder people thousands of times a day. You tear out their eyes with your little claws and you hate, hate, hate.'

Pi stirs next to Fleur. They have already established that he has to leave early to get back to London to take Nina to ballet. Pi's wife, Kamala, known as Kam, could do it, but she has a hair appointment. A cut, blow dry and a whole head of highlights, apparently, as if anyone in the world even cares what Kam does to her hair. So, for the sake of a ballet class and hair appointment, Fleur will have to tidy up by herself, and grieve by herself, and cry by herself, and make her own tea, and fetch her own tissues. She'll find out what Ina has to give her, and then she'll have no one to tell about it. Why, why, *why* is it so impossible that on this day when Fleur actually needs him, Pi could not just ask his wife to reschedule her hair appointment and take her fucking daughter to fucking ballet herself?

Can Nina not just order a cab? Or go on the tube? She is fourteen fucking years old. Although since that is apparently not old enough for her to be able to cope with any kind of separation or divorce, it probably isn't old enough for her to make it to ballet on her own. Poor, stupid Nina. When Fleur was fifteen she flew to Bombay on her own. And met Pi, and brought him into the country, and made him a book of English sayings to help him settle in. If only their plane had crashed and none of this had happened then everyone would be happier. If Pi just died now, Fleur could be free. Except she wouldn't even be able to attend his funeral. And he is – secretly of course – her fucking PARTNER. Fleur thinks of the mice in the tree stump.

This is what she is doing to Pi, of course, what she always does to poor Pi. She is tearing out his eyes with her little claws. He is at least honest with her. Except for the part about leaving Kam when Sai, the elder daughter, went on her gap year. That never happened, because he realised that in fact he can only leave Kam when Nina goes to university, which is not for another FOUR YEARS. Can Fleur do this for another four years? She sighs. She's not sure she can do it for another four hours. Or even four seconds.

He deletes all her texts, which in any case he encourages her not to send. He tears up the birthday cards she sends him, and the silly but sweet Happy Monday cards, and the little notes she puts in with his tea blend – which she invented just for him. When she asked him why, he asked her what she would do in his position. What would she *do*? Apart from the fact that she would have left her partner the very instant she realised she was in love with someone else, she would have rented a diamond-plated safe, or a tiny but beautiful room somewhere, in which to keep everything her lover sent her. Somewhere perhaps to sit and reflect. A sort of temple of love. In a place like this he could keep a mobile phone on which she could text him at any time, although of course he'd never be in this place because he'd always be taking Nina to school, which is what happens every weekday morning, or, after that, working in his study at home with Kam popping back from the hospital for lunch sometimes. WHY he can't just get an office somewhere in London where he could have some privacy is a mystery. OK, well, not a complete mystery, as it would cost a fortune, and he has only had one bestselling book and that was over ten years ago. But the book was basically all about Namaste House – which Fleur now owns, which is an odd feeling – and all the things Fleur taught him and gave him and HAS SHE BENEFITED FROM IT AT ALL? She was not even in the acknowledgements. It would have been natural for her to have been acknowledged, given that she did help with the book and they virtually grew up together and everything. But he said if he couldn't put her first, and if he couldn't dedicate the book to her (it is dedicated to his dead parents) then he didn't want to mention her at all. Although of course back then it was all about his aunt and uncle, and Sai, and then suddenly there was Nina, despite him supposedly not really ever having sex with Kam. Suddenly Nina, and eighteen more years of hell. But Fleur knows now that Pi will never leave Kam. She isn't stupid.

Even Oleander's funeral ended up being scheduled around Kam and Nina. How would they feel if they knew that? It had to be on a Thursday or Friday, really, because Pi comes to Namaste House most weekends, to visit his uncle and aunt, to write and also, of course, to screw Fleur, which he likes to do hard, in the dark, from behind, when she is not quite ready. A Tuesday or Wednesday funeral would have meant poor Pi having to INTERRUPT HIS WRITING and come to Kent twice in one week. Which is entirely unreasonable, of course. What does Kam think he's doing, every weekend, though, really? Perhaps she doesn't care. She and Nina now spend every weekend with her parents. And this is a good arrangement, of course, for a mistress. To have every weekend with your lover! Fleur should be grateful. But she is not grateful. In fact, she has started hating Pi. She should leave him. When he wakes up she should tell him . . .

He puts his hand on her thigh and pulls her back down under the covers.

'You're gorgeous,' he says to her.

'Really?' she says.

Ollie's Oral B Triumph SmartGuide, a slab of plastic stuck to the wall on his side of the bathroom (yes, such a thing exists), has gone mental. It's haunted, or something, like, literally. It's a Zombie

SmartGuide. Last month, or maybe even the month before, the batteries ran out. Of course, the batteries on Clem's identical SmartGuide have not run out, and she definitely cleans her teeth more than Ollie does. But that's incidental. Ollie's batteries ran out, and so for weeks he's been standing here cleaning his teeth with no SmartGuide because its screen has been blank, dead, kaput, gone, always thinking he should ask Clem for more batteries but always forgetting literally the moment he finishes brushing his teeth. But then, like a week ago, the screen began flickering. A few days later it was back to life. Under normal circumstances, like when it has working batteries, the SmartGuide counts down thirty seconds for each quadrant of your mouth until all four are complete, when it displays a happy face and four stars – actually five, plus a dimple on the happy face if you've used the 'intensive' setting, but who has time for that? – and shows a sad face and a red exclamation mark if you press too hard. It also displays the current time when you are not brushing your teeth.

Now that the dead battery has come back to life it does some really weird shit. For example, it acts out wholly fictitious tooth-brushings in crazed fast-forward. You're pressing too hard! No, you're not! Now you are again! Now you've done three quadrants but only TWO SECONDS have gone by. But now you've done none. Now you're BRUSHING YOUR TEETH BACKWARDS. The face is sad! ☹ The face is happy! ☺☺☺ Now the face is happy but the red exclamation mark is there too !!☺!! Now it's 07.17. Now it's 13.09. Now it's sad again ☹. Now it's 12.23; 14.34; 06.14. And so on. The Zombie SmartGuide works much harder to construct these fictional, time-travel tooth-brushing scenarios than it ever did on normal tooth-brushing scenarios when it was alive. It literally does this all day long. Lately it's taken to showing the transition from 07.16 to 07.17 quite frequently. What's the significance of 07.17 to a SmartGuide? Is that the moment it was born? Is it the moment it will die? Are its selections truly random in a mathematical sense, or only random in the way students mean the word? Basically, is it trying to tell Ollie something?

Imagine you are very poor. One day you return to your grotty bedsit to find a letter. It tells of an anonymous benefactor who has arranged for you to have a luxury holiday in a beautiful hotel somewhere in southern Europe. For the first day it is bliss. All you do is lie on the beach reading books that make you feel good about yourself, and swim in turquoise water with soft yellow sand underfoot and multi-coloured fish all around. Back in your room, you admire the tapestries on the walls, the mosaics in the bathroom, the towels that feel like cashmere on your long-neglected skin. Each day the housekeeper leaves you two chocolates and a flower on your bed. But then one day the flower doesn't come, and you feel inexplicably sad. Suddenly your books don't make you feel good about yourself, and there are clouds in the sky that were not there before. The next day the chocolates don't come either, and you wonder just why that bitch of a housekeeper has decided to ruin your day – no, your life. Suddenly the towels don't feel so great any more. In fact, the next thing that goes wrong is that the housekeeper forgets to replace the towels. The next day the chocolates and the flower are back, but you become so worried that they might disappear again that you wish they'd never been there in the first place.

Fleur waits until Ina has gone and then opens the package. The first thing is a note from Oleander. *Dearest Fleur, it is very important that you read this carefully. If you have this package then it is very likely that I have gone. I hope not to have to come back. You will understand everything when you read the enclosed. If for any reason something is not clear, you must find*

Ina and ask her. Then, wrapped in light red tissue paper is a dark red hardback book with gold edging on the pages like a bible. But when Fleur opens the book, it contains nothing at all. There is simply blank page after blank page. The paper is very nice, soft and slightly porous, and certainly seems like the kind of paper that one would read from rather than write on. It's not a notebook. Or is it? There is a space on the front for a title, but there is no title. What on earth is the meaning of this? Is this one of Oleander's riddles? Too late, Fleur realises she has no contact details for Ina apart from a postal address on the Isle of Lewis. She rushes out of the door and down the gravel driveway until she can see the bus stop. There is no one there. Ina has gone.

Holly's Friendship Tree

It is a chilly spring morning in Hackney, but in Charlie's mind he is somewhere else, somewhere perhaps sub-tropical, definitely pre-fertile-crescent, somewhere where there is no wheat swaying in the breeze and quietly enslaving people. In this place, Charlie, a hunter-gatherer wearing a simple garment made not from cotton but from skin, plucks some blueberries from a tree. He steals a small amount of honey from a bees' nest, perhaps led there by the honeyguide – a bird that evolved along with humans and uses its song to tell people where to find bees' nests in return for the beeswax the humans drop. Perhaps there are some primitive wild oats too – dodgy, but not as bad as contemporary wheat, which studies have shown stimulates the same neurological pathways as opiates. Charlie should use these ingredients to make a simple muesli, in which the nuts and fruits far outnumber the oats, but, even though he knows it is unlikely that you would come across a microwave in this pre-agricultural, sub-tropical wilderness, he still fancies porridge after his run.

Charlie was brought up to be a proper scientist, and not to fall into the trap of giving evolution by natural selection (evolution on its own has been around for a lot longer) the indignity of consciousness, even though the whole thing sped up almost seems conscious in the same way that the walking palm sped up seems to be walking. He should not think that the honeyguide deliberately *decided* to help the humans in return for the beeswax, because this is not how nature happens. In nature everything is completely random, and the things that work, well, work and so they endure. That's it. Oh, except for the Darwinian twist which is that things only change when life is so dangerous that everything that doesn't work dies. This is why humans are now so pathetic: they have no predators. Since the agricultural revolution 10,000 years ago, which led to barns full of grain, basically *living seeds* that don't want to be eaten, not really, and will get their revenge, but for the time being meant people could stop starving and start political debates, legal systems and wars, there has been no selection pressure on human beings.

Even the obesity epidemic, some believe *caused* by the barns of grain, does not stop people being able to reproduce. There is nothing that kills screwed-up humans before they can fuck, except perhaps online bullying and severe anorexia. Charlie had a very interesting conversation about this with Skye Turner at Oleander's funeral supper last week. Skye Turner and Bryony were talking about high heels, and Skye Turner said that evolution had made people become taller in the last 200 years. Charlie laughed at her, and Bryony glared at him. But he explained that this is simply not true because in that time period nothing came along and wiped out the short people. The gene for being short was not destroyed. In the history of civilisation there has never been a famine that favoured tall people (and presumably also giraffes?) by providing food that only grew at the tops of trees. In the last 10,000 years, Charlie said, he would guess that very few short people have died because they can't reach fruit, or catch fish or kill enough prey or because they get eaten by taller things. Short people just go to Sainsbury's like everyone else.

'So why did people get taller, then?' Skye asked him.

'Phenotypes, baby,' said Charlie. 'Expression of genes.'

And even though Bryony kept glaring at Charlie, Skye Turner lapped this up to the extent that, OK, she did give him her number, which meant he could have fucked her. A pop star! With really a very nice . . .

And then Fleur glared at Charlie as well, which meant he threw the number away, and in her kitchen bin too, hoping that she would notice. As Charlie opened Fleur's bin to do this he was taken aback by how elegant, colourful and exotic its contents were: the dark yellow wrappers from her homemade hibiscus truffles; the pieces of bright green lime from the cocktails; the poppy leaves smeared red with saffron. Yes, Fleur manages to have a beautiful bin. How is that even possible?

Charlie makes his porridge with bottled spring water, of course, as Palaeolithic man would not have had access to anything resembling North London tap water, that in any case often tastes of bleach, metal, hash and/or semen and in which traces of cocaine have recently been found. Of course, Charlie's double espresso is also not quite authentic, although he reckons that Grok, which is what nerdy people on the internet call the ideal primal man, would not exactly have turned it down if some other caveman had offered it to him. The big question, of course, is whether Palaeolithic man had sex toys. According to some evolutionary psychologist whose name Charlie has forgotten, and who was actually a bit of a twat, once fire was discovered, women agreed to cook stuff for men in return for their protection, thus beginning the first ever dysfunctional nuclear family. And as if men couldn't cook for themselves anyway. But in this scenario all you have to do is go 'Ug, ug' at another caveman every so often and in return you get hot food and fucking. But what kind of fucking? In the shower Charlie imagines his really quite young cave girl on all fours with one dinosaur bone in her cunt, and one up her arse, sucking his cock, while a fire burns in some sort of primitive cauldron. He is halfway through really quite a nice wank when he hears his phone bleep a text message. Izzy? He's dreading facing her this morning, and a friendly message would just . . . But when he gets out of the shower he finds it's just his daily text from his bank, telling him he is nearing his overdraft limit.

Someone call a fucking mathematician! Ollie's To Do list (yes, since he turned forty he has To Do lists) is taking so long to write that it's becoming clear that even writing the list is going to have to be one of the things on the list. Can a To Do list contain its own construction? Can it exist as a set within a set, or an instruction within an instruction, as a recursive positive feedback loop or whatever? Ollie imagines himself at a dinner party with Derrida, and this is what he's saying to him, and Derrida is nodding and laughing in a French way and saying that this is the most insightful thing about a To Do list that he's ever heard. Barthes is there too, saying that if he could only come back to life and rewrite *Mythologies*, then he would include this concept of the To Do list, and Ollie's reading of it, and use it as a way of defining and, yes, OK, *almost* satirising (if close reading can be satirical on purpose, which Ollie actually doubts) the whole of the work-mad early twenty-first century.

So Ollie does add *Write To Do list* to his To Do list, partly as a philosophical, mathematical, metaphysical joke, yes, *joke*, but mainly so that he can, in theory at least, start the day by crossing something off. Ollie has never, ever seen Clem write a To Do list, but if she did write them they'd probably be specific, achievable and so on. Ollie's To Do lists are not like that. They always contain everything that he intends to do with the rest of his life, more or less, or at least the next two years, and he makes no distinction at all between short-term goals and long-term goals, or between things to do today, this week, this month and this year. As a result, Ollie can not only never finish writing his To Do list (all right, yes, keep laughing, Derrida, you big-haired fucking French genius) but has to keep infinite fragments of To Do lists strewn around his desk because Ollie can never cross off all the items on any To Do list he ever makes, because they always contain things like *ANSWER ALL EMAILS* and *Organise next year's teaching* and *Apply for big grant* and *Book dental appointment* and *Overhaul Eighteenth-century website* (which would give Derrida another laugh, if you think about it).

Did Derrida have to *blow-dry* his hair like that, or did he in fact . . .

There's a knock at Ollie's door. Ollie's door is always closed, because he always has things to do. Other colleagues leave their doors semi-open if they don't mind being disturbed, which is probably what Clem does all the time, not that Ollie is allowed to visit her at work because it might be seen as unprofessional or too domestic or something. Ollie can't possibly ever have his door semi-open because he is never even semi-available because he has SO MUCH TO FUCKING DO, as evidenced by his To Do list, to which he has just added, as well as *Write To Do list*, *Read papers for USC*, which he has to do by half one today. As well as that, he has to, as usual, *ANSWER ALL EMAILS*. At this moment, Ollie has 3,000 emails. Yes, literally 3,000. Well, 3,124. And what the hell is he supposed to do with 3,124 emails? He spends literally all his fucking time filing his emails, replying to (some of) his emails, and deleting his emails, but they always come back. There are always, give or take, 3,000. They are probably zombie emails. That is why they cannot die.

One of Ollie's favourite jokes is this: a woman, let's call her Jacqueline, goes for a night of passion with an elderly wine enthusiast but is disappointed to discover he only has a Semillon. Do you get it, Derrida? Of course you do, you high-cheekboned dreamboat. Ollie never remembers jokes, but he has remembered this one so he takes out his iPhone and brings up his Note called Jokes and adds it. He'll tell it to Clem later, despite the fact that he has probably told it to her before. He needs a system not just of remembering his jokes, but who he has told them to and when. Maybe a kind of spreadsheet.

The only way to approach 3,000 emails is to file them by sender and then basically play Asteroids with them, blasting them in clusters. Everything from Amazon: BLAMMO. Barbican Music: a shame, but they are all out of date anyway, so KER-POW. British Gas: those cunts deserve to be BLOWN AWAY. Virgin Wines: GONE. Every single email from the new secretary, Zelda (really), not exactly shot down in flames but brought under control and imprisoned in Ollie's ADMIN folder. If Zelda really needs those 131 things, like, REALLY, REALLY needs them, then she can fucking well chase him for them. Ollie does not work his way through the alphabet logically. In fact, the emails he is trying most to avoid are under D for David, the Director of the Centre for Eighteenth Century Studies (known colloquially as CECS, obviously pronounced SEX), and also F for Frank, the Director of Research, who keeps wanting to know why Ollie has not yet had any books published, despite being in the department for SIX YEARS. Clem hardly ever sends him emails, and when she does they are usually Re: Alison or Re: Shopping or, most recently, Re: Granny. Still, he has never, ever deleted anything she has sent him. Nor has he ever thrown away anything she has given him. He has every ticket of every concert, art exhibition and play they have been to. Often he has to go and get her ticket or stub or sometimes even – yes – *programme* from the bin in her study, which otherwise only ever contains tissues and pencil shavings. It's not because she doesn't care that she throws things out. It's just how she is. She literally throws everything out.

Another knock at the door. FFS. Who could it be?

'Come in,' he says in a low, nonchalant, just-wrapped-up-another-bit-of-admin sort of way. Ollie's PhD supervisor, whom he misses more than he thought possible, had a lovely reassuring voice. He was from some ex-colony that messes with your vowels so 'come in' always sounded like 'come un' and those two words, spoken by that one man, was, at that time, the most comforting thing Ollie could ever hope to hear. His supervisor had huge plants in his room – also ex-colonials, creeping up the walls and around the windows. He also had a really good coffee maker and one spare mug available at all times. How anyone would manage to keep one clean mug in their office at all times now, what with the REF and USC and MARKING is anyone's guess. 'Come in,' he says again, more loudly. It comes out as a passive-aggressive singsong. Who ever decided that the more you sing a word, the more sarcastic it becomes? Have you swept the floor yet? *Ye*-es. Have you remembered to . . . ? Yes, I *ha*-ave. Life is a musical comedy.

The door opens. OMG, it's an undergraduate. Not just any undergraduate, but *her*. Charlotte May Miller. Yes, she uses both forenames, and yes, it's very cute. And, OK, she has that sulky expression they all have, but she enhances it with a strange, wet-looking, vulva-pink lipstick. She wears the kind of clothes they all do: skinny jeans, boots, tops; but hers are clearly more expensive and are never crumpled or muddy. She wears a cologne that smells faintly of Earl Grey tea. And she is thinner, much, much thinner than the others. She is clean; she is rich; she has an iPad.

Ollie used to prefer the grubby ones, but that was back when he still had a sex drive. This is different. Charlotte May has remained more or less the same for the three years he's been teaching her, which makes her a total freak. You can print out a sheet with the students' pictures on at the start of term so you can pretend you've learned their names, but in fact they should give a HUGE CASH PRIZE to anyone who can even match up *one* student with *one* photo (apart from Charlotte May, obvs). The ones with glasses don't have them any more or are wearing their contacts today. The ones with long hair have just had it cut, and the ones with short hair have had extensions. The thin ones have become fat, and the fat ones have become thin and muscular and now turn up to seminars in VESTS in the middle of winter. A crash diet, a bout of intense depression or a trip to the hairdressers: all these can render undergraduates unrecognisable. They are masters of disguise. But Charlotte May always looks the same. She looks like, she looks like . . . OK, TBH she looks like something from the cover of *Cosmo Girl* magazine. Ollie has never read *Cosmo Girl*, or even *Cosmopolitan* magazine. Sometimes *Harper's Bazaar* makes it into the house but it's more likely to be *The New Yorker*, in which all women wear glasses and have wispy greyish hair.

But whenever he browses the covers of women's magazines at train stations or airports, which he obviously only does when he has literally hours to wait, it's *Cosmo Girl* that he likes most, because the girls on the cover look so cheerful and fresh and young. They are exactly the kinds of daughters he'd like to have.

It's quite new for Ollie to feel broody at work. Usually when he contemplates, say, his second-year class and imagines that one of them could be his child – his sweaty, stupid, clumsy, unfashionable, underachieving, semi-alcoholic, pasty, boring child – and he could be paying £3,000 a year (rumoured to be rising to £9,000) for this child to divide its time between working in a coffee shop, being in a band and shagging someone even uglier than it and spending maybe fifteen minutes a week preparing for its seminars ON WIKIPEDIA and using words like 'incidences', he is almost glad to be infertile. Surely the parents of, say, Mark from the Tuesday group, who sometimes turns up in his football kit and thinks all eighteenth-century novels are 'too long' and 'just didn't do enough to keep me interested' and 'could have got to the point more quickly', secretly wish they hadn't had him.

But then there's this one, with her neat blue skinny jeans and her little leather jacket and her PINK LIPSTICK on those lips and that cute diamond in her nose. She has the same handbag as Bryony, the one she's always going on about that cost almost a thousand pounds. How could a student pay a thousand pounds for a handbag? But Ollie realises that if he had a little girl with those sulky lips, who, like Charlotte May, was liable to intense panic over small things like where she left her pen, or what time her train goes, or where she can get a DVD of *Les Liaisons Dangereuses*, and who uses those big blue eyes really rather skilfully and, let's be honest, knowingly, to make people do things for her . . . If that little girl belonged to Ollie, he realises, he'd do *anything* for her. He'd buy her ten handbags. He'd pick her up from nightclubs in the rain. He'd tell her how beautiful she looked.

He'd buy her dresses, and encourage her to wear those rather than jeans. He'd build a castle for her to live in and he'd lock the gates and . . .

'Have you got five minutes?'

In fact, for the first time ever, Ollie understands why some of the adults from his own childhood – and particularly his childhood books – required children to be clean and polished and presented to them in stiff little outfits. After all, if you happened to have a girl like this and you'd had the good sense to call it something beautiful like Charlotte May (if Ollie and Clem had a child it would have to have a botanical name of course, so perhaps Lily Anne or Briar Rose, although wasn't that the name of Fleur's evil mother who KILLED everyone and RUINED everything?) you would want it looking beautiful and shining and polished at all times. You would never, ever want it to build dens or climb trees or step in dog shit or pick up its food with its hands. You would buy it handkerchiefs, and get the uniformed nanny to IRON them.

'Of course.' Ollie swivels a little in his chair. 'Sit down.'

Last time Charlotte May came to see him it was tearfully to confess just how much she wanted a First. Since then Ollie has bumped all her 68s up to 72s, and, just to make sure, all her 72s up to 75s. He has always marked her up by, on average, two marks anyway, just for being so pretty and having such a lovely name. The students are always going on about having more anonymisation so that this kind of thing can be eradicated, but what they don't realise is that full anonymisation would mean everyone would get lower marks. In this age of grade inflation and league tables and increased fees and MUMSNET, of course the students get marked up, and if the prettier ones get marked up a little more then it's because, in aesthetic terms at least, they deserve it. And, after all, that's what will happen in the real world. In the real world people like Rihanna and Beyoncé did not succeed because they had OK voices and turned up to sixty per cent of the things they were supposed to and tried quite hard. That is not why Microsoft Word now automatically adds the acute accent at the end of Beyoncé.

Charlotte May sits down softly on the edge of Ollie's sofa. Other students will often spend up to three minutes removing or adding layers before sitting down or standing up. They come in wet, or covered in snow, or muddy, or having spent the last seven hours FRYING PORK (which is what it sometimes smells like, literally). They unwind their scarves and put them on one of Ollie's pegs, which is wrong, wrong, wrong, because those pegs are HIS; they belong to HIM, in the same way that his desk belongs to HIM, but that doesn't stop some of them actually crossing the room to lean on it and put things on it, despite it being HIS DESK. Ollie has taken to liberating scented candles from the house and placing them in the exact spots in his office that students want to touch, or put things down on or interfere with in some way. Charlotte May never removes any item of clothing or interferes with anything. She is like a doll who has emerged from the workshop already dressed, with her porcelain clothes permanently attached to her porcelain body. She sits neatly with her knees together and her handbag at her feet and writes the date in her Moleskine notebook with her silver Cross fountain pen.

'I wanted to talk to you about the Undergraduate Studies Committee.'

'USC? Why?'

'Oh, well, I'm the new student rep.'

'*Why?*'

'For my CV?'

'Isn't working towards a First going to be far better for your CV than serving on a pointless committee? And USC! It will take literally years off your life. Do you know the meetings typically go on for fifteen hours?'

Her blue eyes puddle a little. 'Really?'

'Well, three hours. I'll give you a tip. Say you HAVE to leave at half past two and just go. I thought you wanted to do your masters anyway? You don't need to worry about your CV yet.'

'My dad isn't sure about me doing my masters. It's quite expensive.'

What a cunt. 'That's a shame. He does know you're headed for a First?'

'He doesn't really believe I'll get one though.'

Twat. Knob. Prick. If Ollie had a daughter who wanted to do a masters there would be no discussion. NO DISCUSSION. Ollie's daughter would do a masters *and* a PhD and he would pay for it because that is what you do. Clem told him the other day about people holding up the queue at the train station because they could not agree on whether to pay an extra ten pounds – yes, only ten pounds – to upgrade their daughter's train ticket, a return from Canterbury to LEEDS, to first class. In the end they decided not to, in case she 'got used to it'. What utter cunts!!! Clem hadn't understood Ollie's reaction at all, and went a bit funny when he said that people like that should be compulsorily sterilised because they do not deserve children. But let's face it, their children *would* be much happier if they were taken away from them and given to people like Ollie and Clem who would line their cots with real fleece and pay for them to travel first class every single day of their lives if that was what they wanted.

'You do know that the chair of the committee is literally insane?'

More big eyes. A tiny giggle.

'And that the last student rep ended up on tranquillisers after having to attend a FIVE-HOUR faculty USC meeting with him and then explain to him afterwards what had happened because he: a) doesn't understand any kind of data at all, whether it's presented numerically, graphically or in some other format; b) can't read without at least four pairs of glasses; c) can't hear anything; and d) is always drunk.'

Another minuscule giggle, like a doll hiccupping. 'I really don't . . .'

'I'm probably exaggerating a bit, but only a little bit. Save yourself!'

The hiccupping stops and now the huge eyes drop to the floor. 'OK, look. I'll be honest. There is something else.'

'Yes?'

She reaches in her bag for a tissue. 'It's just . . . well . . . I'm supposed to get involved in more things because I don't have any friends.'

'How is that possible?'

If she was his daughter he would KILL, yes, KILL anyone who did not want to be her friend.

A fragile smile. 'Well, no *real* friends. I mean, not any more.'

'Because?'

'And my doctor says I'm suffering mild depression.'

'But why?'

'It was like a drug thing. It doesn't matter. MDMA.'

'Right.'

'And I . . .'

'What?'

'Well, I sort of tried to kill myself.'

Ollie is surprised by how he finds himself feeling about this. Does he laugh? No, you can't laugh at someone who has just said they tried to commit suicide. As a conversational moment, though, it is unexpected, and moments like that do make one laugh, or scream, or gasp, or something. If this conversation were a walk along some cliffs then it is as if Ollie has gone too close to the edge and . . . Or is it that she, Charlotte May Miller, has gone too close to the edge, and he is watching and he . . . ? But of course if he was watching he would be the one to save her, or shout something to her or, let's be honest, not let her go anywhere near clifftops at all. A series of images go through Ollie's mind: her seminar group without her; her funeral; finding someone to blame (the doctor? Could the antidepressants have caused this?) and then KILLING them; talking to the press; crying at night because you can do all sorts of things to students but you can't actually LOSE them; they cannot DIE. Then it all clears and Ollie has something like a pure orgasm of sadness. It moves through him in a rush of hot authenticity that is unlike anything he has ever felt before. He wants to cry. He still, stupidly, wants to laugh. He also wants to hit Charlotte May Miller, really to beat her quite violently, for making him feel this way.

'What made you contemplate something so stupid?' he says.

'Just, like, a bad combination of drugs. MDMA comedown plus antidepressants plus some pill that someone gave me to try to help but actually made it worse.'

'Who gave you this pill?'

'I don't know. I was pretty out of it.'

The sadness orgasm starts again, somewhere in Ollie's toes. He literally can't bear to have this conversation any more. He imagines this girl, this pure, beautiful, shiny girl, being so 'out of it' that 'someone' could give her 'a pill' and she could know hardly anything about it. What else did this 'someone' do to her? You'd be able to do anything to anyone who was in that state, rag-dolled and pathetic on some nightclub toilet floor, or on someone's horrible sticky sofa.

'What did your parents say about this?'

Her eyes crawl somewhere off under Ollie's desk. 'They don't know.'

'But how . . .'

'And you can't tell them. I'm over eighteen.'

Ollie can't take much more of this. There's only one thing for it.

He smiles. 'And you really think USC is the answer? USC has made plenty of people . . .' suicidal. Boom, boom! But you can't really joke about suicide, can you? You can't joke about suicide to someone who has recently given it quite a good try. 'Uh, depressed. USC is a very, very depressing committee.'

'You'll be there.'

'That is true. And look, I mean, do you have anyone grown up and sensible you can go to when things like this happen?'

'It won't happen again.'

'But if it does.'

'I've got an older sister, but she's about to give birth, like, any minute.'

'And you really can't tell your parents?'

'I could, but they said if they ever found out I did drugs they'd take away my car.'

'Right.'

'Well . . .'

'Look, can I give you my number? In case you do need someone.'

'No, honestly.'

'Please. I'd never forgive myself if something happened to you and I could have helped.'

'Are you sure? I mean I won't need it, but . . .'

Ollie gives her his mobile number. She immediately missed-calls him so he has hers too. In his mind Ollie goes back to Charlotte May's funeral scene, with someone asking him if he suspected anything. 'Yes, I knew all about it,' he is saying. 'I even gave her my mobile number just in case, and I told her she could call it day or night, but she never did. She never fucking did.'

Izzy is not in her office. Izzy is not in the tea room. Charlie eventually finds her in the Herbarium, looking through old broomrape specimens.

'Oh, come *on*,' he says, when she glares at him. Why are women always glaring at him? '*What*?' More glaring. But she agrees to accompany him to the Palm House, which even people who work at Kew have to agree is romantic. Charlie's favourite glasshouse is the Princess of Wales Conservatory, because of the orchids. But he does not want to be distracted by orchids today. He finds it bizarrely exciting that Izzy is so cross with him. She is cross with him in such a way that she is making a thing of it. If she really hated him she would surely just ignore him. She would certainly not make a thing of it.

'Nicola is very vulnerable,' she is saying now.

'So am I!'

'You are not vulnerable. I cannot think of anyone less vulnerable.'

Above them, one of the palms is in the final stages of hapaxanthy. It's very beautiful but also a little sad, like a young princess who has decided to wear all her dead mother's jewels at the same time. In a couple of weeks it will be dead too.

'Well, there are things you don't know about me.'

'What things?'

'Just things.'

Izzy sighs. 'You're going to have to phone her.'

'I'll drop her a text later.'

'If you don't phone her, I will never speak to you again.'

Somewhere in the world there is a magical book. What does this book do? It simply changes itself to become the book you most need at this point in your life. If you are poor, perhaps it transforms into a very expensive book. But this is unlikely, because your soul knows of all the things you really need, and it is unlikely that wealth will be the most pressing thing. Does such a book really exist? Of course, it is impossible to tell for sure. And even if you had it, it would be so easy to lose and more or less impossible to find again. What would you search for on eBay? To you it is one particularly essential book; to me, something else. If I gave it to you as a gift I would not even know what I was giving you. Not that anyone in their right mind would give such a valuable book away. Or maybe they would. Maybe, once enlightened, which of course does not just mean seeing the light but also becoming lighter and less weighed down, they would leave it on a bus. How long would it stay there? It would not look like a magic book. It would look . . . off-putting religious? Dull? Perhaps even too light? Maybe it would be *The Seagull* by Chekhov. Perhaps it would be a book of spells. Perhaps it would be *A Course in Miracles*. The *Upanishads*. If you have ever not picked up a book left behind on a bus, it is almost certain that you ignored The Book. You ignored your destiny. You ignored your chance to get out of this bloody universe once and for all. But that's what most of us spend every lifetime doing, so it's no big deal. But just imagine if you found the book. What would it look like? Would you even know you were reading it?

Bryony really needs a potato.

Don't think about it; just eat the potato. Don't beat yourself up about it; just eat the potato. Don't tell yourself 'I'm a worthless, gigantic sack of lard'; just eat the potato. That's what the book said, pretty much. It was very comforting, and also solved a lot of the mysteries about Bryony's life. Does Bryony, when faced with a plate of freshly cooked chocolate chip biscuits (the book said 'cookies', but whatever) that are still warm: a) act cool; b) not eat any if she is not hungry; or c) bruise her mouth by stuffing them in so fast that she can hardly breathe? We all know the answer, but the *reason*, according to the potato book, is that Bryony is addicted to sugar. It's not her fault if she's a fat, nervous wreck: she, like all Americans (the book only covers Americans, but Bryony assumes it's the same for people from Kent) is addicted to sugar, the silent white killer, which . . . Hang on. *Is* she a nervous wreck? Not exactly, but she is fat and she would eat the chocolate chip cookies, which is two out of three, and that means she has to have a potato now. There is a very long process that Bryony should have gone through before getting to the potato stage: roughly a month of small lifestyle and dietary changes until she is more or less carb-free during the day. She should also have stopped drinking for several weeks, and certainly not had a bottle of Côtes du Rhône while reading the book.

The book only arrived today, but Bryony read it the way she would eat the fictional cookies, and so can't remember a lot of it. She does remember though, she was supposed to eat breakfast (*tick!* she always eats breakfast) and have lots of snacks (*tick!* Bryony always manages to snack). Anyway, it's bedtime, which means potato time, because a potato before bed gets your serotonin going or something Bryony can't remember but basically WHO WOULDN'T WANT A POTATO BEFORE BED? Bryony is prepared to cook a potato (well, let's say *some* potatoes, because no one normal cooks just one potato) from scratch, but it turns out that there are still some roast potatoes in the fridge from last weekend. Because of Bryony's diet, she hasn't eaten any of them. But that was before she found out that they will actually help her lose weight. Bryony knows that each of these potatoes is at least 100 calories, and with the goose fat James cooked them in probably more like 200. But who gives a fuck about silly numbers when what you want is more (or is it less?) serotonin. She puts four – no, five – in a bowl. While they heat up in the microwave, she cuts some cheese (which she doesn't weigh, but is around 150g, which is another 500 calories).

James comes in.

'You still hungry?' he says. 'Didn't you like your dinner?'

'Of course I liked it. It was lovely.'

Because Bryony is on a diet, James has started using more organic chicken breasts and other lean cuts from the butcher. Tonight they had Moroccan chicken stew with apricots and pomegranate seeds, served with giant couscous from a women's cooperative somewhere in the Middle East. Holly only ate the apricots and the pomegranate seeds. But the others did seem to like it. James doesn't say anything. The remains of the stew are still in the pan on the stove, but now cool enough to clingfilm and put in the fridge along with all the other leftovers that James is always trying to persuade the rest of his family to take to work or school in lunchboxes.

'I'm not that hungry at all, actually.'

'So . . . ?'

'Well, I've got this new book that says that having a potato before bed stops you being depressed. And helps you lose weight. So I'm having a potato before bed. Well, a couple, as they're quite small. You don't question it. You just do it. And in fact . . .'

James puts the old whistling kettle on the Aga. 'Are you depressed?'

'I don't think so. Well, I mean, maybe, now I've read this book and I know what some of the symptoms are. But the main thing is, I think I'm addicted to sugar. It's very serious and affects loads of people, and so I basically have to gradually stop eating all carbs apart from potatoes before bed. Skye Turner said that most days she just eats steak and salad. Although I don't think she does the potato thing. And of course there's Charlie with his Paleo diet, and look at him.' Bryony had a great time with Skye Turner at the funeral supper last week. She sat next to her for basically a whole hour talking about clothes and diets and gossip, and not in a pathetic, shallow way at all. Skye Turner gave Bryony a few beauty tips, like putting Canadian haemorrhoid cream, which is essentially shark liver oil and yeast extract, which makes the whole thing a kind of shark Bovril, under your eyes to get rid of dark shadows and wrinkles. Bryony had known about the haemorrhoid cream, but had no idea it worked, or that it had to be Canadian. Then Bryony told Skye all about the seed pods and how you could probably kill someone with one of them if you wanted to and no one would ever know, because the plant does not exist, has never been officially identified.

'What about cake?'

'I think there are still cakes you can have.'

'What, without sugar?'

'They use Stevia or something. Anyway, I'm just going to see what it's like. In the meantime I'm also going to try this potato thing.'

'So you don't want any carbs except potatoes?'

'Just at night. Before bed.'

'And eating potatoes at night is supposed to make you lose weight?'

'Don't say it like that.'

James sighs and closes the fridge door. 'Like what?'

'What is wrong with you?'

'I'm just . . .' He sighs again. 'I'm not talking about this now.'

He leaves the room.

What just happened? Bryony should follow him. She should. And she does, once she's finished all five potatoes and the cheese, with a tablespoon of mayonnaise and some chilli flakes on top. She waddles – well, that's what it feels like, suddenly – through to the front room. One of the cats looks as if he might be about to catch fire: he's virtually lying on the dying embers inside the inglenook fireplace. James is reading the *Guardian* in that angry way he does sometimes, where it may as well be upside down for all the attention he's really paying it. James knows everyone who writes in the *Guardian*. They all follow each other on Twitter. Bryony follows them all too, but hardly any of them follow her back. After all, she is little more than a cipher in James's column: a character in a life much funnier and simpler than the one she's actually living. What would the last five minutes look like if James wrote it up as his column?

My wife is unhappy. She is unhappy because she is fat. Completely ignoring the fact that I love her curves . . . No, he wouldn't write 'curves': that's *Grazia*-speak, in which he is not even conversant, let alone fluent, despite quite a lot of exposure. Mind you, sometimes he appears in real life not to know this kind of thing and then it crops up in his column. *I have told her time and time again that her tits are fabulous.* No.

I love her body. God, that sounds dry. *My wife's body is beautiful, but she just can't see it. At least, nothing from the waist down. My wife . . . My wife has decided . . . I love my wife. Every inch of her. Trust me, that's a LOT of love.* It's actually quite hard to write a column like James's, especially when you are not James but in a room with him and he is not even looking at you, let alone talking to you. *So my wife has basically decided that the best way to lose a lot of weight fast is to eat as many potatoes as possible. What a stupid, fat bitch.*

Eventually he does look at her.

'What?' Bryony says. 'What have I done?'

'This potato idea is stupid.'

'I know.' She pauses. OK. No more potatoes. But she'll still do the low-carb thing just like Skye Turner suggested, which is going to mean eating amazing things like smoked salmon and eggs for breakfast, or huge omelettes made from five eggs and butter, although to be honest Skye Turner said these should be egg-white omelettes with no butter, but who could really eat an egg-white omelette made with olive oil? Anyway, Charlie has butter all the time. She looks at James. 'But this so obviously isn't about that.'

'Why don't you just read it?'

Of course she knows what he means, but she still says, 'What?'

'I just can't believe that you actually have your father's journal from back then and you haven't even opened it. I thought you wanted to know what happened.'

'I thought I wanted to know what happened too.' She sighs, leaving a space for James to ask a sensitive and loving question.

'Like I said, I could read it for you, and . . .'

Bryony surprises herself with the force of her reply. 'No.'

'Why not?'

'Well, for one thing he obviously didn't want us to read it. Otherwise, why would Oleander have had it for all this time?'

'But it might have something about your parents' deaths in it.'

'I know! Which is exactly what I don't think I can handle at the moment.'

James sighs. 'You don't trust me. It's just like at the funeral.'

'When?'

'When I wanted to go for a walk and you got into a huff with me.'

'Well, I'm sorry, but who just "goes for a walk" when everyone's waiting to be called in for a funeral? I mean . . .'

'I was trying to support you.'

'By abandoning me?'

'I thought you'd want to come for a walk too.'

'And leave Fleur with all those journalists? And not help with the whole Granny situation? I just can't believe you went anyway.'

'It was just really claustrophobic in there. I felt . . .'

'What the fuck do you expect? It was a funeral. They're not supposed to be, I don't know, *light and breezy*.'

'And you completely ignored me at the supper.'

'I was sitting next to Skye Turner! Plus I was still totally pissed off. First you abandoned me to go for a sodding walk, and then you suddenly had to go off to make curries with Fleur. You'd basically ignored me all day anyway.'

'So you thought you'd get back at me? That's mature. We're a married couple with two children; we're not teenagers.' He looks at the wall for several seconds, and then back at Bryony. 'I'm still not sure you understand what that means.'

Another pause. 'What?'

'You heard.'

Bryony starts to cry.

'And you're drunk.'

'I'm not drunk. I've had *one* bottle of wine.'

'You're turning into your mother.'

'My mother drank at least two bottles of wine every night, plus . . .'

'Oh, for God's sake.'

‘And, since you knew I did happen to be relaxing with a drink this evening, why couldn’t you have brought all this up earlier? Why did you have to wait until I was, yes, I’ll admit it, a little bit tipsy – but also actually totally tired? I’ve got a viewing at nine o’ clock tomorrow in bloody Patrixbourne. Why do you always leave things until so late? I can’t think properly when I’m tired. I mean I wouldn’t even have drunk any wine if I knew you were upset and needed to talk.’

Serotonin should be flooding into or out of Bryony’s brain right now. Or whatever the book said. But basically she should be feeling good, not bad. Could she be crashing from the potatoes already? But they’re not supposed to do that. Maybe she had one too many. Maybe the real problem here is sugar, the silent white killer, which was in the cake James made earlier but that Bryony wasn’t supposed to have. Maybe . . .

‘I’m not upset.’

‘Well, you certainly seem upset.’

‘I’m not upset.’

‘Well, you’re annoyed with me, then.’

James sighs. ‘I don’t want to be. I just think . . .’

‘Look, I think it’s obvious that we all have too much sugar. I think you’re crashing from the cake you had before. I probably overdid the potato thing. We’re so emotional. Just look at us!’

The first time Charlie and Fleur had sex, she lay quite still while he put his penis into her vagina and moved it in and out. There not being an internet yet, the only way they could look at porn was via one very well-thumbed magazine that Charlie got at school. This, combined with articles in *Cosmopolitan*, led to their second sex session involving some ball tickling, Charlie’s first blow job (you don’t actually *blow*, silly) and a bit of ‘clitoral stimulation’. The third time, he licked her out, which was the way you said it then. While Charlie did this, he also squeezed a nipple quite firmly between his finger and thumb, and the more firmly he did it the more he liked it and the more she liked it, and so the fourth time they had sex he made her bend over the bed and he spanked her. The fifth time they had sex, she was tied up with silk scarves. This idea came from *Cosmo*, not the porno magazine, and sounded quite tame, what with the scarves being silk and soft and 'gently tied'. But tied up is still tied up. When your arms are free you can pull your lover closer or push him away. But without your arms, he is completely in control. The sixth time they had sex, Charlie brought along a cucumber from the garden, and when Fleur saw it she blushed and giggled and shook her head, but once the silk scarves were in place she wriggled only slightly as he pushed it into her. He fucked her with the cucumber, and she whimpered and looked tiny and that just made him want to hurt her, but in a pleasurable way that he couldn't quite describe and that he knew she shared.

The day after this was when Augustus told Fleur that he was her father, and whatever she was doing with Charlie would have to stop. That night, Fleur put on a lot of black eyeliner and an almost completely see-through floral summer dress. It was Bryony's eighteenth birthday and there was to be a big party at the Grange. Fleur met Charlie a couple of hours before the party began, in the old summer house, and asked him what he thought the worst sexual thing was. 'Worst' in this kind of conversation obviously meant both worst and best. He chose two things: buggery, and rape. Do them both to me, said Fleur. And don't stop if I scream, or say no. Hit me, if you like. I don't care where. I'll say I walked into a door. Did Charlie go too far? When he replayed that afternoon, as he did thousands of times afterwards, and which he could not ever do without becoming aroused again, because it was the single most intense sexual experience of his life, he couldn't find the one thing that must have ruined it all. She didn't scream. She did say no a few times, and sort of pleaded with him to stop, but in the same tone of voice that someone not playing a sex game would say yes and plead with you to carry on. It was obvious that she didn't really want him to stop. Was she disturbed that he actually did all that she asked and didn't ever say that he didn't really want to hurt her? Was it when he slapped her face? When he pulled her hair? He did cringe for years afterwards, though, remembering some of his dialogue: 'Suck my cock well, whore, and I'll be merciful,' for example. Where had that come from? He wondered for a long time if it had been that. Or even, sometimes, if the whole thing had actually been too tame. It was not until years later that he discovered what the problem really was.

Imagine that one day you decide that you need to multitask more, and therefore while doing something boring like cleaning your teeth you will add some other boring thing like doing your daily calf raises, where you stand up on your toes first on one leg and then on the other for say 25 reps on each side x2. This you think of as a good use of time. In fact, for these two minutes of every morning it feels as if you have enslaved time, you have got one over on it. You are winning the war against it. In fact, you get so used to doing your calf raises while cleaning your teeth that you now can't clean your teeth without automatically going up onto first one leg, then another. The mere buzz of your electric toothbrush gets your calf muscles quivering. You are Pavlov's dog. But this is a good thing, because you are cheating time. Or so you think. Imagine that the act of cleaning your teeth while doing your calf raises becomes so automatic and unconscious that you can now do a third thing as well, further demonstrating your mastery over time. Perhaps, as well as doing your teeth and your calf raises you imagine what you'd do if you won a million pounds on the Lottery. Perhaps you write a To Do list in your head. A letter to someone from long ago . . . How aware are you now of the calf raises? How many have you done? Does it matter that this action, like so much else in your life, has now become so unconscious you don't even know you are doing it? What other things did you begin doing long ago, long before the calf raises, that you do not feel or even know about any more? Who were you, before you forgot?

The first-class quiet carriage is almost full. Skye Turner is incognito, sort of. Wearing no make-up and with her mauve cashmere hoody pulled loosely over her head she looks more eccentric than famous, although anyone who watches MTV would know it was her, especially with the blue hair and those cheekbones. Can normal people who watch MTV afford to sit in first class? Not usually, but it's only ten pounds to upgrade at the weekend, which is, when you think about it, actually a good reason not to travel at the weekend at all. Then again, a tenner is a lot to some people. Skye remembers when a tenner was food and fags for a whole week if you shopped at Lidl and got your tobacco off Prince Albert in the Ship. Can you even travel by train if you're properly poor? Not really. Skye Turner had never even been on an InterCity train before she'd done her first gig. And she never went first class until she had her first number 1 single. Anyway, there are no other young people in the carriage, so she's safe.

The train pulls into Newton Abbott station and a youngish woman gets on. She's about the same age as Skye Turner and she's saying goodbye to her parents, just as Skye Turner has recently done, although these parents look homely in their elasticated-waist trousers and fleeces, and probably smell of sprouts, whereas Skye Turner's mum now refuses to wear anything that is not 100 per cent cashmere, linen or silk. The woman's dad mouths 'I love you' through the window, and the woman gets out a tissue to dab at her eyes, but does not do it while they are still watching. She doesn't notice Skye Turner because she's too upset. Poor thing! Skye tries to send a beam of love to the young woman, and another one to the parents, now walking away hand in hand as the train pulls off. Skye thinks of her own mother, Tash, who rarely leaves the house now, and her father, Karl, who does not suit being rich, because it renders all of the activities he has ever really enjoyed – scavenging from skips, renovating broken guitars, going on endless demos including spending three months at Occupy, volunteering for the CAB and so on – completely useless and/or ridiculous. The Turners used to complain about the rich all the time, provoked by the internet, the *Daily Mirror*, *Have I Got News for You*, and the *Class War* pamphlets that Communist Mike used to drop through the door, but now they are rich they haven't even got anything to complain about except how low the ceilings are in the £750k chocolate-box cottage in Dartington that Skye bought them. Skye wants to buy her dad a football team or a guitar shop so that he has something to do, but she's recently realised that she is running out of money and if she doesn't get to the studio soon to record the new album and get another tour booked, then basically she's going to have to stop living in hotels, kick Greg and his mates out of the flat and then sell it and – worst-case scenario – actually go and stay in Devon for a while to get her head together.

But it won't come to that, especially if her accountant can hold off the Inland Revenue for another few weeks until the next big transfer hits her bank. And if she gets some ideas. Or if she decides to record other people's material, which means giving them most of the money and losing the small amount of credibility she has left. Lately, Skye has been visiting her parents in Devon every weekend. It's certainly a lot cheaper than staying in London hotels. In fact, since the Turners 'lost' their cleaner, Skye often arrives on a Wednesday and does a bit of cleaning herself. It's quite soothing after the rush and buzz of

London. And somebody needs to do it. And then there's the neighbour of course, or, to be more accurate, the neighbour's son, who is all of twenty-one and kind of pale-haired and spotty but has those adorable legs, and who keeps texting her . . .

Skye Turner tries to send another beam of love to the woman. She's openly weeping now. Skye doesn't look – she knows what it's like to be looked at all the time, including when you don't want to be looked at because you are crying. She goes back to the mindfulness book that Fleur recommended and reads a line or two about approaching every day with loving kindness. The woman picks up her white iPhone and starts typing. Poor thing; she obviously doesn't realise it's the quiet carriage, because her keyboard makes that tap-tap noise that anyone who isn't – let's be honest for just a second, mindfulness aside – *a complete fucking idiot* switches off the minute they start using an iPhone. Maybe she's a bit deaf or something, like that friend of Greg's who can't hear anything at all that is not a loud drum sound. Perhaps she's composing a message to her now-surely-weeping-too mother, thanking her for a lovely weekend and her Yorkshire puddings etc. (Tash Turner has never really cooked because Karl used to do it all from the stuff he found in skips and stole from farms, and now they have a fridge full of M&S Gastropub meals, but Nanny Barbs made beautiful Yorkshires.) Skye Turner tries to send another beam of love, but it misses, rebounds off the wall of the carriage, flips back over Skye's shoulder, goes out of the window and hits a cormorant drying her wings on a rusted, wrecked boat on the River Exe just past Starcross.

At the end of the carriage, four people have loudly cracked open a bottle of champagne and are making excited noises and talking about how much liquid you can take through security at Heathrow. The weeping woman has stopped weeping now. She picks up her phone again. Tap-tap-tap-tap-tappety-tap, like a fake typing-pool sound-effect in a black-and-white film. WHY is that noise so annoying? It's only a little noise. It's only because Skye's hearing is so good that she's even heard it. She slips her feet out of her sheepskin boots and rests them lightly on the seat in front of her. Then she takes out her hardback notebook because she really should try and write a song before they reach London, but who can write a song with all this tap-tap-tap-fucking-tap going on? Skye breathes. She can smell dead animal wrapped in carbs. Fantastic. Some fucktard is eating a pasty. She thinks that if she were any good at mindfulness she just wouldn't notice the sound or the smell. She'd be thinking much higher thoughts.

Outside the window an egret takes off and flies over the estuary towards Exmouth.

White bird. I thought you heard.
I thought you heard me. White bird.
You soar, and ignore me.
White bird . . .

If she carries on, this is going to be either the best or the worst song Skye has ever written. Apart from anything else, it has *ballad* written all over it. Skye Turner doesn't do ballads. She doesn't do songs about birds. But people have written great songs about birds. Like . . . OK, like those I'd-rather-be-a-sparrow-than-a-nail guys. Or whatever. And, er . . . Before she can think of any more, some guy by the vestibule starts listening to Phil Collins. That's it. That is the very end of her concentration. Since everyone else in the quiet carriage is now making such a fucking noise, Skye decides to get her head-phones out. She puts on the Arctic Monkeys at medium volume and imagines herself looking good on some dance floor while some guy she doesn't know but who looks a bit like the neighbour's son but without the spots gets a massive hard-on just from watching her. 'But is he rich, babes?' asks Tash Turner, the imaginary, archetypal version, who is basically exactly the same as the real version.

In this brief fantasy, Skye Turner is five years younger and is wearing a cheap silver dress from Topshop. The problem, Skye Turner realises, and she has known this for a long time, is that she shouldn't be sitting in first class at all. What about the time she played Korova in Liverpool and got the 5 a.m. train back to London the next day with all those commuters while totally still coming down off MDMA? She vomited in the toilets, what four, five times, and looked amazing the next day: thin, pale and wasted. She still has that guy's number somewhere, not that she ever rang it. Then she went straight to a photo shoot in Spitalfields where the stylist gave her a double espresso laced with a bit of speed to pick her up. The problem now is that she doesn't actually have a life to write about. If someone gives her their phone number now it's because they want her money, not her soul. At least that's what Tash always tells her. But even back then she was writing about her past because no one talks about the present when it suddenly involves: a) drugs, but not in a fun, young way but more in a president-of-something-or-somewhere kind of way, i.e. to straighten out more than get wasted; b) £5,000 beauty treatments; and c) an unfathomably deep loneliness that no one would believe in because if you are rich you can buy anything.

Skye does not even have caffeine now. That's how unreal she has become. That's how far away she is from the eight-year-old girl she used to be who preferred sweet tea to any other drink. She carries her own rooibos teabags around with her and asks for boiling water whenever the trolley comes around. (Other things she carries with her at all times include Diptyque fig-scented candles, a cashmere blanket and her stuffed rabbit.) She's been on this train for hours now and there has been no trolley. The train conductor keeps making dark-sounding announcements apologising for the lack of space in standard class and telling everyone to take any bags off seats so that the *many* people standing can sit down. Skye Turner has her bag on a seat. But then there's no one waiting to sit down near her. No one else wants to upgrade to first class for a tenner. Or do they? If there are people *standing* . . .

The conductor appears and gestures for her to take her headphones out.

'This is the quiet carriage, you know,' he says, pointing at the signs.

'But . . .' MINDFULNESS. 'OK. Sorry.' Hey, universe, look at this girl go! Check her *out*. 'When's the trolley coming round?'

'No trolley on a Sunday. You'll have to go to the buffet like everyone else.'

Like everyone else? WTF? Has he recognised her, or is this some kind of dig at first-class passengers in general? Never mind. Breathe. Good. Karma *ker-ching*! Now that Skye's headphones are out, though, it's back to the tap-tap-tappety-tap of the woman who *must* have finished emailing her distraught mother by now and who therefore can now only be doing something less important, like tweeting. Skye Turner uses her train app to check when the next station stop is. It's not for fifteen minutes, so she can get to the buffet and back without anyone needing her to move her bag or her coat or her packed lunch that she made this morning but needs a cup of tea even to be able to contemplate: five hard-boiled eggs with the yolks taken out (and given to the half-witted poodle Leon) and replaced with tuna mixed with fat-free yogurt and Tabasco. She also has roughly a quarter of one smoked mackerel fillet, three cherry tomatoes, one black olive, half a brazil nut and a jar of caviar.

Behind her, the conductor is explaining about the trolley to an elderly woman who wants a gin and tonic. Skye thinks the conductor should offer to get the old woman a gin and tonic, but he doesn't. Skye should offer to get her a gin and tonic, but she doesn't either. It would make everything too complicated, and it's complicated enough already.

The buffet car is heaving. There is a very long queue that is taking up most of the carriage, but there are also, at the far end, a group of foreign students sitting on the floor, with grubby rucksacks and unbrushed hair. These are the kind of people who would recognise Skye Turner. The queue runs back along the train towards standard class. To get to the back of it, you'd have to fight your way past all of it. Anyway, it doesn't matter because Skye Turner only wants a cup of boiling water, so she joins the queue at the front and waits for the man to notice her. But when he does, he simply gestures towards the other end of the car.

'There *is* a queue,' he says.

'I only want a cup of boiling water, though.'

'You've still got to queue just like everyone else.'

Just like everyone else. What is it with people today? Skye Turner thinks of the elderly woman. She thinks of all the people in first class who have paid more money for a better service. The conductor appears behind her.

'This system's stupid,' she says to him. 'How am I supposed to even get to the back of the queue from first class?'

'I've already told you you've got to queue up like everyone else.'

'But this just makes it *worse* if you're in first class. You basically have to push and shove all the way from here to the end of the queue. That's not . . .'

He chuckles. '*All the way*. You don't know you're born.'

'Excuse me?'

'There are no privileges on this train. You can either queue with everyone else or not. It's up to you. Everybody else is queuing without complaining.'

While Skye Turner is queuing, with her pulse going at around 170, and her eyes filling and refilling with tears, because she thinks there *should* be privileges on this train, for people who have paid more to receive them, but can't work out why, or what this would have to do with mindfulness, or what her father would say if he could see her now (she knows what Tash would say: she'd make Skye report the conductor to First Great Western and ask for compensation), the conductor declassifies first class and personally escorts the foreign students to Skye's carriage and seats one of the most smelly ones in the seat next to Skye's, which involves touching her jacket, her cashmere cardigan, her bag of rooibos teabags and her packed lunch, which she will probably have to throw away when she comes back.

When Skye Turner got her first big cheque (which she would think of as a small cheque now – for a mere £8,000) she bought a pair of sensible boots (but from Donna Karan!!!), and a shearling jacket and a new sofa and a holiday to Morocco for her and Tash. Tash told her to save some of the money, but Skye had a good feeling about her next single and the gigs she had lined up so she didn't bother. With the next cheque she bought her parents' council house outright. She threw out basically everything she had ever owned except her stuffed rabbit. All her Body Shop make-up went, even the green eye-shadow she'd only just started. Her polyester, fire-hazard duvet, stained from all the times she used it with no cover: out. Her lumpy pillows: gone. She even threw out every book in the house (there were fewer than twenty) and bought newer, shinier copies from Amazon. All her old shower gels and moisturisers: dumped. She even got a skip so that she could throw away her old life in one go, because she realised that for her whole life, that was all she'd ever wanted to do.

They weren't due to take the skip away for about a week, and said they couldn't come earlier, so, after two nights of looking out of her bedroom window at rain pouring on what she used to be, she checked into a hotel in Marble Arch and ate three cream teas in a row. Then she threw them up and got on with her life. She has never looked back. Except for sometimes when she's drunk and she cries over her old Topshop silver polyester dress, and the covers of her old Enid Blyton books (and the fact that in the new ones the children aren't called Dick and Fanny but Rick and Frannie). Decluttering is always a work in progress, of course. Skye loves cashmere jumpers, but can't spend her whole life at the dry cleaners, so every garment she owns that cost less than £500 (there are limits) goes in the washing machine – on the silk programme, of course, if it's delicate – and it either survives this, or it does not survive this. As a result there is about £3,000 worth of shrunk cashmere-blend (pure cashmere does not shrink) jumpers in the back of one of the wardrobes at the flat. Skye cries sometimes when she thinks of those too. But most of the time she realises that with cashmere it has to be survival of the fittest and that's just how nature is. It's not a decision she made. If she was in charge of the universe, no jumper she bought would ever shrink.

The first time Fleur had sex with Piyali, it was actually supposed to be a massage. It was her idea that he should learn how to become a masseur. Now that he was eighteen, why shouldn't he pay his way at Namaste House, just like everyone else? When Fleur wasn't making teas and remedies she was selling them at the local market. And this was as well as her yoga classes. Even the Prophet had started running some dodgy mail-order thing from his room that no one liked to ask about, but which Oleander said more than covered his share of rent and expenses. Ketki and Ish both offered massages and various other treatments, but neither of them got much return business. Fleur thought that a certain type of middle-aged woman might like to be massaged by Piyali, what with that jawline and those shoulders. So one afternoon she made him put down his book – probably Hemingway, perhaps *The Old Man and the Sea* – and come and learn how to be a masseur.

She explained to him about the paper panties, and putting a towel over the woman's breasts. She got him a bottle of wild rose oil – that she had made – and lay down on her front, naked except for the paper panties, with her head in the massage table's hole, giving him a few basic instructions as he began with her feet, and then moved on to her calves, thighs and buttocks, parting her legs only slightly so that he could get to as much flesh as possible. He soon had the technique down so well that Fleur wondered if he had done it before. But how could he have done? He'd left India at fourteen, and his parents had not exactly been into this kind of . . . By the time he reached her inner thighs the panties were damp and the only thought in Fleur's mind was, *Go higher. Please, go higher. I'll do anything*. This thought turned into more thoughts. Pi would take her from behind. He would thrust all his fingers into her and she would let him, no, she would PAY him, and he would say 'Fuck your money', and then screw her really hard to punish her for . . .

'Turn over,' he said, once he'd finished her back.

He looked at her tits. He forgot to cover them with the towel. She forgot to remind him. He started at her feet again, and once again gently parted her legs so that he could reach around. Could he see anything? Fleur sort of hoped so. She parted her own legs a little more, to help, but also perhaps to tell him something. He seemed not to notice. His hands swept up! And then down! And then up! Oh, actually, perhaps that time they did sweep a little higher but . . . Now it seemed to be time for him to massage her abdomen, which is not something that usually happens in massages, but actually it was rather interesting, and certainly not something worth stopping. Higher, higher his hands went, carefully avoiding her breasts. His hands swooped this way and then that way until inside her mind she was begging him to . . . And then, suddenly, he *was* massaging her breasts. Both of them at once, kneading them as if they were balls of dough, but with his thumbs gliding over the nipples in an ambiguous way.

Should she stop him? If he had pulled out a contract at that moment asking her to sign away all her possessions and even her soul in order for him to keep going, she probably would have done. So no, she was not going to stop him, even if she should have done. Was this even sexual? She knew that Indians saw the body differently from Europeans. Massaging women's breasts is not *necessarily* transgressive or even sexual. But then he started again on her inner thighs. This time she let out a little moan and parted her legs a tiny bit more than you would if you were just being helpful. His hands went higher. His thumbs brushed up against the edges of the paper panties. His hands moved higher still, and this time they went just inside the paper panties. Swoop, swoop, a little higher each time until his hands were further inside the paper panties and eventually both thumbs were inside her and then on the next swoop he pulled her to the edge of the massage table and she heard his zip being undone and . . .

The second time they had sex, Pi had made his massages a bit more mystical. He prayed over every one of Fleur's chakras and even put gemstones on some of them. Fleur didn't find this especially arousing, but once he put his hands on her it was the same as before. Was he teasing her? It seemed to take an awfully long time for his fingers to enter her panties, although she enjoyed the tit massage more this time, because she knew, or at least reasonably hoped, that it was the build-up to more.

The third time they had sex, Pi had installed chains in his treatment room. These enabled him to walk on the backs of his clients without hurting them, or, at least, without hurting them more than the maximum amount they were willing to pay for. By this stage he was seeing almost all the middle-aged women and, judging from the return business they were getting, he was fucking most of them. Did they tip him? Did he charge them for extras? Or was the sex completely free? Did they use condoms? Fleur didn't know how to ask all these questions. This time he walked on her back, and her legs, and her breasts and pushed her legs apart with his feet.

'I'm going to make tea for the window cleaners.'

She says this in a way that totally implies that he should be doing it. Her very neutrality is utterly condemning. She doesn't have to add any tone. She can do all sorts of things without tone. He is a man. He should do it. To reverse years, no, *centuries* of . . . But it's too late. She's gone to the front door. Whenever Ollie has to talk to builders or window cleaners or the postman he can't help putting on a faint how's-yer-father accent that is reminiscent of granddads and cousins from his Working Class Past. Clem has no such thing in her background and can only sound low-voiced and posh, but in that soft pancakey way. Or probably crêpes rather than pancakes. Or whatever. Anyway, what she's doing now is intriguing. She's speaking to them in her normal, posh, authentic way but what she is saying is like something someone else would say.

'White with one,' she's saying, 'and white with none, right?'

She may even be smiling and raising an eyebrow. But here's the thing. *She has remembered how they take their tea.* And she's saying it the way they would say it, not the way she would say it. 'White with one'! WTF??? One what? One sugar, yes, but she'll have to use caster sugar as usual because she and Ollie are far too posh to have sugar in their tea, and therefore in their cupboards, although caster sugar is different because it goes in cakes, which are different from sweet tea in some way that Ollie has never fathomed. She has made it sound as if she takes orders for working-class tea (Ollie has been banned from calling it 'Builders' Tea') literally every day. If any of Clem's friends come round and she offers them 'tea' and they accept, they get loose leaf Earl Grey in a yellow teapot. Ollie made that mistake when he first visited the Grange. Earl Grey is a perfumed monstrosity, designed to repel rats, and anyway . . .

Clem comes back to the kitchen and puts the kettle on.

'What?'

Ollie is laughing at her. 'Nothing. Just . . .'

'What?'

'*White with one and white with none*.'

'Yes, all right, I know.'

'It's like the beginning of window cleaner porn or something. *White with one and white with none*. You should be standing there in a pinny with a pink feather duster or something. And no knickers.'

'I was aiming more for something like Land Girl, to be honest.' She goes to the baking cupboard for the caster sugar. Ollie does not acknowledge the existence of the baking cupboard, and if he ever has to wash up the rolling pin, the pastry brush or any of those round metal things you cut biscuits with, he leaves them on the side for Clem to put away. 'Or like comforting-warden-of-air-raid-shelter or something. You know, kind of matronly but not in a completely asexual way. But . . .' She smiles. She laughs. 'Oh.'

'But? Oh?'

'One of them was different. I remembered a different window cleaner's tea order. But I didn't realise he was different until he said he wanted two sugars.'

Ollie laughs too. 'You've reduced the window cleaners to their tea order.'

'Yes.'

'To you, they *are* just their tea order.'

'I know.'

'You're a posh bitch.'

'Yes.'

'Come here.'

'I'm kind of . . .'

Ollie sighs. 'Of course you are.'

'Maybe later?'

Like this plant thing, yeah, like a kind of pod.
Peas in a pod
More like a kind of vanilla pod like
Ice ice baby . . .
Lols yeah whatever but not exactly like it's really, really oily
Like thing your mum puts in rice pudding
Not my mum but yeah
You touched one?
Yeah.
Washed your hands afterwards.
For real.
And then you got one?
Not yet but it would be totes simple if I did want one there's this guy and
They're like actually deadly yeah?
Yeah, like really, really deadly.
Lols – really deadly!
???
Like dead is dead
Yeah but I told you these people talk about like different levels of death
Which is bollocks right
But
Like death is the end
But OK right . . .
If death is not the end I don't know what is
Yeah but they say you come back but they don't want to come back
If there woz a choice I would want to come back
And then there's like the bit I can't tell you because it's so nuts
Go on
I did not make this up right
Whatever

These plants have a flower and if you look at the flower it might look like Jesus or Buddha or like some other religious thing.

That's not even possible

No

Like the laws of physics or whatever

I know

These people are tripping man

Yeah totally

And why Jesus anyway?

Like if you're enlightened you see other enlightened people

Sounds like you almost bought this shit

They are totally believable man even though obvs they are also bananas

You're a hippy man

Not if I do this ☹

What do you mean

Like peace and love and

Well, you could just tell Greg to leave

Holly feels a bit funny between her legs, or at least she's trying to feel a bit funny between her legs because that is what the book says she should feel when thinking about someone she knows at school – male or female – who she would like to kiss. But there isn't really anyone she'd like to kiss because kissing, or at least what Chloe told her about kissing – grown-up French kissing, where you have to rub tongues together with a boy, inside his actual mouth – is disgusting and she wouldn't want to do that with anyone. The book says, *Have you ever put a pillow between your legs?* And *Did it feel good?* And *Did you squeeze?* And you have to put a tick in a box next to the things you did feel or do, and Holly's not sure that what she feels between her legs is what you are supposed to feel, and she's also not sure that this whole thing isn't just REALLY GROSS and she would absolutely die before she showed this book to anyone but sometimes she just can't help herself and she has to get it down off the shelf and read it again.

This book has pictures of willies in it, which Holly likes looking at; at least she likes them more than she likes thinking about kissing. There are lots of little boys with little willies, but her favourite picture is of an erection, which is a big, more adult willy sticking up, which Holly has never seen in real life. Obviously if she did ever see one she would have to shut her eyes and maybe even giggle a bit because it would be SO gross, but in that tingly way that some gross things are. Because of this book, Holly now imagines the characters in her Famous Five novels with willies (the book says penises, but that's just revolting) and vaginas, and sometimes she imagines them all being captured and forced to strip while some smugglers take photos of them naked and then send the pictures to a newspaper which puts them on the front page by accident so everyone in the entire world sees them!

Here's another thing that could happen: George in the Famous Five is often mistaken for a boy, so perhaps she will get locked in a boys' only cell by some gypsies or pirates and then the gypsies or pirates will say something like 'Prove to us that you are really a boy', and George won't be able to, and then they will pull her knickers down and see that she has no willy, and then they will examine her really closely with whatever implements they have to hand, probably a pencil and a ruler, just to make sure, and then they will spank her bare bottom with the ruler as a punishment while Julian and Dick and Timmy the dog watch. And Julian and Dick will have had their pants pulled down too, to prove they are boys, and so George will be forced to look at their willies for the whole time this is going on.

'Holly! Lunch!'

Oh no! Not her dad's voice. Not while she is thinking . . . Anyway, Holly doesn't even want lunch. The very idea of lunch makes her feel sick. Her dad puts so much garlic in everything, and horrible green stuff like coriander or basil – although Holly quite likes basil on garlic bread, which also has garlic in it, so maybe it isn't garlic she doesn't like after all. Maybe just at lunchtime. And too much ground pepper, basically. And sourdough bread, which tastes like envelopes with puke inside them. And goat's curd, which is just like that stuff that gets in people's arteries when they smoke, which Holly saw on a school DVD and now can't quite get out of her mind. Not that she doesn't like her dad's food. She wouldn't say that even if a man came in now with a gun and said, 'I'll shoot you between the legs unless you say you hate your dad's cooking.' Or maybe just, 'I'll shoot you in the head'. Something about the feeling that may or may not be between Holly's legs, and the feeling she definitely does not feel about her dad's cooking, do not go together at all. The thoughts about all these things are now churned up in her head like sick.

'Holly!'

Her door bursts open. God! She tries to slip the book under her pillow but she's too late. Ash skips across the room.

'What's that?'

'A-A-ASH!' She draws out his name into a kind of indignant yell, making it into at least two syllables, maybe even three. 'MUMMY!'

He reaches for the book but she can't let him see it. It's her private book and it's not suitable for young children, or for boys, or for little brothers in general. But Ash has pointy, searching, often sticky, little hands, and so the only way she can prevent him from touching her book and seeing – actually, she can't think those thoughts now about what he might see – is to whack him on the arm really hard. Twice. She finds herself gritting her teeth as she does it, sort of enjoying the pure hatred she feels in this moment. She wishes Ash would die.

'Ow! DADDY!'

Now Ash pulls Holly's hair sharply – at least having forgotten about the book – and starts to cry. If you made the stupidest sad-face expression right now, with your lip-edges pulled down as far as they could go, and then if you pretended you were in a slow-mo scene or something and said the word D-A-D-D-Y as slowly and as sadly and as loudly as you could, then you'd sound just like Ash. Holly really, really hates him. She REALLY wishes he would die or at least become suddenly paralysed and have to live in a wheelchair forever.

Bryony comes in.

'What on earth is going on?'

'Mummy? He pulled my hair.'

'SHE HIT ME.' Again, in this loud, low, pathetic, sob-wracked voice.

'Did you hit him?'

'No! Well, a tiny slap because . . .'

'We don't have hitting in this house.'

'BUT, MUMMY, HE IS IN MY ROOM.'

'Holly! Ash! Lunch!'

'Daddy's been calling you for lunch for ages now.'

'Well, I was on my way down and then this little freak came in and attacked me. I had my *Private Keep Out* sign on my door as well. But it's impossible to get any bloody privacy in this place. I don't want any lunch anyway. I don't feel very well.'

'We don't say "bloody", Holly. What's the matter with you?'

'I don't feel very well.'

Now Holly starts to cry.

'Well, if you're ill you'd better stay in this afternoon. You'd better not go to tennis today.'

'But, Mummy!'

'Well, if you want to go to tennis this afternoon you'd better have some lunch. Did you even have any breakfast?'

'Yes.'

'What did you have?'

'Daddy made me porridge.' Which everyone knows is toenail clippings mixed with snot. Which is about as gross as . . .

'But did you eat it?'

'Yes! Most of it. At least one big spoonful.'

'Well, you're not leaving this house until you eat a proper lunch. It's no wonder you feel like this if you're not eating properly.'

'I feel like this because Freakface came INTO MY PRIVATE SPACE AND THEN PULLED MY HAIR. It's so unfair.'

Ash doesn't like being called Freakface, so he tries to give his sister a dead arm by punching her as hard as he can. He completely forgets that his mother is standing right there.

'OW! Get your bloody hands off me, you little freak.'

'Right,' says Bryony. 'No lunch for you until you apologise, and extra lunch for you, madam. Downstairs, both of you, now.'

Sunflower seeds. A hundred million sunflower seeds. Each one handcrafted in porcelain by one of many workers in a rainy town in China and now poured by the sackful into the Turbine Hall of the Tate Modern, London. It used to be possible to walk on them, or lie down in them, or pour hundreds of them through your hands. Presumably you could also steal them. But now, due to concerns over the dust produced by the porcelain, you can only look at them from the viewing area to the side, or from above. Given the themes of the exhibition, it seems both ironic and fitting that rich Londoners are now protected from the dust created by trampling the work of Chinese people who are so poor they leave price tags on items of clothing to show their value. But it is frustrating not to be able to touch the seeds. They look so very touchable. Charlie reads something on the wall about each seed being hand-painted. Nearby, a film is playing, showing how this happened. Three or four strokes for every seed. That's around

350 million strokes of a paintbrush. 'Presumably not the same one,' jokes a middle-aged woman in an anorak.

'This is interesting,' Charlie says to Nicola.

'Hmm?'

'I hadn't noticed this before. In the Cultural Revolution, Chairman Mao was always depicted as the sun, and the people were the sunflowers turning towards him. It also says here that in times of poverty people used to share sunflower seeds, which meant . . .'

Nicola reaches into her bag for her phone.

'It would be better if we could touch them,' she says.

'I know, but . . .'

'It's quite boring otherwise.'

'I wouldn't exactly say that.'

She smiles. 'Sorry. I'm dreadful with art.'

'Right.'

'Anyway, Izzy's texted. Her ballet class has just finished. She wants to meet us in Covent Garden. OK with you?'

'Sure.'

~

When Bryony goes to the kitchen to look for some chocolate, James is holding the seed pod she inherited from Oleander. Bryony stuck it in an old ice-cream tub and put it at the back of the highest cupboard when they got back after the funeral supper. She only realises now that she has entirely forgotten ever doing this. She must have been quite tired. But anyway . . .

'Oh my God.'

'What?'

'What the fuck are you doing?'

'Just looking. Smelling. I mean, these things really smell quite . . .'

'Put it away. Now.'

'God. Chill, Beetle. It's only a seed pod. It's lovely. Here, look.'

It is long, black and oily-looking, very much like a vanilla pod. But . . .

'Right. OK. One of those probably killed my . . .'

'You don't know what . . .'

'*One of those probably killed my parents*.'

'Calm down. There's no need to shout.'

'For fuck's sake.' Bryony starts crying. 'Just put it back.'

'It's just a plant, Beetle. Just a plant.'

'Oh Christ, I hate it when people say things are *just* plants, *just* herbal . . . If my parents taught me one thing, it was . . . Look, do you have *any* idea, have you ever *really* stopped to think about what plants do? Would you be happy standing there holding deadly nightshade or a piece of a fly agaric mushroom? Or, I don't know, hemlock?'

'This is just a seed pod.'

'Right. Like seed pods are never dangerous. Have you ever heard of an opium seed pod? Yew berries – well, they're really cones, but whatever – will kill you in a few minutes, and then there are castor beans, which you can use to make ricin and . . .'

'This is not an opium seed pod, or a yew berry or whatever.'

'No. It's probably much, much worse.'

Bryony starts sobbing now. This is so frustrating. And he won't even give her a tissue. Not that she wants anything he's touched after he's been holding one of those pods.

James sighs. 'If the seed pods are really that bad then why exactly do we have one of them in the house?'

'Because we – *I* – inherited it.'

'Right, well, if it's as toxic as you seem to think, perhaps it would be a good idea for you to hide it from the children?' James replaces the pod in the plastic tub and gives it to Bryony. 'I'd better get on with dinner.'

'Wash your hands before touching food.'

He sighs. 'You are being extremely paranoid.'

'You are being fucking stupid.'

❧

'Oh God, I did one of those phone lines once.'

'No.'

'Yes.'

'What did you say?'

'Just stuff like, *I'm pulling my pink panties off*. Or *Mmm, baby, you're making me so wet*.'

'What, and you could hear them, like, you know . . . ?'

'What, wanking? Yep. They always wanted me to hurry up, but our instructions were to slow down. We all sat around in cubicles with the heating turned up and the windows open, breathing heavily for hours. You could hear what the other people were saying. Sometimes it was hilarious.'

'Like . . . ?'

'I can't remember now,' says Nicola. 'Mind you, there was this girl who got sacked for getting one of the masochists round to help decorate her flat. I mean, on the one hand, what kind of idiot gives out their address on a premium phone sex line? On the other hand, she charged him three hundred quid to steam a load of woodchip off her walls, which is so not fun, while she hit him with a riding crop – provided by him – and called him a worthless faggot.'

'I hate woodchip,' says Charlie.

'You'd hate our place, then,' says Izzy. 'We totally need to get a masochist round.'

'It took days to get rid of mine.'

'Maybe more than one masochist, then. Can you hire them in groups?'

'Someone should do a kind of sex-employment agency.'

'Oh God. Making BDSM actually useful.'

'You'd need a spreadsheet.'

'"Spreadsheet" sounds quite rude now, when you say it like that.'

'I know.' Giggling. '*Spreadsheet*.'

And so the afternoon goes on.

❧

If you discovered that you were the only person in the world, and everything you see around you was in fact a part of you, dramatised, how would that change what you are doing now, right this very instant? What would you stop doing? What would you start doing? What would suddenly not matter at all?

❧

'We'll go through the main doors,' says Beatrix to Bryony and Clem.

They always go through the main doors, because it feels more historic and because, well, they are the nicest doors. Why go in through doors that are second best or, worse, that open onto Street Fashion, where you can get three badly made T-shirts for ten pounds? Why not make a proper entrance?

'I do love Selfridges,' says Bryony. And she does, she really does love Selfridges. She loves walking in through the main doors, feeling a bit like a celebrity in her huge Chanel sunglasses, carrying her Mulberry handbag. Her feet already hurt, though. Why did she decide to come shopping in high heels? They're not even very expensive high heels; they cost £200 rather than the £600 or so you'd pay for a pair of Louboutins upstairs. The good thing about these shoes is that they make Bryony feel ever so slightly more like SJP, or even Skye Turner. The bad thing is that they make the balls of her feet feel as if they have had all the flesh removed from them. She may have to take out the Converse trainers she has in her handbag sooner rather than later, which would be a shame, especially as her Converse fit into her handbag rather better than her high heels. Her Converse have been in the washing machine so many times that they have a faded look and holes that are seen as really very stylish among middle-class mothers of East Kent. But perhaps that will not quite hold in Selfridges, or with Granny.

Bryony's very favourite shoes are a pair of delicate Dior diamante strappy sandals that she bought off the internet one time after watching *Sex and the City*. They are beautiful, but impossible to walk in. As well as them, she has maybe twenty pairs of high heels that she has worn on average three times each. James doesn't like her in high heels. He laughs at her and mimics her wobbling. Fleur can wear high heels without wobbling, but spends most of her time barefoot or in those ridiculous toe socks that she gets all her celebrity yoga students to buy. Fleur gave Clem several of one of the celebrities' prescription painkillers to take before wearing the shoes she'd bought for the Academy Awards ceremony. Apparently that's what they all do. It means they get more of a buzz off the one glass of champagne they are allowed, too. Maybe three Nurofen is the answer. Or perhaps . . .

'It's not too loud down here for you, Granny?' asks Clem.

Over the speakers, Skye Turner is singing about the pain of leaving the guy she fell in love with (OK, shagged) last summer while she and Greg were on a 'break'. 'Too Perfect For Me' has just reached number 1 in the singles chart. Or whatever they call it nowadays.

'No, darling. I rather like this song. Now, where's Mulberry?'

Beatrix always likes to visit 'her' brands: the companies she has invested in on the basis of what she reads in *Vogue*, or what her granddaughters tell her – although increasingly they are too old to know. Bryony, though, can be a fairly reliable marker for what is 'hot' right now. Bryony is not at all forward thinking. She will buy a Mulberry handbag right at the exact moment that everyone else does. But certainly before investors are aware that a great fashion event is happening. Beatrix bought Mulberry for 562p in November after reading yet again about their handbags in *Vogue*. Today they are on 1,361p. Beatrix bought shares worth £10,000, which are now worth around £24,000. Of course, she'll have to decide when to get out, which is part of the reason for these trips. Mulberry could now 'tank', or it could keep going. It may have reached the top of the market, or it may not. It's hard to tell.

You can quite easily see which brands have 'it' and which do not, though. No one needs the *FT* to tell them which fashion brands are doing well when they can just walk into Selfridges and see for themselves. This was one of the reasons Beatrix dismissed her old broker last year and began trading online. He knew, to put it in a modern way, fuck all. Beatrix has a lifetime of knowledge of the fashion and cosmetics industries, and what she knows about science is certainly not redundant either. But this is the part of investing that Beatrix loves. She loves the way it smells: of leather and gardenia and fine crushed powders. There are always a lot of people crowded around the cheap brands, whether they are doing well or not. But which of the more expensive brands is 'doing something'? You can tell just by the atmosphere. Do they have new products? Limited edition lines? Are the staff happy and helpful? Would Beatrix, or at least her twenty-five-year-old self, actually *want* this product? Or . . .

'Oh my God, I want everything!'

'But why, darling?'

It's too late for sensible conversation. Bryony has taken off and is now moving around the display of handbags like a large tornado moves around the east coast of the USA. She's only around seventy per cent predictable, and could arrive anywhere, without warning. She ends up looking at make-up bags. Why would someone want a prestigious make-up bag when the whole point of buying these expensive products is so that everyone sees you with it? Why indeed? But then why does Bryony sit around in ball gowns on the rare occasions that everyone's out, wearing her most expensive shoes and drinking champagne? What she does in public is VIEWINGS and COURSEWORK and HOUSEWORK and CHILDCARE. It's what people do in private that makes money for investors.

Clem is looking at an Oversized Alexa in oak soft buffalo. She's trying it across her body and then over her shoulder. It would rather suit her: it does look like something an academic would carry. She could put her laptop in it, probably, and some books. At least these handbags are not covered in gold chains and unnecessary detailing, or 'hardware', like the ones a couple of seasons ago. Clem looks rather elegant with the big brown bag slung, once more, across her body. She visibly checks that Beatrix and Bryony aren't looking, and then pouts, ever so slightly, into the mirror. Beatrix would have bought one of these handbags when she was twenty-five, she realises. She would have saved up for one. Now? Now, of course, she still uses the Hermès Kelly bag she bought in 1956. Well, all right, not exactly the same one, which eventually collapsed under the weight of tissues, paperbacks, mints and Guerlain lipsticks. But one that someone never used and ended up at auction for just under £3,000.

Bryony is handing over her credit card for a make-up bag. Clem seems to have lost interest in the Alexa and is looking back towards cosmetics. Beatrix likes to have lunch early, and her favourite restaurant is just above the bags. She moves towards the stairs, with Bryony sort of following but trying to organise her purse at the same time with her handbag still undone. She is a horrible crumple of train tickets, old receipts and free coffee vouchers. And when she could be so elegant, with her shiny Mulberry carrier bag done up with a beautiful mauve ribbon.

'Can I join you in a moment?' Clem asks. 'I just want to smell something.'

'*Smell* something? Oh, scent. All right, darling. Shall we order you a salad and a glass of something?'

'I'll choose when I get there. I'll honestly only be a moment.'

Beatrix uses her watch to time exactly how long it takes for the

Spanish-looking waitress to notice them, and from then how long it takes for her to actually come and see to them. It is, as always, far too long. Still, the chef here is wonderful, and last time they visited Beatrix had something called 'credit crunch ice cream' which made everyone laugh. Another rather disgraceful amount of time goes by before the waitress brings a menu.

'I want everything,' sighs Bryony.

'Be sensible, darling.'

'Granny! For heaven's sake. I'm not really . . .'

Clem returns, slightly breathless. Bryony wrinkles her nose.

'What is that?'

'Angel, by Thierry Mugler.'

'Gosh, darling, it's rather . . .'

Bryony frowns. 'It's horrible.'

'I know.' Clem smiles and sits down. 'Have we ordered yet?'

'No. And I'm . . .'

'If you know it's horrible, then . . . ?'

'I'm wearing it ironically. Well, no, actually, that's not really it. I suppose I *know* someone who wears it ironically and so I'm wearing it in honour of her. A kind of non-ironic homage to irony. It's quite pretty when it settles down.'

'Pretty?'

'Well, sort of. Actually, sort of *dirty*. A bit sluttish.'

Clem has never been a good indicator of anything but very niche markets.

'What's everyone having? Bry?'

'It all looks so nice . . .'

What Bryony should be doing now is choosing something low-carb, for example the spiced chicken salad with avocado and coriander. What she really wants is steak and chips. Of course, the classic low-carb meal is steak and salad, which Bryony has been having quite often recently, and is on the menu here. Or – wow – buttered green vegetables. But how many carbs are there in chips, really? After all, potatoes are vegetables, not grains. No one would fatten a cow on a pile of potatoes. They can't be that bad. But then again what about pudding and/or afternoon tea? Bryony had sort of decided that since today was a special occasion she was going to allow herself one, just one, little carby treat. She had thought that a scone with cream and jam would be nice, with a cup of Earl Grey, for tea. So now she should have steak and salad. She'll just have steak and salad and . . . It would help if someone would just come, before . . .

Beatrix is craning her neck around looking for someone to come and serve them. When she does spot someone she starts trying to hail her as if she was a taxi. Eventually the waitress arrives.

'Can I help you?' she says, with a strange element of surprise in her tone, rather as if they had knocked on her door in the middle of the night. Her accent is perhaps Polish, not Spanish. What on earth does she think they want?

'We'd like to order some lunch,' Beatrix says, adding, 'if that's not too bizarre a request.'

'I am sorry. You like to order . . . *what*? I do not understand.'

'LUNCH.'

'Oh, lunch.' Only now does she get out her little pad. She sighs.

'Steak and chips, please,' says Bryony, 'with a side of sourdough.'

'Avocado and chilli on toast, please,' says Clem.

'Oh, that sounds nice. I'll have that too,' says Beatrix. 'And we'll have a bottle of Nyetimber to share. That all right with you, girls?'

'Oh, thanks, Granny,' says Clem. 'That's lovely.'

'Can we have some sparkling mineral water as well?' asks Bryony. 'Oh, and a large glass of Rioja for me.'

Bryony sees an afternoon of extreme shopping ahead. Just one more day like this, she tells herself. Just one more day. How much harm can that do? And then tomorrow she'll be different. A thousand pounds. She won't do more than a thousand pounds. Not counting the make-up bag. So, one thousand *more* pounds. And she won't have more than three cakes later.

'We only do medium – one seventy-five.'

'That's fine.' Four cakes, then.

'You'd think that, of all the words in English, she'd recognise "lunch",' Beatrix says when the waitress walks away.

They don't do credit crunch ice cream any more, so afterwards Beatrix and Clem have peppermint teas, and Bryony has another glass of Rioja and some double chocolate ice cream to help soak it up. Beatrix and Clem are planning to go around the rest of Beatrix's companies (Prada, Dior and the LVMH brands) and then find a pair of noise-cancelling headphones for Beatrix and an anti-ageing face cream for Clem. Bryony arranges to meet them for afternoon tea and then lurches off down the stairs rather like a container ship that has just been launched in a harbour slightly too small and shallow for it. Bryony will dock for a few moments on the ground floor. She will begin and end here, with some quick refuellings, before going upstairs to take on a load of fine goods.

What some people don't realise about shopping is that if you do it right it does what heroin does, and what alcohol does, and what smoking does, and what a litre of ice cream, or a whole box of chocolates or three tubes of biscuits or two large packets of cheese can do. It changes your body chemistry and gives you an *actual hit*. Even though it's just shopping! For example Bryony really needs a moisturiser – unlike Clem she has been using anti-ageing creams for years, not that she needs to as her fat makes her look about fifteen, but when she's thin she will be glad she did it – and so goes straight to Crème de la Mer and buys a 60ml jar of Moisturizing Gel Cream for £190. If this is the physical-hit equivalent of a refreshing pint of beer after a long day, then the £40 Lip Balm that Bryony adds at the last minute is a little vodka chaser and the £230 Radiant Serum she adds at the very, very last minute is quite a good hit of cocaine in the toilets and . . . and . . . Fuck. That's already £460, so maybe it's time to start again. Right, a thousand pounds starting from now.

That feeling, *right there*: that's the one. Oh . . .

Breathe. One nude Dior lipstick to start things off again. Escalators.

Bryony can't buy clothes in Selfridges because she is too fat. But there are lots of other things she can buy, and the main thing she can buy is also becoming her favourite thing: shoes, which they always have in a size thirty-nine. But not just shoes. Bags, scarves, jewellery: a lot of stuff does not have a size at all. Which should make it possible to actually buy it without too much trouble, but . . . She waits for approximately seven minutes at Marni for the thin, beautiful and rather snotty shop assistant to come back and inform her that they don't have a floral print shopping bag without that strange streak on it and ask her if she wants one anyway. For £195. Er, right. Whatever. No thank you, skinny bitch! On to the shoe galleries and into Prada where Bryony is hoping not to bump into Clem and Beatrix. Ankle boots, ankle boots. But where is the fucking assistant now? Bryony sighs, rolls her eyes and sighs again. The assistant emerges.

'Hello. How are you today?' An Asian with a child's voice. Happy, happy.

'Fine, thanks.'

But now she's gone to fiddle with some shoe on the display as if . . . Basically as if Bryony is too fat and not fashionable enough and not even from the suburbs but so far outside Zone 4 into the fucking COUNTRYSIDE where Hunters that only cost around £100 are regarded as expensive footwear, whereas Prada ankle boots cost £500, and . . . Bryony sighs and rolls her eyes a bit more.

'Can I help you?'

'Well, yes, I actually wanted to buy a pair of those boots.'

See, you happy little tiny nobody, how you JUDGE people and then those people turn out to be RICH and then you have to do what they want no matter how fat they are, or where they live. See?

'You want try?'

'I want to BUY. In a thirty-nine, please. And I'm in quite a hurry.'

'You want buy without try?'

'Is that not something you do?'

OMG. She has turned into her grandmother. But never mind that . . . Obviously Bryony will try them in the toilets and return them if they don't fit. She's not so drunk that she's forgotten that she doesn't have space in the eBay room for any more stuff, any more mistakes, any more abandoned things. And £500 gives you such a great hit when you spend it all at once that it sometimes is worth returning the item so you can get the hit again somewhere else; a bit like throwing up, having a big glass of water and starting again. Not that Bryony has ever thrown up on purpose, of course. But anyway, these boots are beautiful. They are a perfect shape with a heel, but not too high. And they're not made out of some old piece of leather that's just been found lying around somewhere; no, some soft baby animal has been *skinned* for these. And then the skin has been pierced with a few hundred silver metal studs. OK, on second thoughts maybe the heel is rather high, but there is a platform, which helps. And a little hole for her toes to peep out of, which is very S/S11. Maybe they are a bit car-to-bar, but . . .

Bryony pays for them. Breathes. Tornadoes slightly wonkily with her Prada bag and her Mulberry and Crème de la Mer bags down the stairs to Vivienne Westwood where she holds out her white iPhone to show the assistant the picture she took of the magazine page with the perfect pink Get A Life silk/wool blend scarf. The assistant sends her to the OTHER Vivienne Westwood concession which is miles away upstairs but where Bryony finds a delightful male assistant who beams, yes, actually beams, at her as she approaches.

'Do you have this?' she asks him, holding out her phone really quite boldly, feeling for a second like Kate Moss, or maybe Kate's stylist, or perhaps someone who knows her stylist's mother slightly but definitely lives in London and has a job that requires her to live on sashimi and spend her lunch hour sewing up the backs of things and buying tights and crying over love.

He takes her iPhone. Scrutinises it. 'Oh,' he says, a touch of colour appearing in his cheeks. A bit like in real life when you show a real-life person a picture of a kitten. But that's it. *Oh*. And he keeps looking at the phone.

If a tornado, or a large ship, had eyebrows and was able to raise them . . .

'Oh?'

'It's beautiful,' he says.

'That's what I thought. Which is why, I, well, thought I'd . . .'

'And I *stupidly* didn't order any. But now, well.'

'Well?'

'I can see I should have ordered it. It would look beautiful on you.'

'Thank you.'

'You *need* this scarf.'

'I know.'

He swivels, quite abruptly. 'Now obviously you know where the main Viv shop is, yeah?'

'Well, obviously . . . Actually . . .'

'But I'll write the phone number down for you in case you want to ring ahead. Unless you've already . . . ?'

'Not on this phone, unfortunately.'

He catwalks over to the desk where he pulls out a yellow card and starts writing on it, very slowly, with a black Muji biro. He hands it to Bryony as if she is a serious genuine person who is actually going to buy this scarf. This must be the kind of thing that happens to stylists and fashionistas. This kind of thing has never happened to Bryony. She has never had an actual conversation with an actual fashion person that has not ended in her crying, swearing at them or spending approximately £500 to £1,500 to prove that it is better to be rich and fat than thin and working as a shop assistant, which she doesn't even believe. She suddenly can't move. This is the only shop assistant she has ever, ever . . .

But of course she's not going to actually go to the Vivienne Westwood shop! She doesn't want the scarf that much. She just likes showing people pictures on her phone and saying 'Have you got that?' But now she'll have to pretend to leave Selfridges if she is to continue this rather marvellous . . . And of course the only way to pretend to leave Selfridges is to actually leave Selfridges, which she is not going to do before she has eaten four cakes, and probably a couple of the little sandwiches they bring with the cakes. And a glass of champagne. Or maybe two. Although if she really, really wanted that scarf she would leave now. She would fly to Conduit Street (he did write out the address as well in the end) on magical wings, with her Prada, Mulberry and Crème de la Mer bags weighing her down only ever so slightly.

'Thanks,' she says. 'I'll ring, I think. I'm meeting my grandmother and my cousin for tea soon, and I might just have to go back to Céline first too. There's a, well . . .' He now gives her such a camp look that she giggles. When did she last giggle? 'A bag . . .'

'Oh, darling! The new yellow snake clutch?'

'How did you know?'

It was actually a nude tote, but whatever.

'You'll already have the Boston, presumably?'

'Of course.'

'Oh.' There is a very long pause. A slight eye roll. The flush again. 'I know people who are still on the waiting list for the Boston. What colour did you get?'

'Well . . .'

'Don't tell me.' He mimes 'being a clairvoyant' for a few seconds but then frowns.

Bryony laughs. 'The nude.'

There must be a nude. There always is. Or something that can be called nude, depending on what colour you are, and what colour you think nude is, or ought to be.

'Oh, darling.'

Over to Céline, then. The clutch is basically £1,000, but Bryony buys it because, well, everyone else obviously wants it, and she has the money, sort of, so why not? Bryony thinks for a second about her bank accounts, but the thought feels wrong when she is so happy and having so much fun so she stops thinking it. And she also doesn't think that she wanted the nude tote as a book bag for university, but only if it was less than £500 and she could pass it off as 'something from Primark' to the other students, and that she basically doesn't have anywhere to take a yellow snakeskin clutch, however beautiful it is. But by the time she has had afternoon tea, which in the end includes three glasses of champagne, only small ones of course, she feels better again. And when she leaves she is – and this is hilarious, but so wonderful – *thinking of Nietzsche*! Which just goes to show that shopping and drinking and eating all day does not make you shallow and ruined but actually takes you to the Dionysiac EDGE of things and makes you see things that ordinary mortals do not see. It prevents you from being timid. Timid people scuttle around like small mammals looking only at things on SALE RAILS and wearing anoraks and cheap trainers and VISCOSE. They buy things from catalogues and Peacocks. They do not have the guts, or the money, to buy things made out of snakes, and they SHOP AROUND for things when everyone knows that half of what you pay for in a place like Selfridges is the atmosphere – which, frankly, they ruin anyway with their existence – and when we are all going to die anyway what is left apart from atmosphere? What really matters apart from how you feel? And at this moment, Bryony feels fucking amazing. Totes amazeballs.

Taxi to St Pancras station – *whoosh* – where Bryony has just missed a train. That doesn't matter! Bryony loves just missing a train at STP because there is just so much to do there. For example, you can sit at Sourced Market and have a small glass of Petit Chablis while watching the world go by (more timid people in viscose pathetically queuing for train tickets or egg mayonnaise sandwiches while Bryony flies high above the world like an eagle or maybe Concorde, or something magnificent anyway) before popping over to M&S for one of those plastic glasses that come already filled with wine, and a large bar of salted caramel-filled milk chocolate. Oh, and a couple of bags of Percy Pig sweets for the kids. Then – quickly – into Boots for some hair bands, bamboo tights, Nurofen and . . . Bryony realises how mundane, how TIMID are these purchases and so immediately adds three of Clinique's new Chubby Sticks, one each of Mega Melon, Whopping Watermelon and Super Strawberry.

On the train there are some football fans drinking cans of beer while Bryony drinks her glass of wine. It feels companionable. Here she is with her weekend afternoon fun, and here they are with theirs. When she gets up to change at Ashford, one of them actually speaks to her. Even though she is fat and old!

'Someone's had a good day,' he says.

'Not her husband,' says one of the other blokes.

Bryony giggles. 'It's my money. Anyway, it's just shoes and a bag.'

The first guy groans. 'Shoes and bags, eh?'

'No worse than football.'

'Fair point, love, fair point.' He nods sagely.

'Anyway, you must like it when your wives wear beautiful shoes and carry beautiful bags. And they do have to come from somewhere.'

'What does that say on there? *Prada*. Pretty flash. Bit beyond my missus, I reckon. What's Céline?' He pronounces it 'saline'.

'Oh, that's much worse,' Bryony says, and giggles again.

'Reckon I'd give my missus a bit of a slapping if she came back with all that.'

'Start having to charge my mates to have a go,' says one of the others.

'You love it really,' Bryony finds herself saying to them. 'You love shoes and bags as much as we do. You love it when we look sexy. You know you do.' She tosses her hair slightly. When did she last toss her hair?

They laugh, but in a nice way, and Bryony gets off the train wondering why everyone does not drink all the time because it really makes life a lot more pleasant. Onto the train for Sandwich, although – shit – isn't the car parked at Ramsgate? Fuckfuckfuck. Bryony could have stayed on that train. Although should she really drive in this condition? Might she be, by now, a tiny bit over the limit? She'll have to ring James. Also, this train has a first-class carriage in which Bryony can now sit and think about what would have happened if she had stayed on the other train. She imagines going to the toilets, and the ugliest bloke – the one who talked about slapping his wife – following her. She imagines him following her in, shoving her roughly against the sink and then, well, having his way with her, despite her fat, and her age, and everything else. She imagines him being quite rough and . . .

Before she knows it, Bryony is in the toilets trying to masturbate, which is a challenge partly because of the uniquely sour Southeastern trains toilet smell, and partly because it's so small. In the end she has to get her feet up on the wall in front of her to be able to spread her legs wide enough that she . . . Oh . . . OK . . . *And all his friends*. Imagine him charging fifty pence each time one of them fucks her. And this happens every time she buys anything from Prada, which means she does it every week and does not feel guilty. Not that she feels guilty now, but anyway. Two of his friends at once. Maybe three. One in her mouth, and . . . Bryony whispers, 'Go on, fuck me, then, you disgusting fat slob,' because the men in her fantasy are disgusting fat slobs, like the ones you see on paedophile exposés on Channel 5, and then comes, convulsing slightly while someone coughs outside.

Back in her seat. What was that? WTF *was* that? Was that actually totally HILARIOUS or, basically, fucked up? If it was fucked up, was this in a Nietzschean way or not? Do men really do that to their wives? Of course not. It's just a fantasy, just a harmless . . . But what about what those guys said? They were joking, right? Oh God. Bryony giggles again, just to herself. It was funny really. Imagine telling . . . OK, you can't *really* tell anyone that you had a wank in a Southeastern train toilet while imagining being domestically abused and raped by yobs. Can you? Not really. Not unless you were very pissed. Bryony opens one of the packets of Percy Pigs and eats them all. She lies back in her seat and realises she does not know what to think or do next.

Then, out of nowhere, the feeling comes to her that she is completely invincible. If a yob came to rape her she would simply crush him in her fist: she would crumple him up like a used tissue. She would rape *him*. She could do that. She imagines herself stepping calmly out of the train – yes, just melting through the window while it is still going along, because that is how invincible she is – and picking it up – yes, the whole train – in her right hand and hurling it deep into the universe. Life is a joke, she suddenly realises. Here she is, sitting on this train and following all the rules of being a puny human when in fact she is a cosmic badass. She can step out of the train, out of life, out of the universe, whenever she likes. But she doesn't do it now; for now, being a puny human is, well . . .

Back at home, and James has taken the kids around junk shops and to auctions ALL DAY LONG and Holly wanted to play tennis instead and Ash is hungry and Holly now has yet another box of books that look far too old for her and Ash has a bruise from where Holly pinched him, but Holly only pinched him because he hit her first and kept calling her Lolly for no apparent reason. Bryony's headache begins at the front of her head and spreads around to just above her ears. She remembers the one remaining bag of Percy Pig sweets and gives it to the kids to share. But Holly throws the whole packet to Ash, deliberately mistiming it so that it hits him on the head.

'Holly . . . !'

'Whoops. *Sorry!* He can have them all anyway. And, Mummy, I thought you knew that Percy Pig sweets are actually made from pork gelatin, which means they are made from grinding up pigs' feet and bones, which means they are actually made from dead pigs that may even have been called Percy, which makes them totally one hundred per cent gross. And each one is thirty calories, which means that if you ate ten you'd have to do six hundred sit-ups to burn them off again.'

'Who told you that?'

'No one. I read the packet. Anyway, Mummy? You smell a bit funny.'

James raises his eyebrows. 'You do smell a bit like a brewery, Beetle.'

Bryony smiles. 'Oh, you know what Granny's like. I suppose I had one more glass than I should have over lunch. I think I'll go and have a bath.'

One of the interesting things about getting as fat as Bryony is now, is that you only have to run half a bath because you fill the rest of the tub with your flesh. And Bryony's flesh means something to her. This roll of fat here: that was Holly. A lot of fat came with Holly. And that one, the next one down: that was Ash. Bryony gained around three stone in the year following her parents' disappearance, but that parachuted in slowly and silently, billowing onto her in creamy folds at night while she was asleep, so she didn't notice what was happening at first. Instead of just getting a bit of a tummy, like Clem, she got larger all over, in the way that digital images increase when you pinch them outwards. In the bath, Bryony now feels immense, like a sea creature or a space monster. It is not an entirely unpleasant feeling. It's actually . . . Bryony drifts off to sleep and only wakes up when the water goes cold. She needs another drink.

But before that: out of the bath. Fluffy towel. Make-up off. Three more Nurofen. Fuck it: four. Now it's time for moisturiser. Bryony unwraps the £190 jar of Crème de la Mer Moisturizing Gel and rubs some carefully on her face. But what about her neck? Granny has always moisturised her face in what she mysteriously calls 'the Continental way', but her neck looks like an elephant's leg. Bryony applies moisturiser to her neck, perhaps a bit more than you'd really need, but enough to prevent elephant-leg developing, at least overnight. Then she moves on to her décolletage. There was something in some magazine about celebrities with 'dodgy décolletage'. Surely Crème de la Mer will be good for this area too? And what about her arms? Her breasts? Her stomach? Bryony finishes the pot of moisturiser, which was too expensive anyway, by rubbing some into her knees.

My perfect girlfriend:

1. Long straight black hair, no frizz, worn down, in low ponytail or bunches.
2. Blue eyes – dark, not that insipid watery blue. No weird flecks.
3. No glasses or contact lenses.
4. Good skin. Pale. Not too much foundation. Does not need concealer.
5. Must be under 8 stone. Ideally 7 stone 10.
6. Thighs must not meet at the top.
7. Fat distributed as follows: small amount on face, mainly lips, cheeks. Small tits – roughly a handful (must not be able to hold pencil under them). Tiny stomach is nice. Do not want to see abs. All of rest of fat on bum. Bum firm but wobbles a little when she walks. But not too much.
8. Pink nipples with no hair on them.
9. Natural or no make-up. Mascara is fine.
10. Interesting botanical name.
11. Intelligent but never boring.
12. Must like the Waterboys, World Party, Van Morrison, The The.

13. Square cut short fingernails with v. dark or clear polish.
14. Lip-balm rather than lipstick. Very light pink lipstick is OK (red lipstick on cock is disgusting).
15. Must have watched *Ferris Beuller's Day Off*, *The Breakfast Club* and other John Hughes films.
16. If she plays lacrosse she will play First Home. If she plays netball she will play Goal Shooter. Will like scoring goals more then running around.
17. Does ballet and/or yoga.
18. Can do the splits.
19. Toenails painted pale pink.
20. Some freckles on nose but nowhere else on body.
21. Wears perfume very subtly. NOT Poison or anything like that. Something unusual and a bit mossy like Givenchy III.
22. Writes long letters in real ink. Blue ink better.
23. Hates grunge music.
24. Hates Bros.
25. Hates *The Word*.
26. Has a London or neutral accent. NOT from North.
27. Wears floral dresses with bare legs and ballet shoes or plimsolls.
28. Has ripped 501s. But not deliberately ripped with scissors.
29. Likes wearing my sweatshirt.
30. Has been to India at least once.
31. Wants to do science at university. Preferably biology/botany.
32. Is clean and does not smell. No fishy odour.
33. Does not fart.
34. Never burps.
35. Does not eat more than one course at a three course meal.
36. Does not smoke or do drugs. One glass of white wine or champagne OK sometimes.
37. Does not like football, rugby or cricket.

38. Makes friendship bracelets in subtle colours.
39. Does not like dolls, soft toys etc.
40. A pony is OK.
41. Small ears.
42. Must be quite artistic but not in an art school way.
43. Sometimes eats only a small amount of chocolate or fruit for lunch (but not both at once).
44. Understands what it is like to lose mother.

The morning of the day that Piyali inadvertently ruins, no, *saves*, no, maybe just *changes* his life begins normally enough. It is a Monday and so he wakes up in Fleur's cottage with that sick feeling that always comes on a Monday. If the feeling was a word, then the word would be 'late'. Pi's homeopath – gasp, breathe, is he seeing her today? Because if he is then he is extremely late, but no, breathe out, it's OK, he moved his appointment to Thursday because of the thing with the car – tends to work on the level of the word. Each person, she says, has one word that sums up their central theme, or essential dilemma, their whole problem in life. It's similar to a writing theory that Pi read about where each character has an objective that you can boil down to one word: power, control, safety, success. Knowing this word means you can focus your character, keep them on track, not lose them.

The idea in real life, or at least with his homeopath and certainly at Namaste House, is to get rid of your word, to zap it, delete it, find-and-replace it with love or peace or some other soft frilly thing. And then what? Go through life with a soppy smile on your face chanting and wearing unflattering clothes and making everyone else feel bad? What is actually wrong with normal, honest suffering? Suffering means you are alive, you are real, you are free. Mindfulness – which is what Fleur has gone to teach this morning, leaving Pi alone in the big feather bed that smells of her perfume and her hair – seems intended to turn you into a docile animal that stands in its field all day never complaining and never smashing down fences and . . .

Pi does not write on the level of the word. Some people manage to do that. Their sentences trot along like happy horses until, suddenly, one horseshoe-nail word appears that makes the horse bolt, throw its rider and run away. It's clever, but anyone with a good dictionary can do it. Pi used to want instead to write on the level of the sentence, like Hemingway and Carver – although didn't it turn out that Carver's sentences were created by someone else? His editor, whatshisname? Yes, yes, of course, and Pi was going to look at it with his creative writing students last year and then forgot to order the photocopies in time and . . . When Pi writes now – which is rare, because life gets in the way so bloody much – it is on the level of the scene, like Tolstoy and his mushrooms, which is something else that he should photocopy in fact, but . . . Pi yawns. At least mindfulness stops all this chitter chatter. But he still hates it. Although he did send that student off for yoga classes last week. Which means nothing. Yoga is suffering too. It's fine. It's just all this other crap that is a problem.

Pi does a headstand to prove he still can. Tweaks his back coming down.

A hot shower. Hotter than Fleur can take it. Does he turn the setting back to where she has it? No. Let her suffer a little too, next time she gets in. Fleur doesn't have real breakfast food, just a lot of raw birdseed and cold, thin yogurt, so once he is dressed he walks across to the main house and finds Bluebell in the kitchen already making the dal for lunch. Late. Late. LATE! Yesyesyes, but seeing Bluebell is soothing and eating a real hot breakfast means he won't need lunch and so he is in fact saving time and in any case he doesn't actually have anything to do today except begin his new novel again and do the shopping so that Kam has the ingredients for supper and Nina has something for her packed lunch, which is what she says now, rather than tiffin, and when he suggested that they visit India together she just said something like 'Yeah, Dad, whatever', and then began a long moan about bikinis and bare shoulders and how impossible it is going on holiday to these backward places where you can't even get a good suntan.

Bluebell makes medu vada, his favourite. Hot, soft, savoury doughnuts made from black dal and spices . . . South Indian, which means they are specially for him. All those recipes she found and learned when he arrived at the house years ago, to try to make him feel at home, which he never did. He suspects that the medu vada are deep fried, which means he shouldn't have them, but lentils are always healthy, right? She serves them with coconut chutney and a sambar with a tiny bit too much tamarind for Pi's liking. Then a bowl of fresh fruit with just half a pistachio kulfi, today the front section of a Tardis. Two cups of coffee. There will be nothing on the ridiculous train he has to catch because he has no car. And Fleur can't even drive, which means she doesn't even have a car to lend him. Women!

There's a familiar person at Sandwich Station. At first Pi can't place him. He is wearing different clothes from usual. This ensemble, complete with jaunty trilby hat, is clearly a London Outfit. But underneath the hat it is definitely James Croft, hen-pecked husband of fat Bryony. Pi goes to the other end of the platform in the hope that James will not see him. It is over two hours going to London this way and who wants to have to talk to someone for two hours? And anyway, Pi has his book, and the *LRB*, and he doesn't like the way that his nervous cough comes out when he has to speak to someone new. But, oh dear, here comes James down the platform towards him.

'Hello,' he says. 'Been visiting?'

No, I've just arrived from space. 'Nice hat,' says Pi.

'Oh, thanks,' says James. And then he rabbits on and on about his hat so that they are still talking when they board the train, which means it is natural for them to sit together, and it turns out that James is actually a very serious and warm person – a writer too, in fact, which Pi had almost forgotten – and on his way to meet his editor, on whom he admits to having a slight crush, harmless of course. And then that deep sigh. He asks Pi about women. How does one cope with women?

'At least you only have one to cope with,' says Pi.

And then, for reasons he later can't understand at all, he tells James everything.

The gym is full of old people. They all sit there watching MTV Dance, which has so far only shown music videos with extreme close-ups of women's arses in Lycra, denim or plain cotton, wiggling, twerking, on a motorbike, a bed, a zebra, or some combination of these. It's not entirely unappealing, although who knows what the old people think. One man has brought a hardback library book, which he reads with a towel over his head, but everyone else just looks at the screen nearest to them because, well, because the screens are there, and what they show is quite arresting. For example Lady Gaga, at this moment wearing only a pair of white knickers and a bra, singing about being born this way, looking as if she could die of malnutrition any minute, but actually making Bryony wonder why *she* wasn't born that way, which is probably what you're supposed to think. And presumably you are also supposed to wonder what would happen if you went out wearing only a pair of white knickers and your period started or some yellow discharge came out or you realised you'd forgotten to wax your bikini line or you had waxed your bikini line but an ingrown hair had become infected or you just peed yourself a little bit . . .

'Hasn't got a pretty face, though, has she?' says one of the old women to the old man on the next exercise bike.

This is Bryony's third session at the gym. During the first two she learned never to attempt any of the following ever again: the rowing machine, on which she managed a bare thirty-two seconds, despite her exercise plan suggesting ten minutes; the treadmill, on which she reached a maximum speed of 6kph before asking the fitness instructor if there was any way of making it go downhill, which did not make him laugh at all; anything in the weight room, full of young men with tattooed necks and almost certainly shrivelled dicks who did not look at Bryony even once. Not even once! And she is prettier than Lady Gaga, objectively, sort of, despite weighing approximately four times as much. According to the magazines that they keep on the filing cabinet in the corner, which are too lowbrow for Bryony to ever actually buy, but are one of the few pleasures of coming to the gym, even Kate Moss is now fat. What hope is there for anyone else in that case? Surely that is the point where the editors of these magazines would decide to slash their wrists or drink a bottle of bleach because, well, if the most beautiful woman in the world cannot live up to the standards of even the thinnest, cheapest, crappest magazine, then . . .

But the true-life stories are quite funny. And they often feature people fatter than Bryony, for example the woman whose husband lost half his head – his actual head – in a blender. And the man who grew a nose on his forehead. And the fourteen-year-old who has already had liposuction, a tummy tuck and a gastric band. The only people who are thin in these magazines accompany stories like 'I lost both my arms to heroin', or 'I gorge on crisps and chocolate but only weigh four stone'. Everyone else is fat, even the woman who didn't let disability stop her from selling her body. Actually, another semi-pleasure of the gym is that several people who go to it are also fatter than Bryony. There's one now, being helped onto the treadmill. Bryony wonders when he last saw his dick. At least her fat doesn't stop her having sex. She simply gets on all fours. Or she could if she wanted to. But what if you were a man and you were so fat that your penis actually disappeared?

When MTV Dance is not showing Lady Gaga or Rihanna videos it shows endless ads for companies called things like Wonga and QuickQuid – really – that will give you £200 until payday and charge you £50 interest, which is 326% APR; or you can get a loan of £1,200 over ten months at a cost of only £1,631.34, which means you have to pay back £2,831.34, which is an APR of 1,362%. Bryony thinks of how happy Granny is whenever she makes ten per cent on something. Or when vendors realise that the value of their house has gone up by fifteen per cent. These places must be raking it in. Except that the saps who would go for such a bad deal are presumably so poor that they can never pay it back. Imagine being that poor. And really fat. And losing half your head in a blender.

Bryony is on one of those bikes with big seats that recline, so you can read a magazine and feel almost like you're relaxing, except for the fact that your legs are going round and round. But there's so much to watch in the gym. Lady Gaga, dickless men, the cartoon old people who go to Wonga, as if any old person would ever borrow anything apart from maybe a cup of sugar, and of course all the ridiculous 'challenges' that the fitness instructors pin up on the noticeboards to encourage all the hopeless, morbidly obese losers who come here. At the moment they have a challenge to see how many Easter eggs you can burn off before Easter. A Cadbury's Creme Egg apparently has 180 calories. A Flake Easter egg has 810 calories. A large Dairy Milk Easter Egg has 1,800 calories. Some twat has made little stickers in the shape of these different-size eggs that you can add to your chart to show how much exercise you have done. You'd think you could then go and eat what you've burned off, but no: the chart informs you that instead of, say, two Cadbury's Creme Eggs, which would be really quite a modest amount of Creme Eggs to eat in one go, let alone in one day, you should really eat a small steak and some broccoli. Right. Bryony has been on this exercise bike now for fifteen minutes and has burned only eighty calories.

This whole exercise thing does not add up. It must be wrong. Bryony really needs a drink.

Monday morning in the Alpine House, where miserably tiny plants cling to barren-looking rocks in an artificially cold and dry climate. It is everyone's least favourite glasshouse, although schoolchildren are always taken there first, perhaps as some sort of punishment. When will people learn that the only things kids want to see at Kew are the pitcher plants and anything else that is even slightly carnivorous or looks like a dick? A surprising amount of plants look like dicks. More, of course, look like vaginas, but kids aren't quite as used to seeing the insides of vaginas as they are to seeing dicks. Or maybe they are now, what with the internet, and . . .

'So?' says Izzy.

'This is stupid.'

'What?'

'I feel like I'm reporting to you.'

'Well, she won't tell me what happened. She just keeps going on about how *amazing* you are.' Izzy raises an eyebrow. 'And how *gorgeous* your body is . . .'

'Why does it matter what happened?'

'I need to keep an eye on you. Lest you transgress. Again.'

The only remotely interesting thing that ever happened in the Alpine House was when a crime novelist came for a whole week to observe the plants and atmosphere so that she could set a murder there. The easiest way to murder someone in the Alpine House is simply to make them stay there for quite a long time until they die of cold or boredom. It was amazing that the crime novelist herself survived. Or maybe she didn't. Charlie can't actually remember what happened next, or if the novel ever even came out. Maybe she's still in here somewhere.

'I still don't know what I'm supposed to have done wrong in the first place.'

Izzy sighs and rolls her eyes. 'Oh, never mind.'

Fleur has one celebrity in the guest wing and another one in the attic. There is a further celebrity in the eco-treehouse. The Prophet has been instructed yet again not to walk around in his underpants, although he is increasingly unpredictable in that respect. It is only week two of the new yoga term. Fleur can't cancel everything, basically, and just run off to the sodding Outer Hebrides after some woman who left her a blank book instead of . . . what? She tries to talk to Ketki about it, tries to ask what Oleander meant to leave her, but the old woman just clicks her tongue at her. Fleur has no idea what she has done this time and Ish won't tell her. They didn't inherit seed pods from Oleander, but it can't be that, surely. First, who wants a deadly seed pod? Second, the house is full of seed pods and has been for twenty years. Fleur got one too, from Oleander, wrapped in turquoise tissue paper. It looks exactly the same as all the others. So what the . . . ?

Ketki and Ish are not supposed to know, but they do know. They know about the boxes. And of course Oleander knew too, even though she never got involved, barely even spoke to the Prophet after everything that happened with Briar Rose and something to do with a magical book that he stole.

Fleur still doesn't ask where the boxes are sent.

And then Skye Turner appears with red eyes and some stuff in a carrier bag and a link to YouTube, on which she is a huge star but totally the wrong sort, and she can't afford to stay in Namaste House any more and even if Fleur didn't charge her one of the other celebrities would probably say something to someone and then the press would arrive, and so Fleur hides her in her own cottage and they drink tea and talk into the night about their mothers and the seed pods and weird shit about money. Skye suggests tasting the seed pod, but instead of this Fleur gives her some special tea and explains again that the seed pod is likely to be very deadly indeed. Skye asks why they all have them in that case. What is the point of them? They are valuable in some way that no one quite knows, Fleur says, and her mother probably died for them. Fleur is all shrugged-shoulders about the whole thing but Skye keeps asking questions because it is interesting to talk about late at night. Skye offers to teach some of Fleur's yoga classes for her, which is ever so sweet, really, but she's still all over the tabloids, and then she's ringing the neighbour's son, just a bit of phone sex because she is so lonely, and maybe the odd fantasy about murdering Greg, and, OK, she leaves him ONE voicemail saying where she is if he wants to send that demo, and then suddenly there are journos camped out in the estate agent's garden behind the eco-treehouse because that's where they think she is and if only she could get some peace and sodding quiet somewhere . . .

The man's face is such a strange shade of grey that it refuses to be lit. The student Clem got in to do the lighting has already burned her hands on the barn doors, so Clem is lighting him herself. Clem apparently never does pre-interviews; she always records her subjects a little cold, so they feel disempowered and a bit Petri-dished, and more likely to tell the truth. She told Zoe all about it in the car on the way over. Zoe half listened and half drove, at one point trying to impress Clem by chasing an ambulance halfway down the Commercial Road while smoking a roll-up that may have had a tiny bit of hash in it.

In one way, making documentaries is entirely different from making drama, because of course it's the truth, and drama is made up. But documentary is made up too, because it has scripts and storyboards, and interviewees are often chosen on the basis that they will say the thing in the script, for example that grey squirrels are evil or that pencil skirts are big this autumn. And fiction attempts to get at the truth in a different way. All of which everyone already knows, obviously. But then there's that insanely magical moment in both forms when the characters 'take over' and say things you'd never thought they would say, and they say them so perfectly that you never could have thought of them yourself. When Clem's characters – who are real people seated on knee chairs to make them not just comfortable but also a little uncomfortable in the way that leaning forward for a period of time does, with the overall effect being that they look oddly wistful and a bit confessional – start speaking, Clem will either look very bored or very fascinated. She looks bored when the character is saying something great, and fascinated when they aren't. This is deliberate. It gets more out of them, apparently.

'Zoe, would you mind just holding this white sheet up over there?'

And documentary makers even do their own white-balancing, which Zoe didn't even know about until this week.

Is Clem nervous? It's always hard to tell. Today's subject is the main protagonist in her documentary, so she probably is. Zoe can't remember his exact name, but he is the first person to have created life in a laboratory, from scratch. He looks a bit like a god, or someone's father, oldish and bearded. Much of what Clem said in the car went over Zoe's head, especially as Zoe was not just driving but imagining what might actually be between Clem's legs, and under what circumstances she would be able to see it, or even touch it, and . . . But there is one fascinating detail that she does remember. Basically, this god-dad scientist builds up genes into sequences of his own devising, which is fucking creepy, but creepier still is that the genes each have letters and can be turned into a code and . . .

'Is what you do essentially like microchipping a pet?'

The interview has started. Clem asks questions like this deliberately in the hope that the subject will begin the response by using the wording of her question and this, when edited, will look as if he has come up with it himself. *What we do is in no way like microchipping a pet . . .* But he doesn't fall for it this time.

'Not really,' he says.

'Explain to us in your own words, then, how exactly you use your genetic code to identify your creations.'

'Well, genetic code is made up of four letters: G, T, C and A. Now, if you think that a whole system of communication can be based on simply a dot and a dash – Morse code, of course – or a one and a zero – binary – then you'll understand how simple it is to create a code from four letters.'

'And you ended up using this code in quite an innovative way.'

'Well, yes. Of course the principal use of the code is to create a genotype, which will manifest itself as a phenotype. In other words the code dictates eye colour, hair colour, the way an organism stores fat. Although, our organism is so simple that it does not have eyes, hair or fat of course. Our organism is not really more than a few cells bunched together. But it is also possible to create genetic code that rather than doing something, *says* something. One can use it to communicate.'

'Can you go on?'

'We refer to it as "watermarking". It enables the creation to be traced back to the creator. We are able to write email addresses and URLs inside the genetic code so that future geneticists can see at once that this organism they have is synthetic, or a descendant of a synthetic organism, and they can find out information about the creator of that organism and even get in touch with him or her or visit their website.'

'You seem fond of this term "creator".'

A shrug. 'I suppose I have become interested in the term "creator".'

'And what do you feel about creating something that can never read its own genetic code?'

'Sorry?'

‘What do you feel about creating an organism, a living thing, that can never read its own genetic code?’

‘We are talking about viruses. Algae. Why would algae want to read its own genetic code? How would algae be able to access the internet, or use an email address?’ He laughs.

‘You’re saying that you have created life that is intrinsically incapable of becoming self-aware. Life that cannot ever know its creator, or communicate on the same level as its creator. What if the algae evolves? Becomes conscious? Finds it has “junk” DNA . . . ?’

He laughs again. ‘I am a god of algae . . . Interesting.’

Zoe notices the nice pause between ‘algae’ and ‘interesting’. She already knows enough about the way Clem works to hear the sentence without its wry ending. *I am a god of algae*. She could see this being remixed by a DJ. Maybe even featuring in her next screenplay somehow. A club scene, with everyone dancing to this new tune that begins with a manic laugh and those words: *I am a god of algae. And I give you . . . slime!* Or maybe something . . . Zoe is a little stoned, she realises.

Think about all the time you spend asleep. Now add to that all those painful last ten seconds of holding a yoga asana, or competing in a 5k race, if you have felt these. Add to this every second in your life you have wished something would just hurry up. Add all those minutes, indeed, hours, you’ve spent waiting for trains. Add all the minutes ON trains, unless you’ve been reading a life-changing book, or talking to someone you love. Now add all the minutes you spent reading books you’ve forgotten, or that turned out to be disappointing, or that didn’t change your life. Books where you believe the author may have ‘rushed the end’. Now add minutes spent talking to people you only thought you loved, but no longer speak to. Add all the time you spent on the phone to them, dressing for them, writing things especially for them, crying over them, holding them while they cried. Add any orgasms you've ever faked, or not enjoyed as much as the ones you have while masturbating. Add all the time you've spent masturbating. Now add minutes at work. Minutes spent on holidays that you thought would be more exciting then they were. Any minutes spent anticipating anything at all that did not live up to your expectations. All those times you wished you were somewhere else. What about all the time you spent shopping for things you later threw away? Childbirth, your own birth, death, grieving, mourning, hoping, the unreal euphoria of being intoxicated. All those minutes can go. But of course by now you must be wondering what is left when you take those minutes away from your life, all those minutes that the ego made for you, and then made you undo. What indeed?

Bryony really needs a beautiful vagina. She needs her vagina to be like a celebrity's vagina. She'll want a landing strip, of course, which will probably come afterwards. But there needs to be some reason for landing in the first place, and therefore the main thing is that Bryony's vagina should smell like summer meadows or spring rain or basically something really expensive and non-vaginal. And she has the money to pay for it; that is not the problem. The problem is that she has Googled 'intimate wash' and so far the only things that have come up are medical-looking bottles called things like Vagisil and Femfresh and SebaMed. Bryony knows how Skye Turner gets rid of bags under her eyes, but she really wants to know how she cleans her cunt. No one uses soap, presumably, because of thrush. But what else are you supposed to use? This has not, as far as Bryony knows, been covered in *Grazia*.

The next thing she Googles is 'expensive vaginal wash' but all that leads her to is articles by well-meaning petit-bourgeois housewives saying things like 'Who needs an expensive vaginal wash? My daughters and I simply use vinegar.' FFS. Vinegar. Right. Who, exactly, would really put vinegar up their cunt? And how would they even do it? One of those thrush-cream syringes, probably. But this is not what Bryony sees in her mind when she imagines softly soaping the inner and outer flaps of her vagina. She does not see herself standing in the shower in the en-suite – which, frankly, has been, along with its mould patches, removed from Bryony's fantasy life and replaced with something more like the shower they had that time in the Langham – with some kind of vile plastic syringe, inserting *vinegar* into her vagina. She sees a pink frothy mousse, not unlike her Guerlain foaming face wash, costing at least fifty pounds. For a moment she imagines herself on that TV programme, presenting her new product idea to a panel of . . .

'Mummy?'

'What?'

'*When* is Uncle Charlie coming?'

It is literally always the same. Ollie stands in line at the fishmonger, or what he thinks is the line, except some other fucker always crosses that line, or ignores it completely, so that even though it is Ollie's turn, Spencer, the son in Marsh & Son, will turn to the other guy with a cheery 'How are you today, Mr Collard?' or 'How's life, Ben?' or simply 'What can I do for you, mate?'

Ollie has been coming to this fishmonger – tucked away on a backstreet in Herne Bay – for the last THREE YEARS and isn't even sure that Spencer recognises him. Spencer has been cheery with him only once, last time he came in, on a cold Friday afternoon. Ollie has tried going at different times. Eleven a.m., just before Spencer has his first cup of tea of the day, after starting work at 4 a.m. (you learn these things just from being in the queue), is the worst time. Late afternoon can be all right, because Spencer is in a good mood because his working day is almost over, but of course there are hardly any fish left by then. Early morning is best. If you go to the fishmonger early in the morning they take you seriously, as if you are a chef, or someone with a real man's job. After all, anyone who convincingly calls other men 'mate', drinks things from cans and carries cash in his back pocket will have completed all important transactions in his life by around 8 a.m. These people count as real men in some unfathomable way that would not make sense in, say, a university or bookshop, but does make sense on a building site or in a fishmonger.

These men, often booked to come and look at the boiler in 'the morning' or to put some shelves up at 9 a.m., invariably turn up at 7.45 a.m. wanting a cup of tea (*white with one, white with none . . .*) and a shit. Then, having knocked off work as early as possible, all that is left for these men to do is go for a nap in a lay-by, or hang around the local tip chatting about SHELVES or SCREWDRIVERS or the COUNCIL, or go down the bookie's. These are the kinds of men Spencer respects. He is also partial to people in wheelchairs, old ladies, old men, the retarded, pretty girls, children and dogs. Ollie is so obviously a middle-class twat with a professional job that it's no surprise that Spencer treats him so cruelly. He is literally at the bottom of Spencer's list. On the odd occasion – usually a Saturday morning – when Ollie has turned up at around 7.45 a.m., Spencer has been almost nice to him. Once he even gave him a recipe for a monkfish-cheek stir-fry with lime leaves and ginger, even though Ollie didn't want monkfish cheeks and doesn't really know how to cook fish anyway, because cooking fish is Clem's job and it is only buying fish that is Ollie's job. Then there was the perplexing, but not unpleasant time when Spencer said to Ollie, 'You like all the expensive fish, don't you? Like my sister used to. I prefer the cheaper sort, me. Cheaper the better. I can take or leave the halibut and bass myself. But my sister, she was just like you.'

And last Friday was also strange. Just as he was leaving, with approximately seventy-five pounds' worth of tabloid-wrapped fish in three separate pink-and-white striped carrier bags, Spencer smiled – yes, smiled – at him and said, 'Got your bottle of wine, have you?' Well, yes, in fact Ollie had just that morning waited in to take delivery of a box from Berry Bros. & Rudd that cost approximately £280, containing old, bloodlike liquids that the following evening Clem would pour from a gigantic decanter into gigantic glasses like something from a fairy tale full of giants and people with big swords. But the result would be somehow disappointing and not taste at all like it looked and Ollie would end up drinking beer instead, as usual.

'Yep,' Ollie had said.

'Nice bottle, is it?'

'I think so.'

'Suppose we won't be seeing you first thing tomorrow morning then?'

'No. No, I suppose you won't.'

HE HAD BEEN REMEMBERED AND ACKNOWLEDGED!!!

But the next time he went in, it was as if this exchange had never happened.

Martin, the Marsh in Marsh & Son, has always been a lot nicer than Spencer. Even though he, also, has never entirely acknowledged that Ollie has visited his shop more than once, despite the fact that his visits must by now be approaching 200, what with all the dinner parties that Clem insists on having, where the starter is often oysters on a plate of crushed ice, or brown shrimp on toast, and the main course is usually pan-fried sea bass, pan-fried halibut, pan-fried red mullet or pan-fried salmon, each with new potatoes and courgettes or butternut squash purée and samphire, when it is in season.

Mind you, there was that one time when Martin said, 'Go and get that halibut out, Spence,' when he saw Ollie coming, which was encouraging. And of course then there are all the conversations that Martin never seems to remember, but are often the highlight of Ollie's day, about the merits of local wild sea bass over the farmed stuff, which always looks small and pathetic anyway, and which Clem once suggested he TAKE BACK, as if you could ever take something back to a fishmonger, especially to one ruled by Spencer; and why you should have a glass of stout with your oysters, and how at Martin's daughter's wedding, which was possibly in Spain, the caterers replaced the dead eyes of the cooked whole sea bass with small pieces of glistening black olive and its greyed gills with cucumber, and served it to look as if it were still alive, or at least raw, and also made a salmon mousse in the shape of a salmon that no one ate because they didn't want to ruin it. The fishmonger also sells poultry and game, so there are always packages of little dead birds and mammals in the display, which Ollie tries not to look at.

Today Ollie has been instructed to get two pieces of salmon, or alternatively a medium-sized sea bass for supper, as well as picking up the dinner-party fish that Clem has ordered over the phone. His original brief was to 'get something that looks nice' but who can operate with such vague instructions? It's like, it's like . . . Aha! Salmon – yes, that pink fish is definitely salmon. The first way not to be humiliated in the fishmonger is to be definitely 100 per cent sure of what fish is in front of you which is: a) not always obvious; and b) not helped by the mispositioning of the little signs which Spencer often throws around when he's in a huff.

'Yes, mate?' Spencer makes no eye contact, as usual. He had already handed over the dinner party fish, which comes to £68.14.

'I'll have a bit of that salmon, please, thanks.' Right. Who says *please, thanks*, FFS? And Ollie dreads the next bit, where Spencer will ask him how much salmon he wants, and Ollie will say just a couple of pieces, enough for two people – two rich people, he will not add, for whom money is no object, unlike the little old ladies with their pensions who scrimp and save for their bit of fish on a Friday – and Spencer will say he has to be more precise and – oh, there's a local sea bass, which is actually much simpler, because if it's the right size then he'll just need it cut into two fillets. The only problem is that Ollie cannot really keep any weights or measurements in his head and can't visualise anything at all fish-related and therefore can only go by price. He knows from trial and error that a good-sized sea bass for two will cost between twelve and fourteen pounds. So, all he has to do is . . .

'Actually, mate, how big's that sea bass?'

Spencer sighs, puts down the salmon, picks up the sea bass, turns it through ninety degrees and puts it down again. Then he goes to wash out his sinks. This is the kind of thing that happens ALL THE TIME. Ollie stands there, sighing and looking at his watch, and Spencer ignores him and washes his sinks. Now he starts on his chopping boards. This is really fucking . . . Then, finally, he turns.

'Have you made your mind up, then, mate?'

'Sorry?'

'I just thought I'd give you a bit of time to decide.'

CUNT. Right. Well . . .

'I was still wondering how *big* it is. I mean by *weight*.'

'Oh, sorry, mate.' Spencer picks up the fish and slithers it onto the scales. He then says something incomprehensible about kilograms.

'And how much is that?'

Spencer says the same thing about kilograms again.

'I meant in price.'

'That'll be thirteen pounds and fifteen pence. Call it thirteen.'

'OK, thanks. Can you do it in two fillets, please?'

Spencer guts the fish and rinses it under the tap before slapping it down on one of his chopping boards and slicing the flesh away from the spine, which is all really quite impressive to watch. He asks Ollie if there's anything else he would like. Yes, there is: he'd like some brown shrimp and some samphire.

'Right, mate. You've got your telephone order, your bass, your shrimp, your samphire. Anything else?'

'What time are you open on Thursday?'

This is not an unreasonable question, as the fishmonger keeps unpredictable pagan hours that Ollie doesn't ever know for sure. Basically, they are closed all day Sunday and Monday because no one goes fishing on Saturday and Sunday. But the rest of the week is a complex arrangement of traditional half-days and non-traditional half-days, and it sometimes changes in summer, but now Spencer looks so deliberately at the 'Opening Hours' sign on the door that Ollie feels like a twat YET AGAIN because of course he needn't waste Spencer's time by asking when he could just, if he wasn't such a posh cunt, look and see for himself.

'Sorry, mate. Didn't see the sign.'

'No, no, you're all right. I've lost track myself, to be honest. You know my sister who went missing last year? They've found a body. Down Hastings way. My dad's gone to identify her and so we're all a bit distracted here.'

OMG. 'Christ, sorry, mate. That's . . .'

'We just heard last week. First we heard there'd been a sighting. Then a particular bit of woodland. Then they did a search and there was the body.'

Fuck. *Fuck*. Poor Martin, lovely innocent Martin who simply laughs when people ask for pheasants in June and asks Spencer to go and put the board back round the right way. Imagine having to go and identify the body of your own daughter. Ollie sees an image of Martin sipping his tea on a winter's morning and taking off his steamed-up glasses and rubbing his hand over his pink face, and . . . And for some reason Ollie now also remembers the one time he saw Spencer in Asda in Canterbury, and how he looked wrong and out of place, like houseplants in removal vans that are suddenly covered in dust, or obviously haven't ever been pruned or watered properly and now have one whole side missing because of a wall that isn't there any more.

'Look,' he says to Spencer now. 'I'm so, so sorry. If . . .' He wants to say something like 'If there's anything I can do'. But he's just a stranger, just a twat with a bad attitude who comes along and pretends to know something about fish when he knows NOTHING about fish, and plays these stupid power games with a fishmonger when he is a university lecturer who lives in a huge house with a study of his own and an interior-designed living area, not that that makes him better or anything, but even so . . . Suddenly he has an overwhelming desire to offer to work for Spencer for free, not that he is sure how that would help. But he could cover the funeral, surely? And if anyone was feeling really depressed afterwards. He imagines putting on a blue-and-white striped apron and becoming a hero, because no one else from around here would even bother to CARE about the death of a fishmonger's daughter . . . Well, TBH, they might care a bit, and of course they'd be much more likely than Ollie to already know something about it, to have been following the story on the local news and so on, but Ollie has some depth of feeling that these people do not have because he can't actually BEAR the local news, where strangers feed off the misery of other strangers; but *here*, *now* . . .

'Thanks, mate. It's just all happened so suddenly, and . . .'

Whatever Spencer was going to say next is lost, because Ollie drops his wallet and even though he doesn't immediately bend to pick it up, his eyes follow it, and then Spencer says, 'Don't forget your wallet, mate,' and turns back to rinse his chopping board.

'Take care of yourself,' says Ollie, but he isn't sure whether the sound of the running water drowns him out. He wants to say it again: 'Take care of yourself, mate.' Or even better, 'Take care of yourself, Spencer.' He knows his name, of course. Everyone knows Spencer's name. But they've never been formally introduced, and anyway, Spencer has now gone back to his other sink.

The orchid walk begins at the Sandwich Bay Bird Observatory at 10 a.m.

'So, kids, there's a prize for who can record the most plants.'

'But we'll see all the same ones.'

'Not necessarily.'

'Well, what's the prize?'

James sighs. 'Um . . . cake. Yes, the winner chooses what cake I make this afternoon.'

'Can the winner choose no cake?'

'Christ, Holly, get into the spirit of this.'

'Daddy, don't swear.'

'And we're having roast lamb first.' James tickles Ash under his ribcage. 'Yum!'

Holly just sighs.

Bryony and Charlie are still inside looking at books. They come out with the guide, a large man with a moth-eaten jumper. Bryony is wearing huge sunglasses, like something from a magazine, which is sort of embarrassing. There are around ten other people waiting to begin the walk, including a woman who looks like a witch, with grey hair, a large mole and a bright red anorak, and a woman who is wearing a lot of make-up and new wellies, but at least no sunglasses. There are two boys with their dad. One of the boys is eating grass. No one is stopping him. Holly writes the date in her notebook: 28 May 2011.

'Excited?' Charlie asks Holly.

'Why would I be excited?'

'You're going to see wild orchids!'

'Right, whatever.'

They set off with the guide. Holly writes down plant names: silverweed, granny's toenails and black medic. Then they see the first marsh orchids. Charlie throws himself on the ground and gently touches the pale mauve flowers. The boy who was eating the grass starts eating some of these flowers, but no one notices. Holly wonders if he might die. The orchids are nice but quite small. You could definitely miss them if you didn't know what you were looking for. But up close the flowers are amazing. It's hard to explain why, but they just look nicer than other flowers. As if they were drawn by a better, more imaginative artist. There are also green winged orchids, which look a bit like the marsh orchid with extra green bits. The guide tells everyone not to touch or pick any of the wild flowers, and says you can go to prison if you do. They see yellow rattle, which, in autumn, has seed pods that actually rattle; lady's bedstraw, which smells of honey and can be used to help people give birth; lesser bedstraw; evening primrose . . . The group scrambles through a meadow and then an alleyway and then onto a strangely quiet housing estate.

Holly catches up to Charlie, who is talking to the guide.

'And then some divvy actually *mowed* one . . .' the guide is saying.

Charlie shakes his head. 'How could you not realise . . . ?'

'There,' points the guide. 'Up ahead.'

Charlie sighs with anticipatory pleasure. They walk towards a grass verge outside a large house. There is a single orchid. It is bigger than the ones they have already seen, pale green and pale purple, and the flowers have long things coming out of them that look like lizard's tongues. There are another two identical plants just a few yards away.

'This is the lizard orchid,' says the guide. '*Himantoglossum hircinum*. It is very rare. Although we have up to a hundred plants growing in the Sandwich Bay area, we are actually one of very, very few sites around the world that support this wonderful orchid. It's a real beauty. Look carefully. Don't touch. Smell the flowers – they have a powerful scent: some say like goat.'

'Flowers that smell like *goat*?' Holly says, but Charlie is on the ground again.

Holly drifts off to look at one of the other lizard orchids. The two boys and Ash follow her. The boy who was eating the grass snaps a flower from the plant.

'Don't do that,' says Holly.

The boy gurns at her and eats the flower.

'You spastic,' says Holly. 'I hope you die.'

She smells one of the flowers carefully, without touching it. It smells of socks.

Soon they are right by the sea. Here they find seaside daisies, yellow-horned poppies, sea beet, sea kale and white bryony. There is stuff growing everywhere! Then back across fields and meadows. Charlie and Bryony walk together, talking urgently, with their heads down. At one point Holly creeps up behind them and hears something like 'If you don't tell her, I will'. Which sort of sounds like it could be to do with a birthday surprise, but had an odd, un-birthdayish tone about it that made Holly reluctant to ask them about it.

'And this,' says the guide, pointing to something that looks like a really, really huge orchid, 'is Himalayan balsam. It'll be six feet tall by the end of the summer.'

'Aren't the RHS asking us to cut that down?' says the woman with the make-up and the shiny wellies.

The guide frowns. 'Not here, they're not.'

'But we're all being asked to cut it down everywhere. It's invasive! It chokes rivers, like Japanese knotweed. You want to cut it down. Dig up the roots. It drinks all the water, and . . .'

'How much water do you see around here?' the guide says, laughing. 'This has been growing here for the last twenty years. I'm not going to cut it down.'

The group moves on. The witchy woman in the red jacket walks next to the welly-woman.

'That's rosebay willowherb anyway,' she says.

'I know.'

They both laugh.

'And some fucking cunt doing sidestroke. Who does sidestroke nowadays? With plastic bags occasionally falling out of his pockets. And three fat women wearing fat women's perfume which, as you probably know, can travel a hell of a long way in a swimming pool. Just because you are in the water does not mean you no longer smell of anything. And then the porno children. Don't look at me like that. You've clearly never seen rhinestones on a four-year-old's bikini before. Maybe they don't do that kind of thing at the golf club. It's no wonder they ban photography. I mean, with only a camera and an internet connection you could set up quite a profitable child porn site without actually doing anything that illegal or really even going very far out of your way. OK. You're not saying anything again. *What?*'

'Shut up and pass me the roasting tin.'

'I'm having *déjà vu* . . .'

'Whatever. Can you just . . .'

'Yes. Here.' It's the right tin. Ten points and a gold star! But . . .

'OK. I am not going to nag . . . I *said* I wouldn't nag.'

'Wouldn't dream of it, I know.'

'But, well, pudding . . . ?'

'I'm on it.'

'Are you sure?'

Imagine you have just been reincarnated, but instead of ending up back on Earth, you end up on the far side of the universe on some brown, rock-like planet that you don't understand. In some way, you remember being human. Whatever you are now – a worm, or an insect, or a grain of sand – in your heart you are still human. Now – close your eyes if you like – and imagine the person you hate most, now, in this life. Back to your rocky world, where you are all on your own, with no one who understands what it is to be, or to have been, human. And then, all of a sudden, from behind a tree or from the undergrowth, or whatever they have there, out walks, or flies, or crawls, your hated person. How do you feel about them now? If you were the only two organisms on a distant planet, how would you be with one another? What would matter, and what would not matter? Now ask yourself: is that person on the rocky planet your higher self or your lower self?

~

When they get back from tennis, the house is full of the smell of lamb stuffed with garlic, which is disgusting. It is disgusting and grey and wet and flabby, like a dirty flannel dipped in oil and blood. If you eat it, that's what you end up with in your tummy, for days and days, until you poo it out. But you can never poo all of it out; some of it will stay inside you forever, and will actually become you, even things like your eyeballs. Imagine having sweaty, garlicky, flannelly, dead baby creature IN YOUR EYES. Holly wants to be sick. But in sort of a good way that she couldn't really explain to anyone.

Charlie comes back from his shower and arranges himself on one of the sofas with a pile of weekend supplements: travel, foreign news, features. Holly does twenty press-ups on the floor by his feet and then manoeuvres her way onto his lap.

'Uncle Charlie?'

'Yes?'

'I think you are the loveliest man in the world, apart from Daddy.'

'Thank you, Holly.'

'I can't marry Daddy, so can I marry you?'

'Hmm?'

'We could get married in four years.'

'You're not twelve yet.'

'I'm almost twelve.'

Charlie pinches her arm gently. 'We all know when you're going to be twelve, Holls.'

'Anyway, when I'm sixteen, you'll only be . . .'

'I'll be very old indeed.'

'But you'll still be very nice.'

'Thank you.'

Holly kisses Charlie on the neck: it's a little tiny winged kiss like a fairy landing on something soft like a cloud. No response. She does it again. She does it all around his neck like a fairy necklace. And then up and under his ears. He smells sweet and a little bit of the cinnamon soap in the spare bathroom.

'Uncle Charlie?'

'Yes?'

'Am I good at kissing?'

'You're *very* good at kissing.'

'Am I better at kissing than your girlfriend?'

'I don't have a girlfriend.'

'All right, then. The last person you sexed.'

'Much better.'

'So basically there's no reason for us not to get married.'

'Unfortunately, I believe it's still illegal to marry your uncle.'

Bryony comes in holding two glasses of white wine. She gives one of them to Charlie.

'What on earth are you talking about? Holly, stop mauling your uncle.'

'Your charming daughter has proposed to me,' says Charlie. 'And as she's such a good kisser I am inclined to accept, except . . . surely it's illegal to marry one's uncle?'

'He's actually my second cousin, once removed, isn't he, Mummy?'

Bryony sighs. 'Oh, I'm sure marrying her is legal somewhere in the world. Holly. Off. Now.'

Charlie takes the glass of wine. Holly wrinkles her nose.

'Uncle Charlie? Why are you drinking wine?'

Bryony rolls her eyes. 'Leave the man alone, Holls, for goodness sake.'

'Because I'm a grown-up,' says Charlie. 'And it's Sunday.'

'But is it Paleowhatever?'

'It's made from grapes, which are fruits that grow in the wild.'

'So you'd find some wild grapes and jump up and down on them? With your tribe?'

'Holly, give it a rest.'

'I suppose we're not married yet,' Holly says. 'So you can do what you like.'

'What else won't I be allowed to do when we're married?'

'Don't encourage her.'

'Well,' Holly says, 'obviously no drinking or smoking. No cakes. No McDonald's. Nothing deep fried at all. No staying up too late. No watching sport. Oh, I suppose except the London Marathon, you can watch that. And tennis, of course. No bird watching. And no real sexing, just kissing. Because I'm still quite young. And . . .'

'Holly!'

'What?'

'That really is enough.'

'Sounds like quite a normal marriage to me,' says Charlie.

Ash has been helping James in the kitchen. Now they both come in, James carrying a glass of local cider, and Ash with his apple juice.

'Who bets that I can't do a hundred sit-ups?'

'Holly, for goodness sake. Can't you sit *down* for five minutes?'

'All right. I bet you can't do a hundred sit-ups,' says James.

Bryony glares at him. Holly gets down on to the floor and tucks her toes in under the sofa that Charlie is sitting on. She starts doing sit-ups.

'I bet I can do a hundred sit-ups too,' says Ash, his timing off as usual.

Holly sighs. 'All right. We'll start again. Uncle Charlie, you can count and see who can do the most.'

'This girl does not need more exercise,' Bryony says to James.

'Ten, eleven, twelve – come on, Ash, don't give up!'

'Everyone needs more exercise, Mummy.'

'Apple pie? OK . . . I mean, I suppose it's quite retro and . . .'

'According to the Chicago Smell and Taste foundation, just the smell of apple pie increases women's genital sensitivity by twenty-four per cent.'

'Where on earth would you find out something as ridiculous as that?'

'*Men's Health* magazine.'

'And are you planning some kind of orgy?'

'Well, now you mention it . . .'

'Right. So we'll just get everyone to throw their car keys in the middle of the table?'

Silence.

'I mean, why do we need our guests to have increased genital sensitivity?'

'Not our guests.'

'What?'

Sighing. 'I just want you to want me.'

James keeps going on about Holly's birthday present, but will not confirm that he has bought her the Wilson Steam tennis racquet she so desperately wants. Even Bryony is no longer sure that he has done what was required and gone to Canterbury and bought the racquet. But he must have done. It was basically the only thing he had to do for Holly's birthday, since Fleur offered to make food for the surprise party and bring it over in secret while Holly plays tennis with Charlie – with her new racquet – in the morning. Bryony is glad: at least she knows Holly will eat some of Fleur's delicate and beautiful cakes, biscuits and chocolates. At one point James rather ridiculously suggested a hog roast, which is perhaps the least likely thing that Holly would ever eat. How can he not see that? But he now seems to be planning to make up for it with this secret present that *must* be on top of the tennis racquet, could not possibly be *instead* of the tennis racquet. It's all very worrying. Bryony had been considering buying a back-up racquet herself and hiding it in the boot of her car, but that's silly and she trusts James, but now Holly's birthday is tomorrow and it's too late even to order something on Amazon.

'You'll never, ever guess,' he says now to Holly.

Dinner is over and everyone is in the sitting room. Bryony is supposed to be reading *Tristram Shandy* on her iPad but is actually reading *Grazia*. *MasterChef* has just finished and she is eking out the last of a rather nice Syrah. She can't really get away with opening another bottle now, just for one small glass. Maybe she'll have some white instead. Just a drop to help her sleep. Although it's not bedtime for a little while, and . . .

'OK,' says Holly, rolling her eyes. 'Is it a tennis racquet?

'Come on,' says James. 'Show some imagination.'

'Is it a tree?' says Ash, in that random way that he does sometimes.

James makes a face at him.

'What?' he says. And everyone realises it *is* a tree.

'Did he know?' Bryony asks James later, in bed.

'No. I mean, he can't possibly have done . . .'

'Oh well. It'll still be a surprise. What kind of tree did you get?'

'Guess.'

'Hmm. A holly tree?'

'God. I *am* transparent.'

'I think it's a lovely present. Where will we plant it?'

'At the bottom of the garden. It'll be her special tree.'

'It'll look beautiful.'

'And . . . No. Actually, I'll leave the next bit as a surprise.'

'What next bit?'

'Oh. I found a lovely Emily Brontë poem to read before we plant it.'

'"Love is like a wild rose briar . . ."'

'You already know it.'

'Yes. Of course I do.' Breathe. 'Look, James. This is all lovely and everything, but I do have to ask you . . .'

'What?'

'You did buy the tennis racquet, didn't you?'

'This is so much more . . .'

'You DID buy the racquet, didn't you?'

'Well, actually . . .'

Bryony sighs. 'Fuck.'

'What?'

Bryony gets out her iPad. 'It's Sunday tomorrow as well. The shop in Canterbury is closed. Bluewater won't open until ten in the morning. Oh Christ, what am I going to do?' She looks at her watch. It's gone eleven. How on earth . . . ? She can ring Charlie and get him to stop at Bluewater on his way tomorrow, although that will mean pushing everything a bit later and . . .

'What? She has a tennis racquet already.'

'Do you know *anything* about tennis?'

'Do you? What happened to being given what you need, rather than what you want? What happened to birthdays being more than just a shopping list you give your parents?'

'She only wanted ONE THING. I couldn't even get her to make a list. All she wants is that sodding racquet.'

'Which is a good reason for her not to have it.'

Bryony shakes her head. 'I just don't get you.'

James raises his eyebrows. 'I could say the same.'

'Yes, but anyone in their right mind in the entire world would agree with me.'

James sighs. 'Well, you would think that.'

'Even her tennis teacher said she was ready for a new racquet.'

'OK. Well, I didn't know that. No one told me that . . .'

'And I even rang up and got them to hold the racquet in Canterbury! It was simply your job to go and pick it up. I mean, I could have done it, but you said you would. Your job was not to CHOOSE Holly's birthday present, just to collect it.'

'Which is always the way, isn't it?'

'What is that supposed to mean?'

'Why can't I choose something for Holly for a change?'

'I just don't understand why you are deliberately wrecking her birthday.'

~

'I have no idea why everyone thinks nature is so benign and glorious and wonderful. All nature is trying to do is kill us as efficiently as possible.'

Distant giggling. The clinking of glasses. A plane flying over the Channel.

'Isn't that a bit of an out-of-date view, though? Nature being "red in tooth and claw" and all that. And didn't people use that as an argument in the nineteenth century to basically control nature and exploit it for its value?'

'OK. Number one: nature in this sense is not red at all but sort of golden. And no one has ever controlled nature. The people who think they are most in control of nature are the ones being most controlled by it. We only really do what plants make us do. We are like huge bees in a way, moving around not just pollen but seeds, fruits, whole plants. And we think we are doing it because we want to, but we are actually doing it because the plants want us to.'

'But hang on. Plants are not conscious.'

'Aren't they?'

Laughter. 'No. Don't be so . . .'

'But consciousness takes different forms. Why is ours the best? Why is ours the only possible form? What we call consciousness is, after all, just a lot of cells that are not conscious doing things in harmony with one another. When people try to find the thing we call consciousness in there, they can't do it.'

'OK, but you're not saying that a poppy sits there thinking and plotting?'

'No. But if you put together every poppy in the world, then you have a plot.'

~

'Well, that was embarrassing,' Charlie says to Bryony.

It's warm in the garden so everyone has stayed outside after watching James plant the holly tree. The occasional blue tit visits the bird table regardless of the guests. There's one there now, nibbling something, and then a robin comes and shoves it out of the way and . . .

'Yep.' She sips her champagne.

'I mean, if you can choose one poem that will freak out the maximum amount of people . . . I mean, it's not just that it's our poem, but now all the stuff about the wild rose briar sounds wrong. Fleur's face.'

'He didn't know. And Fleur's mother was Briar Rose. But still, it's close enough.'

'Yeah. Well, at least Holly got her racquet.'

'Yes. Thank you. I totally owe you one.'

'She's bloody good, you know. You should come and watch her.'

'I know. I must do. I'll try next week.'

'I mean, she thrashes me.'

'But you let her, right?'

'Nope. I'm very competitive. I wouldn't be able to . . .'

Ollie drifts over with an unlit cigarette hanging out of his mouth.

'Who's competitive?' he asks.

'Me,' says Charlie.

'Want to do a triathlon, then?'

Charlie laughs. 'What?'

'Seriously. Well, maybe not. Well, anyway, there was a sign on the way here. The Walmer Triathlon. You swim Walmer to Deal, then run to Fowlmead, and then it's a few laps on the bike.'

James comes over. 'I heard the word "bike",' he says.

Which is lucky, thinks Bryony, because if he'd come over a few minutes earlier he would have heard the word 'twat'. Although she hopes she said it so quietly that no one could possibly have heard. Maybe she just thought it.

'Fancy a triathlon?' says Ollie, lighting his cigarette.

'Sorry?' says James.

'Twenty-fifth September. You fancy it?'

'You're not serious?' says James.

'Actually,' says Charlie, 'I run, Ollie swims and you ride a bike . . .'

'Nice,' says Ollie. 'We *are* a triathlon.'

'So . . .'

'The Walmer Triathlon. It's like a fun thing. The swim's only a mile. The run's 5k and the bike ride is only 20k.'

'20k!'

'What?'

'I normally use my bike for going to the shops in Sandwich. Or to ride with Ash to school.'

'You've ridden to Canterbury,' Bryony reminds him.

'Once. And I had to get the bus back.'

'I think it would be fun to have something to train for,' says Bryony.

'I'm in,' says Charlie. 'Although I'd prefer it if the run was 10k.'

'I'm in,' says Ollie.

'James is in,' says Bryony.

'Game on,' says Ollie.

Skye's dance routines have fucked up her knees big time so she sometimes spends over an hour on one of the pink foam rollers in Studio B, the only place in Namaste House with frosted and very high windows, lying on her front, going up and down and up and down her thighs, often with tears of pain rolling down her face. When the fronts of her quads are done she does her iliotibial bands, down the outer edges of her thighs. She moans and groans her way through this while Fleur sits with her back against the mirrored wall, writing. She's not writing into the actual book, not yet. Because that might not be what it's all about at all. That might be totally fucking wrong. Anyway, she can ask Ina quite soon. The plane tickets are booked. She and Skye are going on a trip! To the Outer Hebrides! Apart from anything else, poor Skye needs to get away and hide somewhere more remote than Studio B. The tabloids won't leave. And with Piyali suddenly stalking the cottage because Kam has 'gone away', and Ketki growling her way around the main house it seems to make sense for both of them to hide out in the studio; but obviously it can't go on forever. One of the celebrities is doing the Silent Retreat while the other two have opted for the Get up and Glow package. People are having trouble remembering which is which. Ish keeps talking to the silent one – the cricketer – about betting scandals and leg-spin bowling. This is the sort of stuff Oleander used to control.

But for now Fleur is only interested in what Oleander used to say.

'How did you first hear about Oleander?' Fleur asks Skye.

Of course Skye was Oleander's client originally. Then, when she needed someone to meet her in London, Fleur would go. And then there was the swapping of dresses and lipsticks and the hair brushing and recently Fleur telling Skye things too, which would be wrong if she had ever had any training but of course she has never had any training and . . .

'One of my aunts. *Mail on Sunday*.'

'Oh, that thing.'

'Like the Madonna thing.'

'Madonna never even came here.'

'Yeah. Nice publicity, though.'

'OK, anyway, so what was the most helpful thing Oleander ever said to you?'

A long pause. Up and down on the left ITB band. A low groan.

'She said that giving love was the only way to receive love. No.' Skye shakes her head, and her hair tumbles over and then – ouch – under the foam roller. Fleur wonders if this could lead to a really gruesome accident, but now Skye retrieves her hair, scrunches it into a brown band, sits up and rearranges the foam roller so she can lie on it lengthways. She breathes in and then starts rolling her spine up into a lowish bridge. 'Actually, that's wrong, because she always said that you would receive love anyway, no matter what you did, even if you'd, like, murdered someone or run them over or whatever. But this was more like a short cut or something.'

'Yeah. But you can't see it like that.'

'No. Exactly. It has to be genuine.'

'You have to really love the person in that instant.'

'Which is when you realise how hard it is to love someone else, really.'

'And how fucking hard it is to love yourself.'

'Which is the same thing.'

~

They go to Deal, even though Granny doesn't like it because it is full of homosexuals. There's a westerly blowing gently, so it's even quite hot walking down the pier. It's Bank Holiday Monday, which means that everyone has come out to complain about the weather, but the weather is actually rather nice so no one has anything to talk about. Except . . .

'The turnstones!' says James. 'They're still here.'

All this toing and froing that birds do. It must be quite tiring. Why not just find somewhere the right temperature all year round – like Benidorm or Auckland – and stay there? But everyone loves the turnstones, even though they are known for eating anything, including used condoms. They look like a proper water bird, with black, brown and white feathers that work with shingle and stormy weather. They also have nice orange beaks with which they supposedly turn stones, but around here are more likely to use to turn chip packets and drink from dirty puddles. They scurry along the pier in quite a cute way, though, trying to steal the fishermen's bait, or their catch. They are supposed to only be in Deal for the winter, but it's no surprise that they have not left somewhere that has such rich pickings and – usually – can't be that much less freezing than wherever they'd normally go.

'Didn't they say on *Springwatch* that some of them have started . . .'

'Look,' says Ash. 'That one's only got one leg.'

'Started what, Granny?' Bryony needs a drink.

'Staying for the summer. Gosh, he has only got one leg, poor thing.'

'We'll call him Hopalong,' says James.

'It's got a leg, stupid,' Holly says to Ash. 'It just doesn't have a foot.'

They walk around the end of the pier, where Bryony gets a text message welcoming her to Belgium. This happens all around the coast here. More often it's France, which at least you can see from the end of the pier. This is usually funny enough to tell people, but she's too hungover, and Granny won't understand anyway. Then back. And there's Hopalong again.

'He's following us,' says Ash. 'Maybe he likes us.'

And then he's down by the fishermen again. And then on the bench. Hopalong is everywhere, it seems, hopping along with a stump where his foot should be. He certainly has no difficulty in getting around, poor thing.

Then Bryony realises. There are four or five turnstones on the pier and each one is missing a foot. Now there are six, now seven . . . Dark piano chords thump painfully in Bryony's mind. They are all footless. Which means . . . ? They have some disease that will spread and wipe them all out? Or maybe they are being snagged on fishing lines. Maybe there is some psychopath who . . . In any case, what if they are not migrating because they can't, because like so many other organisms in this sad, crumbling universe they have ended up broken and stuck where they are? But when she looks up she sees that no one else has noticed, and Granny is now offering to buy the kids ice creams and Holly is asking if she can have a new can of tennis balls instead.

Posters have gone up around the public areas in Namaste House: the entrance lobby, the spa and the gift shop. GROUP READING: THE BHAGAVAD GITA. BEGINNING WEDNESDAY 8 P.M. Who is doing this? Pi is doing this. Pi is still here. Kam, having 'gone away', has not come back. Kam's sister, it turns out, got on the same train that Pi and James were on, because she lives in Folkestone, but they didn't see her. Bluebell has been muttering over her condensed milk about a possible divorce. Ketki is still not talking to Fleur. Anyway, it's not that it isn't lovely having someone else around the place helping with the activities. It's a bit like the old days. Pi has started an advanced men's yoga group, which Fleur thought was ambitious until men actually began turning up for it: a tennis coach from Deal, a hipster with a bright orange beard from Canterbury, two triathletes from Sandwich, a gym instructor and two very flexible sixty-somethings who had been going to Fleur's yoga for years but came and told her that in fact they prefer Pi's approach because it is more 'intellectual'.

Pi has offered to cover all Fleur's sessions – except the 'mindfulness crap' – while she and Skye are away. Which is so incredibly generous, of course, but then Fleur has a dream that when she comes back he has changed the locks and painted the house yellow and had her cottage shipped to Kansas. Which is obviously WTF in the way all dreams are, but also: what if he does take over? He's already acting all man-of-the-house with Bluebell and Ketki. What if Fleur is sidelined? She might own Namaste House on paper, but in reality everyone knows that no one owns anything and everything just runs on invisible lines of power and personality. Usually when she touches the frankincense tree each evening she offers it some of her energy and she feels the tree take it, in the way an elderly person accepts a seat on the tube. But the last couple of nights it has offered some back. What does that mean?

During meditation Fleur's thoughts, which are clouds floating past that she should observe without attachment, or bubbles floating around her head that she must pop, have become unkind. For example all the thoughts about how it is probably easier to love a millionaire, which is what Fleur now is. Or that now she has Namaste House she finds that she does not want to share it. What a selfish bitch! That she particularly does not want to share it with the man she supposedly loves is problematic.

She wants to share it with the man she really loves and . . .

Pop-pop-pop, go her thoughts.

The Outer Hebrides

June, 1999

Dearest Charlie,

I know you will think I am a coward for not telling you this in person, and especially for not telling you this in person months ago, but anyway, I am telling you now. Here goes. I am lying in my hospital bed holding my beautiful daughter and I just have to tell you that she is yours too. I never meant this to happen, but I am holding OUR beautiful daughter. How do I know? You'll see for yourself when you meet her. I have known for a while now, mainly because of the timing. I'd like to say we have been unlucky – after all, there was just that one time – but honestly, Charlie, she is so beautiful that you will not think it bad luck at all, but good luck, and you will forgive yourself for what we did, just as I have forgiven myself. James knows, and has agreed that he will bring her up as his own daughter. He says he already loves her as much as if she was his own child. We will let her believe that he is her father, at least at first. I do hope you will accept that this is the only thing that can happen. He suggested not telling you (which may give you some idea of his state of mind), but I couldn't not let you know. What will you do about Charlotte? Obviously you are not long married and we certainly don't want to rock the boat at this end. Perhaps you'll be happy to become a very special Uncle Charlie? Or

perhaps you'll never speak to me again. Anyway, I also wanted to let you know that I have named her Holly. Do you know the Emily Brontë poem 'Love and Friendship'? *Love is like the wild rose-briar, / Friendship like the holly-tree—/ The holly is dark when the rose-briar blooms / But which will bloom most constantly?* That's the beginning. There is more. Anyway, I wanted her to be a celebration of our – hopefully – enduring friendship. Perhaps a child made more from friendship, albeit a rather passionate moment in that friendship, than from love will have some particularly special qualities. I'd like to think so. As you can imagine, James is taking some time to come to terms with what we did. But once the storm passes I would like you to come and meet your daughter as soon as possible.
In loving friendship,
Bryony

Who would put Fleur Meadows and Skye Turner in the emergency exit row? Seriously? Just look at them. Look at their eyes. Look at their lipstick. Actually, both of them could put lipstick on straight in the CERN particle accelerator if they had to: Skye from sheer practice and Fleur because it matters in ways that she can't quite . . . But here's the point: *no one* wears lipstick on a plane from Glasgow to Stornoway. What would you be needing lipstick for, in Stornoway? And would a properly rational person have even let them, these lipsticked, drunk, ponytailed *disasters*, on the plane at all after seeing the way they reacted to it at Glasgow airport, doubled over in laughter, calling it, among other things, a toy plane, a miniature plane, a 'shrunken shrinky-dink plane you could put on a keyring'.

But here they are. Fleur by the window or – to be more accurate

– door. Skye is next to her, with a preposterously sharp high-heeled shoe sticking out into the aisle. They are both wearing huge sunglasses. They look a little bit as if they have each been allowed to take one thing too many from the dressing-up box. Have they read the instructions as they were asked? Well, sort of. Well, Fleur has tried. There's a picture of a man being attacked by a red arrow that seems to want him to jump from the plane. It's a bit disturbing, actually. But to be honest the more compelling thing to look at, right now, is the way that only one black, plastic propeller seems to be moving, and the other one is obviously broken and the whole thing is increasingly like a toy: but more like something you'd put in the bath than something that could actually fly.

The plane is so small that it has only one steward, or cabin crew, or whatever, and then one guy with a moustache in charge of flying it. He's called Dave and she's called Maggie. Fleur counts the seats in the plane: thirty-six. How would something like this take off, though, really? And with only one propeller? Could she open the emergency exit by mistake while they are flying along? Could she fall into a dream-like state and do it by accident and KILL EVERYBODY? The plane taxis to the runway. At Heathrow they saw a hawk hunting on a strip of grass right there with planes waiting to take off. Here there are mountains, well, hills, and lots of other places for hawks to hang out. And – excellent – the second propeller has come on. And now the engine, which is surprisingly loud, and . . .

'Little thing goes pretty fast,' Skye says.

But Fleur can't reply because taking off makes her feel amazing but a bit sick, especially after all that Chapel Down she managed to drink on the BA plane. She doesn't usually drink very much, and neither does Skye, but apparently it really helps with air travel, which Skye does a lot and Fleur hasn't really done since she was fifteen and went to Mumbai, then still called Bombay, to get Piyali. It's a little bit like coming up on opium, although really . . .

Dave seems to be avoiding the clouds as he works the little plane up into the sky, penetrating it slowly, and really quite gently. It's like, it's like . . .

'It's actually a bit like a bicycle with wings.'

Maggie comes with the trolley.

'Cup of tea?' she offers. 'Biscuit?'

'Have you got any wine?'

'Just tea, love, sorry.'

'Are they chocolate biscuits?'

'Yes, love.'

'OK. What is the maximum amount of biscuits we can have?'

Maggie drops her voice. 'I can let you have two each,' she says. 'But don't tell.'

'Make it three?'

Maggie sighs and gives them five biscuits to share. They turn out to be those things that the posher housing-estate mums used to put in kids' lunchboxes back in the early eighties. They are basically several layers of polystyrene and sugar wrapped in the kind of chocolate that the EU used to want to condemn and call 'vegolate' on the basis that its cocoa density was so tiny. They have shiny red and silver packaging that is half open on all of the biscuits.

The cloud clears a little as they fly over Ullapool and then a bit of Atlantic, with the Stornoway ferry chugging along beneath them. When they begin their descent it turns out that they are on the wrong side of the plane so they abandon the emergency exit row and take new seats by the opposite windows while other passengers tut and complain about who will open the doors in an emergency. (In an emergency, in an aircraft, what use are doors really?) But it's so beautiful, coming in to land on this island that really looks like an island, with edges like on a small jigsaw puzzle piece.

Landing at the airport is like landing on someone's driveway. All right, a celebrity's driveway, but still. The airport itself fits neatly into one large room. It's actually great if you're wearing shoes like Skye's or even like Fleur's. You can stumble down the steps off the plane and then by the time you've righted yourself you've fallen through the door to baggage reclaim, which is a bit of a joke really, as you can see your bags coming off the plane and being wheeled around to a hatch and then loaded on to the carousel when they could just basically hand them to you. There is no security and no customs. Fleur buys a postcard of the plane. Skye buys twenty Marlboro and a box of chocolates with a picture of a different, even smaller plane landing on the beach at Barra. They get in a cab and give the female cab driver the name of their hotel. On the map it had looked as if this hotel might be maybe ten minutes from the airport, but in fact the cabbie says it's going to take forty-five minutes to get there and will cost fifty pounds. On the way there they see houses that are bare and basic and grey. They see rocks. They see sheep. They see an egret a bit like the one Skye Turner saw from that train, just before everything that happened happened.

'Holiday?' asks the cabbie.

'Research,' says Fleur.

'Oh, I thought you looked like . . . I'll tell you what I thought. I thought to myself, Maybe TV. We do get TV people here sometimes, but they never stop for long and they never come back. Are you TV?'

'No.'

'Film?' She says it 'fillum'.

'We're botanists.'

'Oh aye.' There's quite a long pause. 'Really? You'll know all about the orchids then.'

'Yep.'

'You know, the Hebridean spotted orchid?'

'Yes, of course.'

'Who else comes here?' Skye asks.

'Walkers. Artists sometimes. We had a novelist last year. Mind you, we've already got a novelist living here, so . . .'

On one side of the road there's a huge rock. On the other side a sheep eats a thistle. There is barely anything on this island apart from sheep, rocks, ugly houses and thistles. What's missing? Something's missing. There's . . .

'And you'll know about the Sabbath,' says the cab driver.

'No.'

'Everything closes. No buses, no taxis, no nothing. No restaurants, although you'll be all right because your hotel'll serve food all day, but for residents only of course.'

'So there are restaurants?' Skye imagines cute little fish places on a cosmopolitan, charming, bustling waterfront that looks not unlike Nyhavn in Copenhagen, where she went once for some reason she's forgotten. She imagines eating a dozen oysters and drinking champagne while watching the sun set over the Atlantic. Just around the next corner there could be anything, there could be . . .

'Oh aye. Back in Stornoway. In the hotels. Some of the pubs serve food.'

'And shops?'

'What will you be wanting to buy?'

Shoes, lipstick, *Vogue* magazine, spiritual and/or uplifting books, deodorant, mascara, socks, probably, and also some hiking boots, more cigarettes, nail varnish, a new blusher brush, a tea set, some interesting wallpaper, art, ironic souvenirs, ethnic rugs/throws, Diet Coke, Vaseline, a meditation cushion, an eye-pillow, an iPhone charger, an iPad charger, some toothpaste. The last hotel Skye stayed in had vending machines for everything, from champagne to diamond tiaras. It was a thing. Is this a thing? What kind of thing is this? There has not been one single establishment that would sell you anything in the twenty miles they have already covered. Not even a petrol station for milk and fags. How do people even survive here?

'Er . . .'

'You won't really be finding a shop that close to where you are.'

'Right.'

'Do either of you drive at all?'

Skye shrugs. Fleur shakes her head.

'You do know you're going to be a bit remote, then?'

'We'll be fine. Thanks. We'll call a cab if we want to go anywhere.'

'Och aye, well, but not tomorrow, remember?'

'Right.'

The hotel, which costs over £100 a night, looks oddly like the working-men's club that Karl and Tash Turner used to go to of a Saturday night after *Gladiators*. It had almost exactly the same swirling turquoise and orange carpet. Its bar had the same smell that this bar has. It, too, had no open fire or anything quaint or touristy about it at all. It, also, had Radio 1 playing behind the bar, and chicken Kiev on the menu. It did not, however, have 200 different single malt whiskies.

'Which one do you recommend?' Skye asks the barman.

'To be honest, love, they're all about the same.'

Fleur orders a double Jura Superstition. Skye has the same. They go through to the hotel lounge, which is a posh version of the bar area done out in a mint green colour with a sofa facing a fireplace with candles in it. Why is there no open fire? The room smells cold: of grease, fly spray and furniture polish. There is a vacuum humming faintly upstairs somewhere. On the wall are pictures of stags and thistles.

'Why have I heard of Jura?' Skye asks.

'It's where we're going after this. Meet the others at the lodge.'

'Oh yeah. *Duh*. Didn't someone burn a million quid on the Isle of Jura? Some pop group from the nineties?'

'Did they?'

'Yeah. The K Foundation. Or the KLF. Whatever.'

'I'd like to burn a million quid.'

'I sort of have.'

'Yeah, well, me too I suppose. Sort of.'

They clink glasses. Skye sighs.

'Everyone hates me.'

'It'll be all right. Look what happened to Rihanna.'

'She was a victim of something. I'm more like . . .' Skye lets a space open up in the air in which both of them replay their own version of what happened on that train. Fleur wasn't there but has heard all about it, of course. Skye has edited her version slightly. For example she has written out the phrase 'fucking fuckbag gyppos' and the bit where she threw the cup of boiling water at the man in the corner who had not done anything more innocuous than just play Phil Collins on his new (now ruined) phone. All the bits she has written out were, obvs, in the video on YouTube that has so far been viewed over two million times.

'What about Kate Moss? It all looked like it was over for her back in whenever. You know? With all the coke and stuff. And now . . .'

'I'm not Kate Moss.'

'Yeah. Well.'

'Kate Moss did not keep dead birds in her bath.'

'No.'

They sip whisky. Skye thinks about the tabloids getting into her parents' place. Quite why they had to choose the day that Skye's alcoholic aunt decided to collect all the dead birds from around the house – which is weird enough, admittedly, but it's just the age the cats are and how frisky they have been since coming to Devon, and how little clearing up Skye's parents ever do – and . . .

'This is like an old people's home.'

'I know.'

'Are there really no shops, do you think?'

'There'll be something. We'll look in the morning.'

'What about the Sabbath thingy?'

'There'll be a Londis or something.'

'Have you got a map on your phone?'

'No. You?'

'Yeah, but the battery's flat.'

'Charger?'

Skye shakes her head.

'What about your iPad?'

'I've got like thirty per cent battery left. I thought I'd better ration it.'

'Charger?' Silly question.

'Why . . . ?'

'What?'

'Why don't you just take your chargers when you go away?'

Skye shrugs. 'It's like my ritual when I arrive somewhere, like buying new ones. I don't know. It gives me something to do. Probably stops me feeling lost and lonely or whatever, you know, if I have a mission. Or maybe deep down I don't want to charge them up, because . . . Anyway, you've got your phone presumably.'

'Yeah, but my phone's just a phone.'

'We so need a proper map.'

'We'll get it off your iPad while you've still got battery, and copy it out or something. Do you want another drink?'

~

Clem's drunk, which is the first unusual thing. The second unusual thing is that she has rung Ollie from her hotel in Edinburgh rather than just texted him goodnight. The third thing is that she has rung Ollie to TALK ABOUT HER FEELINGS. To whom does she normally talk about her feelings? Fleur? Bryony? But they've both been wrapped up with other things since the funeral – and, indeed, aren't they both on different Scottish islands at the moment anyway? – and so now Ollie is in with a chance to be supportive and impressive and, well, a bit of a metrosexual (does that mean thoughtful, or actually just gay?) hunk. But this is something of a sticky problem.

'So you're upset because no one wants to rape you?'

'No! Of course not. Don't twist what I was saying . . .'

'I wasn't . . . I was just . . .' Ollie has no idea how TWISTING, which is always a part of their arguments, but never a part of any kind of supportive chat (do therapists *twist* things? Do counsellors and priests *twist* things? Well, actually, well, never mind . . .), has suddenly come into this. It's, frankly, a bit much. But she's off again.

'I was just saying that I feel so fucking old. And so ugly. And even though I feel sort of semi-glamorous at work – except compared with Zoe of course – that's only because, on reflection, everyone at work goes around in soup-stained jumpers with no make-up on. Here, here . . . *Here*, basically I'm just a washed-up academic with orthotics, for God's sake, not that anyone can see them, but even so, and a three-month old haircut, and a paunch, and wine-stained teeth . . .'

Clem does have a small paunch, it's true, despite all the swimming and everything. Heaven knows which ironic god decided that the best way to lay down fat on the wife of an infertile man would be to make her look three months' pregnant all the time. There's no real fat anywhere else on Clem, just on her stomach. Apparently someone once even asked when her baby was due, which Clem told Ollie: a) while LAUGHING; and b) without any shame or embarrassment; and c) without really thinking first.

'I love your . . .'

'Anyway, what I was saying was, I hope, a bit more profound than that I am upset because no one wants to rape me. I was just thinking about all the times I've got cross with you for not locking the back door before going out and leaving me on my own, or leaving the kitchen windows open or something, basically because I thought that there were always, at all times, *bushes* full of desperate men in the garden just waiting to clamber in any open window, no matter how small, with, I don't know, huge red shiny bell-ends sticking out of their vile stonewashed jeans – what a horrible image, sorry, I am a bit pissed – and willing to do anything to fuck me, like go to prison or be stabbed to death with a bread knife or *anything*. And yet here, no one will even look at me. I could lie on the floor with my legs open and they'd just step over me. So I realise that, once again, my mother was wrong. I mean, maybe men would have risked life and limb to rape *her*, and of course someone actually did rape Fleur's mother – although maybe I wasn't meant to tell you that, so just forget I said it – but me? No way. And yet I was brought up to believe I'd be raped all the time if I didn't actually make the effort to avoid it.'

'Stonewashed jeans? *That's* the thing you'd notice? You are so posh.'

'I mean, obviously I still blame the woman-hating film industry, which is basically the same film industry that made me grow up believing that a beautiful woman must not enter a car park or a kitchen or go on the roof of anything or accept a lift from anyone or go outside on her own ever because she will get murdered, which really means raped, although they're too worried about certification to show any of that . . . That's the same industry that is here now and fucking ignoring me. Oh well, at least they have good wine. Although of course anyone who is anyone is doing drugs, and at another party altogether. It's just like the Oscars all over again.'

Ollie knows that the one response he can think of to all this will not be welcome. He knows he should not say it. But the invisible, unnamed troublemaker that exists right at his very heart is poking him and whispering, 'Go on . . .'

'Well, I'd want to rape you,' he says. 'If I were there I'd Rohypnol your drink and everything.'

'You are such a dick. I don't even know why I rang you.'

But he has sort of got away with it because at this moment she almost needs him. And she did ring him. Imagine that. It wasn't him ringing or texting first but CLEM doing it.

'Anyway, I think what I'm saying is partly that I hate my mother and partly that I hate celebrities and . . . Oh.' She laughs. 'I really am drunk. Sorry. It's just . . . why does no one want to speak to me?'

'You do sometimes look a bit forbidding . . .'

'Not here I don't. Here I look like the cleaner, or someone's mum.'

And of course the last thing you'd want to look like is someone's *mother*. Because of course motherhood is forbidden, and banned, and disgusting, and taboo, even though adoption would in theory be possible. But Ollie doesn't say this. He files these thoughts away somewhere with the latest email from David, and the latest episode when he used the other flight of stairs so that he wouldn't bump into Frank and then it turned out that Frank went the other way and . . .

'I don't think you look remotely like Alison,' he says instead.

'Well, you wouldn't know. When did you last see her?'

Ollie is so scared of Alison that he makes sure he is at work or swimming or at the gym every time she is due to come round, and if he gets home and sees her car parked on the road outside he usually goes and parks in the cricket ground for half an hour and either has a little sleep or blasts some emails on his iPhone. But Clem isn't supposed to know that. Clem is supposed simply to think he is a bit stupid in that masculine way and basically not at all interested in anything to do with the cleaner.

'Anyway, I'm actually quite pleased that Zoe gets here tomorrow. At least I'll be able to talk to her.'

The earth is black. The dark green grass frizzes on top of it like a seventies afro.

'Is this peat?' asks Skye.

Fleur shrugs. 'I guess so.'

'I don't think I've ever been anywhere this wild before.'

'It is kind of remote, I agree.'

They have set off from the back of the hotel and are walking towards the sea. They have a map, sort of, drawn in biro by the hotel owner. It has one squiggly line to represent the coast, and then an arrow showing which way they should go. There is a faint blob representing the village they are looking for. It is not to scale.

'But you're used to the countryside, right? You live in it.'

'Sort of. We have shops. Sandwich is a town – you know that, you've been there loads of times. Anyway, what about your parents' place? That's out in the wilds of Devon somewhere, isn't it?'

'We have a pub. It sells everything. There don't seem to be any pubs here . . .'

'And I live five seconds from a bus stop . . .'

'There are bus stops here, I suppose.'

'No buses on the Sabbath, though.'

'What the fuck is that all about?'

'Yeah. I don't know.'

'I quite like walking on this stuff, though.'

'I know. It's like . . .'

'It's like walking on a giant's pubes.'

'The pubes of the universe.'

They walk up a small hill and then down the other side. There are little piles of stones that have a special Scottish name that Fleur has forgotten, and jagged edges of cliffs and soft blurs of heather and gorse. Ahead of them is the deep blue sea that goes all the way to America. Above them, low cloud. There are pink flowers growing out of the peat. Fleur bends down.

'This must be the Hebridean spotted orchid,' she says. 'Look at the leaves too. Charlie would love to see this.'

The leaves are green with black splodges that seem to have been flicked on by a creator in something of a hurry. The orchids are everywhere. And all among them are the ubiquitous white dabs of cotton grass, making the landscape look as if it had recently gone through the wash with a tissue in one of its pockets.

'Where do we go now?' Skye asks Fleur.

'I thought we should turn right up the coast.'

'Cool.'

'Right.'

'I have a horrible feeling this is going to take hours.'

'I know.'

'How are your feet?'

Skye is wearing the hotel owner's daughter's wellies. Fleur is in MBTs.

'Fine. Yours?'

'Yeah. For now.'

They smell the village before they find it. Peat fires sending what smells like thousands of shots of Laphroaig into the air. Skye's feet are bleeding. Fleur's legs and arse are almost completely numb. The blackhouses are made of old stone and thatch and look as if they are sinking into the ground. Smoke curls from chimneys. A woman in tie-dyed dungarees comes out of one of the houses and lights a cigarette; she is followed by a bald man with a yin and yang symbol tattooed on his head. Fleur looks at the number on the door. It's a five. It's the right place.

'I thought Ina lived alone,' Fleur says.

'Maybe these are tourists,' says Skye.

'Why are they in her house?'

'Hello!' says Ina, when she sees them. 'You're just in time for the retreat.'

'Retreat?'

'Well, you're three hours late. But that's OK. We'll do a recap.'

'But . . .'

Ina drops her voice. 'It would be good if you would make up the numbers, just for the rest of today at least. We can talk tomorrow. Although tomorrow we're at Sylvia's place. Tomorrow evening.'

'My feet,' says Skye. 'I need to sit down.'

'Good,' says Ina. 'I'll put more water in the kettle.'

They come by plane.

James had wanted to come on the boat. He said it would be more authentic. But the plane looked much simpler – Ramsgate to Saint Pancras, Circle line to Paddington, Heathrow Express to Terminal 5, BA to Glasgow, Flybe to Islay (pronounced Eye-la), ferry to Jura. And all to see this ancestral pile that everyone has inherited and that no one really remembers. Charlie is coming later. Fleur might drop by as well. Of course James moaned about aircraft fuel, although really, how much fuel does it take to fly a thirty-six-seater over a couple of islands and mountains, compared with how much it would cost to drive a car all the way from Kent to remotest Scotland? Not to mention the sheer mental torture of going more than five miles in a car with Holly and Ash. And James, sweet, innocent James, even bothered to moan about Glasgow airport, with its tiny amount of shops and bars and basically – albeit on a small scale – everything Bryony likes about airports. All those clean, happy, disposable things shelved outside of real life, in a place where, let's face it, everyone is waiting to die and therefore anything goes. But no one is allowed to eat any of the lovely, shiny crap because James has brought packed lunches. To go on a fucking plane! OK, Bryony did feel sorry for him when they confiscated the cartons of organic apple juice he'd so lovingly packed for them all, but not so much when he then said loudly, 'Do we really look like the kind of people who are going to bomb the plane with cartons of organic apple juice?' as if he was the first person ever to have thought of that joke. Bryony pointed out that however much everyone secretly thought that the only people who should ever be searched in airports were brown men with peculiar beards, it would be kind of wrong if that actually happened, and equality in the world depended on James being treated exactly the same way as everyone else, and then HE accused HER of being racist!

But whatever.

Bryony manages to stash three small bottles of red wine – for sale in the Starbucks just beyond security – in her handbag AND sit next to sleepy Ash rather than prying Holly AND end up behind, rather than in front of, James. *Result*, as the kids say. Epic. Elephant poo in China.

When they land on Islay it's like landing on a picture from a book of perfect islands. There are vast beaches of yellow sand, and mountains, and grass. You can't get lost on Islay: there are only two main roads. And it must be even easier to find your way on Jura, where apparently there is only one. The sun is shining. Things twinkle. James drives the hire car past old walls and cottages and trees. Over the brow of a hill and there in the distance are the Paps of Jura. A pap is, apparently, a breast. These ones are at least DDDs. Bryony realises that if she didn't have her dissertation to do, life would be perfect. And also, actually, if James wasn't such a total arsehole. No, arsehole is wrong – too damp and earthy and pungently sweet for James. Ollie is an arsehole, and Charlie, quite obviously, is a cock. James, at his worst, is more of an elbow. Or maybe an earhole or a nosehole. Or a plughole. WTF??? Bryony's thoughts are tumbling out as if it's closing time and they've all got to go home but they can't quite remember where they live . . . Bryony shouldn't really drink any more until this evening because she drank enough on the journey to have a real headache now, but the ferry doesn't go until . . .

'What time is the ferry?'

James shrugs. 'You're in charge of this journey,' he says.

Bryony sighs. 'Right. Well. Um . . .'

The ferry timetable is on a website on her iPad, but she didn't look at it closely because she assumed it would be one of those back-and-forth kinds of ferries and they'd just get the next one when they arrived, but now there's no 3G or any kind of mobile signal at all so she gets out of the car to look at the timetable pinned to the wall of the ferry office. But what it says can't be right, so she asks a woman sitting in the sun leaning up against the ferry office with a book.

'Are you waiting for the ferry?'

'Yes.'

'When does it go?'

'Six thirty.'

'But that's over an hour from now.'

The woman shrugs. 'Sunday service.'

'Oh, *Mummy*,' Holly says when Bryony tells them. 'I knew Daddy should have organised this.'

And Daddy can drive a fucking ferry, can he?

Port Askaig, where they are stuck, has about five houses, a pub and a shop, which is closed. Through the window it is possible to see stickers saying *I ♥ Port Askaig*, and postcards and tea towels of local whisky distilleries. Opposite, there is a tiny beach, where clear, cold-looking water laps nonchalantly at some bright green seaweed.

'Ow!' says Holly, adding at least one unnecessary syllable as usual. 'Ow!!!'

She starts swatting at the air. These must be the famous Scottish midges that they have heard so much about. Whenever James makes them all watch *Springwatch*, which is set in Wales, but same diff, the presenters are always complaining about being attacked by midges. You can see why. Bryony thought they'd be smaller, but they are like normal-sized flies, and they bite quite hard.

'Ow,' says Ash. 'Get off! Mummy!'

Bryony has packed seven different types of insect repellent: Citridol, Jungle Formula in 'Natural', Jungle Formula in 'Outdoor and Camping', Boots own brand in 'Natural', DEET from the camping shop, tropical strength Ultrathon and, hilariously, Avon Skin So Soft, which was raved about on TripAdvisor as being a cult product used by all Scottish fishermen, workmen etc. as well as people in the Caribbean, even though it's supposed to only be a body moisturiser and is not designed to repel insects at all! Bryony grabs the DEET spray as it's the nearest and also the most horrible-looking.

'Oh. My. God. Mummy, that's disgusting. It's in my mouth!'

'My eyes!'

'MUMMY!'

James, of course, refuses insect repellent.

'Shall I get us some drinks?' he asks.

'I'll get them,' says Bryony.

She knows she should appear with only a mineral water, which is why she has a double Laphroaig at the bar. After all, it's made on Islay, and when else do you get the chance to drink a single malt on the island it comes from? But the rest of the family probably wouldn't understand that. So it's a Diet Coke for Holly, which she usually isn't allowed because it gives you cancer, or at least gives cancer to rats – but they are on holiday, which everyone knows makes you immune to cancer – and an apple juice for compliant little Ash, who does what he's told far too much for it to be good for him, and the same for James, except now he's sticking his head through the door . . .

'Actually, Beetle, get me a half of something local.'

'OK, I'll join you, I guess.' She smiles.

She considers getting half pints of whisky, as that's the only thing that's really local, but then it turns out that there's something called Islay Ale, so she gets that.

Back outside and those midgey things really are persistent. Bryony is sure she's being bitten, regardless of the DEET. But when she looks again there are no red marks, so who knows what is happening? James and the kids paddle in the water and then walk around the little port looking at ropes and creels and boats. When they come back they are full of stories of cormorants and seals. Seals!

'Why didn't you tell me?'

'You never like looking at nature, Mummy.'

After waiting for an hour and fifteen minutes they drive the car onto the ferry for the five-minute journey across the Sound of Islay. And then they are on Jura. It's all craggy shoreline, sparkling blue water, dark green bracken and acres of pink foxgloves. But where are all the people?

'We're here!' says Ash.

'Yep,' says Bryony. 'Only about another twenty-five miles to go.'

~

The bald guy speaks first, straining his face as if it were a muscle about to reach failure on a set of very hard reps.

'OK, so the basic thing – do you know the basic thing? No? Right. OK, so the basic thing is, well, did you ever have that thing when you were a kid and you wondered how there could be a God when everything in the world is so shit? I did. I remember watching the famine in Ethiopia on the news and going into RE the next day at school and asking the teacher, and the teacher saying that God moves in mysterious ways, and then all the other kids were making Ethiopian jokes anyway, and basically that was the first time I contemplated suicide because I could not bear to live in a world that cruel.'

'I was already trying to be a Buddhist then,' says the woman in dungarees, who is called Mog. 'My teacher – what was her name? – anyway, I remember very well her saying that the starving people must have accumulated so much bad karma in previous lives that they had to suffer through this one. I thought that can't be right. I mean, I got all the stuff about reincarnation and karma but I didn't see why it had to be so . . . Yes, I suppose the word is cruel, like Joel said.'

'Evolution did it to me,' says Tony. He looks like a garden gnome. His wife is called Mary but has not yet spoken.

'Why evolution?' asks Ina.

'Maybe not evolution, exactly, but nature. When we went on our gardening trip last year, that was when I first realised. The whole thing's a bloody competition. Every beautiful garden is the result of dreadful violence and mass slaughter. And it's not just stupid things killing other stupid things, like bindweed versus penstemon, or blackfly versus sweet pea. All the snails, slugs, aphids, weeds. Humans kill those. Who decided that these things do not deserve to live and other things do? I gave up being a vegetarian when I realised that animals eat each other, that it's "natural" to kill things and eat them. But it's horrible. I don't really want to eat a sandwich made out of something that could fly, and had feelings, and probably felt very frightened at the moment that . . .'

'I look at the birds on my bird feeder,' says Edith. 'And I think, You poor little terrified things. They take one mouthful of food and then look around for predators. Another mouthful, another look. Eat, look, eat, look. Imagine having to eat your dinner like that? But of course some people do, in Africa, probably, or the Middle East.'

Stan looks like a giant novelty candle. He is very, very fat, and from New York. He has been living on the Isle of Lewis for several years and met the others in Stornoway at the Amateur Dramatics society. Apparently they did *Midsummer Night's Dream* together, then all signed up to a herbalism course with someone called Rainbow, then the gardening trip, then Reiki (also with Rainbow) and now this. And with Ina offering these retreats right here on the island, well. And they've all read the book, *A Course in Miracles*. Well, most of them have. Well, they've bought it at least, off Amazon: £37 for the hardback edition or £6.99 for the Kindle version. It's a pretty strange book, to be honest, though, which is why you need a retreat to understand it.

'I hate the human body,' he says. 'I mean who came up with the idea of having to go to the bathroom every twenty goddamn minutes? And carrying your waste around with you in an internal sack like some kind of sausage full of shit until you can find a hole full of water in which to . . .'

'Are we losing the concept of God in this?' Ina asks.

'This is the bit I have trouble with,' says Mog, sighing.

Fleur and Skye exchange a look.

'Who can bring Fleur and Skye up to date?'

Joel frowns. 'OK, so it's pretty difficult for any of us to believe in a cruel God who zaps people and makes earthquakes and cripples and stuff, right? So we might wonder, if God didn't make the universe, then who did? For years I thought no one made it, that it was just an accident. Just a few bits of crap swirling in a void, colliding and retreating, expanding and contracting, all for no reason whatsoever. I was your basic atheist. But if atheism is right, then what is to stop people just raping and murdering whoever they want? All the good moral stuff in the world comes from religion . . .'

'A hell of a lot of bad stuff too,' says Stan.

'Yeah, of course. But . . .'

'I think what Joel is saying is that the world as many of us see it is a paradox,' Tony says. 'One where half of us – actually a lot more than half of us – throw ourselves on the mercy of this entity who is supposed to be all-knowing and all-loving but in fact is cruel and brutal and seems to want to humiliate and belittle us, and the other half pretend that life is spiritually meaningless, and that "this is it", and that although in theory we are just part of a pattern that includes, I don't know, hedgerows, say, and pecan nuts, and polar bears, in just the same random way that it includes us, in reality we teach our kids a bit of religion just in case, and base our legal, political and moral systems on notions of "good" and "right" and "equality". Meanwhile, the God that is supposed to represent the pinnacle of enlightenment in fact demands that we get down on our knees like the scum we are, and sing tuneless hymns at him every week, and send prayers not full of love but full of worship, as if he was just another mad dictator demanding more palaces and statues. Meanwhile, the atheists have started going to church to sing the praises of their cleverness, their nothingness . . .'

'I think what Tony is saying is this: What if God did not make the world? But what if it isn't random either?'

'Surely that just means there's another God,' says Skye. 'Like if the universe is not random then something must have created it. And if there's a creator then they have to be nice or horrible, but you'd kind of hope they were nice, although I totally get your point about earthquakes and stuff, and . . .'

'There's another solution,' says Ina. 'Joel? You look as if you're about to say something.'

'The central idea is this,' he says. 'God didn't make the world. God made us, and then *we* made the world, and that's why it is so fucking awful.'

'But there is actually only one of "us",' says Mog. 'The idea that we are separate is just an illusion. In fact, the whole world that we made is only an illusion. None of it is real. Just like the Hindus say, and the Buddhists, more or less.'

'The reality,' says Ina, 'if you can call it that, is that we are imagining everything. This world is a bad dream. Think of it like this. There we were, blissfully happy with God, the most contented, pampered child you could ever imagine, far beyond space and time, where no one ever dies and nothing bad ever happens and everything is perfect, and will be for all eternity. But then this child wondered what it would be like to be separate from God. What if he went off and did something on his own, away from the creator? This tiny, awful thought was really the beginning of the ego. The ego is the part of us that thinks, "Maybe it would be better if . . .", or, "Perhaps I could have more . . ." or, "Wouldn't it be exciting if things were different?" or, "I have to prove I am better," or even, "Where is the drama?" But this ego-driven desire to be separate from God, the most loving entity imaginable, led to a flash of guilt so tremendous that it became the Big Bang that made this universe, in which we are now trapped, fragmented and disparate, trying to find ways to come back together and remember who we are so we can switch the whole thing off. But in the meantime the ego has taken over. War! Shopping! Sex! Violence! And if anyone turns up saying that things could be different they get crucified for it. Or people simply find them boring. And then everything they ever said gets written down wrong and people end up using messages of peace as excuses for war and turning the son of God – who is all of us, who represents all of us together – into jewellery and swearwords and Christmas cards. And here I am now getting angry about it, feeding the ego, when . . .'

'You have to forgive,' says Joel. 'That's the only thing to do.'

Ina now laughs. 'Which is easier said than done, of course, as we'll find out.'

Halfway down Jura's one road, Craighouse nestles in a beautiful bay with more sparkling blue water and an old stone jetty that curves back towards land like an elbow that someone has rested there while they have a long chat with their neighbour. The Small Isles poke out of the sea like pieces of something's spine. They are, in all seriousness, and according to an information sign by the jetty, called Flat Island, Rabbit Island, Goat Island and Useless Island. Craighouse has a shop (closed on Sundays), a village hall, a hotel and the Jura whisky distillery. It's very charming, but they are not staying.

'But why not, Daddy?' asks Holly.

'Yeah,' says Bryony. 'We may as well have dinner here, surely?'

'I think we should press on. Fleur said there were supplies at the house.'

'Right, but Fleur's idea of supplies is likely to be . . .'

'And you must be curious to see it?'

'I suppose so.'

'Where is Fleur anyway?'

'On some mad spiritual quest to the Outer Hebrides.'

'Aren't we in the Outer Hebrides, Mummy?'

'Jura is the Inner Hebrides,' says James.

Ash doesn't say anything because he is asleep.

~

After everyone leaves, Fleur, Skye and Ina sit together in front of the peat fire. It's impossible for Skye and Fleur to walk back, and Ina doesn't have a car. Somehow she manages to survive on this vast shopless island with just a bicycle, and the bus. Skye is bathing her feet in hot salt water. Fleur has a blanket around her shoulders. It's cold in the evenings here, even in July. Ina gets them each a nip of single malt.

'So, I've really come about the book,' Fleur says. 'And, I suppose, the seed pods.'

'The book?'

'You gave it to me after the funeral.'

'Oh, Oleander's copy of *A Course in Miracles*. That makes sense, although it's odd that you managed to find out about the retreat . . .'

'The book was blank.'

'What?'

'The book wasn't *A Course in Miracles*. It was blank.'

'Can I see it?'

'It's back at the hotel. I should have brought it with me, but I didn't realise . . .'

'We'll find someone to drive us over and get it once the retreat is over tomorrow. We'll have a proper look at it. I mean, you're absolutely sure?'

'Yes.'

Did Bryony come here with her parents once, or did she just imagine it? No one is exactly clear how Jura House came to be in the family, except that Fleur seemed to think it had something to do with the Prophet. It wouldn't have looked then as it does now. It's been an extremely expensive holiday let for years. But even now it looks like something other than it is: it is a hyperreal vision of what someone in London thinks that someone coming on holiday here thinks that a hunting lodge should look like. And it's all been put together with a slightly raised eyebrow, with, if Bryony's honest, a bit of a metropolitan sneer that may even be very slightly camp. But you can analyse these things too much. Who really cares that the herbarium specimens hanging in the front parlour are written in French, and are from Southern France, rather than Scotland? And surely no one really minds that the boy riding the goat in the painting in the white bedroom is from a different century, country and socio-economic class, let alone family, from the ankle-socked girls in the large framed photographs in the dining room? It is all tremendous fun, as Granny might say. And now, she – well, she and James, or maybe let's go back to she – owns a third of it.

'How do you feel with all this God stuff going on?'

'Kind of weird. How about you?'

'Yeah.'

‘Oleander never did the God thing. The ego thing, yes. But not the God thing. But so much of what they are saying here is like the stuff she used to say, so how can she not have done the God thing?’

‘Maybe she just didn’t call it that in her head.’

‘Maybe . . .’

‘I mean, they talked a lot about “the universe”, right? What’s the difference between the universe and God?’

‘Yeah. Nothing.’

‘I keep thinking about that bird thing she used to say.’

‘What bird thing? Oh, the thing from the *Rig Veda*?’

‘Two beautiful birds living on the same tree . . .’

‘The *selfsame* tree, is how she put it . . .’

‘One eats the fruits of pleasure and pain . . .’

‘While the other just looks on.’

‘Yeah. I like that.’

‘Me too.’

‘I’d still rather be the one that eats all the crap though.’

‘Me too. Although . . .’

‘What?’

‘Maybe you’re supposed to be both? Like it’s the ego and the self together?’

‘Yeah, maybe. Oh well. Goodnight.’

‘Night.’

The plane banks slightly to the left, and Charlie can see that below him the landscape is beautifully wounded, as if it were a troubled teenager with a razorblade and a whole afternoon alone. In places the red is streaky or slightly clotted. But every so often there is a perfect square of it, and it is the most wonderful red you could ever imagine. It is actually far redder than blood. Can people make red like that out of binary code or melted-down plastics? No. This is not Pantone 186 or 711. The only thing that is red like this is summer poppies. There are fields and fields of them, annihilating the wheat, and overdosing any insects stupid enough to try to eat them.

Charlie remembers being maybe twelve or so, which meant Clem, Bryony and Fleur would have been about ten. They were driving somewhere together. Perhaps it was someone's birthday. Yes, perhaps Aunt Plum's. Bryony's mother. There was a two-car convoy: his father Augustus driving one and Uncle Quinn driving the other. He remembers a silly race down country lanes. Going over a small humpback bridge and at least one of the cars actually taking off and all the grown-ups laughing about it afterwards. Some village pub that he forgets, and perhaps a picnic in some woodland, although maybe that was another occasion altogether. But he particularly remembers coming around a bend on a high ridge and seeing below a huge, perfect square of red that at first looked like the roof of the biggest barn imaginable, but set at a funny angle. He remembers his mother and his sister begging Augustus to chase the red, to find out where and what it was, how it began and how it ended. At each bend they would either lose or find the red. And when they did glimpse it, magical and intense and always so maddeningly distant, his mother would sigh and say, 'It's poppies, darlings. Poppies everywhere.'

Doilies.

Lots and lots of doilies. Some of the doilies have little statues of the Buddha on them. Some of the Buddhas are covered in a kind of gold foil. Also covered in gold foil are the chocolates, which are arranged on various cake stands around the room. There are framed photographs of rainbows with angels superimposed on them. Mog and Joel have not come to Sylvia's for the second part of the workshop, and it is as if they have taken some light away with them. The remaining delegates, if that is what one would call them, all seem to be wearing polyester. There is a smell of sweat, and, vaguely, mostly from Stan's direction, faint wafts of urine. Fleur goes into the kitchen to see if Sylvia wants help with the tea. Also to get away from the smell. Ina follows her.

'It's your own fault,' says Ina, when Sylvia pops out to the car for more pink wafers.

'I'm sorry?' says Fleur.

'If you actually believed anything at all that I have said, or that Oleander used to say, you would not have made all this so remote and, well, so unattractive and horrible. You've made it much worse today than it was yesterday. Why?'

'I don't understand.'

'This is all an illusion, right? Your illusion. Sort it out.'

'How would I do that?'

'Forgive everyone. Forgive yourself.'

'Right. Look. If I forgive everyone for being old, fat, smelly, boring and ugly then I won't mind any more that they are old, fat, smelly, boring and ugly. So for all you know I might have already forgiven them.'

'So then why are you making us have this conversation?'

Fleur sighs. 'This is doing my head in.'

Sylvia comes back with the pink wafers.

~

'So I read that midges are point six millimetres, which is obviously really tiny, right, but the things that keep biting me are' – Bryony holds up her forefinger and thumb with approximately two centimetres between them – 'this long. What are they?'

'They're called clegs. They're like a horsefly.'

'Clegs?'

'Yep. Horrible things.'

'They don't seem to respond to insect repellent.'

'Have you got Avon Skin So Soft?'

'Yes.'

A young woman now joins in. 'Did you get the blue or the pink bottle?'

'Blue.'

'That should work,' says the man. 'Mind you, it works on me but not on my wife.'

'You see,' says the girl, 'you've got normal clegs and then you've got deer clegs . . .'

'They chased us off the beach,' Bryony says.

'Well, yes, they'll do that.'

'Right.'

'What you need is Smidge.'

'Smidge.'

'It's the only thing that works on local clegs.'

'Brilliant. Thanks. Well, I'll take one . . .' What? Tube, bottle? Bryony looks around.

'We're out of stock, unfortunately. We'll have more in on Thursday.'

It is Tuesday. Bryony can literally not stand outside for more than two seconds without feeling that horrible pinch of something biting her and then looking down to find yet another black insect sucking out her blood. Yesterday they went on a bus tour of the island and Bryony wore jeans, socks, shoes, a hat and a long-sleeved top. They got out to look at an old graveyard and one of the fuckers bit her THROUGH HER TOP.

'Where could I get some now?'

'You'd be needing to go to Islay if you wanted some now.'

Islay. What seemed like a tiny, insignificant island when they arrived has since been revealed to be a buzzing metropolis compared with Jura, with its one shop and one road. The only thing you can reliably get all the time here is whisky. It seems that by the beginning of each week the tiny shop has run out of all its fruit and most of its veg. It does have an amazing range of everything else you could possibly imagine, however, and James certainly didn't need to bring a lunch box full of garlic and herbs and cinnamon sticks, because they have all those things here. And the shop does sell wine, but not after 5 p.m., and nothing even remotely drinkable that isn't a five- to ten-pound Shiraz. Bryony has already been to the island's only hotel and bought their last remaining bottle of Châteauneuf-du-Pape and both bottles of their second wine, a rather nice Côtes du Rhône. But where has it all gone? She had been resigned to buying village-shop wine – yes, yes, she is a snob, but no one is here to see her or to care, so whatever – but actually now she has an excuse to go to Islay . . . There probably isn't an off-licence on Islay either, but there is a Co-op, Bryony remembers, which probably means cut-price Château Sénéjac or Château something else . . . And a nice hotel too, that will presumably do a good lunch for one. Or maybe Charlie will want to come too . . . ? And she did promise Holly she'd try and find a tennis court. There are none on Jura.

But in the end it is just Bryony who goes to Islay. And yes, the nice hotel can fit her in for lunch. The others have decided to go off to find the house where George Orwell wrote *1984*. And here's the thing. Even though they are her children, her husband, father of one child, and her cousin, father of the other, Bryony secretly wishes that one of them will, well, not *die*, exactly, but get injured so badly that they have to be airlifted from this wild and dangerous place where insects suck your blood and crabs nibble your toes and wild deer loom everywhere. Just to prove . . . Well . . . *Why* is it only Bryony that is allergic to this stuff? She orders another glass of wine and tries not to scratch her biggest and most uncomfortable cleg-bite, which of course is right on her arse. She sips her wine. Outside, boats bob in the cold blue harbour, and birds shiver from one side of the bay to the other, and Bryony realises she is the only person in the dining room, perhaps the only person on this island, perhaps the only person left in this whole entire ridiculous world.

~

'Right. Forgiveness. So everybody needs to choose someone they hate.'

'Like Hitler, or something?'

'No! Hitler will be far too hard. Just choose someone in your life who has annoyed you a lot, someone you really feel pissed off with in some way.'

'Maybe my mother?'

'Parents are usually too difficult as well.'

'I don't hate anyone,' says Mary.

'Yes, you do.'

'No, actually, after reading about the *Course* on Wikipedia I realise that I already do all the things it says. I'm not even really sure I need . . .'

'So if someone came in here and murdered your husband . . .'

'Oh, thanks,' says Tony.

'Well, how would you feel about that?'

'What do you mean?'

'I mean, would you be able to forgive them?'

'Of course not. What a silly question.'

'Out of interest, what do you think should happen to murderers?'

Mary frowns. 'Well, I must say I do believe in bringing back hanging.'

Gasps. 'You don't!'

'All right, all right . . . Back to forgiveness. The main thing about this sort of forgiveness is that it does not assume that I am better than you, and you need forgiveness and I am superior and therefore I can give it. That is definitely NOT what we are trying to do here. Forgiveness is more of a gift of love. If your beloved dog drops her tennis ball in the river, you might feel momentarily annoyed, but actually you then find you think it is quite sweet, and rather funny, and very *her*, and when you get home you'll tell your wife and you'll both ruffle the dog's fur and say something like "Oh, you silly thing", but in a loving way. You *forgive* her for losing the ball. It's real forgiveness. It's not grudging, or done for show or for some reward. Or what about when someone you love falls over on the way to the kitchen to fetch your birthday cake, or make you a cup of tea, or feed the cat? You don't laugh, do you? You want to help, to love them. You *forgive* them for looking stupid, and almost making you have to drive them to Casualty. When you see someone you know and love in an unexpected place, say in a secondhand bookshop, the delight you feel when you greet them and say how well they look . . . You *forgive* them for holding you up, being in your way, changing your plans for the day. Forgiveness means being able to apply these loving feelings to all human beings at all times, not just your loved ones at times when you are feeling affectionate towards them. What if you saw everyone the way you see that old friend, relative or lover in the bookshop? What if you treated the most annoying person in the supermarket with the love you show to your dog?'

'You'd end up acting like a loony!'

'You'd get arrested.'

'You certainly can't just go up to strangers and ruffle them . . .'

'No, well, exactly, but . . .'

Afternoon tea at the Caledonian Hotel, Edinburgh, costs fifty pounds, which is more than what Zoe is paying for her whole room in the Travelodge. Clem orders two, assuring Zoe that the festival will cover it. Apparently they are covering all her expenses, including her laundry.

'I actually put a clean pair of socks in by mistake,' she says. 'But who cares, right? I think I might get a massage too.'

'If I tried to get a massage at the Travelodge they'd probably send round a prostitute.'

'Stay here with me if you like. I've got a massive bed.'

'Really?' That strange feeling again.

'Of course. Well, I mean, I'd have to let you in, obviously, and I'm out until so late at these events, but presumably you'll be at more or less the same things, so actually . . .'

'No, don't worry. I really am fine where I am.'

'Well . . . I suppose there's Ollie's possible arrival to think about as well.'

'And all the Swedes are at the Travelodge anyway. They've got loads of hash.'

Zoe sees a look flick across Clem's face. She's too old. She can't keep up. Could it even be *cooler* to be staying in the Travelodge? Clem can impress Zoe with her CV, and her huge house, and the fact that she employs not only a cleaner but a gardener too, and actually pays her council tax and TV licence, and would never consider doing something as vulgar as playing a videogame or having a duvet day. Zoe is almost certain that Clem would not know what a duvet day even was. But Zoe's life is hard and real and authentic. So whose life is more impressive really? Is Clem's life better? Just because Zoe is impressed and wants to impress Clem back does not mean any of these things are objectively impressive. But it's hard to tell whether Clem actually cares or not.

'All the other judges are smoking in their rooms,' Clem says. 'It's become a thing.'

'What, hash?'

'No, just fags. Even though all the rooms are non-smoking. One of them takes her own handmade mother-of-pearl ashtray everywhere with her and just relies on the fact that she's so famous no one will bother her about it. Another one smokes out of the window. Another one smokes in the bathroom with the shower running full blast and hot, and then flushes the evidence. You're not still smoking?'

'Only hash. Only sometimes.'

'I wish Ollie would give up.'

'Mmm.' Does Clem realise that she has started comparing Zoe with Ollie like this, out loud, making it totally obvious that . . .

'I mean, breath mints never work, right? People just smell of mint and fags.'

'Oh, that sort of reminds me. My chillies are actually growing!'

'Oh, how cool.'

'It was amazing. The little flowers dropped off but behind them was this green swelling kind of baby chilli thing . . .'

'That's the ovary.'

'What do you mean?'

'When you pollinated the flowers, you sort of made them pregnant. The next thing is that the ovary swells and . . . Why are you making that face?'

'It's just that, well, you have to admit "swollen ovary" sounds pretty gross.'

Clem laughs. 'I never thought of it like that. All fruit is basically swollen ovaries.'

'What, like apples and pears and cherries and . . .'

Clem laughs again. 'You're just like my students.'

'OK. This is basically how the ego works. It convinces us that, rather than being fragments of one perfect being that needs to come back together, we are separate beings, in competition for everything from food, shelter and land to love, power and dignity. In order for one person to feel good – having, say, got a hundred per cent on an exam, or been asked to join the hockey club, or bought some amazing shares – someone else must fail the exam, be excluded from the hockey club, sell the shares. Now, I'm not saying that everyone should always succeed and everything should be wonderful all the time. In this world that's impossible anyway. Not everyone needs to join the hockey club. Failing a test can be a sign that you should be doing something else with your life. But this is actually about the feeling you get when you do something better than someone else. That little pumped-up feeling, that swelling, that inflation . . . Perhaps you don't realise it, but this is actually a feeling of violence. Because on some level, you don't just want to beat your rival, you want to smash them into the ground. And let's go further. You want failure to be punished. You want people to CRY because you beat them, or even because someone else did. You think you don't, but if you search your heart you'll find that you do. And when you find yourself behind a hearse at some traffic lights, and you see that the one man inside has his head bowed, you hope that he is crying – not completely consciously, but you do – and you hope that he feels more alone than anyone ever thinks possible because that means you are OK, somehow, you are better than him, and you are *winning* . . .

'Meanwhile, if you are winning, then the losers want *you* to die. And you want anyone more successful, wealthy and powerful than you crushed, brought down to size, found out as a cheat, a fraud, a con artist. The popular crowd at school, the people who bullied you and laughed at your hair, wouldn't it be great if they were all in a plane crash? What about that teacher who was always mean to you? What if he was caught smoking crack with a prostitute and had to resign and then KILLED HIMSELF? How about rich people, beautiful people, anyone with a castle or a private jet? The Royal Family? You loved it when Diana died. Everyone loved it when Diana died. Diana's death had all the deep, warm pleasure of a great tragedy but with the added excitement of being real. Marie Antoinette said that stupid thing about cake and didn't understand poor people so of course SHE SHOULD DIE . . .

'Let's face it, YOU are a better driver than that fat bitch who just cut you up. She should die. As for the slow, old people in the supermarket – hurry up and die! And what about the ticket inspector on the train who made you get your railcard out even though it was obvious you were asleep. If he'd woken up the next day with terminal cancer, wouldn't that have been a good thing? Wouldn't he have deserved it? And you don't *think* you think these things, but if you search your heart you'll find that you do.'

'I definitely don't think any of those things,' says Mary.

And of course at that moment everyone sort of wishes she would die.

'But the first step in forgiving others is to forgive yourself. To stop feeling guilty about having these thoughts and just accept them. Let them go. Give yourself a break. It is only by doing this that we can forgive others. Only if we recognise the other as, in fact, the self, can we achieve enlightenment, and leave the cycle of birth and death forever.'

'But surely thinking those awful things is . . . I mean, we should try to stop doing it, right? Not just do it and accept it?'

'If you truly believe that the person cutting you up on the road is just a part of yourself, how do you think you'd feel about them then? Wait – it's not obvious, this one.'

'I'd basically feel the same. I'd still hate them. Possibly even more.'

'Exactly. Our hatred of others really stems from a hatred of ourselves. If we stop hating ourselves, then we automatically stop hating other people. If we beat ourselves up and feel guilty all the time then we hate ourselves, and by definition we hate other people. Even if we don't ever come to accept that we are in fact one being, one organism, we'll have a much better time here.'

'What do you call a deer with no eyes?'

'I don't know.'

'No idea. Get it? No. Eye. Deer. What do you call a copulating deer with no eyes?'

'Don't know.'

'No fucking idea.'

'Charlie . . .'

'They've heard the word "fucking" before. Anyway, last bit. What do you call a copulating deer, frozen in the moment of orgasm?'

'Do deer have orgasms?'

'Do you give up?'

'Yes.'

'Still no fucking idea.'

'Hilarious. Fucking hilarious.'

'*Children*.'

The pff-pff sound of sit-ups pauses. 'You are both really, really disgusting.'

'Mummy? Were all these pieces of deer part of a real deer once?'

'Lots of real deer.'

'Deers.'

'*Deer*.'

'Whatever.'

'Right, one more. You'll like this one, kids. So a man kills a deer and brings it home for dinner . . .'

'Do they do that here?'

'Probably. Anyway, his wife cooks it . . .'

'Why can't he bloody well cook it himself?'

'In the *joke*, his wife cooks it. They serve it to the children but don't tell them what kind of meat it is. "Mmm," say the children. "This is delicious, Mummy. What is it?" And so she says, "All right, I'll give you a clue. It's what I call Daddy sometimes." The children immediately scream, "Oh my God, we're eating arsehole!" Boom, boom.'

'That's actually quite funny, Uncle Charlie. Although . . .'

'If James killed a deer and brought it home, I think these two would notice.'

'G.R.O.S.S.'

When the retreat is over, Sylvia drops Ina, Fleur and Skye back at Ina's place. They go via the hotel and pick up their stuff. Ina has said they can stay with her, and her place is so much nicer than the bland hotel with its nylon sheets and see-through curtains. If this is all an illusion then Fleur really has made Ina's little part of it rather enchanting, with the beautiful peat fire and the nips of dark, earthy whisky and now this gorgeous dinner of thick, creamy Cullen skink followed by haggis, blue cheese and fruit cake.

The only problem is the book.

'It was definitely blank before,' Fleur says.

While they were out, someone has clearly been into their hotel room, stolen the blank red hardback and replaced it with the blue hardback that Ina thought it was in the first place: *A Course in Miracles*.

'It was *A Course in Miracles* when I gave it to you,' says Ina. 'Which means . . .'

'Fleur's gone bananas?'

'No, dear. I think we have The Book back.'

'The Book?'

'Yes. It needed to become blank to get you here. Very clever.'

'How much do you actually know about your parents' disappearance?'

'Not much,' Fleur says. 'In theory I should know more than anyone, but I don't really know anything. All I remember is Oleander giving me two passports – mine and Piyali's, which I'm pretty sure was forged by some acquaintance of the Prophet's – and then half packing a bag and being taken to Heathrow in the dead of night. It was 1989. I was fifteen. Then Bryony's dad, Quinn, met me at Bombay and took me in some weird rickshaw to another airport and on another plane to Cochin. I didn't even see my mother. And I didn't know why I was even going to India. I thought they'd been on some island – they called it the Lost Island? – in the Pacific. I spent half a day waiting in a room above a spice shop in the most intense heat . . . Bryony's mother, Plum, gave me a sealed parcel to put in my suitcase and take back to Oleander. Grace – Charlie and Clem's mother – was there too. They introduced me to Pi. I had to say he was my cousin if anyone asked . . . My mother was supposed to be catching the next plane home with the others. That's what Uncle Quinn said. But . . . that was the last anyone ever saw of any of them.'

'Do you know what was in the parcel?'

'I guessed it was seed pods.'

'And you realised that Piyali's parents – Ketki's sister and her husband – had just been killed.'

'Yes. But it was all a total blur. I didn't understand any of it. Pi didn't speak much on the plane. I guess he was in shock. He spent a lot of time with Oleander when we arrived. At some point he became fine, although I suppose he was never totally fine. He never really mentioned his parents. I guessed it was the seed pods. But to be honest I was more worried about my mother. I kept expecting her to come back and then she never did. And then that anthropologist, Professor May, went to the island and they weren't there and . . . But how are you connected to all this?'

Ina sighs. 'I was – am – an anthropologist too. Obviously I'm retired now, although I still see some of what I do here as a kind of participant observation, although I try to integrate and, ha ha, forgive. I first visited the Lost Island in the seventies. I heard about it when I was doing some fieldwork in Northland, New Zealand. There was this rumour going around about a US airman who'd lost his mind and claimed to have crash-landed on this island full of magical plants and weird shamans and a tribe full of immortals he called the Enlightened Ones. You couldn't get there by boat because of high cliffs, and there was no runway for a plane, but you could in theory fly there in a helicopter. It wasn't long after the Philippine government had invited anthropologists to go and study the Tasaday people on the island of Mindanao. Even though the Tasaday tribe was later found to be a hoax, basically a bunch of normal islanders with loincloths over their usual underwear, every anthropologist wanted to find their own lost tribe. Anyway, for various reasons I came back to the UK, and, not long after, had a pretty spectacular nervous breakdown. I went on a retreat at Namaste House – one of the first ones, actually. At first I told myself I'd do a participant observation thing there, you know, an objective study of tie-dyed freaks smoking pot and talking about the time George Harrison dropped by for tea. Then I, well, I basically became one of them. Went native, as they say. Oleander and I became great friends.'

'Wow. OK, so . . .'

'Well, I couldn't shake off this idea of the Lost Island, and when I ended up back in Northland for another lot of fieldwork I took a couple of boats out to an island closer to where the Lost Island was supposed to be. Then I managed to find a guy with a helicopter to fly me out there. It took us three attempts to find it. Basically blew my whole budget. Anyway, in July 1978 I decided to go for a month. The idea was that this would give me a chance to see what was there and learn enough of the language to make sense of the people, and then I could get back for the new university term in September with a view to writing a proposal for further study. I arranged with the helicopter pilot that he would come back for me on August twenty-second. I paid him in advance. He asked if I was sure about all this.

When we landed on the island there seemed to be no one there at all, and I don't think he thought much of my chances. But in those days I knew how to survive in places like that and I actually didn't much care if I lived or died – I just wanted to write a great book about a great tribe and make a name for myself. Anyway, of course the pilot never came back . . .'

'What! How long were you there?'

'Ten years, give or take. That was how long it took the next anthropologist – dear old Professor David May – to hear the rumours, charter a helicopter, find the right island. By then of course I was indistinguishable from the other Lost People. When I spoke to him in English David May just assumed the language had been passed down from a missionary or something. But there were never any missionaries there. You literally couldn't get there without a helicopter. Anyway, David insisted I travel back to London with him, although at that point I think I'd resigned myself to remaining on the island forever. I went back to Namaste House and told Oleander what had happened. Briar Rose – your mother – and Quinn and Plum Hunter were very interested in my story. They had started calling themselves ethnobotanists by then – basically drug hunters. And they were into the whole rave scene and the 1988 Summer of Love which meant drugs for pleasure, not finding a cure for cancer or anything like that . . . Oleander became interested as well. She wanted stuff for her retreats.'

'But what was it like there? On this island for ten years? Did you go mad?'

Ina shrugs. 'It's almost impossible to describe. I did end up considering it my home but I'm not sure I'd go back. The first year was hard. Sex rituals. Psychedelics that left you feeling upside down for days afterwards. But the main thing was the plants; the island was full of plants that did impossible things. The seed pods that you inherited – they came from the island. You know what they do?'

'They kill you instantly but you get enlightened as well?'

'Yes, that's right. And of course enlightenment means being free of the cycle of birth and death, so although you die, this is a final death. This death releases you from the universe.'

Skye shudders. 'I'm not sure I'd want to be released from the universe . . .'

'The pain, apparently, is worse than anything you could ever imagine. But then you are free.'

'To do what exactly?'

'Perhaps you get to go back to the creator. Experience ultimate peace and harmony. Lose the ego forever. Anyway, we'll come to that. There was another plant that a particular shaman used to threaten me with. He liked orgies and, well, I was different from the tribeswomen, and he and his friends particularly liked to have orgies with me. One night I refused, and he said he'd make me, and I said he could kill me, and he said he could *really* kill me, and I said I knew all about the seed pods and the final death and I didn't think it sounded that bad. It definitely sounded better than what he and his friends had in mind. Then he led me to his garden and showed me a tall plant with a pale blue flower. That, he said, is the plant with which I will poison you if you do not do this. He then explained what it does. If the seed pods free you from the illusion, then this blue-flowered plant keeps you trapped in it forever. Imagine that. But worse, each death you suffer takes you further from enlightenment. Just like with the seed pods, the plant is toxic and you die. But when you are reincarnated you come back in a worse state than before. Every life you have is more painful and abject than the last one. Eventually you become a wild animal, then a caged animal, then a farm animal, then a lab animal. Then a fish, a shellfish, a barnacle that someone steps on while clambering over rocks that are the only home you now remember. Eventually you come back as the very plant that did this to you in the first place, with no soul left at all.'

'Did you believe him?'

'Oh yes.'

'But isn't this all just a load of . . .'

Ina shakes her head. 'It's complicated,' she says. 'But it is real.'

'What do you get if you cross Bambi with a ghost?'

'What?'

'Bamboo!'

'I totally don't get it.'

'So what did my mother and Quinn and Plum and the others want from the island? It sounds awful. I mean, the plants don't sound like plants anyone would want to have. I mean, that is where they went? Or . . . ?'

'That is where they went. They were annoyed that all I brought back with me from the island was The Book. The shaman who liked the orgies mellowed over time. He enchanted it for me as a gift before I left. I read it on the plane and then gave it to Oleander. But the others wanted the plants. There was a theory that you could make the seed pods safe and get the enlightenment effect – temporarily – without dying. Your mother wanted to create a kind of religion pill, the ultimate drug.'

'How?'

'Well, that's the bit they never found out.'

'And why India?'

'Because none of the Lost People would tell your mother how to make the pods safe. They had given her a taste of a liquid, apparently made from seed pods steeped in a secret ingredient. The effects of this liquid were so staggeringly wonderful that she – and the others – became determined to find out what the ingredient was. Ketki's sister was a famous herbalist in Cochin, and so Oleander arranged that your mother and the others would take samples to her and see what she made of the whole thing. Whatever she did, did not work and she died, along with her husband. Briar Rose, Quinn, Plum and Grace left pretty quick after that, as you would imagine. Pi was brought to the UK so he wouldn't be able to function as a witness. It was a horrible, horrible time. On the other hand it was clear why people were going crazy over the seed pods and this liquid.'

'And this Book. It's this one here?'

'Yes. Oleander gave it back to me to keep for you.'

'And it supposedly changes from one thing to another and . . .'

'I'm surprised you never knew about it. You must have heard Oleander talking about The Book?'

Fleur screws up her face. 'The whole thing with the Prophet . . . ?'

'That's right. He stole the book, became enlightened and then, being enlightened, brought it back and started working for Oleander for free.'

'The Prophet is *enlightened*?'

'Well, sort of. He's a complex case. Anyway . . .'

'So this Book thing is real?'

'Everything is real.'

'What does that mean?'

'In the illusion, anything can be real if you want it to be – or even sometimes if you don't. That's what I've learned. I have also learned that the more complicated and strange and knotty the illusion seems to be – for example what you believe to be a law of your universe being broken or violated without any real consequence – then the closer you are.'

'The closer to what?'

'To it all loosening up. Unravelling. Enlightenment. Leaving the cycle of birth and death. Going home.'

At the word 'home' something odd inside Fleur tingles, fizzes and is then gone. This is all really fucking . . .

'So you can get enlightened with these seed pods, which is why everyone wants them, but you have to die too unless you have this mysterious liquid, which is a bit of a leap of faith, or . . .'

'Or The Book, right?' says Skye. 'It sounds like you can get enlightened with The Book too?'

'That's right,' says Ina. 'The Book becomes whatever you need it to be to find enlightenment your own way. It's not instant. In fact, it's usually bloody hard. *The Upanishads* and the *Bhagavad Gita* are beautiful and sacred texts, but their basic instruction is to meditate through several lifetimes. And have you ever tried to read *A Course in Miracles*? It makes no sense. No sense at all. It takes years to study it. Years of undoing the brainwashing of the illusion. Years of re-educating yourself to basically look, act and think like a lunatic.' Ina picks up the blue hardback and touches the edges of its pages. 'The main part of the book is a more or less impenetrable text that sounds like Sunday School with a hangover, full of stuff about Jesus and the ego, followed by a "Workbook for Students" which you take a year to go through. The first lesson? You have to sit in a room and repeat the words "Nothing I see in this room means anything". And then you have to go around the room finding things and repeating "This table does not mean anything", "This chair does not mean anything", and so on. The Book used to turn into herbal manuals, great novels, books of poetry. It used to be the *Upanishads* quite regularly. I believe it spent a year with a friend of the Prophet's as *The Master and Margarita*. When I first read it, it was a strange memoir about a lost martial art. But apart from its brief spell as a notebook – which at least brought you here – for the last few years it seems to have wanted to be *A Course in Miracles*. Regardless of who it belongs to.'

'So, as usual it turns out that enlightenment is basically impossible,' says Fleur.

'Oh, it can be quite easy if you want it to be,' says Ina.

'What, like in those Buddhist stories where some old woman

whacks you over the head with a poker and you suddenly see the light?'

'Kind of. Or there is another way . . .'

'Right.'

'But it involves the seed pods.'

~

'What did the deer say after he left the gay bar?'

'Who knew there were so many deer jokes?'

'No, that is not what he said . . .'

'And this one sounds particularly unsuitable.'

'Shut up, Mummy. What did he say?'

'I can't believe I just blew fifty bucks back there. Ha ha!'

'Uncle Charlie, that sounds kind of disgusting, but you're going to have to explain it.'

'Good God, Charlie.'

~

'What plant are the seed pods from exactly?'

'You don't even know that? I thought you were more or less running a factory down there.'

'The Prophet does all that. I try not to know much about it. Are they orchids of some sort?'

'Have you seen the flowers?'

'No. Well, yes, but not in the way I think you mean. I've heard the myth, but these flowers aren't exactly . . .'

'This is what you were all talking about at the funeral,' Skye says.

'What myth?' asks Ina.

'You know. About the flowers being in the shape of religious icons. Images of Jesus, the Buddha, a cross . . . My mother told me about them once when she was stoned, before she disappeared. She said I had to look out for these flowers, watch out for them . . . Of course I've seen the plants around the place. The Prophet's so good at growing them that they are everywhere. I think we've even got a couple in one of the treatment rooms. They basically look like orchids you'd buy in Sainsbury's.'

'And the pods are just like vanilla pods, right?'

'Clem Gardener's growing plants from her seed pod to see what they are. I think she's making some kind of documentary about it. Charlie Gardener has already had his identified at Kew. It's either vanilla or doesn't exist. They weren't sure.'

'Clem's growing plants from the pod she inherited?'

'Yeah.'

'Interesting.'

'Why?'

'Do you know how the pods you inherited are different from the ones the Prophet grows, or that Clem is now growing?'

Fleur shakes her head. 'No.'

'Are they from the actual Lost Island?' Skye asks.

'Yep,' says Ina. 'They are. They are much, much more potent.'

~

'And what do you get when you cross a bear with a deer?'

'Er, let me guess, Uncle Charlie. Maybe a BEER?'

'You are too clever.'

~

'Do you know what a mimic orchid is?'

Fleur thinks. 'The ones that look like bees?'

'Yes, exactly. But there are lots of others. A number of orchid species mimic things. The bee orchid is in the *Ophrys* genus, where all the flowers mimic insects. There's also the *Dracula* genus, which contains orchids with flowers that resemble vampires, monkeys, even mushrooms. This is all pretty easy to understand. The flowers want to be pollinated and so they fool insects into landing on them, one way or another. But our orchid, the lost orchid . . .'

'It pretends to be religious icons because . . .'

'Because religious icons attract people who want to be enlightened. And it promises enlightenment, of course, just with this unfortunate side-effect that you die. You see a flower that looks like Jesus. Of course you will want to taste its fruit so you pollinate it, which is what it wants – the lost orchid only has human pollinators . . .'

'What does that mean?'

'It relies on humans to pollinate it. You see a flower that looks like Ganesh or the Virgin Mary and you touch it, you learn what it does, you make it fruit, you eat it, you probably die. And the seeds are buried with you. But before that, in a final strange twist, the lost orchid mimics one last thing.'

'Which is?'

'If you are destined to eat the fruit of the plant and die – whether this is in the next five minutes or the next thousand years – the lost orchid flower begins to look like . . . Well, it starts to look just like you.'

'Seriously?'

'Seriously.'

'And this isn't just a load of . . .'

'No.'

'OK, then. Bears. You'll like this one. This is a good one. More of a life story than a joke.'

'Yeah, whatever.'

'OK, well, two guys are camping in the forest in Canada or something. Somewhere there are bears.'

'Are there bears in Scotland?'

'No. Anyway, these two guys have just fallen asleep when they are woken by grunting and shuffling sounds. It's a big grizzly, looking for food.'

'Do grizzly bears eat people?'

'Yep. So there is food, but the food is in the tent and has just woken up and . . .'

'Charlie, this is a bit gruesome just before bed . . .'

'And one guy peeks out of the tent, kind of gulps, and says to the other, "Do you think you can outrun a grizzly?" And the other guy says, "I don't have to outrun a grizzly. I only have to outrun you." Think about it . . .'

'Here.'

It's the following day and everything has gone strange, just like when they went to Sylvia's, with the doilies and the pink wafers. Rain pounds the windows. Fleur feels more hungover than she should after just a few small nips of whisky the night before. Ina passes a photo album to her. Who has photo albums these days? And this one seems particularly cheap: the cover is imitation maroon leather, cracked in places. Inside are prints that look like bad photocopies, each one stuffed loosely inside its crackly plastic wrapper.

'What am I looking for?' Fleur says.

'Just look, and you will see.'

'I'm seeing some flowers,' Skye says, 'but . . .'

'You can't see . . . the crucifixion? Ganesh? Shiva as the cosmic dancer?'

Again Fleur and Skye exchange a look. Yes, OK, one of the flowers does look a bit like a crucifixion. A crucifixion created by a ten-year-old on Photoshop. And the Ganesh flower is ridiculous. A pinkish, orangey blur with a peculiar trunk coming out of it, again looking as if it has been airbrushed on. Shiva is a blue orchid with limb-like petals that make it look more like a common clematis than a cosmic dancer. Fleur feels hollow, suddenly. Everything she has learned here swirls like dirty water around a plughole and is gone. All at once she feels a deep and bitter hunger for something she knows does not exist. It is as if she has turned up to the biggest banquet in the world to find only bread and water. This whole thing is a joke. And it's not even funny. Are these pictures just projections of what she really thinks of all this? Or is this whole thing just utterly stupid? Fleur feels tired. Tired of this life, of all the others, and of this bloody universe, whatever the hell it actually is. She just wants to go home.

'You're not seeing it,' Ina says. 'The illusion is blocking it. You have to be able to see through the illusion. You have to learn, somehow.'

'Right.'

'Would you want to see it, if there was some way . . .'

Fleur shrugs. 'I don't know.'

'I want to see it,' says Skye.

'I just don't think I'm actually very good at sex. Sorry.'

'But what about your husband? I mean . . . ?'

'We just got into the habit of not doing it. It's been a relief. And, oh God, this is going to sound horrible, but he is just so grateful to even see me naked that just lying still and moaning a bit made me an amazing lover in his eyes. I mean, if I gave him a blow job he'd be happy for *months*. But with you? I realise I'm lacking in skills. I am really sorry. I think I'm actually a bit lazy. A bit heterosexual probably. I just want to lie back and let you be the guy.'

'That is so not how it works.'

'I know.'

'Go down on me.'

'What?'

'Go down on me.'

'Now?'

'Yes.'

'If you want a really good time, go into a church.'

'Right . . .'

They are still sitting at Ina's kitchen table. Somehow another day has passed. The rain has stopped. Moonlight is shining on the copper pans Ina has hanging above her range. The smell of peat is there, as always. The photo albums are back on the shelf. On the table is a small medicine bottle containing a clear liquid. This is the last bottle, Ina has been explaining. This is the substance that Briar Rose was trying to re-create. This is what everyone died for.

'And you say it's simply the result of steeping a seed pod in . . .'

'Yes, in the tears of one of the Enlightened Ones.'

'A Lost Islander?'

Ina shakes her head. 'Anyone who is enlightened will do.'

'What, like the Prophet?'

'Maybe someone a bit more enlightened than the Prophet.'

'Do enlightened people cry very much?'

'No. Which is why . . .'

'I see. So it's a paradox. Impossible.'

'Well, sort of. It's . . .'

'And you always knew this?'

'Yes.'

'And my mother never knew?'

'No.'

'And you didn't tell her because . . . ?'

'Look. Deep down your mother was a good person, as we all are. But she was trapped in a beautiful body. People would do anything for her. Piyali's parents' deaths . . . The Prophet losing his arm. She would have gone on and on trying and failing to create a sort of synthetic bliss. I mean, I'm not knocking it exactly but I don't think it's the best way for us to get out of the illusion. Not ultimately. Oleander agreed in the end too.'

Fleur gulps. Breathes. Her mother died for information that was right there all along. But then what would Briar Rose have done to try to get hold of an enlightened person's tears? Where would she have stopped?

Skye looks at the bottle of fluid. These are someone's actual tears? This is . . .

'So what's special about a church?' she asks Ina.

'You simply won't be able to bear the bliss, at least not at first.'

'In a church? Like, just a normal church?'

'Yes.'

'Seriously? This kind of sounds a bit, um . . .'

'Try it and see. You're extremely lucky. I wouldn't give this much of the last bottle to anyone else, but of course if it wasn't for your mother I wouldn't even have it. I mean, she brought the original pods back. And . . .'

'So what exactly happens in a church?'

'It's hard to describe, but basically it doesn't seem boring any more. In fact, you can look at anything you found boring before and it will now be entirely the opposite. The world will be turned inside out. All the shiny things the ego loves become dull. Shops seem grey, cold and pointless. Success is a big yawn. Everything expensive or difficult to obtain appears cheap and easy. But suddenly just sitting on a park bench looking at strangers is as exciting as watching the latest film which, in turn, now appears pointless and slow and fake. You won't be able to go to graveyards at first, because you will get lost among all the spirits still there. But as time goes on you'll learn to enjoy visiting them, in the same way good mediums do. You will be able to attend their great feasts and hear their incredible stories. But it's impossible to describe. You really have to try it.'

'And we won't die?'

'No. Well, it's very unlikely. No one has. Not from this bottle.'

'OK. Well . . .'

Fleur and Skye look at one another. This feels a little like queuing for hours for a fairground ride and then trying to change your mind at the top. They are here now, and so they might as well . . .

'There's just one more interesting side-effect.'

'Which is?'

~

'I can fly . . . !'

'Me too! Oh, oh, oh . . . OK. This is . . .'

'Breathe, girls. Breathe.'

'Oh. My. God.'

When Fleur says the word 'God' it feels ticklish inside and kind of orgasmic. It suddenly seems like too much for one word. Too much to say again, unless she really means it. Which is impossible, because . . .

'Where are we going?'

'To Calanais, to look at the standing stones.'

'And this won't wear off while we . . .'

'No, dear. It won't wear off for, oh, about a year.'

'A year!'

'Well, give or take. You can squeeze a bit more out of it if you regularly meditate and remember to practise forgiveness. The initial exhilaration fades into a more comfortable kind of bliss after a day or so. You'll still be able to fly, though. But most people forget that. Most people forget the whole thing afterwards, in fact.'

The word 'forgiveness', when Fleur hears it now, means something rather different from when she heard it before. Before, it was a bit blah blah and also quite vast: a remote, dark purple mountain of a word with dangerous edges and a pretty steep drop on the other side. Now it is a beautiful, soft gift with silk and ribbons – the spiritual kind – that she can't wait to give to someone else. But of course it's just the same if you keep it . . . In fact, everyone has one anyway, and no one ever tires of opening it and looking inside it, and the contents never get dirty or boring or old. All Fleur wants to do is lie down and shut her eyes and relax into this feather bed of feelings. This is a Sunday morning for the soul that could last forever and ever and . . . But she needs nothing, she realises, nothing at all. She feels like a ball of pure energy bobbing around in some make-believe world that is so very sweet in some ways but also a total joke. The world has become a child's drawing, something knocked up before lunch in a cosmic nursery, just like the pictures you find in an old cardboard box after your parents die or divorce or move to somewhere smaller. What a nice effort, you think. But, well, ridiculous, all the same. Blue people! And a green, not even totally round sun. And everyone hand in hand. Bless . . . As Fleur thinks this, the world completely fades out for a second, and there is a bright white light that feels – ouch, oh, stop, oh, more, no, wait – too much like . . .

'She's passed out,' says someone very far away.

'Fleur?'

When she wakes up she is flying over the Atlantic. Calanais is only a few miles down the coast from Ina's place. But why not fly around the world when you suddenly find you can? Fleur skims New York, its ghostly Twin Towers still there as an energy force, bright spectres of the past, emitting more light than anything else below her. Fleur realises that if she looks down in a certain way, with her mind as well as her eyes, she can see all of history embedded in the landscape, all fresh from a vast 3D printer, and she can see all the fish in the sea, and every scale on every fish, and all the atoms in one scale of one fish and all the electrons in one atom and all the quarks and – bang – there's the white light again . . .

When she wakes up this time she is flying over desert. Her mouth feels dry. She wishes she could discard her body, just peel it off like the set of clothes you were wearing that afternoon when you got caught in the rain. But it's not time for that yet. It is much, much too early. 'Take me to Calanais,' she says to it, in the end, and then, just like that, she is lying on the ground somewhere between the tourist information stand and the public toilets. This is the best sat-nav in the world! But she feels slightly sick. Skye and Ina are looking down at her.

'You OK?' says Ina.

Skye looks a little how Fleur feels. As they walk up the path towards the standing stones, concealed behind a mound (although Fleur and Skye can now see through things like mounds it turns out to be quite tiring, so they have stopped their brains from doing it all the time), she whispers to her, 'Where did you go?' 'I went all around the world,' says Fleur. 'What about you?' Skye smiles. 'I went inside geometry,' she says, 'And then I wrote fifty albums. Oh – and a symphony! And I heard the cosmic song . . .' And it all makes sense to Fleur, and everything is beautiful. The darkness around them is simply a curtain they can pull aside whenever they want to, although the light behind it is too dazzling to be of much use. So, with only a tiny crack in the curtain they walk up the path some more until they can see the standing stones in the distance. From here they look like a freeze-frame of a breakout session at a convention of giants. But as they get closer, Fleur sees that the beings they represent – no, *are* – are not giants but archetypes. Here is every possible shape an ego can inhabit. There is the great mother, with her cape swirling about her. And right in the centre of everything, the patriarch, acting as though everything is very important indeed. There, the little girl and the little boy who do not want to stand still, and beyond them all, the stranger who comes to the door in the middle of the night and changes everything. The outsider, the freak, the loner, the mistress, the forbidden lover, the criminal. Fleur sees herself first in this figure. She walks over and tries to touch the stone, but that ticklish, painful, orgasmic feeling returns and she finds she can't even get close to it, because it is like touching her own insides. But gradually she realises she is all of them. She is mother, father, daughter, son, maiden, crone, hero, witch . . .

And then the white light, again.

Back at Ina's, Fleur asks for another look at the photo album. And now she sees the lost orchid as Ina sees it. There, indeed, is Ganesh, and Shiva, and beautiful, mellow Jesus, first as a too-wise young man and then at the end. Now when she looks at it the crucifixion goes from being painful and real to being something different entirely, not a joke, exactly, because she realises how much he needed to concentrate to do it, and how much it was supposed to mean, and not a trick, exactly . . . Something like a proof. This is how little the body means. You can do anything to me and it does not matter, because I am not of this world and beyond it I will always be free. And whatever we do to each other, through this eternity and the next, you are me and I am you, and in the end none of it matters at all.

~

'When I read those Judy Blume books when I was a child I was so confused all the time. I mean, what is baloney? What is a baloney sandwich?'

'It's a gross kind of salami. Like a huge sausage.'

'How do you know that?'

'Well, obviously I Googled it, Mummy.'

'Are you sure that book isn't too old for you?'

'It's too late now anyway. I've read it. It has a penis in it called Ralph.'

'Oh, Holly.'

'If someone would find me a tennis court I wouldn't need to read unsuitable books.'

Or perhaps the proof is that there is no God, not here, not in the illusion, because what God would be the author of *this* story? What God would kill his hero in such a thoughtless way? What God would let anything he created suffer so much . . . ?

We do this to ourselves. There is no one else involved.

No one else is even *watching*.

'Apparently if a man turns up on one of the islands claiming to be the seventh son of a seventh son you have to put an earthworm in his hand.'

'Gross. Why?'

'Because if he is telling the truth then the earthworm immediately dies.'

'But why would anybody want to be the seventh son of a seventh son?'

'Because you get supernatural powers.'

'What, to kill earthworms? L.A.M.E.'

The clue is always, always, buried deep in the boredom . . .

Where do you feel most bored? Go there.

'Of course, everything you do is better than what everyone else does.'

'What is that supposed to mean?'

'Well, all this wholesome crap about walking and fishing and swimming, as if everything anyone else wants to do is inferior. WHO exactly decided that swimming in ice-cold water having your face bitten by clegs is better than watching TV all afternoon? I almost added "an old film" to make it more acceptable to you but what I am trying to say is that I am SICK of doing that. If someone wants to watch, I don't know, *Teletubbies* all day then why do you feel you have to stop them?'

Bryony thinks of that odd conversation she had with Fleur, when Fleur said that basically nothing you do in this life matters at all and has already been decided anyway. In which case Bryony had no choice other than to watch *Australia's Biggest Loser* for five hours straight while the others tried to climb one of the Paps of Jura. She still feels tearful thinking of the woman who got so fat she could not ride her horse, and how lovely it was when . . .

'Well, if that person is my child, then I do feel I have a responsibility to . . .'

'And you think you're so fucking healthy!'

'What?'

'All this coconut milk, and butter and cream in everything. All the fucking cake. James, look at me. Do you think I need cake? I have never needed cake. But you've shovelled it into me virtually daily for the last ten years. And now I look like this. It's almost as if you intended me to be . . .'

'I don't pour two bottles of wine down your throat every evening.'

'Not this again. You know I only do that on a very special occasion!'

'There were two bottles on the side this morning. *Again*.'

'Well, Charlie . . .'

'Charlie has about half a glass. Anyway, why does everything always have to come back around to Uncle sodding Charlie? Why is he always here? I never thought I was signing up to this.'

'This is not about Charlie. It's about you.'

'OK. One last joke. An island one.'

'Will it really be the last one?'

'Good God . . . Right. There's an Englishman, an Irishman and a Scotsman who are stranded on an island after their boat is shipwrecked.'

'Like in *The Tempest*?'

'Yes, except that all the characters and the whole situation is completely different.'

'Except for the shipwreck.'

'Yes, except this is more of a little boat. So anyway, there they are on this desert island, and they find a magical bottle with a genie inside it. The genie offers them each a wish. The Scotsman goes first. "I wish to be back home with my family with a nice roast dinner in front of me," he says. And, *poof*, he is gone. The Irishman has a similar idea. "Take me to Dublin, to the finest restaurant, and put a beautiful woman there with me." And, *poof*, he is gone too. Now the genie turns to the Englishman. "What do you wish?" he asks. "Well," says the Englishman, "it's a bit lonely here on my own, and I need some help gathering food and firewood. I wish my two friends would come back." Boom, boom!'

'Whatever.'

'Shit,' says Bryony, when she gets off the phone.

'Who was it?'

'Clem. From Edinburgh. We've got Granny problems.'

'What's happened?'

'She's got into a dispute with a noisy neighbour.'

'I fear for the neighbour.'

'Don't joke. And she's lonely, apparently.'

'Everything all right?' Fleur comes in with Skye Turner. They both look oddly peaceful at the moment. Have they been meditating too much? Fleur in particular looks like one of those silvery pears with a pink flush down the side, and . . . And how did they even GET here, to Jura, from the Outer Hebrides, or wherever it was they went? They say they flew, but not how they made it from the airport to the front door with basically no transport at all. And why is Bryony the only one who finds this weird?

'Oh, everything's fine. Well, except that Granny Beatrix is threatening to move in with one of us.'

'Or Augustus,' corrects James. 'The Grange does belong to her after all.'

'What's the problem?' says Skye.

'Oh, she's been abusing her neighbour. She lives in a very, very posh apartment in the Royal Crescent in Bath. The kind of place where you don't abuse your neighbour. Although apparently the neighbour has been playing music very loudly, and . . .'

'Beatrix is beautiful,' breathes Skye. 'I adore Beatrix.'

'That's right. Didn't it turn out that she had bought . . .'

'*Downloaded* . . .'

'. . . one of your albums?'

'Well, you can move in with her if you like,' says Bryony.

The universe does a tiny pirouette. Almost trips, and then rights itself.

'You know what?' says Fleur. 'That's actually . . .'

'Could I really?' says Skye. 'I mean, it would be . . .'

Disgraced pop star hides in old lady's flat. But what if she *could* hide from the tabloids this time? She knows now to keep her voicemail switched off at all times. If they can't listen to her voicemail, they can't find her, right? There is nothing in the world to connect her with Bath. And she does sort of adore Beatrix. And she can fly to Sandwich to see Fleur whenever she wants. Because she does remember. Even though Ina said she wouldn't, she does.

❧

'How was your meal, sir?'

'Are you just being polite, or do you really want to know?'

'Ollie . . .'

'If you have feedback, then we . . .'

'OK. Well, since this is about the twentieth time you've asked is everything all right and are we enjoying our meal I am assuming that you do really want to know. Let's begin at the beginning. Your *amuse-bouche* was not amusing. It was pretentious, surprisingly bland and a very off-putting shade of green. Like everything else, it needed much more seasoning. And more heating. The starters looked pretty enough on the surface but the cucumber was too cold. It was also unpeeled and unseasoned. The salmon was fine, but then it would be, since all the chef had to do was open the packet. Ditto the salad, which needed dressing. And if you are going to have green beans arranged like little crucifixion scenes around the plate then they should not be overcooked and flaccid. The main course was far too ambitious. I did not need to have venison two ways: one way would have been fine, if it had been cooked properly and somehow kept hot until it reached our table. I believe restaurants have ways of achieving this. Deep-frying things does not automatically render them edible if they would otherwise be inedible. For example your fondant potato, and your ridiculous "string" French fries that, remarkably, do taste of string. If I did not need venison two ways I definitely did not need parsnip three ways, once of which was simply "boiled, 1950s style" and the other two of which were indistinguishable from one another and also from the strange lumps of celeriac I kept finding strewn around my plate. I could not identify the pink cubes. As for the puddings, of course we only had ice cream, which you only had to spoon from a tub, but the reason people serve ice cream in little bowls rather than on saucers is because it is really impossible to eat ice cream from a saucer unless you are a cat.'

'I will pass your comments to the kitchen.'

Triathlon

'You said the word "Ollie" in your sleep last night, by the way.'

'Did I? Are you sure? It wasn't something else?' Brolly, trolley, folly . . .

'It was definitely Ollie.'

Dolly, volley . . . ? Don't push it. 'Peculiar.' Bryony yawns.

'Was it a university dream?'

'It must have been. How odd.'

'Oh well. I'll go and make the tea.' James kisses her on the cheek and gets out of bed.

Bryony's dream begins to come back. It was her birthday, and James had arranged a surprise for her. When she went downstairs, every surface of the house had been covered in pink, silver or gold tissue paper. James had also installed glass cabinets everywhere. Inside the cabinets and on all the surfaces were all the things she could ever dream of buying. For example scores of pairs of beautiful shoes, all in her size. And several ranges of cosmetics. And cookware, for some reason: five different heavy frying pans. And beautifully bound books, and handbags, of course, and pens and board games and silk scarves. A basket of grey kittens. The idea was that Bryony could choose the things she wanted and James would send the rest back. He loved her so much that instead of giving her a voucher, or cash to take on a shopping trip, or one or two presents that she could take back if she didn't like them, he had spent *all* his money on *everything*. And he would simply take back what she didn't want. He had, he said, kept all the receipts. The effort, the expense, the time involved in setting this up . . . Bryony could not imagine being loved more than this. It was just so amazingly, beautifully . . . And then she came to a set of upright coffin-shaped glass cabinets containing men. All the men she has ever slept with. And it became clear to Bryony that she had to choose one of these too. And then James was there saying that she could still keep all her other presents, even if she didn't choose him. And then she chose . . .

'Here you go.' James returns with a mug of tea.

'Thanks, love.'

The guy is blond, pure muscle, a tennis player, Australian? Or maybe Swedish. He can't believe Fleur has not seen him on TV. He has won a couple of Challengers, whatever they are, but has not yet ever gone past the first round of a major, which is a big tennis tournament like Wimbledon. They also have them in Paris, New York and Melbourne, apparently. Fleur will need to talk to Holly about this, maybe offer Holly a few minutes with him in return. Anyway, he's seen sports psychologists, more sports psychologists than you've had hot dinners, not that Fleur looks like someone who has had a lot of hot dinners anyway, which he actually SAYS, which makes her blush and look at his crotch and then out of the window, and she realises that he is definitely Australian and not Swedish, and then he explains that he is sort of in hiding because NO ONE trains in the UK, because why would you?

'And what's the problem exactly?'

'I get so tight I choke and lose my forehand.'

'I don't know what any of that means.'

'That's why I need you. This is not a sport thing. This is fundamental.'

'Right. OK. I really don't even know what a forehand is.'

'It's usually someone's best shot. Usually your strategy is to play to the guy's backhand, but all the guys on tour know to play to my forehand. Sometimes just one shot hit to my forehand makes me choke because I know that he knows, and he knows that I know that he knows and it's like all a big fucking mind game and you must know about mind games?'

'I know about mind games.'

'So what do I do?'

'You breathe.'

'Right.'

'This is called the Fishing Game.'

Ollie wonders if it will be like the fishing game he plays with Spencer at the fishmonger in Herne Bay every week. Or used to play. For various reasons, he and Clem have started buying more fish from Ocado lately. Anyway, this fishing game is happening at the university, in the glass-and-stone building usually reserved for VIP visits and executive group meetings. It is part of a day of activities and team building on the theme of 'co-operation in the university'. Why is Ollie at something so redundant, lame, and, what with it being run by a sodding anthropologist, probably ideologically unsound? Why indeed. It was someone's idea that Ollie should represent the junior, or as they are known now, 'unpromoted' staff from the School of English. Alongside him in his team are David, Frank and Megan, sometimes known as Mystic Meg, who teaches Magical Realism and has somehow made it to Senior Lecturer before Ollie. These are all people that Ollie wants to impress. Except for Mystic Meg, whom he wants, in some unexamined way, to crush.

Although Ollie wants to impress David and Frank, he nevertheless spends quite a lot of time and energy avoiding them, perhaps because he believes his absence to be more impressive than his presence, at least until he finishes his book. For example he never, ever goes up the stairs to the main level of the School of English building. He has an arrangement with one of the prettier secretaries that she will post the contents of his pigeonhole to his house every day. The only other reason for going upstairs (apart from to see people, but who needs to see people when you can email people?) is to use the School of English kitchen, which is a zone fraught with danger and a high likelihood of conversation, not just with David or Frank, but indeed with any of Ollie's colleagues. If Ollie wants a cup of tea and has scheduled roughly two and a half minutes in which to make it he really does not want to have to take part in a fourteen-minute conversation about someone's dog, cat, illness or – horrors – baby. He does not want to look at pictures of people's grandchildren. He does not want to have to make yet another witty comment about the teaspoon amnesty. He doesn't want to smell things that other people are microwaving.

The anthropologist is droning on about a Nobel prize-winning economist called Elinor Ostrom. After about ten minutes of waffly introduction he says that in fact he doesn't want to say too much about the fishing game because he wants everyone to see for themselves how . . . The Vice Chancellor clears her throat. She is on a team with other members of the Executive Group. Ollie is terrified just looking at her. This is humanities day. The winning humanities team will go forward to compete against other winning teams from around the university. But from what the anthropology dude is saying, winning is not that simple. You have to decide how many fictional fish to catch, but if everyone catches too many there won't be any left, which means that winning can actually become losing and . . .

The other way of getting a cup of tea is to go and queue for it somewhere on campus. But this always takes approximately nineteen minutes – even longer than talking to colleagues – and you never know who you could end up queuing with. And there's the guilt about the paper cups, and, of course, the cost. And the weather. And the likelihood of running into students, as well as colleagues. And of people laughing at you or accidentally throwing a Frisbee in your face. Ollie has therefore designed a system that is almost perfect. He has had a kettle in his office (Sainsbury's Basics: £5) for a long time, but never used it because using it involved going to the School of English kitchen to fill it, empty it, wash mugs etc. And the thing you wash the mugs with is always over a year old and stinks and has been regularly TOUCHED BY POSTGRADUATES. But every problem is just a question looking for an answer. Now, each morning he takes in a bag of clean cups, plates, knives, forks and teaspoons, and each evening he takes home a bag of dirty cups, plates, knives, forks and teaspoons to go in the dishwasher. He buys a six-pack of two-litre bottles of cheap spring water each Monday with which to fill his kettle and, when he has to, empties old water from his kettle out of the window. He has also bought a mini fridge (Amazon: £49.99) for milk and storing his packed lunch. All so he doesn't have to see the two men he is now sitting next to.

After quite a lot of fiddling, the anthropologist shows a YouTube film explaining the concept of the tragedy of the commons. Well, OK, at least tragedy is something humanities people get. A cute drawing of a meadow appears. The meadow, probably in pre-enclosure England, is common land, explains the American voice-over. Every farmer in the village can graze his cows on it. If one farmer decides to double the amount of cows he has, he can double his profits (profits??? In pre-enclosure England? A few people titter at that, including Ollie, but you're clearly not supposed to, and indeed this is GETTING AHEAD and CHEATING) without increasing his overheads, so obviously he does this, because there is nothing STOPPING him from doing this, so then the other farmers decide they may as well do the same and before you know it the cows have eaten all the grass and shat everywhere and the MEADOW IS GONE. It's the same with fishing without quotas, apparently. A bunch of selfish cunts ruin everything for themselves and everyone else. Obviously they should be KILLED, but . . .

Apparently old-fashioned economists thought you needed lots of laws to stop people fucking up their meadows. Then some other economists thought that people should be left to fuck up their meadows if they want to because once you have made a profit from this meadow you can always leave and find another meadow. Neoliberal twats.

But what if . . . what if . . . Ollie yawns and drifts off. Wakes up again.

Quite what the fuck any of this has to do with the university is anyone's guess.

The anthropologist enlists help from a couple of historians and hands out three sheets of instructions and figures. He starts talking about tribespeople fishing in a shared lake just outside the village. The lake is the same as the meadow, right, like a *tribal version* of a meadow, like a shared resource, a COMMONS, and . . . When Ollie's sheets arrive he feels queasy. He can't do maths! Who, in English, or indeed in any of the humanities except maybe politics, can do sodding maths? Of course, now he thinks about it, both David and Frank are excellent with figures, especially when it comes to massaging the incomprehensible student satisfaction survey stats. There are groans around the room and other noises and gestures of confusion. It is as if a woman wearing a leopard-print outfit has just walked past the big cat section of a zoo. The animals recognise it, they just don't understand why or how . . .

'Is that clear?' finishes the anthropologist. Fuck. 'Decide how many fish you are going to catch and write the number in the box.'

Silence breaks out.

'What are we supposed to . . . ?' says Ollie to Mystic Meg.

'Shush!' says the anthropologist. 'No communicating – yet.'

'It's like a game,' Megan whispers back.

'Oh, I forgot to say,' says the anthropologist. 'There's a prize for the winning group, and a prize for the winning individual.' He holds up a bottle of champagne and a big box of chocolates.

Ollie likes games. He likes champagne. He really likes chocolates. But more than any of that, he likes winning. He loves the feeling he gets in the swimming pool on the rare occasion that someone else is doing real lengths, and not just randomly dribbling snot or bobbing up and down with a visible erection, and he easily overtakes them – as he always does – feeling a little piscine himself, if he's honest, with a clean, sleek, scaly power that makes him feel almost as if he has merged with the water. If he wins this, then he will not just get the usual buzz of victory, but will be able to accomplish something for the School of English despite the fact that he has not yet completed his book. And he will be noticed by the Vice Chancellor. So . . .

What do you have to do to win? Ollie scans the sheet in front of him. It seems that the basic idea is that people put in 'orders' for fish, or in other words tell the anthropologist how many fish they intend to catch. Even though the fish are free, because they come from your shared tribal lake, in this exercise they have a price, but the price is not determined until everyone has put their order in. So it's all a bit of a gamble. The orders are secret, says the anthropologist. No one knows how many fish their neighbour is secretly catching . . . But everyone knows that overfishing has a severe cost, which in this exercise is represented by the price of each fish going up dependent on the total amount of fish caught. So it's in everyone's interest to catch only a few fish, because then they will be affordable for everyone. But since everyone knows that, and everyone is therefore likely to catch only a modest amount of fish, then why not be the ONE PERSON who catches a lot of fish just when everyone is expected not to catch a lot of fish?

Ollie doesn't quite realise this until the second round, which is when everyone else realises it too. BLAMMO! The meadow is gone. All the fish are dead. It's the tragedy of the commons! It's also the Prisoners' Dilemma! It's that situation when no one gets their kids vaccinated because they assume everyone else will . . . *Ha ha*, goes the anthropologist. *See.* So then for the next round everything is different. In the next round you can *talk* to your team members. You are still playing as an individual, though, and your order is secret. Your order is still *secret*. That can only mean . . . For a second it's as if the other guy swimming laps has got cramp and Ollie can glide past him like a calculating cold-water salmon . . . This is basically his chance to win it for himself, but also for his team, none of whom will do anything quite so . . . And of course the system needs someone to do what Ollie is going to do now. And all the people sitting around him are so soft and liberal and *Guardian*-reading that they probably think winning is vulgar and all they are thinking of is SHARING their fish, and perhaps giving them away to poor people, and maybe going vegetarian and not even eating fish at all.

'So we agree that we'll get twelve fish each,' says Megan.

'I think fifteen is fine,' says Frank.

David is replying to messages on his BlackBerry.

'I definitely think twelve,' says Ollie.

And then he orders twenty. After all, they'll be at a very good price . . . And of course he is sacrificing himself, and his own integrity, only to help prove this clever theory of the tragedy of the commons, and how there will always be someone who will come in and order more fish than they are supposed to. And win.

The orders are in, and the anthropologist adds them all up.

The next round is the same. This time, when the anthropologist adds them up he frowns quite a lot.

'You are definitely all talking to each other, right?' he says.

David looks up from his BlackBerry. 'Someone's cheating,' he says. 'The numbers are wrong. If we're ordering only twelve fish each, the price should be less than this.' Then he goes back to his BlackBerry. But . . . OMG. The way he said it. The way he said, 'Someone's cheating.' Like saying 'Someone's going to have to go.' Or 'This research record just isn't good enough.'

He calls over to the anthropologist. 'Someone cheating, right?'

The anthropologist nods.

How, exactly, is trying to make a profit and trying to win, when those are the terms of the game, cheating???!!! But Ollie doesn't say this. Ollie looks down at the desk and pretends to doodle, even though he isn't a doodler. In meetings Megan often doodles flowers. He starts trying to do one of these now: a circle with petals around it. But he does his petals too big at the start and has to finish the whole thing off with one that is tiny, stunted and all wrong.

'It was you, wasn't it?' says Megan.

'Of course not,' says Ollie.

But now he's sweating. The Vice Chancellor has realised that Someone Has Cheated and is frowning and looking around the room, sort of peering at people. One of the pro Vice Chancellors whispers something to her and she looks at David.

'OK, well, apart from a small blip there, that worked quite well. But before we discuss what you should have noticed, let's now open it up to the whole room. You can now discuss with everyone what your fishing plans are. Let's see what you can achieve now.'

Oh fucking fuck. So this was an exercise designed to *disprove* the tragedy of the commons. To prove that in real life people don't tend to fuck up their meadows. To prove that people are essentially good and nice and capable of managing their own resources. To prove that real communities communicate and cooperate and would probably stab someone like Ollie to death with a pitchfork or a boning knife or a tribal implement. Shit, shit, shit. Ollie has never felt more of a total cunt than he does now. Well, maybe when . . . He starts sweating more heavily. He has cheated in public. He has cheated in front of his line manager, and *his* line manager and . . . But OK, maybe it's not too late. The only way to compensate for what he did before is to act in the opposite way now. Now he will be a *Guardian*-reading fish hugger too! Especially given that he does actually read the *Guardian* and does (sort of) believe in community and sharing and being kind and good and . . .

'It was you, wasn't it?' asks David, after approximately three minutes of this.

'Well, I just thought that someone had to . . .'

David looks away, shaking his head.

At the end of the exercise each team is required to add up their total profit. The Executive Group has made a total of 55 units of profit. History has managed 42. English has somehow only got 42 as well, despite Ollie's efforts. But the winners overall are Theology, with a grand total of 398. The anthropologist presents them with the chocolates and the champagne. The overall winner, some chick from Divination called Kimberley, immediately opens the chocolates to share – get ready to vomit – not just with her team but with the whole sodding room. Ollie would have taken them home to share with Clem. And Ollie is of course feeling too slimy and wrong at this moment to even bring this up with anyone but, actually, he can't resist saying to Megan . . .

'It's so obviously because they added up their fish wrong.'

She rolls her eyes and starts packing away her things.

'I mean, Theology is not known for its maths skills, is it? I mean, don't they think the universe was created four thousand years ago or whatever?'

Here Megan should laugh or make a joke back. She doesn't. She simply says, 'See ya,' in a flat, dead way, and then leaves.

When Ollie turns around, Frank and David have gone too. No one in the room is making eye contact with him. But he was just . . . Of course, someone had to . . . He imagines telling Clem later, and what she might say, but then he realises he won't tell Clem later, that he will never, ever tell anyone he did this.

~

The young couple are beautiful. Like something from an ad for jeans shown after 9 p.m. on Channel 4 or any time on MTV. But the big question is: will they fit into this village? Of course not; the whole idea is fucking ridiculous. But what does Bryony do about it? What can Bryony do about it? Of course, she wants to sell this house because she wants, and sort of needs, the commission. What she does not want is for a house to be under offer to two people who no doubt have no mortgage arranged and are going to end up as the weak link in a chain now probably also containing PEOPLE FROM MARGATE and at least one mobile home parked somewhere in the White Cliffs Holiday Park.

It's 12.15. Bryony has had, so far today, three espressos and two and a half croissants from Allotment, the cute little organic shop that has just opened virtually next to her office. She has the remains of a latte in her car, and the remains of a breath mint in her mouth, and she is due to meet her business partner Emmy, to whom she hasn't properly spoken for *days* despite their offices being next to each other, in the Black Douglas at 12.30, and she should really text her to say she's going to be late, but if these two would just hurry up and realise that this village is full of white *Daily Mail* readers who are over seventy and they would not possibly ever fit in here then she might just . . .

'Oh, babe. A real Aga.'

FFS. Bryony takes out her phone.

For the price of this house, a four-bedroom detached with a paddock and orchard in Worth, this couple could buy a fifteen-bedroomed house complete with ground-floor Chinese restaurant if only they would look in Margate or Ramsgate or Herne Bay. But no. Bryony realises that the girl/woman half of the couple is wearing an actual Barbour and not the version you can get from Dorothy Perkins. This is serious. She texts Emmy.

Bryony met Emmy roughly ten years ago, when she and James were considering putting their house on the market and moving somewhere far away and rural so that James could write a different book from the one he is writing now. Or maybe it was sort of the same one. It was before he got the Natural Dad column, anyway, and before women started giving him That Look in the street and sometimes even writing to him to tell him how perfect he is and offering to take him off Bryony's hands. On more than one occasion he has been asked to send women pictures of his biceps. His biceps! James has no biceps. Well, not real ones. Not like Ollie's. Perhaps James should send women pictures of Ollie's biceps. Or perhaps Ollie should just send . . . OK. One too many espressos. And that dream last night . . .

By the time Bryony gets to the Black Douglas it's gone one. Given that it's Friday, and given all the stress of just having to live through Monday to Thursday with staff appraisals and a broken photocopier, they get a bottle of Sancerre as a special treat. But after two glasses Bryony still looks sort of serious, and a bit . . .

'God, babes, what's up? You look tired.'

Bryony sips her wine. 'Family problems.'

'Really? Not with lovely James?'

'Well . . .'

'But you two are soulmates. I mean . . .'

What utter bollocks. When Emmy is pissed – in fact, she does not even have to be pissed – and within a five-mile radius of James she seeks him out and flirts with him so outrageously that people who have not seen it before tend to sit there open-mouthed – literally – and sometimes even say something. Last time Emmy came round for supper Fleur was there, and Clem and Ollie actually, and even Ollie noticed Emmy nudging James and winking at him and announcing to the table, 'We've got so much in common, me and James,' and, 'I adore poetry. James loves poetry too, don't you, James?' In fact, wasn't that the night . . . ? Yes, that must have been the night when Emmy was in full flow, reminiscing about the time she and James first met, and how romantic it was, and of course it was just because she was really pissed – and yes, OK, she does obviously fancy James, but that's flattering, right? – and so Bryony smiled and opened another two bottles of wine and let it all go until Ollie said, 'Are you just going to let her fuck your husband then or are you going to do something about it?' and then Clem got embarrassed and they left. Is that what happened? Did Bryony maybe dream it? No one tells you that once you pass thirty – or, say, your 3,000th bottle of wine – you begin to forget even important things like what music you had at your wedding and the date of your youngest child's birthday, let alone what happened at a dinner party two years ago. Anyway, Emmy doesn't mean it.

'He just . . . I just . . .' But how do you explain to a single person the intricate tiny fuck-ups in a married life? And how would she even begin on all the stuff with Holly? Like for example when James was pouring his homemade lemonade yesterday – and this is something Holly will actually drink, possibly because it tastes sour and faintly medicinal – he gave Ash almost twice the amount he gave Holly. Why on earth all the men in Holly's life are conspiring to starve her is a bloody mystery in any case, and . . .

'Are you fucking regularly? That's the main thing.'

'Regularly as in once a year?'

Big eyes. Huge eyes. 'Nooooo? You're not serious?'

'No. It's not quite that bad. But . . .'

'Maybe you need new underwear? Trip to Fenwick's?'

'Selfridges, darling.'

This is why people have affairs. Yeah, Bryony could buy new underwear. But if she does it'll be another one or two hundred quid that could have been spent on the children, or put aside for repairing the dishwasher, or put towards the fucking forest fund, which still somehow exists even though Clem, Bryony and Charlie have decided not to sell the house on Jura this year. Why encourage your actual wife to buy new underwear when you could just install her in a forest and then go out and get a whole new person with a whole new wardrobe full of clothes you have never seen before, that you do not resent in any way because none of them were bought at your expense, and none of them cost twice what you get for your column and in any case if they did it would be exciting, not threatening, and . . . But James won't have an affair. He'd be too scared.

'A man goes to the doctor. "Well," says the doctor, looking grave. "I'm afraid this is serious. The best thing you can do for your health is to give up smoking, drinking and fatty food, and to take up some exercise." The man looks concerned. "I hear you, doc," he says. "So what's the second best thing?"

'That one is *almost* funny, Uncle Charlie.'

'You are very hard work sometimes.'

'Are we there yet?'

A plane comes in to land overhead. 'Yep. We must be close.'

'Are we lost?'

'Of course not. I know London like . . .'

'Yes, I know, like the back of your hand.'

'Actually, I've got something else that Oleander said to me when I was feeling guilty once.'

'Go on.'

'OK, so it wasn't long after my mother disappeared, and I'd taken on loads of jobs at Namaste House to make sure that I was indispensable and wouldn't get thrown out. Anyway, one of the things I thought of as my "job" was feeding the birds. Silly really, because I'm not sure Oleander even noticed the birds. But I definitely felt that having a garden full of real birdsong would be extra relaxing for the clients and just, well, beautiful. I wanted to make everything beautiful then.'

'You still do.'

'Mmm. I suppose so. Anyway, at the start I didn't really think about the birds or know anything about them. I was just feeding them for my own reasons. And they did pretty well out of it. So we were all happy. And they sang and sang, and I carried on feeding them, for several years. But then I started forming relationships with individual birds, particularly a robin – he still comes, actually. Anyway, feeding the birds gradually began to feel like an obligation. One week, I suppose a couple of years ago now, I went to London on business – ooh, maybe even to see you! – and didn't feed the birds at all and when I came back I felt so guilty. I didn't see the robin for a couple of days and I was so scared he'd starved to death. I shared these fears with Oleander. This is what she said to me: "How do you know what the birds want?" I looked at her, a bit bemused. I said something about how all animals want to survive and how in the winter the birds need quite a lot of food, and then she just cut in, looked me right in the eyes and said, "How do you know the birds wouldn't rather be dead?"

'That should definitely go in the book.'

Holly is windscreen-wipering the ball with her Wilson Steam 25 racquet. Her opponent, who is called either Alice or Grace, does not know how to windscreen-wiper the ball, which means her shots are weak and flat and pathetic and often kind of slicey in a bad way. Her opponent also stands in no man's land pretty much all the time, which means that all Holly has to do is land the ball at her feet and with all that topspin of course she can't hit it and the whole thing is totally predictable – 15–0 and 30–0 and 40–0 – and actually also really embarrassing, and on the first day here, when Holly didn't let her opponent get at least one game, the other girls at the David Lloyd Tennis Centre called her a lesbian and a fucktard and didn't tell her you needed to change out of your tennis clothes for dinner, which meant she was the only spaz at dinner still in her whites.

Holly windscreen-wipers the ball really hard into the net on purpose.

Forty–fifteen. She serves and the other girl stumbles. It's an unintentional ace.

Holly runs up and touches the net before taking her place back on the baseline to receive serve. This is a way of burning around two more calories every point, which is quite a lot over the course of a match, especially if you intentionally do not win all the points. Another thing is to do squats. Three if you win a point and four if you lose it. In any match, the coach told them today, more points are lost than are won. It's just a fact. This is one of the profoundest things Holly has ever heard.

The David Lloyd Tennis Centre smells of the rubber inside tennis balls. It is full of echoey, squeaky sounds, like tennis shoes changing direction on the acrylic courts: rubber against rubber. One of Holly's teachers at school is known for giving a punishment that requires pupils to write about the inside of a tennis ball (it may have been a ping-pong ball, but whatever), as if that was the most boring thing in the world. But the week Holly has already spent here, and the week to come, are basically that: being trapped inside a tennis ball. And obviously it is brilliant, and it costs LOADS, and Uncle Charlie was very generous to give it to Holly as her birthday present. You get to play tennis for about eight hours EVERY DAY. And the coaches teach strategy as well as just hitting. For example you can move someone back behind the baseline and then drop-shot them. You can actually choose to do that, and not just do it by accident. And you also have to wait for the short ball before going to the net. And play the percentages, although Holly still isn't quite sure what that means. And you can serve and volley, except apparently you also have to be a complete lesbian to do something as bold and aggressive as that.

In the breaks between sessions all the kids are allowed to go to the bar and order snacks and drinks. Charlie has given Holly ten pounds for each day, which is generous. The other kids all get Cokes, which cost £1.89, and are full of sugar, caffeine and empty calories. For lunch they all get huge baguettes with crisps and a chocolate bar. Holly gets a glass of skimmed milk for only 79p. And she never buys crisps, which, as well as being expensive, are basically bits of old potato dunked in boiling hair grease, but instead gets two apples: one for her snack and one for her lunch. If she wins every single match she plays in the little championships they have each day then she allows herself a Freddo bar, which is a whopping ninety-five calories but OK as a reward every so often. Sometimes Holly throws a game on purpose so that she doesn't have to eat the Freddo bar. There's something about Freddo bars that means that if you do have to eat one, you should do it as quickly as possible.

So far Holly has saved over fifty pounds! Uncle Charlie has told her that he will double whatever she can save from her daily ten pounds and then she can spend it on something nice from the David Lloyd Tennis Shop, which is the kind of place kids are not really allowed in on their own, and which also smells of rubber, but in an expensive, frightening kind of way. Holly has no idea what she will buy in there, but imagine, just imagine, having around £200 to spend on anything . . . Probably another new racquet. Having two racquets means that if you play in a tournament and one of your strings breaks, you just get out your spare racquet rather than forfeiting the match.

But you should not use a crappy old racquet for this: all your racquets should be amazing. Perhaps Holly's second new racquet will be a Babolat, which is what the Angel plays with. If Holly could never eat again in order to save the money to be twenty per cent of what the Angel is then she would. She would do anything.

The Angel is actually called Melissa, but that is the wrong name for her really. She is too perfect to have a human name. She is quite old, maybe seventeen, and is the best tennis player Holly has ever, ever seen. She turns up for her coaching sessions in very short shorts, which are strangely silky looking, like footballers' shorts, and an old pink sweatshirt over a tight white T-shirt that shows she has basically no fat. But it's not even that. She is very strong and when she hits the ball she seems to be flying through the air like a warrior from one of Uncle Charlie's martial arts films. Not that Holly likes those films. They are very, very lame and boring and unrealistic. But when Melissa flies through the air, that's different. Melissa is the captain of the U18 Middlesex county tennis team. Middlesex is where the David Lloyd Tennis Centre is, even though it's really in London. Holly knows she would pass out if Melissa ever said anything to her. Melissa is going to play at Wimbledon next year.

When Holly defeats what turns out to be Alice, not Grace, one of the coaches says something to one of the other coaches and looks at her and sort of nods. There are three games going on simultaneously, and on the far court Melissa is flying through the air and making only a little grunt – nothing like the ghostly wail of some current tennis stars. Melissa's grunt sounds like an angel sighing. She's hammering the male coach she's playing: really annihilating him. What is it about seeing a thin girlish girl with long blonde hair like in a fairy tale hitting the ball like that? And beating a man? It's so, so deeply ace. Holly loves beating Uncle Charlie, but she also loves beating the boys here, which is really, really easy. But the girls are so . . .

'Watch out,' says fat Stephanie, walking into Holly and shoving her.

A ball hits the back of Holly's knee from where someone has thrown it 'at the basket' which is about three metres away. Yesterday Holly didn't just drop a game to Stephanie, she actually gave her the match. It was quite an odd feeling, like being God or something – not in a weird spazzy way – but Holly knew exactly where Stephanie was going to hit the ball every single time she hit it. For most of the points Holly just kept getting the ball back, but that was a risky strategy because Stephanie would make a mistake fairly quickly usually, going for the winner when she should be just hitting middle and deep. On the other hand, long rallies mean more calories burned. And if you give your opponent the chance to run you around the court, then . . . but Stephanie is not very good at running people around the court. She certainly doesn't like running herself. There is nothing she can do, no shot she can play, that Holly can't retrieve. When Holly wants to lose a point her favourite method is hitting it in the net because at least that's controllable. And sometimes she does what Uncle Charlie would call taking the piss. She will get 40–0 up in a service game by playing normally, and then serve the most outrageous double faults for the next two points and hit it into the net for deuce.

Occasionally, though, when she tries to serve a fault, she actually serves an ace, which is really, really weird but might have something to do with the *Inner Game of Tennis*, which is a book that Fleur got Holly for her birthday and says that instead of telling your body to do things you should let it do what it wants because it knows how to play the right shot and if you keep telling it what to do you are only interfering.

The big question now is what to do about the next match with Stephanie. Holly would like to beat Stephanie this time, especially as losing to her does not seem to have stopped her bumping into her and saying horrible things to her at lunchtime and in the drinks breaks. Yesterday there was this long conversation about deodorant that Holly didn't understand but seemed to be aimed at her. On the other hand it would be nice not to have to have a Freddo bar. The idea of a Freddo bar seems quite exhausting at this moment. The Good Holly who lives in Holly's mind frowns at her for a moment, shakes her head, and then turns her back and goes to sit down for a nice roast dinner with a blurry family that may or may not be Holly's real family. Anyway, the Holly that exists in the world is different from her. What if she ate two Freddos? Which is ridiculous, when she doesn't even want one! Or *five*? Where is this coming from? Who, apart from a real fatso like Stephanie, would eat five Freddos?

'Actually, Holly . . . Holly?'

The nicest coach, Dave, who is a Geordie, is talking to her.

'Yes, you, flower,' he says. 'Can you get over to court 4?'

Court 4 is where Melissa is playing. How can she possibly . . . ?

'And hit with Melissa for a bit?'

'Sorry?'

'Hurry up! Don't keep her waiting.'

'OK.'

Over on court 4, Melissa is drinking something from a silver bottle. She raises an eyebrow at Holly and then sort of half smiles before getting up, only slightly tightening her by now very loose, long blonde ponytail. On court, she nods at Holly to feed the ball in. Of course Holly hits it straight into the net – and not even on purpose. Maybe she is doomed from all those other times. 'Sorry,' she says. But after that the hitting is great. Melissa windscreen-wipers the ball much more than Holly does and her balls fly over the net like spinning meteorites in a slightly stronger gravitational zone than Earth's. Holly is fast. She can get to Melissa's wider balls, but only just. Every so often, when Holly hits short and weak, Melissa kills the ball breathtakingly hard, just like she probably does in real matches, and then grins at Holly. But most of the time she just hits it back hard but straight, and the two of them dance a faraway waltz with one another, and with the ball, sidestepping, pointing and windscreen-wipering, and soon Holly finds she is making a little grunt just like Melissa's and hitting the ball harder and deeper than she thought she could. And it's as if the ball will never go out, will never fade, become bald or die . . .

Afterwards, Melissa offers Holly a sip of her drink. It's sweet and herby.

'Don't ever say sorry again,' Melissa says. And then she leaves.

Dave comes over. 'That was more like it,' he says.

'Thanks.'

'So what's the problem when you play Stephanie?'

Holly shrugs.

'I mean, why are you throwing the . . .'

'I'm *not*.'

'You won't do that when you're in the county squad, will you?'

'I, uh . . .'

'Twelve, aren't you? So you'll be in the 13Us.'

'The *county* squad?'

'Yep. Do you live far away? We'll need you here on three week-nights, sometimes four. And get you an address here so you can play for us. We've got another girl doing that, so don't worry. Anushka. You'll like her.'

'I live in Kent.'

He frowns. 'Kent. Could be worse. OK, I'll call your mum.'

'Oh my God! Thank you. Thank you. I'll train all the time . . . I'll . . .'

More sit-ups. No more Freddo bars. Only green vegetables. Maybe a touch more protein. Lots of squats and lunges. Resistance-band work.

'I don't want to ever see you throw a point again. No matter who is bullying you or what they are saying. Kill them on the court. Don't be anyone's bitch.'

'I, er . . .'

'I totally shouldn't have said that. Anyway, if I see you throw a point again you'll be out of the squad. Got it?'

'Yes.' Holly frowns. 'What if it's by accident?'

'You can lose a point, flower. You just can't do it on purpose.'

It isn't then that Holly passes out, as she thought she might do when Melissa spoke to her. It isn't after her hot shower that evening, although she does feel a little faint then. It's not at dinner, because she doesn't go, and no one makes her, and it's not when the pizza she has ordered through the hotel does not come. Holly goes to sleep empty but happy. Happier than she has ever, ever been. It's at breakfast the next morning when she hits the deck, right at Stephanie's feet. And she doesn't wake up for a whole day, and when she does come round, there are Uncle Charlie and her mum and her dad standing by her hospital bed and they all seem to be cross with one another.

Reasons for giving up smoking:

Live longer
Better breath, especially in a.m.
SWIMMING – lap times will improve
Annoying cough will finally go
Will not have to be slave to something
Not have to worry about cancer any more
Not have to stand outside in the rain
End embarrassment at work – must not be caught by D again
Smell in office/on clothes/in car will go
Will not have Del Boy feeling on holiday
Can attend long meetings w/o cravings
Also not get stressed in cinema, theatre, flights etc.
No more staining on fingers

Will be able to speak more clearly, and project voice more in lectures
Will save money
Will be more attractive to C?

'You think that lettuce just sits there innocently on the ground hugging itself with its soft billowy leaves and dreaming of nothing more ambitious than being part of a salad or a mildly soporific soup? All lettuce wants is sex. And violence. Just like all plants. It wants to reproduce, and it wants to kill or damage its rivals so they don't reproduce. Of course you're welcome to think that lettuce does not "want", that lettuce does not desire. But if you watch it, and other plants, sped up I am pretty sure you will change your mind. The walking palm seems so dignified, struggling along, alone, right? But if there was another, weaker plant in its path it would not go around it. It would trample it. It would mow it down.'

'Really? This is what the film will show?'

'Yes.'

'All you need is a new time-lapse camera?'

'Yep.'

Let's say that in one lifetime you have a difficult relationship with your mother. Like, *really* difficult. Not one of the many lifetimes where she does not quite understand you, or makes the odd mean comment about how you never became a doctor or a lawyer, or does not buy you a pony. This is one of those lifetimes where she sleeps with your new husband while you are in the pool, or sells you to a man with a turquoise turban who calls at the house looking for beautiful young girls, or lets her husband rape you every Saturday night after *X Factor* is over. How would you forgive a mother like that? It would be impossible, right? And how would she ever get over the guilt? You might not think that bad people feel guilt, but they do. And of course in the next lifetime she is the little girl and you are the rapist, however much you try not to be. And in that lifetime perhaps you come to think life is cheaper than you do now. Life is less fair, more brutal. Perhaps you drink? Of course you drink. All you want to do is go back to that beautiful black hole from which you sense you came. All you want is the bliss of oblivion. You'll do everything you can to get that oblivion back, and your eyes will glaze over and your soul will harden like the branches of a shrub cut back for winter and you simply won't see the wounds you inflict on others, even when they bleed onto the floor in front of you.

And then there will be those lifetimes when you do not have a strong connection with this soul at all. Lifetimes where you are a relatively happy graphic designer and she is the one hygienist at your dentist who you never much like visiting. Or perhaps you are a journo on a junket and she is an airport waitress. Maybe you only meet each other once in this lifetime, in a lift, and no, it does not break down, and no, you do not reveal your great secrets to one another while waiting for the engineer. In this lifetime you have no significant relationship at all, but often when you do see one another your feelings, actually based on lifetimes of betrayal and disgust and sometimes deep love, but in the sensory world based on no more than instinct, or feelings of 'instant dislike', seem so far out of proportion that you really wonder whether you might be losing your mind.

'And why exactly was my daughter playing with a seventeen-year-old county player? She's twelve years old, for God's sake. What were you trying to do to her?'

'Mrs Croft, it was just that she was throwing games against kids her own age. We wanted to see what she could do if she . . .'

'Throwing games? Maybe she was just losing.'

'We know what throwing a game looks like, Mrs Croft. And anyway, she . . .'

'But you obviously don't know what a serious eating disorder looks like.'

'A lot of the kids we see are very lean. They do a lot of sports. If you were concerned, then why did you even send her . . . ?'

All right. Advantage whatever-his-name-is. It's true. Who does send their anorexic – Bryony can hardly think the word: it's new, like the word alcoholic, and seems so horribly final – daughter to stay in a downmarket Hounslow hotel for TWO WEEKS on her own with nothing to do apart from play tennis all day? Oh yes, and promising to double whatever food money she saved? Good one, Uncle Charlie. What a fucking twat. What a total, total . . .

'Anyway, how is Holly?'

'She's home now. Back at school. Seeing a counsellor . . .'

'Because we'd still really like to have her in the squad.'

'No,' Bryony says. 'Sorry. You've already almost killed her once.'

'But what does Holly think?'

'Holly thinks she wants to finish school and go to university like a normal person and not throw her childhood away on something as meaningless as . . .'

'Mrs Croft, I really can't stress enough just how talented your daughter is.'

For a moment Bryony hesitates. A tennis match starts playing in her head. A huge, muscular black woman is playing a smaller, sleeker blonde. One of them has some sort of knee brace, like something Bryony saw in the gym earlier, and she is limping between points a little. The camera pans to each of the competitor's families. They look wracked with tension. Eventually one player wins; let's say it's the black woman. The blonde woman cries. Her family look distraught and disappointed. Maybe next time the black woman loses, and she cries, and now her family look distraught and disappointed. Bryony instantly knows two things. First, she is not prepared to give up her life to tennis, even if her daughter thinks she is. She is not going to be in that distraught and disappointed family. And second, what is the point of training for hours every day to be one of the best in the world at something, and then finally to get there, and then to be beaten by another one of the best in the world at whatever it is and then CRY? Even if you become the very best in the world for a while and win everything, it never lasts. And then what do you do? Marry another has-been tennis star and do cereal commercials?

Doctors, lawyers, bankers, vets . . . They are all quite clearly happier than tennis players. You don't go to hospital and find your surgeon CRYING because another surgeon just did a marginally better operation, do you? You don't go to the bank to find all the tellers in tears because Aimee in business banking can count 100 ten-pound notes faster than anyone else. And when someone in normal life does something well in their job, for example a teacher correcting a child's spelling, they don't have to get up and do a stupid dance afterwards or start fist pumping and shouting 'Come on!' There is absolutely no point in sport: Bryony has discovered that in the gym. Not that the people there play sports exactly, but that dead look that comes over them when . . .

'I know that families have pressure, Mrs Croft, but . . .'

'I'm sorry. My decision is final.'

'Well, tell Holly that if she changes her mind, I'll be here ready to coach her. For free.'

'Have you had your lover round?'

'Hmm?'

'I said, *Have you had your lover round?*'

'What do you mean?'

'There're two plates in the dishwasher. You're not very subtle.'

Clem rolls lazily from one side of the sofa to the other.

'Oh.' She laughs.

'You think it's funny?'

'I was trying one of Zoe's macrobiotic brown rice recipes but I put the rice on the plate before I weighed it, so I had to take it off, weigh it, and then obviously I didn't want to put it back on a dirty plate so I got a new one.'

'And two wine glasses?'

'The first one got a bit seaweedy.'

'How can a glass get seaweedy?'

'Well . . .'

'And how do you explain the two forks?'

'I used chopsticks.'

'Aha! And washed them by hand and dried them and put them away to fool me. And then left two forks in the dishwasher to fool me even more.'

'But it seems you are not so easily fooled.'

'And what did you eat with the rice? Hang on.' There are sounds of Ollie opening the bin and looking inside it. 'Tofu. You really are disgusting. You and your lover eating a whole packet of tofu.'

'There's actually half a packet left in the fridge. I thought I'd make sushi tomorrow. Will you get an avocado in the morning?'

'So where did you conceal the other packet? Or does he not eat much?'

Clem rolls her eyes. 'My lover doesn't eat that much. Yes, you're a genius.'

'So you admit it! Ha!'

'It looks like I'm going to have to in the end.'

'Is he really big?'

'Yes. Oh, what, you mean his dick? Yes, he has a really big dick.'

'Bigger than mine?'

'Anyone's dick is bigger than yours.'

This month the stupid challenge in the gym is to see if you can cycle, run, row, cross-train (which is what form of transport exactly?) your way to popular holiday destinations like Margate (17 miles), Calais (37 miles), Amsterdam (175 miles), Paris (237 miles), Blackpool (326 miles), Bilbao (804 miles) Torremolinos (1,356 miles) and, finally, Faliraki (2,309 miles). Then there is a chart to help you convert kilometres, which are used by every machine in the gym, to the miles recorded on the chart. Why did they not just put kilometres on the chart? Anyway, all the usual people have started putting their stats up. Some twat called MIKEY, who rowed his way through a deluge of Easter eggs, has already made it to Bilbao after only THREE DAYS. Is that even possible? Bryony imagines going to Margate, and then having to get from Margate to Calais, and then to Amsterdam, then back to Paris before having to find your way to Blackpool. It would be fucking dreadful. Bryony thinks how much nicer it would be to go to Bath, Edinburgh, Nice, Florence, the Maldives, Kerala . . .

'Sorry to keep you waiting,' says Rich, the fitness consultant.

They go into his little office. There are the scales of doom, that told Bryony how morbidly obese she was last time she was here. And that she was forty-four per cent fat.

'So how's it going?'

'I still hate exercise.'

'OK.'

'I suppose I don't mind cycling. I went up to Level 7 the other day. And I've made a playlist like you suggested. Oh, and I've started doing occasional sprints, which I suppose are quite sort of euphoric, and . . .'

'Well, that's all positive. Let's have a look at your stats.'

Bryony takes off her trainers and socks, and gets on the scales. She has lost a kilogram, despite all the lapses. And she is now thirty-nine per cent fat, which is still a lot, but SHE IS OUT OF THE FORTIES! However, Rich looks concerned.

'I suppose you've put on a bit of muscle,' he says. 'But . . . Well, I would have expected a more impressive result by now.'

How is this not impressive? SHE IS IN THE THIRTIES!

'How have you been getting on with the diet?'

'I've stuck to the calories. Fifteen hundred a day.' Give or take the odd egg or handful of nuts here and there. Oh, and croissants on trains, because what you eat on trains doesn't count. And all the nibbly things she has when she is drunk. And lunches with Emmy at the Black Douglas. And all the bits of James's cakes that she doesn't really eat, but sort of really does. And all the times that she stops looking at the kitchen scales because she doesn't want to know what they actually say, especially when weighing butter. Oh, and that time the battery was running out and would not go beyond five grams however much stuff you put on it. Bryony had a lot of five-gram portions of things that week.

Rich frowns. 'I think you've gone into starvation mode.'

'What's that?'

'Your body thinks it's starving and so hangs on to fat.'

'But I've actually *lost* . . .'

'You need to take your calories up a bit.'

'Right.'

'Eighteen hundred a day.'

'Eighteen hundred?'

'Yep. You getting enough carbs?'

'Ah. Well, actually, that's one thing I have changed. I've gone, well, a bit, because of my cousin who . . . Well, basically sort of primal.'

'What's that?'

'Like a low-carb diet, but with . . .'

'Don't do that. Your body needs carbs.'

'But that's not what . . .'

'People give up carbs on these extreme programmes, but they don't realise that for a balanced diet you need them. Without carbs all you lose is water.'

'But what about all the fat that the scales . . .'

'Go and get yourself some wholewheat bread. And some pasta. Are you losing energy in workouts?'

How can anyone do a workout without losing energy? Bryony can now do eight minutes on the rowing machine on Level 6, and can go up to 8.5kmph on the treadmill at an incline of 1.5 for a total of five minutes. But she does feel a bit knackered afterwards.

'I suppose so,' she says.

'You've hit the wall. No glycogen in your muscles.'

'Right.'

'You need pasta.'

Everything Bryony has read in the last three months would suggest that she does not need pasta, that pasta is the very last thing she needs. But Rich's voice is drowning it all out. *Your body needs carbs. Your body needs carbs*. When she leaves the gym she goes straight to Sainsbury's and buys a French stick, a large bar of milk chocolate and a jar of strawberry jam. And also a packet of six large jam doughnuts. And a family bag of sea salt and balsamic vinegar crisps. Oh, and a loaf of wholewheat bread and some wholewheat pasta.

Gym Playlist

If You Let Me Stay – Terence Trent D'Arby

Sweet Little Mystery – Wet Wet Wet

I Luv You Baby – The Original

We Got A Love Thang – CeCe Peniston
Out Of The Blue (Into The Fire) – The The
Angels Of Deception – The The
This Is The Day – The The
Yes – McAlmont & Butler
Your Woman – White Town
Bonnie And Clyde – Serge Gainsbourg and Brigitte Bardot
On Your Own – Blur
Give It Up – KC and the Sunshine Band
Time To Pretend – MGMT

~

They finish the Everyman crossword in about an hour. Skye Turner had never done a cryptic crossword before coming to stay with Beatrix, but it turns out she has an uncanny ability to see anagrams in her head. And to get those amazing clues like *Of of of of of of of of of of (10)*, which of course is 'oftentimes', a word that Skye Turner is somehow aware of, despite never having used it. Perhaps she has read it somewhere, in some old-fashioned schoolbook. Now she is scanning the *Radio Times* to try to find something for their evening viewing.

'*Downton Abbey*'s on. New series. Do you like that?'

'Vulgar,' says Beatrix. 'Too much about the servants.'

'I've never seen it.'

'It's far too twee for you, dear.'

Skye Turner keeps scanning. What's that thing that Tash and Karl are obsessed with? It seems to involve a group of mild-looking people trapped in a tent with a lot of carbs. Skye has tried not to watch it, partly because it's for old people. Beatrix is an old person. But then again . . .

'I think I might like to look at *Game of Thrones*,' says Beatrix.

'Isn't that all blood and guts and swords and stuff?'

'Have you seen it?'

'No.'

'I read about it in *Vogue*.'

'OK . . . I can't find it though. Is it definitely on?'

'I think I managed to video the series.'

Beatrix does not 'Sky+' things, and would never involve Sky, a company with whom she has an uneasy relationship due to its share price falling from 850p to 692p virtually overnight just last month, in any kind of verb formation. Even though she insists on calling what it does 'videoing', she is pretty nifty with Sky+. When Skye looks, she finds, as well as *Game of Thrones*, several nature programmes, a documentary about perfume, and four episodes of *Midsomer Murders*.

'And I'll have a cup of tea and a date. But only if you'll join me.'

'Pranayama', Fleur says to the tennis player.

'You what?'

'It doesn't matter what it's called. It's just different ways of breathing.'

Ever since she came back from the Isle of Lewis Fleur has had the ability to see what people need; well, more than usual anyway. She knows that Georgina from the Tuesday morning Rise and Shine class needs to drink more water. She knows that Martin, the only man in the Wednesday afternoon group, needs to stop online gambling. In some odd way that she can't explain she also knows that she can't change what will happen to them. But the tennis player has come to her and asked for help, which is different. If Martin asked her for help what would she say? Probably the same thing. Breathe. Sit still, and breathe. It really is the only way. But Fleur somehow also knows that Martin will give up online gambling after his wife dies, and that he has needed to go through this experience in this lifetime, that although it has been incredibly, horribly shit, in some ways it has helped him grow, and he sort of – whisper this bit if you like – kind of *chose* it.

'It doesn't matter where you sit, as long as your spine is relatively straight.'

'Well, you've seen me try to sit cross-legged. That was a fucking joke . . .'

'Can you kneel?'

'What about a chair?'

'No. Let's try you in the Hero pose. *Vajrasana*.'

'I certainly ain't no hero.'

'Yes. Well. We'll see about that.'

❧

'It's certainly no fucking wonder she is so obsessed with food.'

'What is that supposed to mean?'

'You obviously have an eating disorder. Kids pick these things up.'

Eyebrows. 'What, from a second cousin, once . . .'

'You know what I mean.'

'Anyway, *I* have an eating disorder? That's rich. I have nine per cent body fat.'

'You know what percentage of your body is fat! I repeat: *you have an eating disorder*.'

'My blood pressure is a hundred over sixty . . .'

'For God's sake.'

'I am about as healthy as it gets.'

'Physically, maybe . . .'

'What is that supposed to . . .'

Bryony sighs. 'Come on, surely there is more to life than . . .'

'Anyway, you know your body fat percentage too. What was it? Forty . . .'

'It's thirty-six and a half now, actually.'

'Why does me knowing my body fat percentage mean that I have an eating disorder, and you knowing yours mean you don't?'

'Because you don't need to know yours! You've basically got a perfect body.'

'Maybe Holly wants that too. What is so wrong with . . .'

'SHE ALMOST DIED.'

Charlie is quiet for a few seconds.

'Maybe we've all got some level of eating disorder.'

'Maybe we have. But the point is that Holly isn't following *my* example.'

'Thank God.'

'This isn't going to get us anywhere.'

Bryony goes to the fridge. 'Let's sit down with a glass of wine and talk about this properly.'

'Look, Bry, there's not much to talk about. Basically if you don't tell her, I will.'

'It's not the right time.'

'It is the right time.'

'But James . . .'

'What about James?' says James, coming in.

Think of a substance you'd like to give up. Perhaps it's a drug. If it's a drug, it's likely to be a plant. Perhaps it's a food plant that acts like a drug? Decide on your substance now, and visualise it in its processed form, or in the form you take it. Think of all the other people who indulge in this substance. See them walking around. Now imagine the plant (or plants) from which this substance is made. See them growing. What do they look like? What nourishes them? Are they attractive or not? Now think again of all the people who also take this substance.

How many of them do you think would like to give it up? Imagine yourself walking among them, the only one who has broken free of the substance. How do you feel?

'Mummy?'

'Yes, Holly.'

'Mummy? When can I play tennis again?'

'When you're better.'

'And when will I be better?'

'When you weigh at least six stone.'

'BUT, MUMMY.'

'I'm not arguing about this, Holly.'

'Has Dave rung you yet?'

'No. You must have made a mistake.'

'I did not make a mistake!'

'In any case, you don't want to play county tennis. It would completely take over your life. You know, some of those Olympic gymnasts from Russia lost their whole childhoods, and . . .'

'BUT, MUMMY, ALL I WANT TO DO IS PLAY TENNIS.'

'You don't need to shout.'

'It is LITERALLY the only thing I enjoy doing.'

'You enjoy reading.'

'Compared with tennis I hate reading.'

'Well, what about watching films on the laptop?'

'I only like watching tennis matches on YouTube on the laptop.'

'Well, I just don't think tennis has been very healthy for you so far.'

'This is so, so unfair.'

Things Charlie does before running:

Takes 2 Nurofen

Takes 2 Devil's Claw tablets

Takes 3 magnesium tablets

Massages calves gently with Pro-Tech massage stick

Eats one dried apricot

Eats half a tablespoon of honey

Does calf raises

Performs myofascial release on calves with old tennis ball

Applies arnica gel to lower back, knees, shins, calves and Achilles tendons

Puts on compression socks

Performs myofascial release on lower back with spiky massage ball

Puts on Vibrams

Runs on the spot for two minutes

Stretches hamstrings

Stretches quads

Performs myofascial release on quads and ITB with Pro-tech massage stick

Eats one more dried apricot

Stretches calves

Uses foam roller on calves, hamstrings, quads, lower back

Applies Biofreeze gel to lower back, knees and quads

When Fleur and Skye sit together now it is just pure sitting. Skye has the blue cushion and Fleur has the red cushion, although sometimes it's the other way around. And they wear anything. Not the kind of 'anything' that takes thought, preparation, a glance in the mirror. This is not about doing ballet with tights ripped just so and your hair brushed to look unbrushed with nude lipstick and brown mascara. In fact, Fleur and Skye do brush their hair for these sessions. They brush it and neatly tuck it behind their ears. They don't wear make-up: it feels sticky and wrong. But if they did it wouldn't matter either. Today Fleur is wearing pink socks, blue jeggings and a yellow T-shirt with a red heart on it. Skye is wearing denim-effect hot pants with Nike pool sliders and a T-shirt someone left at Namaste House that has hot-rock holes and says 'Rap for Jesus'. Fleur has just finished teaching her Body and Soul yoga class which this week contained ninety per cent arthritic old ladies from Sandwich and ten per cent famous tennis player, and all the old ladies laughed because he still could not cross his legs AT ALL and was even less flexible than them and could not do a headstand because he was too scared. Nice muscles though, they all agreed. Great shoulders. Terrible feet though, with no toenails at all on his left foot, and all that tape . . .

When you can fly, there is something even more amazing about sitting still. When you can fly alone, then sitting with someone else becomes a strange kind of privilege, although this whole thing is becoming harder and harder to describe. They don't always use the meditation room but they do sometimes. Sometimes they do it in water, in the warm spa pool, just standing there looking into each other's eyes. It doesn't matter. Nothing matters. Nothing is matter . . . Skye thinks about when she was first with Greg and they used to sleep tucked up against one another and she deliberately did not breathe when he breathed because she did not want him to think she was copying him, trying to be him. She did not want to be like those cheesy couples who do everything together, have his 'n' hers stuff and beans on toast every Tuesday night. She also did not want to fall into a pattern that he could break. If she let her breathing fall in with his then it was an implicit admission that he was powerful, he was in charge. If her breathing fell in with his and then he changed it then that would be a rejection for sure. So night after night she lay there waiting for his breathing to meet hers and it never did.

And now this.

Fleur and Skye breathe together. They hold hands, create a circuit. They could die now and everything would still be perfect.

They breathe in and breathe out.

The man is, as always, incompt and untrig. He sloggers around his rooms in his black and grey ragtails like an elderly magpie with those bleep bleep noises going all around him, a choir of dying things. The bleep bleep noises sometimes enter the robin's licham and make him abubble and a little gunpowdered. When this happens the robin bobs up and down and sometimes the man then speaks to him. He says things like 'All right, little red breast? Right little raver, aren't you?' and laughs as the robin flies through the window and into his dark rooms. Everywhere in these rooms are thin pieces of deadtree sewn together with lengths of cotton, and the pieces of deadtree have symbols on them, written in the dark liquid made from deadthings. Mostoftentimes the deadtree symbols stay the same but in one deadtreething they change and the man had this deadtreething and then he lost it and it made him all agloom. The bleep bleep noises come from circles made from sap that the man revolves in a box on a table. While he does this, the robin flies into the back room and takes the halfpod that the man has left for him. 'Cheeky little thing,' the man will say, smiling. And the robin will fly back to the leafmoss-hair of his last female's nest and open the pod and . . .

After the pod the robin's flight is swipping and meteorous and he does not need to visit the bird table at all. He is wick! He is fire-swift! He can also sit in stilth and ro for longtimes and mull, and for a time he forgets about the sparrowhawks and pussycats and the long grey squirrel. In his merrow head he hears whirleries of human poetry and other meaningthings from far, far away. But often the meaningthings are too many and the robin must sing ahigh to remove them. After the podseeds the robin hears and knows all ancient songs ever sung, including the cosmic song. The man has been searching for the cosmic song all his life, he told the robin once, and the robin bobbed and nodded and bobbed. Is it true, the man asked the robin, that in this dimension songs sound different but in the dimension above they are all the same? Is that why songs are so similar when you think about it, and why we only have twelve musical notes? During conversations like this the robin always simply bobs and nods.

After he sings the cosmic song the robin tarries quietfully around the grounds of Namaste House – the large red-brick structure with its big doors and windows next to the smaller, cosier cottage with gardens full of roses and papavers – and sees all the things he has ever seen, and all the things all his ancestors have ever seen, at the same nonce, togethers. There is the first one of Fleur's sort, with her long black hair, all cold here after the heat of India. Men with cottonthings and woolthings on their heads. A big argument between the elderlings and then the great one, Oleander, whose name he does know, as he knows Fleur's, making of the big house a vast nest full of songs and smoke and colourful souls with great scurries of feeling. He also knows the name Briar Rose, not just Fleur's mother but, the man says, mother of the podseeds. Ah, Briar Rose. With her bright feathers and her big, soft nest. The robin sees her mapreading and planmaking with other familiar people, now gone, but of whom the incompt man often speaks: Quinn and Plum, the great explorers from the nearby village of Ash, Grace, the botanical artist and Augustus, her botanist husband, he who was longtimes in Briar Rose's nest and made the egg that became Fleur. And the incompt man longed for Briar Rose's nest too, as did all redblood living beings, according to the incompt man.

After eating the podseeds the robin singsandsings, and thinksgreatthoughts and balladsmuch long after darkness comes. He stops to sleep and wakes only when the redbreast man comes on his bicycle with thin deadtreethings and stringthings. Sometimes the incompt man is there to greet him and he takes away podseeds hidden in drearihead murk-coloured cubes of pulplayers. He takes them away! However much the robin sings his great songs of sadness and killing and deep black danger, the redbreast man still takes them away, far away, where they are turned into puffs so ferly and ghastful that no one can ever sing of them, where not only the bodies but the very souls of their victim are rived and betorn forever.

'I think I'd like to buy ITV. They were nice to me when I went on *X Factor*.'

'Very well, dear. We'll just have a look at Level 2 first.'

'Level 2?'

For the last week or so Skye has been learning about how to buy and sell shares, mainly because Beatrix seems so much to enjoy teaching her. She has her own trading account now, and her own monitor, which is the best reason yet for keeping her iPad charged up. Now, instead of endless fan mail and weird shit from Greg and the *Mail on Sunday*, she looks at a screen of red, blue and black with the odd splash of green. When there is activity on a share it highlights yellow, and then red or blue depending on whether the price has fallen or risen, whether it is being bought or sold. Since Skye has had her ADVFN monitor she has felt a good deal less alone in the world because every tiny flicker is, well, the flicker of a person, an action, a desire, a movement . . . Even at night when the LSE is sleeping, she can watch shares ticking over on the NYSE or in Hong Kong or Tokyo. Money never stops moving. People never stop moving it. It's like watching ants carrying corpses and bits of cake around in a tiny garden. But in a good way, because something about seeing those colours moving on that screen makes Skye feel alive in a way she can't quite . . .

'Level 2 is where you can see the order book for a share,' says Beatrix.

'The *order book*?'

'Yes.'

'There is something called an order book for shares?' Skye Turner sees something huge and leather-bound on the desk of a serious-looking God somewhere beyond the clouds. And a scribe is writing in it with the most exquisite . . .

'Yes, dear. Of course. Otherwise how would they know who to give them to? If you can see the order book, then instead of simply seeing the spread you can see all the orders in the market. I went to a very informative seminar about it. It is rather complex. But if you put it on histogram mode you can see all the orders standing up straight in rows, almost marching towards each other, rather like soldiers on a battlefield, and I find it useful to imagine each order bringing down soldiers on one side or the other. Bang, bang, and then . . .'

Skye knows what the 'spread' is. It is the difference between the highest buying price and the lowest selling price on a share. But she thought men in pinstriped suits made up these spreads in their heads. She didn't realise . . .

'Look,' says Beatrix. She opens a new window on the screen of her vast iMac. A box appears. Beatrix types 'LSE:ITV' into it, and suddenly there is a new kind of cascade of numbers. At first it is completely incomprehensible. But you can sort of work it out. There on the left-hand side of the box are all the orders to buy. ITV is cheap at the moment. It has fallen to just under 53p a share. Skye can see seller after seller on the left-hand side of the screen, wanting to offload their shares for 52.9p or 53p each. But the much shorter list of buyers will only pay a maximum of 51.9p for the share so the screen freezes until something changes, and then a cascade of orders are suddenly tumbling over themselves to be filled, and in histogram mode it does kind of look as if the soldiers are flipping over and dying, and the spread drops a halfpence and then a penny and then Sky Turner buys her first shares. Five thousand shares for £2,582.50. At the end of 2013 they will be worth four times that much, but of course by then everything will be different, and anyway, who needs money when they can . . .

'What do I do now?' asks Skye.

'Just wait, dear. Or buy another share. You can watch the Level 2 screen for a bit longer, or look at another share on it. I find it quite soothing to watch shares I don't own, and to watch all the colours change and, well . . .'

Beatrix doesn't have to finish. She and Skye have both sensed that they feel exactly the same way about monitors. Skye looks for LSE: EZY. She has had a soft spot for easyJet since her very first holiday with them. The share price is 307.7p. She watches the flickering of the Level 2 screen for several minutes, imagining planes taking off and landing, and people sitting there in their silly holiday hats and big sunglasses, before she notices something strange is happening.

Skye realises that she is seeing – really seeing – Paul, a retired airline pilot in Manchester, with his copy of *The Naked Trader* and his slice of toast, having set himself up with a DMA account, which means he can put orders directly into the book without going through a broker. She sees him quite clearly sitting there, on a bright red knee chair to help with his sciatica. And then, as soon as his order is met, he is gone. And then she senses a man at a desk in a big open-plan office with empty food cartons everywhere and a strange smell of goats. He stays a little while, sitting on a lowish stop loss, using most of the space on his two screens to trade bonds, which is his actual job. And then she sees beyond into his life, all laid out like a spreadsheet before her. She sees a bathroom with a bright red cactus that flowers every winter, and a brother who never phones. And . . .

❧

It is raining on the morning of the triathlon.

'Well, I suppose you're going to get wet anyway,' Bryony says to James.

He remains under the covers. 'I can't believe I'm actually doing this.'

'You'll be all right.'

'I feel sick.'

'Imagine if you win.'

'Beetle, I promise you I am not going to win. Just staying alive is my goal.'

'Well, OK, what if everyone else dies? Then you'll win by default.'

'It doesn't have to be competitive. I'm only really competing against myself. And like I say, just finishing is my goal.'

'I thought you said staying alive was your goal?'

'I suppose I would quite like to finish.'

'You will.'

'I might not.'

'You will.'

'It doesn't matter anyway. I'd like to finish, but it really doesn't matter.'

'Right. Well, I've been thinking, and I'm going to do the 5k,' says Bryony.

'What?' James sits up.

'You can enter just the 5k on the day as a kind of fun run. I'll do it with Holly. She does so much want to do it, and she's promised to eat a big dinner afterwards . . . And she's so missing her tennis, and, well . . .'

Bryony expected James to be impressed with the idea that his fat, somewhat unhealthy wife is planning to run five kilometres, but instead he sounds annoyed. He's annoyed about everything to do with Holly lately.

'What about Ash?'

'Fleur'll watch him, I'm sure.'

Here's the other thing. What if Bryony wins? OK, not the whole 5k race, because one of the triathletes will certainly win it, but what if, in her age group, and of the people just doing the 5k, what if she wins? She's looked up the times posted in other local 5ks, and found that people actually do it quite slowly, compared with the times she has been doing recently. It's sort of inconceivable, but rather delightful . . . For some reason Bryony is much slower on the treadmill. But when she goes out with her Nike+ wristband on she can knock off a 5k in twenty-seven minutes. Maybe it's the joy of being outside? Maybe the treadmills are a bit old. In any case, winning the 5k would certainly prove to everyone that . . .

'So you won't be waiting for me at the end, then?'

'Yes, of course I will. The run ends at Fowlmead, doesn't it? And that's where the cycling is.'

'I suppose so.'

'Oh, I see. You're worried I'll take all the glory.' Bryony laughs and pinches James. 'Don't be so silly.'

He sighs, but says nothing.

'What's wrong?'

'Nothing.'

'No, really. What have I done?'

'Nothing. I just . . .'

'What?'

'I suppose I was just thinking it was nice that something was going to be about me for a change.'

'Well, isn't it nicer that it's going to be about all of us?'

'Not poor Ash.'

'Ash hates sport. I'm not making him do a bloody fun run.'

'I thought you hated sport too.'

'I do! But you know I'm trying to lose weight and . . .'

'Can't you just be happy with things as they are? Why do you always have to try and change everything?'

'Um. Right. I'm losing the thread of this conversation. I think I'm going to get up now.'

'I just wanted someone there to watch me swim.'

'Right.'

'For God's sake. In case I *drown*.'

'Whatever.'

❧

Skye sees. She sees much more than she should be able to. Like when she puts on a CD, her CD, the first and best one when she wore that flesh-coloured dress, and does that third-eye meditation thing, suddenly she can see all the people who are listening to the same CD in the world right now. When she was a kid listening to Abba or whatever and she wondered how many other people were listening to 'Take A Chance On Me' RIGHT NOW AT THIS MOMENT she thought it might be billions or millions but definitely thousands because the world was so big, but if you think about it, even now there are search terms that no one has ever used on Google. The world is actually small. So small that in fact at this moment there are only 125 people listening to Skye's first album, which is actually kind of awesome if you think about it and better than nothing. It turns out that she can flick through them, flick through these people like a Rolodex, and choose one, yes, *choose one*, not the naked one, and sort of put in the co-ordinates and . . .

❧

All the advice on racing says not to begin too quickly. But running at a comfortable pace, one where she can breathe through her nose and still hold a conversation (who with?), has meant that Bryony is in last place in the fun run. What is fun about that? She can't be last! She can't *lose*. Holly has already broken away and is running towards the front of the pack. An oldish lady, perhaps around seventy and wearing a pink tracksuit, totters past Bryony. OK. She was not in fact last, but she is now. This is ridiculous; this is humiliating. Bryony summons some effort and passes the old lady, who then passes her again. They are vying for second-to-last place. FFS. It is still raining, and a bitter north-easterly is coming in off the sea. Bryony wasn't sure of the etiquette with her iPod but there is no one to even see her if she puts it on now. Her gym playlist begins. And everything is different, suddenly, and more alive. She can do this. She passes the old lady. Keeps going. Spies three fat women ahead with *Mums for Justice* T-shirts. Passes them. She is really doing this!

She is nowhere near Fowlmead when her Nike+ device tells her that she has run 5k. Well, that's just outrageous, to advertise a 5k run that turns out to be way more than that. WTF? Bryony is absolutely fucking knackered. She has run 5k and has not even finished the race! She is wet. She is cold. She needs a drink. If she stops now she might freeze to death. And there'd be no one to rescue her. She has to keep going. OK. Start the playlist again. Except . . . Bugger. *The battery is low*. Stumble. Get up. Put one foot in front of the other. Do Not Cry. No one else is crying.

It's the panting she hears first, the hot breath of wet men coming up behind her. Right. Great. To cap it all, the triathletes are now beginning to overtake her. In first place is some tall thin guy she has seen at the gym from time to time. Then – OMG – it's Charlie! Closely followed by Ollie. Charlie doesn't acknowledge her as he runs past, his face rigid with concentration. But Ollie slows, slaps her on the shoulder and says, 'Come on, babe. Race you to the end? Last one in buys the drinks.' And that is in fact what it takes to get her going again. Of course, she loses sight of Charlie and Ollie quite quickly, and by the time she makes it to Fowlmead they are already on their bikes. But she has done it! She has finished a 5k that actually turned out to be . . .

When she gets her breath back she confronts one of the organisers.

'Not very accurate, is it?' she said.

'What?'

'Your course. More like 7.5k than 5k.'

'And what did you measure it with? That?' he asks, nodding at her Nike+.

'Yes, and I'm sure it's a damn sight more accurate than . . .'

'Did you calibrate it at all?'

'What?'

'Did you calibrate it?'

Oh God. Bryony doesn't know what this means, but she does remember some word like that appearing in all the blah blah of the instructions she threw away, because really, who needs instructions to operate a bit of plastic you stick on your wrist and . . . Actually, she did have to get the instructions back out of the bin to work out how to connect the little thing you put on your shoe to the thing you put on your wrist, but that was surely all you needed to do, and . . .

'Mummy, you are *such* a wally.'

Holly came third overall in the fun run, and first in her age group, but she does look a bit pale. Bryony makes her put on her tracksuit and then gets her a Coke and an ice cream from the van. Then she finds Fleur and Ash.

'Where's James?' she asks.

Fleur shrugs. 'He hasn't come in yet. But the others are going well. It's still between Charlie, Ollie and that guy.'

Poor James. He will finish, but in last place.

'About that drink . . .' Bryony says to Ollie, while James is doing his final lap.

'Well, you're definitely buying,' says Ollie.

'What about graduation day? We could make an afternoon of it.'

'Just you and me?'

'Yeah. Why not?'

'All right. Yeah. Good. As long as you're buying.'

At first, Skye Turner appears as herself. She melts through the windows of teenagers in Detroit and Manchester and Barcelona and appears at the ends of their beds just like that. *Hello, I'm a fucking celebrity, and who are you?* Not that she says this. Not that this is what she even means, but . . . Are they happy about it? Not on the whole, no. They drop their PlayStation controllers in horror. They kick their keyboards onto the floor in fear. They spill their cans of drink. They gasp, they scream, occasionally they throw up. It's . . . well, it's not like having a mini-audience for a personalised gig. It's not the life-changer Skye hoped it would be. It seemed like fun at first to just start singing along with her own song, to be the live version of the CD or the MP3, but most of the kids just thought they were tripping and they really, really didn't like it. They didn't like it that something magnificent, impossible, crazy was happening to them. Let it happen to someone else, for God's sake! They didn't want to see a ghost, an apparition, a freak of physics. Not in their bedroom. Not *now*. So Skye Turner goes through a phase of just watching them, knowing them, learning from them – without ever letting them see her. OK, she performs the odd minor miracle. Hides some kid's pot before his mother searches his room, whispers in the ear of a girl not to go down that road tonight, creates a diversion that stops someone's father beating up on him yet again. She removes bullets from the guns of soldiers – on both sides. Drops money in the laps of the poor. One day she turns up at someone's door looking like a bomb victim, because of a mission that did go a bit wrong in the Middle East somewhere, and she asks this person for a glass of water, and they give her a glass of water and also a meal and a bath, even though she stinks and looks extremely suspicious, and she is so moved and so grateful that she begins to cry . . .

Fruit

The sunflowers! Why does she always forget everything? This morning, driving into Goodnestone, and the sunflowers were up in the PYO field, which means they must be selling sunflowers at the shop, and there was that thing James said about the sunflower he tried to grow as a child and . . . Anyway, it's gone five thirty, so they'll definitely be shutting, but they look open, so . . . But Bryony can't be bothered to turn around. Or . . . OK, but she *is* turning and going back. Perhaps she is a decent human being after all, whatever the fuck that even is. Perhaps this means she can stop crying now? Yes. Bryony will get sunflowers for James and everything will be all right.

There are no other cars in the car park, so Bryony pulls up next to the shop entrance and goes in. There's the guy from last time who looks a bit like a scarecrow. Bryony looks around the shop. It's low-lit, end-of-dayish, and sunflowerless.

'Sunflowers,' she says. 'I was hoping you'd have some sunflowers . . .'

'Only in the field,' he says.

'Oh. Are they pick-your-own, then?'

'Yes.'

Pick your own sunflowers. That's actually very cool. So . . .

'Can I pick some?'

'We're closing soon.'

'How soon?'

'Like ten minutes ago?'

'I'll be really, really, super quick.'

'OK. Well . . .'

'Thank you! Oh, how do you do it?'

A girl comes out. 'I can lend you a spade.'

A spade? WTF???

'I'll be all right, thanks. Except, actually, how do you do it without a spade?'

'You just snap them off with your hands.'

Right. So here's Bryony striding through the field, on what seemed at first to be a short cut, with her ankles actually being stung by nettles, which just shouldn't be anywhere at a PYO, unless people want to PYO nettle soup or nettle tea or whatever, somehow CRYING AGAIN, because all the good sunflowers seem further and further away, and what if when she gets to them they're like the dead ones from that art gallery in New York? Van Gogh, she remembers. Of course. In the Met. And the amazing pumpkin ravioli afterwards, with that Louis Armstrong record playing that she's never been able to track down, and that honey-coloured Chardonnay . . . *Ah, sunflower, weary of time.* Yeah, that's about right. We're all weary of time, baby. Is that what it even means? Bryony remembers the way Ollie said it in his William Blake seminar. *Ah, sunflower*, making it sound like *Arse, sunflower*, which is what he said Blake would have expected people to make of those sounds, which wasn't actually 100 per cent convincing.

Bryony is ridiculous in this field. She is too big for it. Too grey and urban and fat, in her Oska clothes, with her Toni&Guy hair and her bare ankles. But the sunflowers are clothed by angels and their hair is made of free love and weird science and the purity of the silent universe and they stand in the field like a row of Marilyn Monroes, each one playing a contrite farm girl slightly too sassily, with her chin jutting out and her apron hanging half off. *Arse, sunflower*. But what about the youth pining away with desire? That's Charlie, of course.

Or is it? What about constant, taken-for-granted, gentle James, with his ridiculous soups and puncture repair kits, and Radio 4, and finding recipes for date syrup? And he loves sunflowers. Who knew?

The sunflower stalk is so huge that Bryony can't close her hand around it. In fact, everything about these sunflowers seems outsized. They are not like the puny things you get in supermarkets. They're . . . actually, they are really surprisingly hard to break. You can snap the stalk easily enough but the thick fibrous strands that run down it cannot be broken so easily. Is that what the spade would have been for? But Bryony can't visualise it. In the end she pulls and pulls and imagines the sunflower screaming, like in that documentary her parents worked on, all those years ago. She imagines the plant screaming and pleading with her to stop, but still she pulls and pulls and the fibres peel off slowly like thick pieces of skin until they are virtually at ground level, where they snap. But of course the stalk is now ruined. The fibres took so much flesh with them that the sunflower cannot stand up properly. It droops, dying. *Arse, sunflower, weary of time*. Bryony discards it and starts again.

'What are you doing?'

Pi is standing in the doorway in the thick black dressing gown that Fleur bought for him. He is wearing the cashmere slippers that she knitted for him. He is holding an empty Wedgwood mug. The one that she bought for him, specially, to be his mug when he is here. He is still here. Fleur is sitting at her writing desk, writing.

'Hmm?' As well as writing, she is watching the robin, who has just finished his morning bath. What is it about birds when they bathe? They manage to look both comical and fiercely proud. Fleur always feels so happy when a gift she has offered is accepted. For the first few days the birds ignored the birdbath. Now they all use it, even the woodpecker. And also the squirrel, and the estate agent's cat. Elsewhere in the garden, a bee sucks the dregs of nectar from a drooping verbena like it is 5 a.m. at a party in a place with carpet on only the middle part of the stairs.

'What are you doing?'

'I'm writing.'

'You don't write.'

'Well, I am. I mean, just . . .'

'What on earth are you writing?'

'Just stuff that Oleander used to say. I'm getting the Prophet to give me stuff too. And recent clients like Skye Turner. You know, like . . .'

'Oh, I see. "What does your heart say?"'

'Well, yes, and also . . .'

'"What would Love do?"'

'Yes, but as well as that . . .'

'You don't need to write it down. Just go and get a Paulo Coelho book. She was ripping him off for years.'

'Yes, but I think that Oleander's stuff goes a bit beyond . . .'

'And then all the things she didn't say, but just implied, like "Slavery is OK".'

'What? She never said slavery was . . .'

'Come on, in Oleander's world everything is OK.'

'Well . . . I mean, I don't really think that . . .'

'She never even bothered to read the *Bhagavad Gita* properly.'

'Well . . .'

'Anyway, what have you written? Can I see? "Imagine you are very poor".' Pi laughs. 'Yeah, right, but she wasn't, was she? None of your lot are. "Imagine you are a squirrel"?' He laughs again. 'You are insane.'

Imagine you are a squirrel storing nuts for winter. You spend your days scouring fields, woodlands and gardens for acorns or, if you are lucky, nuts from a bird feeder. It takes you a very long time to find food, and then to bury it for the long winter ahead. Morning, noon and night you scurry this way and that, sorting, burying, hoarding. If you are lucky you manage to store ten nuts each day. You have to eat quite a lot to fuel your search, and to try to put fat on before the first frosts.

One day you are roaming through a garden when, beyond a clump of mushrooms, you find a gap in the fence that has not been there before. You investigate. Here is a tunnel you have never seen before. You check right, left, behind you, and then right and left again. You twitch your whiskers. Everything seems OK, and there are calm vibes coming from the nearby orb spider, which is usually a good sign, so you enter the tunnel. It is long and dark, but you can smell peanuts, and peanuts are your very, very . . . Oh my! At the end of the tunnel is a perfect garden. The main thing that is perfect about the garden is the huge pile of peanuts in its centre. There are enough peanuts here to keep you going not just for this winter, but for years and years to come. You pause for a moment, twitching your whiskers. There must be great danger . . . ? But you sense no danger. There are no scents here. No cat scent or dog scent or stinking fox scent. No other squirrel scent. You are alone with the peanuts. What do you do now?

'So how was I conceived?'

Good God. What a question. But ever since Holly has known that Charlie is her father she has been asking these awkward things. How was she conceived? Right. Concentrate. Why is Bryony not here? Then again, this would be even more embarrassing if she was. They never talked about that night afterwards, and doing it now, in front of Holly, would be . . .

'It was at the Grange, in the summer house.'

'That's nice. What were you and Mummy wearing?'

'Not very much, when it came down to the actual act of . . .'

'I know *that*. I mean before.'

'Your mother was looking very striking, I remember, in a golden dress.'

Which he ripped, he realises, pulling it off her shoulder the wrong way.

'Why?'

'What, why was she wearing the dress? She was at a wedding.'

'Whose wedding?'

'Augustus – Granddad – and Cecily.'

'Was she a bridesmaid?'

'No. For some reason Cecily chose not to have any bridesmaids because . . .'

'OK. Whatever. Anyway . . . ?'

What can he say next? He was on his way to the loo when he heard shouting coming from the drawing room and eavesdropped, as usual. For some reason Fleur was shouting at Augustus. Two people who never spoke were suddenly, passionately, shouting at one another. Something about being invisible, not existing. It was all very bizarre. Was she . . . ? With Augustus? That would explain all the . . . When she came out, Charlie followed her to the kitchen garden. There, among the lavender, mint, rosemary, lemon balm and thyme she tearfully told him the truth; that she was his sister, and that his – their – father had made her keep it a secret because he was so ashamed of sleeping with her mother, the evil Briar Rose, who . . . Of course, Augustus knew that Beatrix would never forgive him if it turned out that . . . And Augustus was a coward, and . . . And then the bit that Charlie can't bear to relive. Fleur reaching for him with her shaking, slender hands, needing to be embraced and stroked and comforted, like a little frightened animal that has been locked out in the cold all night. Charlie pushed her away. 'Don't be so disgusting,' he'd said. 'Don't touch me.' For all those long years he had tortured himself wondering why she had rejected him after their time in the summer house, and what he had done wrong. And now, finally, had come the reason. He wanted to throw up. Instead, he left the kitchen garden and headed for the marquee, and a bottle of champagne all of his own. And there was Bryony, with a bottle of champagne all of her own. Where was James? Possibly driving somebody somewhere? Or maybe he was never there. In those days he was often never there. He was always on a deadline of some sort, always writing a book, or on location. And Charlie's wife Charlotte was at work, of course, always at work, always on call.

'Your mother was drinking champagne out of a beautiful crystal flute.'

'From a *flute*?' Holly mimes with her fingers.

'A champagne glass, silly.'

'Did you ask her to dance?'

'Sort of, yes.'

The band had long stopped playing. 'Life sucks,' Bryony had said to Charlie. 'Don't you think?' And then he'd asked her what made her think her life sucked. Whose life could suck more than his did at that moment? Anyway, it turned out to be something about missing her parents, and James not being there when she needed him. She was pissed and feeling sorry for herself. But she perked up when she realised that Charlie was unhappy too. 'Let's get another bottle,' she said. 'Let's be really unhappy together. Let's be unhappier than anyone has ever been.'

'We were the only people left in the marquee,' says Charlie now. 'We looked at each other and suddenly realised . . .' What? That at that moment they were exactly as lonely and fucked up as each other? Or that they both needed to do something awful and stupid and outrageous? 'We realised that even though we were not exactly in love, we were very, very great friends, which is better in many ways than being in love, and your mother looked extremely beautiful, with her red curls tumbling down her back like something from a Rossetti painting, and I was wearing an Yves Saint Laurent tuxedo, and we were younger then, and both sparkling and shimmering, and the moon was shining . . .'

'This is becoming sort of gross, but I like it.'

'We walked across the grass towards the summer house, through the secret garden which was full of this heady, wonderful smell of jasmine, and into the cherry orchard. We picked some late cherries as we went, and we fed them to each other, and kissed.'

And then Bryony went to throw up. And Charlie imagined he could hear Fleur's sobs carried over the garden, and he wanted to go to her but he couldn't, and then Bryony came back and rinsed her mouth with the champagne they were still carrying, and suddenly here was his big, bold, rather beautiful cousin, in whose soft flesh he found oblivion, just for a while. The warmth of her, and the soft scent between her large breasts, and then the sweet earthiness he found between her voluptuous thighs, and then . . .

'And then . . .'

'Yes, and then you were conceived.'

'And was it the very best moment of your life?'

'Well, when you put it like that . . . Of course it was.'

So there's this bloke, right, and he is very, very poor. He lives on an industrial estate in a room without heating, with rats that eat his soap and nibble his toenails while he's asleep. He's a saver, a hoarder, a make-do and mender. He's a big bloke with one change of clothes and an understanding with the guy at the gym with the sauna round the corner. He nicks stuff from time to time: caffeine from the factory;

pills; bits of old radio; but mostly what he does is forage for mushrooms and rabbits and pigeons, and he pickles things, including sometimes himself, ha ha, in cheap gin. He likes a bit of a magical mystery tour, right? Only £5.99 to really not know where you are going, which is not a bad deal and actually better than most drugs, not that you should know anything about that. And he can always get a shag by the seaside, this bloke. Sometimes he has to pay for it, but not usually. He is so dirty that he seems clean, and girls just love the way his tight little balls flob around in his grey tracksuit bottoms. In his favour he also has piercing blue eyes, nice cheekbones and he's always up for anything, pretty much, and girls like blokes that take a risk now and then.

And then one summer's day in nineteen eighty-whatever he gets on a coach to Margate. He has a bag of yellow pills – never you mind where they came from. And he ends up with a load of beautiful posh people at some seafront ding-dong in something called Dreamland or Dreamworld, and everyone does a load of yellow pills and then it's off again, whoosh, up the A2 to the M25 and into a field somewhere where everyone loves everyone but the person he loves most is called Briar Rose, and she reminds him of someone he loved a long time ago, and so he follows her through the field and into a caravan and then, yes, she lets him, she does, right, even though later she says she didn't, and then he follows her back across the field and back around the M25 and, whoosh, down the A2 and all the way to a place called Sandwich – ha ha, stupid name, right? – and into a big house containing a beautiful thin daughter who he is NOT ALLOWED TO TOUCH and a clever old woman running yoga courses and waiting for the Beatles to come back and a witchy friend and their most treasured possession which was a magical book that was a load of bollocks, right, except . . .

He nicked it. Of course he bloody did. What's the point of a magical mystery tour if you don't get a shag and some swag? And he was going to sell it, of course he was, except it turned out to be quite an interesting book when he read it, full of spells and charms and ways of making the universe do what you want. So the man whispered to the rats one night, asked them to leave, and they did. He made offerings to the woodland creatures and spirits, and they showed him all the fruits and nuts and mushrooms he could ever desire. He asked the universe for a big house and he got a set of record decks, but whatever. He suddenly had a long-lost uncle in Jura who sent him whisky and money, and he sold the whisky and bought records and he bought pills and he bought records and he bought pills and he met this bloke called MC Loss so he became a DJ, and the book told him to always leave sugar out for ants and grow flowers that insects like, if you want the insects to like you, that is, and to shag everyone because it does them good and to do what you want because . . .

He ended up taking the book back. They were so upset, all these women, bless them, and then so grateful, and he even got to have another go with Briar Rose, just once, but then everyone was leaving on planes to find drugs and what's wrong with that, so the DJ sloped off to the spare room and did a few repairs and grew a few plants and helped Briar Rose with her Big Project which meant quite a lot of pruning and watering but also a bit of smoking and snorting, and then one Tuesday afternoon not quite dying but waking up without an arm. And then she was gone.

'So what I really want to know is, will you give me another five marks on my essay if I take my top off?'

'What?'

'For ten marks I'd . . .'

'Charlotte May, please. This is not why I . . .'

'It's three in the morning, and I am here, alone, in my flat, and who has come to visit? It's my lecturer, Ollie. Say hello, Ollie.' She holds up her phone.

'You're recording this. Why?'

Now Charlotte May Miller takes off her top. She is not wearing a bra. Her breasts are small, and sort of triangular. The triangularity is emphasised by the last dregs of suntan line from a string bikini. Her nipples are hard, but she strokes each one of them separately to make sure anyway. She jiggles up and down, and her tits – do they count as 'tits' now that she is no longer behaving as a pretty daughter might? – bounce as if she were doing naked aerobics. She stands next to Ollie jiggling and filming herself. He hopes he looks horrified. He tries to look more horrified for the camera. He actually wants to be sick because he knows that this is the end of his academic career, however it plays out. This is the kind of thing that no one can explain. *Why did you even go to a student's flat at 3 a.m., Ollie?* What a fucking twat.

'Shall we see if he has an erection?'

Charlotte May leans down towards Ollie's lap. He slaps her away. Strangely, instinctively, he slaps her face, which is a part of her that should be naked, rather than the other usually clothed areas within reach. It's also, he realises, how he would slap her if she was his daughter. The phone flies out of her hand and lands on the other side of the room.

She screams. 'Ow! Get off me.' She keeps up a pretence of protesting and *ow*ing as she goes to retrieve the phone.

Ollie sighs. 'I am nowhere near you.'

'*Hitting* a student. Nasty. And you were kissing me before.'

'Charlotte May, please. You know that's not true.'

'Come on, Ollie. Ollie. *Ollieeee . . .*' She makes her voice sound like an echo.

'Are you on drugs again?'

'Everyone's on drugs, baby.'

'You are, aren't you?'

'I just really, really want a First.'

'I know you do. Look, how about this. I'll give you fifteen more marks if you put your top back *on*.'

The universe shudders, sighs and is silent just for a moment.

And another sweet thing about James is that he never, ever mentions the eBay room. Bryony has hardly even been into the eBay room for about three years, but however much she ignores it, it never decides to just disappear, or clean itself up. Isn't there some theory that if you don't look at something it doesn't exist? Surely shame must trump quantum physics at some point? But Bryony is, unfortunately, quite sure that behind the door is the same mess of stuff that was there last time she looked. There's the sewing machine, on which, admittedly, she did make one quilt, when she was trying to get over her PND after Ash was born. There's all her quilting stuff: a big rubber mat for cutting out octagons, squares, triangles etc., and a sharp knife, and a ruler, and serrated scissors – but all this was before Bryony discovered that you could order quilting squares PRE-CUT from eBay. Mind you, all the pre-cut squares she ordered ended up smelling of cigarette smoke, and some were covered in pet hair, so they went off into their own zone in the eBay room. They could be thrown out without any problems, but to get to them Bryony would have to wade through all kinds of stuff she just can't handle yet.

For example there is all the yarn that she bought so that she could knit clothes for Ash in a last attempt to bond with him and love him like a real mother from a glossy children's picture book or *Sainsbury's Magazine*. And all the yarn she bought to knit clothes for herself to make her feel better about still not being able to wish she hadn't had him when he was ONE. But in the end buying cashmere cardigans is much easier than making them, even though Bryony went through a phase of walking around shops saying 'But you could make that!' You could, but she didn't. Still, in the weeks and months she spent thinking about knitting she invested a lot of time and money in choosing some really wonderful yarns, including some from a black alpaca called Santos. The balls of yarn came with a picture of Santos and his pedigree and details of the prizes he'd won. Sometimes Bryony gets a bit tearful thinking about Santos. But she will do something with his wool, she will. And in the meantime it will stay in the eBay room.

James did suggest getting a skip at one point. But there is no way that Bryony could ever throw Santos's wool in a skip! Surely it's more realistic for her to become a better person and eventually tidy the room and maybe buy a rocking chair and a wood burner and sit there on winter nights making a lovely big blanket for the whole family to use to snuggle under to watch films or on long car journeys. But the skip conversation led to the moving-house conversation which led to Emmy coming round and in fact THAT was what cured Bryony's PND. She bought some high heels and some blusher and went to work. But of course being an estate agent is not 100 per cent fulfilling all the time, which is why she also goes to uni. But she is definitely not depressed any more. The eBay room, however, still smells of depression. Not just any old depression, but that exact depression. If Bryony ever had to go back there, then . . .

But she is there, now. And there's another smell as well as depression.

Pear drops mixed with ripe lilies.

'Holly?'

She is under the old desk, beyond the still new-looking ironing board and the iron that are there purely for quilting, and pressing darts.

'Holly? What are you doing under there?'

'Reading.'

'We're going to be late. You're going to Aunt Fleur's, remember?'

You can't get cross with Holly any more, because if you do she doesn't eat. Of course, it turns out that she's always been prone to fits of starvation, but Bryony never properly took account of it until recently. Of course now that she has been actually hospitalised . . . Holly goes quite well in the eBay room, actually. Another project that Bryony thought would work but didn't. Something she thought would always be shiny and new, or at least artistically distressed, a bit like a cobwebby shawl made from Kidsilk Haze in a colour like 'Hurricane' or 'Ghost' hanging over an antique doorknob in a contemporary pattern book. But you can't think like that about your own child, and anyway, everything in the eBay room, including Holly, is Bryony's fault. They are things Bryony fucked up. Which is why . . .

'What are you reading?'

'Granddad's journal.'

'And why exactly are you reading Granddad's journal, Holly?'

A sigh. 'Because you won't. And Daddy won't.'

'But it might be private.'

'Mummy, he's probably dead. But if he isn't dead then maybe there are clues about why he and Grandma and Great-Aunt Plum disappeared. I don't think he'd mind. He probably wants us to read it. Although . . .'

'What?'

'There is quite a lot of sexing in it, Mummy.'

'Oh, Holly. You'd better give me . . .'

'Well, I've read it now so it's too late.'

'Well, who exactly is being sexed?'

'Everyone! But mainly someone called Briar Rose.'

'Fleur's mother.'

'Yes. And she had a baby. With Grandpa.'

'Grandpa?'

'Grandpa Augustus.'

'Really?'

'Really.'

'That's actually quite interesting. What else is in there?'

'Lots and lots of stuff about a tribe called the Lost People, who also do a lot of sexing. And praying. Plus, I don't know how to tell you this, Mummy, but you know the seed pod that you made Daddy throw away?'

'Yes?'

'And you know how it's really deadly and terrible and everything?'

'Yes, of course. That's why we threw it away.'

'Well, it was worth ten thousand pounds.'

~

Fleur has not just baked a cake especially for Holly, she seems to have provided her with a famous tennis player as well. Bryony's going to be late if she does not leave now, but this is actually quite . . .

'Do you know what a money shot is?'

Holly shakes her head.

'OK, well, in pornography it's . . .'

Bryony's look is a high topspin forehand to the famous tennis player's deuce corner. The tennis player can reach it, just, but he has not planted his back foot properly and . . .

'It's basically like your best shot. And it's got to be a two-handed backhand down the line. Money shot for everyone, according to Brad Gilbert, who is like a famous coach who worked with Andre Agassi and Andy Murray.'

'I've got a one-handed backhand.'

'Who taught you that?'

'My uncle. Well, my dad.'

'And he thinks you're who? Billie Jean King? Margaret Court? Gotta get with the times, girlie. You seen any woman on the tour with a one-handed backhand? Doesn't exist nowadays. I mean you gotta have a slice, but for your drive you need two hands.'

His blond hair is like something from a fairy tale. The way he talks is like . . .

'Can you show me? Please? Please, please, please?'

The tennis player looks at Bryony. Bryony looks at Holly.

'Do you remember the deal?'

'Yes, Mummy.'

Bryony explains to the tennis player about Holly needing to put on three more pounds before she is allowed to play tennis again.

'Pretty harsh. Can she not just drink a couple big bottles of Evian?'

'That's so not the point.'

'We could weigh her in the morning, perhaps, and decide then?' says Fleur.

'You'd let her go anyway, whatever she weighs.'

'Well . . .'

'I'm going to be late. I think it's probably a no for now, Holls. You haven't even got your stuff here. And anyway, I'm sure that famous tennis players have better things to do than knock around with twelve-year-old girls.' Bryony smiles thinly. Remembers to kiss Fleur goodbye, although Fleur suddenly seems . . . Anyway, it's almost time for a drink. Beautiful, relaxing, restoring. Well, it would be normally. Instead . . .

The drinks menu is at the back. Pages and pages of wine, fine wine, champagne, dessert wine, liqueurs, brandy, port. But this evening Bryony is looking for the soft drinks. She has promised James that for this one meal with his parents she will not drink alcohol. And maybe this will be the start of something amazing. She feels that if only she can prove to herself that she can go just one night, then . . . And if she can just order something as quickly as possible, then . . .

'I see she's gone straight to the back pages,' says the waiter, twinkling. 'Got her priorities right.'

What is it, what the fuck is it, about the simple act of choosing to spend a small amount of your available cash on a glass or bottle of fermented vegetable matter that gets people so excited? Why is it so remarkable, so naughty, so *outré*, to do this, especially when every other woman – fat, highlighted, high-heeled – in this restaurant will be doing exactly the same thing? Look at *her*. Isn't she a one? Isn't she terrible? Ooh, missus, why not have another? She's just like her aunty Trace, she is . . .

'I'm actually looking for a soft drink,' Bryony says.

James gives her a supportive look. He and his dad order a beer each. His mother Lyn orders an orange juice. Bryony wants sparkling mineral water, but . . .

'Do you only do Badoit?' she asks.

'Ah,' says the waiter. 'The finest mineral water.'

'Yes, yes,' Bryony says. 'But it's not very sparkly. Do you do anything else?'

'We do Highland Spring, but only in small bottles.'

'Great. I'll have one of those, thanks.'

'Badoit is lightly sparkling because it's natural, of course.'

'I know. Thanks. But I really prefer something more carbonated.'

An eyebrow. An ironic little smile. 'Like to really scour the tongue, do you?'

'Um, I just like quite fizzy things.'

'What you want then,' says the waiter, 'is a nice bottle of champagne.'

'Right.' Bryony sighs.

James nudges her. Something in her tone or body language is presumably not quite . . . But actually, fuck this . . .

'I'm sorry, but have you not heard of the concept of an alcoholic?' says Bryony to the waiter. 'Or driving? Or Islam? Or Buddhism, Or WeightWatchers?'

'Bryony . . .' says James.

'No, I'm sorry,' she says again, although she is not sorry. 'I didn't realise that this is a place in which drinking alcohol is mandatory. I didn't notice the sign on the door saying that it is impossible to order a glass of fizzy water here without being bullied into drinking something with a percentage symbol next to it. Perhaps it doesn't occur to waiters in places like this that people might not be drinking for a good reason, and that they might be feeling a little fragile or delicate and not want to incessantly *banter* about it. But fine, OK. You win. What's your most expensive champagne?' She starts flicking through the laminated pages of the menu. 'All that fuss, and the most expensive champagne you have is thirty-two pounds fifty. We'll have two bottles, please.'

'Bryony . . .'

'You'll join me in scouring my tongue, won't you, Greg and Lyn? On me, of course.' Bryony looks back at the waiter. 'And you may as well open a bottle of the 2007 Graves too, and let it breathe. If we're going to have to drink alcohol we may as well do it properly.'

'What is enlightenment?'

Fleur laughs. 'How long have you got? What time is your mother picking you up in the morning?'

Holly sighs. 'Why do adults always . . .'

'All right. Look. Do you know the story of Adam and Eve?'

'Yes. In the Bible. They are in a garden with a tree and God says not to eat the apple on the tree and then of course they do eat the apple and it's all Eve's fault and . . .'

'I've never heard someone sound quite so bored by the Bible.'

'It's so old-fashioned. And anyway, if you are God and you don't want someone to eat something why give it to them in the first place?'

'Maybe to prove that they have free will?'

'Right. So, anyway, about enlightenment . . . ?'

'Do you know what Adam and Eve got when they ate the apple, which, by the way was just a fruit. It wasn't necessarily an apple. It could have been a fig.'

'Um . . . knowledge? It was like the tree of knowledge?'

'And then what happened?'

'I can't remember.'

'They put on clothes because they were ashamed of their nakedness.'

'And then God punished Eve with periods and stuff!'

'Well, in a way God didn't really need to punish them. With knowledge they could punish themselves. Knowledge isn't just knowing facts from books. Knowledge is knowing things like shame and embarrassment and fear. It's knowing that you are better or worse than someone else. It's being separate from things. Knowledge is a good thing to have at school, but in this story it's a curse.'

'OK . . .'

'Enlightenment, or at least the way I see it, is a way of un-eating the fruit.'

'What, getting rid of knowledge?'

'Yes. Or what I would call the ego.'

'Right.'

'Holly, do you have a sort of voice in your head that tells you that you're not good enough or, I don't know, that your last tennis shot was really lame, and that you are ugly and a failure and things like that?'

Holly makes a face. 'Sort of. Yes. How did you know?'

'I know because everyone has the same voice.'

A long pause. 'Really? Are you sure?'

'Yes. And does the voice sometimes say nice things, like that you're cleverer than other people, or thinner, maybe? Does it get you to imagine being at Wimbledon, or becoming head girl at school or . . .'

'I suppose so. I don't know. It's not *exactly* the same voice, though. It can't be.'

'I think it is. I think that is the ego speaking to us. And the main thing it does is separate us from one another. Makes us always better or worse. Encourages us to compare ourselves to others all the time. Imagine being exactly the same as someone else. How does that make you feel?'

'Honestly?'

'Yes.'

'Really, really bored.'

'That's exactly what the ego does. It makes true enlightenment and oneness seem kind of boring. But imagine if that feeling was full of love. How would it be then?'

'Still really, really boring. I don't know . . . Maybe . . .' Holly thinks, suddenly, of Melissa, and that time when she hit with her. Neither of them was trying to win. All that mattered was the force and beauty of the shots. If it had been about winning points it would have been less enjoyable. If Holly could be the same as someone else it would have to be Melissa. But would Melissa want to be the same as Holly? Probably not.

'Lots of grown-ups very much want to be enlightened.'

'Why?'

'Some people – Hindus and Buddhists mainly – think that we keep being reincarnated until we find out how to become enlightened, and that being alive is basically about suffering. People want to be enlightened so that they can stop suffering.'

'So they basically want to be dead?'

'People want to be free of the cycle of birth and death.'

'Aunt Fleur, that actually sounds really creepy.'

'I know it does.'

'So what Granddad Quinn said in his journal about the seed pods . . .'

'He's right. They are a short cut to enlightenment. But they kill you.'

'But they make you enlightened first?'

'Yes, but they really, *really* kill you. There's no coming back.'

'Unless you're an animal, apparently. I read that animals and birds are already enlightened and the seed pods affect them in different ways. Granddad Quinn said that sometimes people come back re-incarnated as animals. Is that true?'

'Maybe only if something has gone wrong in this lifetime? But I'm not sure. The point is that if you eat any of the seeds from the pod – and they are very tiny – you don't come back as anything.'

'I feel a bit scared now.'

'Why don't you have some more cake?'

'Do I have to? It's not like Mummy is ever going to let me play tennis again anyway.'

Fleur sighs. Puts the cake away. 'Look, the thing you have to remember about the seed pods is that they are very, very dangerous. You must promise me that if you were to find one anywhere . . .'

'Yes, Aunt Fleur. I'd let you know immediately.'

'And you wouldn't touch it or anything.'

'No, Aunt Fleur.'

'Stop being such a gaylord. Just sit still for two minutes and listen.'

'And then you'll let me help?'

'Yes.'

'You'll let me help find the seed pods?'

'Well, I suppose I'll probably need a lookout. But it'll be very dangerous, so you need to be properly briefed.'

'OK.' Ash sits as still as he possibly can. He can't help humming a little bit though. Why is he humming? He seriously can't stop. Actually, *what* is he humming? It's the New Zealand National Anthem, which he has had in his head since he watched the rugby with his father this afternoon. He hates rugby, but his father says it is traditional and English and brave and a little bit pagan and that he should try to like watching it, even if he hates playing it. The New Zealand National Anthem is lovely and cheerful and makes Ash think of happy children dancing. OK, the children are in uniform, and are doing what they are told, but they are doing it under a bright warm sun with streamers and bunting. 'God Save the Queen' just makes him want to scratch and yawn and . . .

'Ash!'

'What?'

'You can't go to sleep. This is very important.'

'OK.'

'Right. The Prophet goes for dinner at nine o' clock. That's when we can sneak in.'

'Are you sure he's got them?'

'*Yes*, I've told you. He grows them and sells them.'

'But that journal was written in like nineteen eighty-something.'

'Old people don't change their habits as much as we do.'

'OK.'

'So I'll go in because I'm the eldest. You stay at the top of the stairs and watch in case he comes back for something. If he does come back for something you'll have to throw yourself down the stairs . . .'

'No!'

'All right, well, just pretend to faint on the landing then.'

'Like I did in drama club?'

'Just like that.'

'What if I'm scared?'

'Then you will be very brave and manage not to act like a complete fucktard.'

'Holly?'

'Yes?'

'Holly, what are you going to do with the seed pods?'

'Sell them.'

'And then what?'

'Then I'm going to run away and go and live in Middlesex, where I have to play tennis for the county team. It's very important, and the team needs me, and Mummy doesn't understand. If I stay here Mummy won't ever let me play tennis again. You heard what she said before. When I am famous you can come and visit me and I'll buy you a Rolls-Royce.'

Is that what Holly is really going to do? Like, really, really do? Maybe. Sort of. Well, probably not. But she does see herself holding out the seed pod to her mother, who will be pale and trembling and totally shocked by the bravery and determination of her daughter, and she will finally understand how desperate she is and how she will do anything for tennis. Then her mother will be certain to let her hit with the famous tennis player while she phones Dave to find out about the county squad. And of course if Holly has the seed pods, there will be no question of whether or not the family can afford for her to go. She can buy a new tennis dress as well, probably one that comes with its own matching bra and shorts. Oh, and of course another Wilson racquet or two, and a big bag for them to go in and . . .

'I don't want you to go to Middlesex.'

'I know, but . . .'

'Can't you just eat some more? Then Mummy will let you play tennis.'

Holly thinks about this for like two seconds. 'No.'

'Well, can I come with you?'

'Well, maybe; it depends on . . .'

'Holly . . .' Ash begins to cry.

'Stop being so gay. Look. All right. When we get the seed pods I'll give one to you.'

'But . . .'

'Each one is worth ten thousand, at least. Mummy says they are probably worth an awful lot more now because of inflation . . .'

'BUT I AM REALLY SCARED OF THE SEED PODS.'

'Shh. I know. But they're not that scary.'

'But they are.'

'Just don't be a retard and do anything dumb like eat one or put it in your eyes.'

~

The room is surprisingly humid. It smells a little like lizard orchids mixed with earth and that really yellow ice cream you get in Cornwall. It is in two parts. The first part of the room is full of books and pieces of faded notepaper. There is an armchair in the corner and, over by the window, one desk with a computer on it. On the wall there is a calendar with a naked lady sitting on a red car. There's a collection of old, weird musical instruments with a set of bongos, and a huge tambourine-shaped thing. Then there is another table with two record players on it, next to one another. Between them is a large plastic willy which gives Holly a very, very funny feeling, as if . . .

Oh! Horrible! And a pair of lady's breasts, in a kind of pink rubber, and . . .

On the wall there are old, faded posters. One of them is a large, yellow smiley face. One of them has a picture of a yellow pill on it, with the words DJ Profit and MC Loss at the top. There are some photographs of a woman naked in a dark field, holding some kind of glowing stick that might actually be . . . Oh yuck . . .

Holly goes quickly into the next part of the room. This is where the earthy, goaty, vanilla smell is coming from. And, yes, just as she thought, here they are. Lots and lots of orchids with seed pods hanging off them like, OK, to be honest, like nothing that can be described except in a really gross way. One of them has a flower, but before Holly can look at it there is a noise behind her. It is the sound of a door closing. She turns around. Tiptoes back into the first part of the room. But . . .

'Well,' says the Prophet. 'Hello.'

'Hello,' says Holly. 'Sorry! I got a bit lost and . . .'

'I went sneaking around this house looking for treasure a long time ago and look what happened to me,' he says. 'I wouldn't recommend it.'

His voice is like the kind of voice that bad men have in those black-and-white films that teachers and old people like to watch with children around Christmas time. Dickens, or whatever. Or that thing with a flying bed. It's a bit London and a bit broken. It sounds like he has the kind of bad cough that goes with a really old-fashioned illness like TB or something.

What *has* happened to him? It is hard to say. He has grey hair, like all really old people, but it is streaked with red and tied into a horrible ponytail that crawls down his back like a dying snake. His teeth – all four of them – are black. His cheekbones sit so high on his face that he looks like a skeleton. In fact, in a way he looks a bit like all those pictures they showed Holly when she went to the clinic, of girls who ate even less than she did. What a stupid idea that was. The pictures were supposed to scare the girls, but instead they used them as inspiration. *Thinspiration*, in fact, which is a word Holly learned while she was there. Before she went to the clinic she didn't eat because she just didn't really like food and preferred tennis. Now she doesn't eat because she wants to beat those skeletons. She wants to beat the skeletons 6–0, 6–0. The double bagel. But she does not want to turn out like this shrivelled little man in front of her and . . .

'I could use a little girl,' he says.

'Er . . . I think I should go back to Aunt Fleur now.'

'Sit down,' he says.

'But . . .'

'Sit down.'

'Oh God. Look, I'm really sorry I came into your private space and . . .'

'Sit down. I am assuming you can type?'

'Type? Well . . .'

'Since you're here, and since you're not supposed to be here and are therefore in trouble, I'm going to tell you my life story and you are going to write it down for me. It's hard for me to type with ONE ARM MISSING after all. Think of it as a sort of punishment. And in return . . . Well, I'm going to take a wild guess that you're here to steal my seed pods.'

'Well . . .'

'Are you or aren't you?'

Holly closes her eyes. 'Yes.'

'I'll give you five.'

Opens them again. 'Thank you. But . . .'

'Quinn and Plum's granddaughter, aren't you. Read the journal?'

'Yes.'

'So you probably know all about this.'

'Yes.'

'You know how your parents got all that money?'

'Sort of.'

'But you don't know everything.'

'No.'

'SIT DOWN FOR FUCK'S SAKE.'

Holly goes to the computer and sits down. She realises she is shaking. There is another plastic willy next to the computer. She doesn't like it. Where is Ash? Where is Aunt Fleur?

'All right.' He fingers his horrible, straggly grey beard. 'What is the number one question you have?'

Holly thinks. 'What actually happened to my grandparents and Fleur's mother?'

The Prophet roars with laughter. Well, it comes out like a croak. Like a dying toad.

'You think I know that? No one knows that. They went back to the Lost Island and probably got murdered by some shaman who was pissed off with people constantly turning up in his village looking for free drugs.'

'Right.'

'Number two question.'

'Why are the seed pods worth so much money?'

'Good. Better. Intelligent little girl, aren't you?'

Holly shrugs. 'I just . . .'

'Go on.'

'Well, I read that the seed pods kill you and then instead of being reincarnated or whatever, your soul leaves the universe, which a lot of people think is a good thing, but which actually sounds . . .'

'Ever heard of biological warfare?'

It's 15.25. There are no more viewings. Bryony is not having her first drink of today until 18.00 so the big question is what to do between now and then. The obvious answer is admin, but that is very boring. And also quite hard at this lazy, pre-evening, pinkish, oscitant time of day. On the one hand this time of day is exciting, because it is only two hours and thirty-five minutes until Bryony can have a drink, and therefore relax and sink into herself and, frankly, switch off. This isn't a terrible time of day. This isn't, thank God, 10 a.m., the heavy drinker's equivalent of being in Oxford and longing for the sea. But the fact remains that there are two hours and thirty-five, make that now thirty-four, minutes to fill. Make that thirty-three.

Do a pee.

Thirty-one.

Bryony watches a YouTube video of a man hip-hop dancing onto a treadmill and then falling off. She Googles Clem. She Googles Skye Turner. Watches Skye melting down on YouTube for what must be the hundredth time, and admires how thin and beautiful Skye looks even when she is being so embarrassing. She watches it again. At least the tabloids haven't found her at Beatrix's place. She sets the Sky+ for the rest of the series of *MasterChef*.

Bryony three-finger-swipes to her email inbox. It's horrible! Her spreadsheets. Dire! The five – count them – property descriptions she should have finished by this afternoon. No! She three-finger-swipes back to Safari. What else can she do? Outnet or Amazon? Or both? The Outnet is more absorbing, but Amazon gives her that buzzy, clicky, happy feeling in a more immediate way. Just because she has forbidden herself from ever going onto eBay again does not mean that she can't . . . And she could do with some new trainers. So . . . *Trainers* and then *Women's*, and then *Sports and Outdoors*, and then *Athletic and Outdoor Shoes*. Then sort: Price, from high to low. Ooh. There are some trainers that are £258! But they seem to be only for cyclists. Bugger. The most expensive trainers in Bryony's size are made by Ecco, which means they are for old people. So, on to the Outnet. Or, fuck it, Netaporter. Nike Airs or Lanvins? Both. *Ker-ching*!

A brief, small buzz, which fades after about fifteen minutes.

When Bryony feels like this there is only one thing to do and that is get out of the office, get some fresh air and clear her head by going to Two's Company a few doors down the High Street and buying approximately £300 worth of scarves and jewellery. Yes, yes, it's more shopping, but it stops her thinking about wine. When she goes there today she finds a dress that almost looks as if it could fit her. It is a beautiful deep crimson silk with the kind of nipped-in waist and expensive cut that – potentially – makes even someone quite fat look beautiful and arresting, like a woman from a painting with a lot of fruit in it. Could she wear it for her graduation? Might it send the wrong message? Or – worse – the right one? There is also a rather lovely hunting jacket and a crisp white shirt and, OMG, the XL in both the jacket and the shirt ACTUALLY FIT. The shirt is rather billowy, like something from a ship, or the eighteenth century. But the dress, the dress. Whisper it, but . . . *it fits too*. Perhaps she could wear it at home, for a dinner party, with bare feet and a delicate silver anklet, and afterwards she and James . . . But lately thinking of fucking James is as exciting as thinking of replastering the house or getting that blue soapy stuff topped up in the car. She buys the dress quickly to neutralise these thoughts. And a big necklace to go with it.

At 17.47 she takes the small bottle of M&S wine from her office fridge and puts it into her cool bag. She drives to the seafront, as far north as possible where she is less likely to see anyone she knows walking past. It's reasonable, right, to want to have her first drink of the day in peace and quiet on her own? Of course, she has nicer wine at home. And she'll have that when she gets in. But increasingly she needs something to take the edge off walking through her own front door. And also, she needs to be on her own to think about Ollie.

OK. Obviously nothing – as Holly might say, N.O.T.H.I.N.G. – is happening, is going to happen or ever will happen. It's hard to think of a more forbidden love than this, although Fleur and Charlie were pushing it, weren't they, all those years ago? How extraordinary. But a tiny bit of incest, if it's true love and there are no other obstacles . . . That's surely not quite as bad as this, which would be adults choosing to wreck their whole entire lives? Then again, in some ways it is sort of worse. After all, Fleur and Charlie could never marry, whereas Bryony and Ollie . . . If anything ever happened between Bryony and Ollie, that would be the end of the whole family. But they could legally marry. Of course, Bryony is fairly sure that Ollie does not share her feelings. Even *she* does not fully share her feelings. What on earth is she even thinking? That stupid dream. Touching his arm. And now a red dress . . . She imagines kissing him, just once. Could that be enough? Just one kiss? If she could engineer it so that he would . . . No. She loves James. Ollie would be bad for her. She sips her wine. At least she feels normal now.

Fleur waits at the bus stop. She's put the Book in a Thais Are Us carrier bag given to her by Bluebell. The bag dangles from her wrist as if it contains something she's taking back to the library or returning to a friend. When the bus comes she pays the fare to Canterbury. But in fact she gets off at the next stop, and leaves the book to finish the journey to Canterbury on its own. Does it arrive? Does it hitch a lift back? Maybe someone picks it up long before that, in Ash or Wingham. Perhaps it's on someone's bookshelf before Fleur has even finished walking home. Who knows?

It's beginning to rain as Charlie and Izzy enter the Shirley Sherwood Gallery in Kew Gardens. They are miles away from anything. Well, they are quite close to the Temperate House. But they are a ten-minute walk away from their offices, and on a grey afternoon like this one it feels as if they are miles away from anything. It is a misty, low-cloud sort of day in which even London buses look a bit like alien craft emerging from the gloom, with their ascorbic orange dazzle. Not that they can see any buses from here. They can vaguely hear them passing, flashes of their dazzle only slightly visible above the wall. And of course there is the usual roar of planes coming in to land at Heathrow, but no one at Kew hears those any more. Bright green parakeets fly damply from tree to tree and grey squirrels bob up and down. The nights are drawing in, and the last of the wasps have already retreated inside clammy buildings where some will find a sleeve or a gardening shoe in which to sleep out the coming winter, but most will hurl their now heavy bodies against window panes and into fluorescent lights until they die.

Inside the gallery there is an exhibition called the Art of Plant Evolution, but that is not why they are here. Or, at least, Charlie doesn't think it is why they are here. Izzy won't say why they are here. The botanical paintings are arranged in evolutionary sequence. So the first thing is Alexander Viazmensky's painting of *Amanita muscaria*, the classic red toadstool with white spots that has hallucinogenic properties but is also very deadly. Early plants like algae and mosses do not have seeds: instead, they multiply through spores. Charlie wonders for a second why plants bothered to invent such complex reproduction mechanisms as flowers, resulting in fruits containing seeds to make more flowers. What's wrong with just throwing your spores around, like nature's equivalent of having a wank? And especially if you can reproduce that way, well, who needs other organisms? It seems a whole lot less complicated than what evolution eventually produced: vast complex entities that require not just a bit of damp earth and a fair wind but designer clothes, deodorant and a late-night tube service. Charlie and Izzy walk past the algae and the mosses, past a wall full of gymnosperms, with their strange, otherworldly cones. But of course the angiosperms are what everyone wants to see, because the angiosperms have flowers which are beautiful and . . . Here are the lilies and peppers and magnolias.

'I've always sort of preferred monocots,' Izzy says, as they walk on. 'Is that weird?'

Charlie laughs. 'Sort of, with you being an expert in fuzzy, complex leaves . . .'

She shrugs. 'I've never liked working on my favourite plants.'

'What is your most favourite plant?'

'I'm fond of lilies. You?'

Charlie shrugs. 'I'm an orchid fan myself, so . . .'

'What is Nicola's favourite plant?'

Good God. This again. 'How would I know?'

'You've been on lots of dates. You've never been on a date with me and you know *my* favourite plant.'

'Um . . .'

'What do you think it might be?'

'I really wouldn't . . .'

'Do you think she'd like roses?'

'Are you trying to get me to send her . . .'

'No! I just wonder if you can tell things about a person by what plants they like.'

'Maybe it's more relevant if you work with plants, and . . .'

'Roses are quite obvious, I suppose. But then Nicola is a bit . . .'

'Most people don't really know what roses are. I mean, Rosales? Yes, I'm fond of Rosales.'

'The whole order?'

'Yep. All that lovely fruit. Sloe berries and figs and . . . My sister does this thing with her students where she gets them to work out the connection between apples and roses – like, greeting-card roses in a vase, *Rosa damascena* or whatever – and apparently most of them can't get it. They don't know that apples are also part of the Rosaceae family, don't understand that an apple tree grows flowers that look like roses before they fruit. I mean, apparently they don't even know that flowers do fruit. Oh, there they are over there.' There, indeed, in the Rosales section is a painting of three hyperreal-looking apples. They set off diagonally, leapfrogging quite a few evolutionary steps. But then there are the spathes of the *Philodendron muricatum* which make them stop again.

'I do love Margaret Mee.'

'So do I. Her plants always look sort of evil . . .'

'You know that one's pollinated by scarab beetles?'

'Nice.'

'They go inside the spathes and mate all night long.'

'Like little sex booths.'

'So many flowers are basically little sex booths.'

'Of course that's actually an inflorescence, not a . . .'

'Shut up. We're like completely off duty.'

There is no one else in the gallery. It is late, and wet, and grey, and Tuesday. Who goes to look at botanical paintings on a wet Tuesday?

'Right.'

There is a jangle of keys and the bloke from the gift shop comes through.

'I'm going to knock off if it's all right with you guys,' he says. 'I'm sort of on a promise, and, well . . .' He looks at the door leading to the way out.

'You're joking,' says Izzy. 'But we just got here. And it's so wet outside, and . . .'

He smiles. 'You both work at Kew, right?'

He leaves them the keys with such little fuss that for a second Charlie wonders if Izzy actually . . . But no, all Izzy wants to do is talk about Nicola. The last time Charlie saw Nicola was Friday night. She turned up at his place covered in gold sparkle and Guerlain perfume and offered to take him clubbing in Soho. In the end, though, they couldn't be bothered to leave the house. Nicola had some weed with her and so they got stoned instead. Charlie remembers her annoying him by finishing his sentences – wrongly, each time – and then trying to gatecrash the jazz band's practice by claiming to be an experienced blues singer. He still fucked her, of course, but he pretended she was the cave girl from what has become his regular morning wank fantasy, and persuaded her to put her hair in bunches for him to hold while he . . .

'So you've got a list of attributes your perfect girlfriend would have?'

'It's from when I was like eighteen or something.'

That's right. He showed Nicola his list too. He shows all women his list at some point. He has a box of 'amusing stuff from the past' that contains things like his school photo from when he was nine, and a certificate for competence in, of all things, gymnastics. Then there's the list, written in turquoise ink on yellow paper. Both the ink and the paper were given to him by Fleur. The whole list is obviously about Fleur, well, more or less. But basically the list never describes the woman to whom it is shown, which, now he thinks about it, must sort of be the point and . . .

'What's the worst thing on it?'

'Oh, um, quite a detailed description of how firm her bum should be.'

'Oh, Charlie. You should be ashamed of yourself!'

'I was eighteen!'

'So how firm should her bum be?'

And here's the problem. Izzy has exactly the bum he described back then. Basically Fleur's bum, which Fleur still has of course, but that Charlie can never see or touch or think about ever again. How does Izzy know? Why is she doing this? Is this all a complete coincidence, or . . .

'I suppose it is basically your bum,' he says, shrugging.

'Really?' she says, taking a step closer.

After the graduation ceremony, Bryony meets the others in the Abode Hotel Champagne Bar for drinks. Ollie was supposed to text everyone to tell them where to meet but he's fucked it up somehow and so only Grant, Helen and Bryony make it. After two bottles of champagne – paid for by Bryony, even though they got the PhD scholarships and all she inherited was a bit of cold mansion a million billion miles away, Grant and Helen drift off to the house they share with a poet and a postcolonial theorist. Once Bryony is ninety-five per cent sure that Ollie is not coming she switches to a table at the back of the bar, drinks a glass of red wine, eats two omelettes and a large salad, and then leaves.

Without the others she feels strange in her gown, with the beautiful red dress rustling underneath. There is drizzle in the air, and even the Caribbean market stall looks grey and desolate. A fruit seller is trying to flog off the last of his local Cox apples for ninety-nine pence a bag. Schoolchildren trail around soggily in their polyester school blazers, all heading for McDonald's or the bus station. Perhaps Bryony should have taken her kids out of school and insisted that James bring them to her graduation. But then of course she wouldn't have been able to get pissed with Ollie, which she has been looking forward to since they talked about it at the triathlon. Not that there is any Ollie. He was there in the cathedral; she saw him as she walked past: a blur of jeans, stubble, white shirt, crooked tie, cracked iPhone . . . Was he texting during the ceremony? But where is he now? They were definitely, definitely going to meet for drinks.

Can she go to his house? Why not? It's only round the corner.

But if he'd wanted to have drinks he would have gone to Abode, surely?

Unless something came up.

Bryony walks to Ollie and Clem's place and knocks on the door. Nothing. Her phone rings. That'll be Ollie now. Although he never rings her and . . . But no, weirdly it's Clem. Bryony declines the call. She can catch up with Clem later. Talking to Clem right now when she is knocking on her front door looking for her husband would be . . . But this is totally innocent, of course. It's really mainly a time thing, and . . . *Knock, knock, knock*. This is just desperate now. Her phone buzzes a message just as she closes the wrought-iron gate behind her and heads back into town.

~

Fleur knocks on the Prophet's door. There's no reply, but she goes in anyway.

'Hello?'

He's there, with an old Fila shoebox on his lap.

Fleur is holding the scraps of paper he gave her. Which took poor Holly all night to type, apparently.

'This is basically your life story,' she says. 'It's not for Oleander's book. It's for me. I mean, all that stuff about my birth and . . . I sort of understand what you've done, I think. But why?'

The Prophet closes his eyes. Scratches behind his ear. Opens his eyes again.

'You may as well be with the bloke you love.'

'You're very kind. Really . . . But I was like fourteen or something when you first knew my mother, right? There's no way you could be my father. Although I liked the bit about being born at the end of a rainbow, that was really beautiful. And . . .'

'Look, it doesn't matter who spunked in who. There's more to life than that.'

Fleur laughs. 'Well, when you put it that way . . .'

'Your mother . . . I mean, anyone could have been your father. No offence.'

'I just look so much like a Gardener.'

The black hair they all have because of Gita, the beautiful bride that great-grandfather Charles brought back from India and whose portrait hangs in Fleur's bedroom. Fleur looks just like her, which is one of the reasons the portrait has been hidden from the rest of the family for all these years. It's how Oleander knew.

'There was a woman, all right, back in the early seventies. Maybe seventy-three. She was exactly like your mother. Same red hair, pale face and everything. I thought Briar Rose *was* her when I came here. I mean, that's why I chased after her so much. One of the reasons. I'd heard that this other girl got knocked up around the time that I knew her. And for a long time I did think you were mine. I wanted to think it. Thought I'd found you. Like you'd been a princess sent in a basket down a river or something. It's not that far-fetched.'

'But my mother and Augustus . . .'

'Yeah, if you want a loaded father then he's the one to choose.'

'*Was*.'

A low cackle. 'I give all my money away.'

'To me.'

There's a pause. The robin flies in, gets his bit of seed pod and flies out again.

The Prophet shrugs. 'All right, well, you'll have to do it this way.'

'Do what which way?'

'You spoken to Piyali lately?'

This is not a bad question. Everyone knows they are 'together' now. It's even sort of accepted in the house. But do they speak? Not that much. He's now offering Yoga for Athletes and two new reading groups. He's started learning Malayalam and Sanskrit. He's become too busy to speak to Fleur. Except to occasionally criticise the way she runs the house.

'No.'

'He's going back to India, apparently. To find himself.'

'Oh . . .' Fleur is not as disappointed as she would have thought. 'I suppose I had begun to realise that . . .'

'So there's going to be nothing stopping you from having a go with the bloke you really love.'

'Except the fact that he's my brother.'

The Prophet sighs. 'I don't think that matters.'

'Everyone else would think it does, though.'

He gives her the shoebox.

'This was meant to be for you anyway. For the "right time".'

Fleur opens the box. Inside, it contains a tiny glass bottle of clear fluid lying in a nest of shredded newspaper.

'Doesn't stay that potent in sunlight,' he says. 'So I'd keep it in there until you're ready.'

~

And then, through the front window of Abode, Bryony sees Ollie.

'Thought I'd missed you,' he says when she joins him.

He did remember. But he is obviously quite drunk. How long has he been here? It can't be longer than an hour, because Bryony was here an hour ago.

'Thought I'd missed *you*.'

'Not sure I'm going to be very good company, though.'

'Why not?'

'Everything's a bit fucked up, TBH. Clem's left me. And I've been suspended from the university.'

Not only is he drunk, he has obviously been crying.

'Shh,' says Bryony. 'It's OK. Tell me everything.'

What follows is a jumble of stuff about how much he loves Clem and something about a fishing game, and then some video made by a student, but one of Ollie's students, not one of Clem's students, which was all quite hard to untangle, and how the video is on YouTube, just like Skye Turner's video was on YouTube, and, in fact, this one was partly *inspired* by Skye Turner's video, and shows that Ollie offered to give her fifteen more marks on her essay if . . .

'Oh my God,' says Bryony, cringing. 'But why . . . ?'

'It was a total fucking ambush. I'd given her my number because . . .'

'You gave her your number?'

'She said she didn't have any friends! She was suicidal!'

'Right.'

'I have to speak to Clem. Clem doesn't understand. I never even had any sexual feelings about Charlotte May. If anything I fantasised about her being my *daughter*. Which of course I can't say in public because it makes it sound even worse.'

'So why did you offer her fifteen more marks?'

'Because she had her top off and . . .'

'Oh my God,' Bryony says again.

'I offered her the marks to make her put her top back *on* again. If anything it was just for the camera, to show how desperately I did not want to have her topless in a room with me. But apparently offering to give students more marks is gross misconduct whatever the circumstances.'

'So what did Clem say?'

'She said she knew for ages that something weird had been going on with me. But not only that, like everyone else she is sick of me. Apparently I lie, and I cheat, and I'm sexist and I'm racist and . . .' Ollie looks out of the window. 'Shit. Great. Press.'

'How do you know?'

'That cunt's been following me all day.'

'I don't think he's seen you.'

'No. But he will. They hack your phone, apparently.'

'Look. Let's just get a room and a bottle of wine and work this out. I'll pay.'

'Are you propositioning me? Because I think I've had all the . . .'

'Of course I'm not propositioning you. Don't be stupid. It's just practical. Where else are we going to go if you've got press trailing around after you?'

'I suppose I do need somewhere to stay since I've been thrown out of both my house and my office.'

Bryony breathes hard as she climbs the stairs ten minutes after Ollie. She feels light-headed, as if her mind is climbing the stairs faster than her body. It's similar to the way she felt running that 5k, when this all started. Or maybe it started long before that. She thinks about her landing strip and her toenails and how they were all for him. But not really. Well, only sort of. Only sort of for the fantasy version of all this. But it's OK because the reality now is that they are going to sit in the privacy of a hotel room for a while and then . . . Bryony looks at her watch. It's 4 p.m. She has one hour max. Maybe an hour and a half. And she mustn't drink too much before driving home. One more large glass.

In the room there is nowhere comfortable to sit except the bed, so Bryony and Ollie sit next to one another with their legs stretched out. Bryony pours wine. It's a blah blah Merlot that turns out to be a rather nice deep red when poured. The same colour as her dress.

'Things aren't great for me at home either,' she says. 'If that makes you feel any better. I don't really know what to do about Holly, and . . .'

'I'm not sure I'm going to be a great listener, but . . .'

'No, don't worry. I'm not going to offload. Just didn't want you to feel alone.'

For a moment there is just the hum of something. Probably a mini-bar.

'When did you last have sex?'

'Me and James?'

'Yes.'

Bryony thinks about it. 'I think maybe July. On Jura. We had a massive row and . . .'

'I haven't had sex for over a year.'

'Oh God. That's . . .'

'Part of the YouTube experience is a close-up of my erection.'

'What?'

'Through my jeans. But you can see it. Well, just.'

'But why . . . ? I mean . . . ?'

'I am a man. A beautiful girl was jiggling her tits at me. Even if she had been my daughter, I . . .'

'God.'

'But don't you think after a year, I mean, it's not that weird to . . .?'

'No, no, of course. It's completely understandable. So what's wrong with Clem?'

'She just doesn't love me any more.'

'But that's no reason not to have sex with someone.'

'Really?'

'Sex can be about different things.'

'Can it?' His hand moves from his lap to her leg.

She gulps. 'Yes. Um . . .'

'Hmm?' He has his eyes closed.

'Ollie, this probably isn't a good idea.'

'Isn't this why you're here?'

'No! I mean, well . . .'

'I feel as if no one in the whole world wants me.'

'That's not true. I do want you. You know that.' Bryony touches his bicep. 'It's just I'm sort of trying to patch a few things up with James, and . . .'

'I am a bad person.'

'Maybe I am a bad person too.'

'So we're two bad people in a hotel room. My life is fucked anyway . . .'

'What are you saying?'

'Undo your dress. I want to see a real woman's tits.'

'Ollie . . .'

'And I want to see your bum.'

He pulls up her dress and strokes the inside of her leg. Finds the edge of her stocking and gasps ever so slightly. Here's the problem. Bryony can no longer resist this and . . . Her phone rings. What now? She gets it out of her bag. It's James.

'Tell whoever it is to fuck off.'

She flicks the decline button, which is hard to see now that Ollie has his hand . . .

'You bastard,' she says, giggling.

'Am I? What are you?'

'Call me a bitch,' she says. 'Call me anything you like.' His finger slips inside her. 'Call me a whore.'

'What am I? Say it again.'

'You're a bastard.' Bryony struggles out of her dress. Every single thing she is wearing, from her silk underwear to the red crêpe de chine dress, which she now drops on the floor, was chosen with this man in mind. Or, not exactly this actual man but the fantasy version for whom the real Bryony would never really undress. Only the fantasy Bryony would ever . . . But here she is. And here he is.

'You can leave those on.' He nods at her stockings.

'Bastard,' she says again, raising an eyebrow. But she does leave them on. She did that French thing of putting her knickers on after her stockings, which sort of means that . . .

'What else?' He unzips his fly and pulls down his boxers and his jeans. Bryony is now naked apart from her stockings and suspender belt, but he doesn't seem to want to take any of his clothes off. He holds onto a tit with one hand while fingering her with the other. He doesn't seem to have noticed her toenails, but he may have seen her landing strip and . . . 'What else?'

'You're a disgusting bastard.'

He enters her. Which he can do without her having to go on all-fours, which is something she wishes the fitness instructor could see. Or maybe not. He keeps his thumb on her clit. She gasps.

'You're a cheating bitch.'

'You lie and you fuck everything up and no one trusts you because . . .'

'Shut up, whore.'

'Is that the best you can do, cunt?'

'Fat bitch.'

'Sad wanker.'

'Fat slag.'

'Pathetic, ridiculous, small-dicked loser . . .'

They both come.

When Fleur gets back to the cottage, Pi is already packing.

'I thought . . .' he says.

Fleur frowns and sighs. 'It's all right,' she says. 'You should go.'

'I'm so sorry.'

'It's OK. Go and find yourself. You deserve that.'

'At the beginning I was so fucking angry with you because of your mother. Even though you were so kind . . . I haven't always been very nice to you. I'm sorry. If it helps, I did love you, despite everything. Although that made me hate you a bit too. But I know that you don't love me, at least not now.'

'I did love you once. Sort of. I mean, when we were kids here in the house, having to survive, never having any money. All those scams. Your massages . . .' Fleur smiles. 'But then of course there was Kam. I couldn't forgive you for that. I have now though.'

'Do you remember when you used to tell the celebrities' fortunes?'

'Yeah. Although in those days the celebrities had no sodding money either.'

'And our market stall . . . All those little lavender bags that you sewed.'

Pi sits on the bed. Fleur sits next to him. Takes his hand in hers.

Above them the portrait of Gita hangs in its ebony frame. Pi never seemed to notice that Gita and Fleur were so similar. Fleur's skin is paler, of course, all these generations on, but that is the only difference.

'You earned this place,' says Pi. 'You worked for it. Harder than I ever did.'

'Well . . .'

'I went to see the Prophet earlier. He's given me money for the trip. Said you wouldn't mind.'

'It's his money. But of course I don't mind.'

'He says it's your money. Your inheritance.'

'Well, I still don't mind.'

Outside, one of the churches strikes six o' clock. It's getting dark.

'But you can't go now,' Fleur says.

'I've booked a taxi. I arrived here in the dark. I may as well leave the same way. My flight's first thing tomorrow. I'll stay at Heathrow overnight. Better than waking up at two in the morning or whatever.'

So Fleur's last night with Pi has already happened. It is over. It passed without her even knowing that's what it was. What would they have done if they had known? Would they have made love? Would they have cried? As it was she went to sleep early while he read the *Upanishads* on his Kindle. But of course he did know. He'd already bought the tickets.

Pumpkins. Everywhere. Thousands of pumpkins.

Is there nothing you cannot PYO now?

Bryony's hair is still wet from the hotel shower as she steps out of the car into the cool blue October twilight outside the Old Lorry Farm Shop. She has driven beyond Ash, beyond home, trying to dry her hair because it didn't really rain that hard today, and how do you explain . . . And of course she couldn't use the hotel hairdryer, can never use a hairdryer on this frizzy mop that needs particularly gentle teasing and stroking and finger drying . . . She can hear the chainsaws going out the back where the men cut firewood all winter long while an Alsatian barks at everyone who walks past. But at least Holly will have her pumpkin. Quite why it became Bryony's job to get the pumpkin on her graduation day is still a mystery. But it is a reason to be late. Is pumpkin something Holly would even eat? Perhaps in a nice, thick creamy soup, or in a pie. But how can Bryony think about pie now, after what she has done? But of course she is actually thinking about Holly, and Holly is the important thing in all this . . . Holly must have her pumpkin for school, and James will make something out of the insides. Maybe cake. Can she undo what she has just done with Ollie? No. But maybe she can unthink it. Tonight she will be a good wife and a good mother, and . . .

But she can feel the sting from where Ollie was inside her, and of course she can still hear the things he said. But she asked him to say them. Perhaps she should have asked for something else instead. 'I love you, my darling' would have been nicer. But what they did was real and brutal and dangerous, which is how life is sometimes. It just doesn't feel much like that when you are in a field full of pumpkins, and it's getting too dark to see anything, and . . .

'Are you all right, love?' calls one of the chainsaw men.

'Yes, thanks. Just trying to work out how to pick one.'

'Have one of these. Just picked this evening.' He gestures at a table full of pumpkins.

Bryony should pick one herself. It is more real, and will help deflect attention from the fact that she is home very late from a lunchtime drink. But actually what's the difference between a pumpkin you picked yourself and one that someone else picked? She can always say she picked it anyway, and . . .

'Thanks,' she says. After she has paid for it she puts the pumpkin on the seat next to her, like the head of a lover in a horrible car-accident story. She puts her handbag on the floor.

She almost doesn't recognise Clem's car in the driveway when she gets home. Why would Clem be here? Of course. She has left Ollie.

She must have come to stay or something. Which is awkward, of course, but . . . She remembers the message she didn't listen to before. Oh well, too late now. It probably just says what she knows already and . . . Should she say she saw Ollie? Yes. She had a drink with him and the others, and she got the impression that something was wrong, but she doesn't know all the details and . . .

Fleur has made the phone call and now stands in the kitchen watching the garden fade into the soft darkness of a late summer evening. The little bottle of fluid still sits in the shoebox. Next to it is a seed pod, the one she inherited. Short cuts, short cuts, but . . . If this life hadn't already gone so wrong, then . . . If it was OK to love your brother, then . . . If it was possible to meditate your way out of this, then . . . But she's done that. And anyway, she's made the phone call now. Breathe. Steady your hands, girl. Steady. Find something clean. Maybe one of those teacups that Charlie gave her. Yes. In goes the liquid and in goes the pod and . . .

All you can do is breathe, and wait.

Clem has still not looked directly at Bryony. It seems that Bryony pressed the wrong button when her phone rang in the hotel room. It seems that she cannot even work a fucking mobile phone. The room smells bitter with all the emotion that has not been allowed to escape. It's a combination of dried tears, stale breath and children's food plates that have not yet been cleared away. Bryony notes that, despite all the trauma, James has made cauliflower cheese from scratch for them and Holly has left most of hers because, well, who does like cauliflower cheese when they are twelve? It's the colour and consistency of pus. Holly and Ash are in the conservatory watching a DVD, which means that the adults are half whispering and sort of hissing at one another.

Clem was here when James rang Bryony before, when it became apparent that Bryony is not only an immoral alcoholic who BETRAYS EVERONE but cannot – just to repeat this point – even use a fucking mobile phone. In fact, James was ringing partly because Clem couldn't get through. They were so worried . . . Quite why they all couldn't have just left her alone when she was at her graduation drinks, or supposed to be . . . But that doesn't seem to be the point any more.

'Why in God's name did you ask her to listen to it too?'

'Because at first I didn't know what I was hearing. I thought you were being attacked. I thought that's why you had answered your phone but weren't able to speak. Then Clem recognised Ollie's voice and . . .'

'Well, it must have quickly become quite obvious that, no, I didn't mean to answer my phone. How long did you both listen?'

'We are not at fault here,' Clem says. 'Don't try to . . .'

'What would you say if you were me? I've fucked up. I'm sorry. There isn't really anything I can say. I know I can never undo this. I think I'll just . . .' Bryony turns to go upstairs. To go anywhere. To die? If she could die at this moment . . . But she mustn't think like that.

'You are not walking away from this,' James says. 'We really need to talk about what we do next. The kids. The house.'

'Don't be so dramatic.'

'You just slept with her husband. Of course this is fucking dramatic.'

'Mummy,' calls Holly from the conservatory, 'when will we be able to do the pumpkin?'

James wipes a tear from his eye.

'I'll take the kids to Fleur's,' says Clem. 'You obviously need some time.'

'Thank you,' says James.

'I'll stay there too. Give you some space. Let me know later that you're OK?'

'Yes. Likewise?'

For God's sake. How wonderful it must be to be such innocent, self-righteous victims who are THERE FOR EACH OTHER and who have probably hugged at least once already. What about Bryony? Who exactly is she going to let know that she is OK? Who will be there for her? Who will hug her? Ollie won't care. Fleur will be annoyingly neutral. Perhaps Charlie . . . But he won't really understand. Bryony cannot believe this. She needs a drink.

'At least I didn't fuck my own brother,' she finds herself saying. 'Which you could actually ask Fleur about when you see her. Remember when she and Charlie were together? And then suddenly weren't? Well. I'm not the only one in this family who has gone to bed with the wrong person. Not by a long way.'

~

When Fleur looks at Charlie this time she allows herself to feel it, just for a second, and it is like sinking into a hot bath after being trapped in an icy cave for years.

'Charlie,' she says, and she almost does not have to say anything else. Could they speak to one another without words? Probably. But that's for later.

'Tell me,' he says. 'What is it? What's happened?'

'Something big. Well, potentially.'

'Go on.'

'OK. The Prophet. He says that he's my father.'

'What?'

'The Prophet says that he, not Augustus, is my father.'

'How . . . ?'

'My mother certainly slept with a lot of people. The Prophet thinks that he might have met her years before he came here to live, and . . .'

Fleur watches as Charlie's mind slips into the same hot bath and immediately softens. She watches as the warm water washes away the guilt and yearning of the last twenty years. She sees him imagining them together, he and Fleur, walking up a bright green hill wearing soft woollen scarves, with Holly as well, perhaps. She sees him imagine her touch. The very tips of her fingers. To actually be allowed to . . .

But wait. In that case why is he basically still looking in a mirror, and . . .

'Is that true?'

'Honestly?'

The bath is going cold. There is no hill. 'Yes.'

'No.'

'Then . . .'

'He was just trying to be kind.'

Charlie sighs. Rolls his eyes. 'So we are still related?'

'Yes. Sorry. But . . .'

'Fuck, Fleur. Why are you doing this to me?'

'Because – wait, sit down – I think you still feel what I feel.'

'Which is what?'

Breathe in. Breathe out. 'Love.' Breathe out some more. 'Desire.'

'But we can't . . . We haven't been able to . . .'

'The Prophet made me see that we can. When he told me he was my father, I felt exactly the same things that you just felt. All these years of suffocating my true feelings. Of never even bothering to end things with Pi because I just couldn't face having to go out there and find someone who wasn't you. But then I realised. The Prophet may as well be my father. It doesn't actually matter who is anyone's father. I'm not planning to have any children. Are you planning to have any more?'

'You know about Holly.'

'I know about Holly.'

They both pause. Breathe in. Breathe out. Wait for the universe to run its hand through its hair and smooth down its skirts.

'Anyway, no, I'm not planning to have any more.' Unless . . . God, that whole business with Izzy was even more stupid, now he thinks about it. Is she on the Pill? He didn't even ask. All he knew was that he didn't want to do things like that any more. Even as he was fucking her he was regretting it. And she was saying maybe they shouldn't be doing this, but not really meaning it. And she was also saying 'What about Nicola?' And Charlie realised that this was the game, this was the thing, that these two were competing over him as if he were the last size-eight dress in the sale, and that Izzy only wanted him because Nicola had him, but she only got Nicola to have him because she wanted him, but she couldn't want him unless he had been endorsed by someone else, and not unless there was competition involved and . . . And she was pulling him towards her, deeper into her, as if he were a flower and she an insect desperate for his cheap, sugary nectar. And he'd had enough. He had really . . .

'Well, then,' says Fleur. 'We're not eighteen any more. Surely . . .'

'So what are you saying?' Charlie asks.

'I just think that reality is not all it's cracked up to be. Rules, what people think, how people think things should be. Who cares if we're brother and sister? Or, well, half brother and sister.'

'The law?'

'But we're not legally related. Augustus's name is not on my birth certificate.'

'OK . . .'

'I mean, someone would actually have to do a blood test. But there'd be no reason for them to. And anyway, no one knows. So . . .'

Charlie breathes deeply. 'You're actually right,' he says. 'It's so obvious when you say it like that.'

'I mean, I don't even think I feel weird about it at all any more.'

'No. I'm pretty sure I don't either.'

'I did, once.'

'You already knew, in the summer house, when we . . .'

'Yes.' Fleur looks down at the floor. 'I was ashamed of that for ages. But I'm not any more. I just think that on my deathbed I want to remember love and passion and being wildly wrong, not being nice and careful and doing the right thing. I don't even know whose rules we're obeying anyway.'

Charlie walks over and touches her hand. He raises it to his lips and kisses it. One finger, and then another finger, and then . . .

The doorbell. Even Fleur's doorbell is beautiful. It is a real little brass bell that tinkles in the hallway. It tinkles again now.

'Whoever that is has great timing,' he says.

It's Clem, with Holly and Ash. She is carrying a pumpkin. And there is a new, strange look in her eyes that both Charlie and Fleur immediately realise is, among other things, knowledge of them, of who and what they are, of what they did once and now can never do again.

~

'I'll put the kettle on. I think you probably need a coffee.'

James fills the vintage whistling kettle from the tap and puts it on the Aga.

'I think I need a glass of wine.'

'You do not need a glass of wine. I imagine you've had enough today.'

'I don't actually care about my health at this moment.'

'This is not about your health. I want you to be able to listen to me.'

'I can listen to you.'

James sighs loudly. 'Right.'

'Perhaps if you weren't so controlling, then . . .'

'I'm sorry? YOU are the alcoholic, but I am somehow controlling? This is all my fault? What the fuck, Bryony?'

Bryony goes to the fridge. There's nothing there. What about the Wither Hills Sauvignon Blanc that was there yesterday? Surely she didn't finish it? She goes to the wine rack. Empty. Now that is strange. She definitely didn't drink all the . . . But OK, whatever, there is lots more wine in the cellar. But she finds it locked. Oh, great. What the fuck indeed.

'When did you do this?'

James shrugs.

'Good job I've been to Hercules, then, isn't it?'

Bryony goes out to the car, her hands shaking. There in the boot is the box of wine that she meant to unload yesterday. But here's the problem. A red will be a bit too cold to drink, and a white a bit too warm. Which to choose? If she puts a red by the Aga then maybe . . . She walks in with a Barolo. It cost thirty pounds, but this is turning into a thirty-pound-bottle-of-wine sort of day. James hasn't thought to hide the corkscrew, so she opens the wine and pours a big glass while he watches.

'I just cannot believe you are doing this.'

'What, that I have chosen not to give up drinking on possibly the worst day of my life just because you've decided I should? I imagine you're leaving me anyway. What do you care what I do?'

'I didn't say I was leaving you.'

'But you will.'

'Is that what you want?'

Bryony hesitates. 'No.'

'I need you to make a decision. I need you to pour that bottle of wine down the sink. I really, really need you to make a decision now. The wine, or me.'

The kettle begins to come to the boil. The whistle begins low and distant, like a faraway train in a long-forgotten film. Bryony could pour the wine down the sink, of course she could. She has plenty more in the car anyway. And it wouldn't be the first time she has poured a bottle of wine down the sink during an argument. But that has always been *her* idea, to make *her* point. There was that 1965 Exshaw Grande Champagne Cognac that Augustus gave her for her thirtieth. She loved pouring that down the sink in front of James when he suggested she'd had one glass too many. 'See how much I don't care about cognac?' she had screamed at him. Where were the kids that night? Probably in bed. So it can't have quite been a scream, even though that's how she remembers it. After James went to bed that night Bryony ate a whole box of chocolate liqueurs. Are there any more chocolate liqueurs in the house? The kettle whistles more loudly now.

'Well?' James says.

Bryony takes her wine glass and sips from it. 'I just need some space to think.'

'Bryony, it's the wine or me.' James is now shouting to be heard over the kettle. Why doesn't he just take it off the boil? 'Choose.'

'All right. I choose wine. Since you've forced the issue.'

'What?' He starts sobbing. 'What is wrong with you?'

'And please do something about that kettle. It's going right through my . . .'

James picks up the kettle. 'This is how you make me feel,' he says, as he pours the boiling water over his head. At least, he gets halfway through the last word before he starts to scream. 'Help me! Oh God, please help . . .' And then he passes out, melting onto the floor like a piece of butter in a frying pan.

When Clem and the others have gone to bed Charlie and Fleur drink lapsang souchong tea, and Fleur tells him about her trip to the Outer Hebrides and the strange dreams she has had since going there. Her memory of everything that happened is a little hazy, but she remembers being told how to do it again, except that it was impossible to get hold of the fluid, for obvious reasons, but then suddenly this box and the bottle . . .

She shows him the teacup. Tells him how dangerous the seed pod is. That she's not sure about the liquid. It could actually be anything. But if it *is* an enlightened person's tears, as the Prophet seemed to think, then . . .

'Let's do it,' Charlie says.

And so they fly away together, on something that is either a first date or a last night on Earth, or perhaps both, high over the English Channel, not knowing where they are going, or if they will ever . . .

Of course Ollie takes the pod from the time-lapse film set Clem has rigged up in the spare bedroom, and which is still recording. After all, there are not many nature documentaries that end with the suicide of the filmmaker's husband by ingestion of the very plant that is the subject of the documentary. Perhaps Clem really will win an Oscar for this one. Ollie hasn't seen the plant for a while. He should have been interested, but has not been interested. When was he last interested in anything about Clem apart from how she reacts to him? Anyway, it certainly now has fruit. Or what botanists call 'fruit'. It is really more of a bean pod. Like a vanilla pod, perhaps, but larger and not yet as shrivelled. Ollie remembers some dinner party with Clem talking about vanilla coming from an orchid, *Vanilla planifolia*, that Madagascan farmers have to pollinate themselves, because it is just too complicated or tiresome for the plant to do it itself. The vanilla orchid flowers in the morning and if it is not pollinated by the end of the day the flower simply drops off and dies.

Does Clem have any idea how much she has broken Ollie's heart with her words? The one that keeps going through his mind is 'boring'.

Boring, boring, boring. And after trying so hard *not* to be boring. After trying to make life anything *but* boring. But life without a job, without Clem and of course without any children could well become boring. Could Ollie become a priest? No. He is boring, and also not a Catholic. He could adopt, of course, but his children will probably come to hate him as much as Clem does. They will spend all their time with their birth certificates in their hands, trawling the internet in search of their 'real' parents, the people who made them from slime rather than love. The only person who has ever been impressed by him is Bryony. Even she does not know the real, boring him. She just uses him as a screen on to which to project her own fantasy. But then, of course, he does the same thing to Clem. Is that all romantic love is?

Ollie has not yet really looked at the plant's only flower, but he does so now. It is a sort of dark, minky grey and off-white with some spots of black and two peculiar holes. He pulls off the pod containing the seeds and puts it in his jeans pocket. The flower vibrates and then comes to rest. Without Clem here to pollinate it, it will probably just die. The dry calyx at the tip of the pod crackles faintly against the denim. He becomes aware of a scent, perhaps a little chocolatey, a touch of nutmeg or something spicy like cardamom, but also quite otherworldly and impossible to describe. He almost stops everything he is doing, almost manages to stop thinking for a second, because it is the most beautiful thing he has ever smelled. He knows the scent is coming from the pod. Is he sure about this? He sighs. Walks back to the door and opens it. Turns to switch off the light. But does not switch off the light because there, hanging onto the plant, is a ghostly image of his own face. He couldn't see it close up, but now it is obvious. There, spectrally, improbably, insanely, is his high forehead, and his hollow cheeks and even his stubble, marked out in little black dots. The holes, of course, are his eyes. It hangs there for a moment and then drops to the floor.

It is 07.17.

❧

And it's impossible to describe in words what is on the other side. There are no words on the other side. But on the brink, in this cosmic edgeland, you can see eternities of people coming and going. You can see the last moments of individual souls before they melt into the oneness that from the outside seems eternally boring but inside is orgasmic. Ollie pauses now, on this precipice, and sighs long and deeply because he finally knows what real love is. He has left his body behind but calls on his lips, or the great lips of the universe, for just this one final kiss. Who with? Time moves so oddly in this barely-there place with its clocks only faintly ticking that he is able, finally, to make insane cosmic love to Clem without any resistance, indeed with her loving him back, pulling him into her and sweating and crying out for him. At the same time as this he finds he is kissing and stroking Bryony and calling her 'my darling' and 'my love' and breathing out again, long and deep, as every atom leaves his lungs and then his body and the three of them merge into one, into all lovers everywhere and finally into love itself. Holly, who arrives a long way behind them, has kept her whole body, plumper now and brimming with sparkle, has resurrected it in child form, because, as she hangs out on this strange, multidimensional, fizzing edge, she will get to have her perfect hit with Melissa again, for all eternity and beyond, until they merge into one another and into the silence that comes only when the last ball in the universe has bounced for the very final time.

Into this silence they will all go, eventually. Here comes a small, elderly robin, flying steadily, his red breast out, leading the way for his beloved Fleur, hand in hand with Charlie at last. And everyone arrives here in the end, rapists and murderers and liars and cheats, and all their victims, and they laugh and cry with joy because all the rapes and murders and lies and games do not exist any more. None of it really happened. It was, after all, just a horrible dream. The unraped, the unmurdered, the unbound, the uncriminalised, the unpoor, the unguilty: everyone cries with joy and relief because there is no addiction here, and no economies, and no plants of any kind, and nothing that everyone does not know and share. All the drama in the world begins to fade out as this once tragic universe yawns deeply and prepares for its long sleep. When Holly has finished her tennis she runs towards the very edge of everything and in her final instant becomes every little girl who ever lived: blonde and black in jeans and a sari and a gingham dress and pigtailed and glittered and hatted and gloved and socked and naughty and dirty and clean and good and bad but strangely wise, and as Ollie, the last, flickering blink of Ollie, looks at her, at the cosmic little girl, he realises that he is not only now her father, but the great father of everything.

Zoe is bored with hearing the story. OK, the drama was exciting at first, and, yes, she got Clem all to herself for a while and she made cups of tea and poured wine and bought expensive cottage pies from M&S that Clem would not even eat in the end. But what can you really say to someone whose husband killed himself because of a stupid love triangle with a fat cousin who tried, but failed, to kill herself too? Oh yeah, with the weird plant that you grew. Or some other version of it. OK, you can say trite, baffling things like 'This too will pass', which Zoe found on a bereavement website. Or you can offer to listen to the person who is bereaved. You can see if there is anything practical you can do for them. And then you discover that, yes, there is something practical you can do for them: you can help plant, give away, donate and eventually begin throwing out each of the 1,000 strange, almost black *Clematis viticella* plants that Ollie ordered before he killed himself. But what happens when you just get fucking bored with it all? Sex is completely off the agenda. Last time they made love was, well, the day before it happened. Did Ollie know? Clem has never actually said. It's become the thing Zoe can't ask. In fact, Zoe can't ask anything that implicates her in any of it. It's almost as if she can hear her mother's voice: *This is not all about you, Zoe*. But why not? Why can't her shiny new relationship that, OK, has been dropped pretty heavily on the floor, why can't it be all about her? And if you find you are in a relationship that is not all about you then it's time to move on, right?

Ash is alone in the garden when the goldfinches come. Should he be alone? Perhaps not. But Bryony and Holly are buried deep in the spare room, pulling out things to keep and things to go in the big skip outside. His father has asked for all his things to go into the skip but apparently he no longer knows what he is saying so they will go into storage. Holly is carefully putting black wool in a cardboard box and not speaking much. She still doesn't eat. Even after all this. Even after Aunt Fleur gave her a magical book that she has to keep very, very safe. It makes Ash sad. Ash is to collect all the things he wants to take to Jura and put them in a sensible pile somewhere. What does he want? Perhaps photos? Some things are going to Jura on the plane and some are going in a boat and . . .

Ash has a really horrible feeling inside. He wanted to move out of this house, out of this village, and now, well, he is. Does that mean everything is his fault because he wished for it? When everyone was in hospital he stayed with Beatrix and Skye, and Skye told him you can definitely ask the universe for things but you have to be careful how you phrase your requests. You must always ask the universe for positive things. Never say 'I don't want to be poor any more' when what you mean is 'I want to be rich'. Because if you use the word 'poor' then that is what the universe hears and that is what it gives you. But even asking to be rich is problematic because you might become rich because all your family are dead. Ash didn't phrase his request very well at all, and all his family almost did die. Still, when he goes to secondary school on Islay, because there is no school on Jura, it will just be normal. 'Hi, my name's Ash.' Although of course he will never be normal again because of what happened. But as Skye said, he doesn't have to tell everyone, or even anyone, what happened if he doesn't want to.

He hears them before he sees them. They come in groups of between five and ten until there are twenty, fifty, seventy, eighty, a *hundred* goldfinches in his garden, as many of them as possible squabbling over the niger seed in the feeder. There is nothing on the bird table for them, even though some of them do land there. Ash goes into the kitchen, although he no longer feels good or even OK in this kitchen, and looks in the cupboard. There is the unopened bag of sunflower hearts that his mother bought in the spring. He opens the bag carefully, with scissors rather than with his fingers, and takes it outside. All the goldfinches fly into the small holly tree or land on the wall just beyond and watch in silence as Ash reaches for the bird table and pours the entire contents of the bag onto it.

'I hope that keeps you going,' he says to them.

They say nothing. Really, they should fly away. But they don't.

'I probably won't see you ever again,' says Ash.

A gentle wind rustles through the holly tree. Still the goldfinches stay. Ash wonders what might happen if he stands very still, and . . . Then a single goldfinch flies over to him. Something in its little red face looks familiar, as if Ash has seen it many times before. Ash keeps very still and the goldfinch lands on his shoulder. His heartbeat rips through him. Being this close to a bird is the most exciting thing that has ever happened to him. In this moment Ash knows that he is going to work with birds, that he is going to become an ornithologist, and everything is going to be hard, but it is somehow going to be all right.

The goldfinch moves on Ash's shoulder. This is strange, though. Surely he smells wrong to a goldfinch? He must smell of human, not of tree. Maybe it's because of his name. He remains very still. The goldfinch hops up to the place where Ash's shoulder becomes his neck, and it tickles, but still he doesn't move. He can feel a strange energy coming from the goldfinch now, something loving and kind and warm. Ash will never be able even to try to describe this to anyone, but it feels like a soft ball of long-ago things like cuddles, bedtime stories and hot water bottles, and this is what is standing there with its claws now only slightly digging into his neck. Then, just like that, the goldfinch seems to kiss Ash's earlobe. As it flies away he is sure he hears the little bird whisper something. It sounds like 'Namaste . . .' He is sure it is his aunt Fleur's voice. And then Ash runs into the house to get his mother and his sister, but by the time they get outside it's as if the goldfinches were never there.

Family Tree (revised)

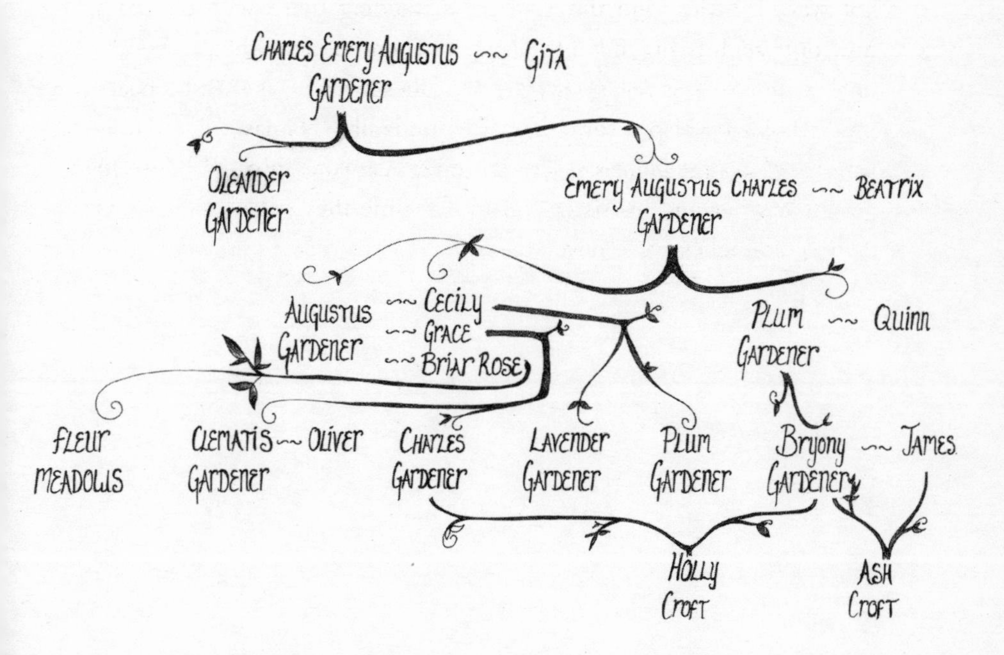

Acknowledgements

So many people helped with this book, but I would particularly like to thank Rod Edmond, my first, best and most demanding reader for his love and support; and my family, Francesca Ashurst, Couze Venn, Sam Ashurst and Hari Ashurst-Venn, for being my longest-standing and most dedicated fans. Nia and Ivy, I am thrilled that you are joining us. To my father Gordian Troeller, many thanks for your inspiration and encouragement. And my other father, Steve Sparkes, who was also a big influence on this book, may you rest in peace.

I would particularly like to thank David Miller, my agent, for being so serious about writing, and Francis Bickmore, my editor and dear friend, for making this all so much fun. Thank you to everyone else at Canongate, but particularly Jamie Byng and Jenny Todd, for the enthusiasm, passion and understanding. Vybarr Cregan-Reid, Ariane Mildenberg, Amy Sackville, David Flusfeder, Emma Lee and Charlotte Webb, thank you so much for your friendship, support and inspiration. Thanks to staff and students on the MSc in Ethnobotany at the University of Kent, who taught me everything I know about plants. Florence and Ottilie Stirrup, thank you for confirming that kids still say the same stuff (more or less) now as they did in the eighties. Christopher Hollands and Toby Churchill, thank you for helping me bring Holly back. Dorice Evans, thank you for introducing me to the *Course*. All my research students teach me something, but particular thanks to the ones who read and commented on my manuscript: Amy Lilwall, Gonzalo Cerón Garcia, Karen Donaghay and Hristina Hristova. I am also grateful to Tom Ogier, Charlotte Geater and Chieko Trenouth for constantly reminding me why I love writing.